A Deliberate Act of Violence

A Deliberate Act of Violence

Violence

Steve McHugh

Podium

Cover design by Istvan Straban

ISBN: 978-1-0394-8912-7

Published in 2025 by Podium Publishing
www.podiumentertainment.com

Podium

LIST OF CHARACTERS

The Assembly
Miles Watson: Arbiter
Church: Vampire-enhanced Doberman. Best girl.
Megan Song: ATO (Assault Team Officer) Commander
Jonathan Holt: ATO (Assault Team Officer) Commander
Mordecai Balderas: Assembly Justice
Karine Beaumont: Assistant to Justice Balderas
Rosa Sanchez: Arbiter handler

House Venator (The House of Justice)
Drest: First Lord of House Venator
Charlotte Henry: First Counsel of House Venator
Gideon: First Librarian of House Venator
Halime: First Captain of House Venator

House Nix (The House of Demons)
Aamir Lazaar: First Captain of House Nix

Templar International
Henryk Greger: Head of Templar International Private Security
Dominik Greger: Son of Henryk
Sara Bakos: Sworn to Henryk Greger
Furio Cappo (Fury): Employee of Templar International

Great Vampire Houses
House Barbarous (The House of Blood)

House Nix (The House of Demons)
House Phalanx (The House of One)
House Umbra (The House of Shadows)
House Venator (The House of Justice)

Minor Vampire Houses
House Bane (The House of Fang and Bone)
House Bestias (The House of the Wild)
House Gravis (The House of Graves)
House Idolator (The House of Faith)
House Meteor (The House of Miracles)
House Nebula (The House of Fog)
House Rampart (The House of Iron Shields)
House Somnus (The House of Dreams)

Expunged Vampire House
House Divinus (The House of the Divine)

A Deliberate
Act of
Violence

PART ONE

Chapter One

Sara Bakos would be the first to admit that she didn't have the most difficult of lives. She was wealthy, she had an important role in a billion-dollar company, and she enjoyed the power and prestige that came with her role. Including a fifth-floor penthouse flat in Marylebone, situated in the City of Westminster, London. She'd considered living in one of the vampire-controlled boroughs, but she hated the idea of the Assembly having any control over the place she called home. Unfortunately, there was one part of her job that she despised, and recently that one part was becoming a full-time occupation.

She'd been about to feed—a lovely twenty-seven-year-old vintage she'd been looking forward to sampling—when the call had come through. *Dom needs help.* Dom *always* needed help. He was basically incapable of doing anything except fucking up and making more work for her.

Sara had told her new plaything to take the night off and had taken the private lift to the underground parking area. Her driver, Philip, was waiting outside of her black and silver Rolls-Royce Ghost wearing a dark grey three-piece suit, with black shoes polished to an almost mirror shine. The suit jacket was designed to cover the holstered gun against his side, and it did a pretty good job. Considering how much she'd paid for the suit, it should have done an excellent job, and she mentally reminded herself to speak to the tailor when she had the time.

"Madam," Philip said, with a slight smile. He had pale skin and was clean shaven, with short dark hair. A scar ran from above his ear to just shy of his temple, the result of his time in the British armed forces. Sara liked Philip and trusted him not to blab her secrets to anyone who asked. She knew he had a family, a son, a little boy called Peter. She occasionally wondered if Philip knew how much danger they were in just by virtue of who he worked for.

"The King's Head, Edgware," Sara said, climbing into the rear of the Rolls-Royce and taking a moment to enjoy the white and orange leather trim interior.

Sara let herself relax a little as they drove, looking out of tinted windows at the still busy streets of the capital of the United Kingdom. Two AM or PM didn't much matter in London; there were still places you could go, still people out and about. Sara wondered how many were vampires looking for a good time in one of the many vampire-friendly establishments, or out to hunt. Probably fewer of the latter. After she'd become a vampire, she discovered that there was very little need for vampires to actually hunt their meals anymore. She'd been quite disappointed about it at the time but had quickly adjusted, and now she was able to make a phone call and have her drink of choice come to her within a few hours.

"How is Peter, Philip?" Sara asked. "Being a good child?"

"Yes, ma'am," Philip said, almost bursting with pride.

"Good, I hope that will continue," Sara said, meaning it. "Do you know Dominik Greger at all?"

"I've driven for his father from time to time," Philip said, his tone utterly neutral.

"Henryk is a hard man," Sara said. "And, in my experience, hard men either produce hard children, or they try to overcorrect their own upbringing. And then they produce humans like Dominik."

"You do not like him?" Philip asked, choosing his words carefully.

"I do not," Sara said with a slight smile. "He is an imbecile. A fact that his father and I agree on. He's little more than a thug and bully. The kind of man who would start a fight and then hide behind his bigger friends. I detest the little shit. But I owe his father, Henryk, more than I can ever repay, so I do what needs to be done. Even if it means holding my nose and getting on with it."

"Will you need my assistance?" Philip asked.

"I hope not. Just stay in the car, keep the engine running, and be prepared to leave quickly."

Philip nodded, his eyes trained on the road ahead.

Sara went back to looking out of the window for the next few minutes until they pulled down a road with a small park opposite an old warehouse.

At the end of the road was a pub, the King's Head. The entrance was illuminated by a streetlight that probably wished for a better standard of clientele. It said *Traditional Pub* on the side in golden letters, which, considering the state of those letters, Sara took to mean *shithole*. It looked like the kind of place the police would hear about on the radio and sigh, or pretend they hadn't heard anything.

"Turn the car around," Sara said. "Park up opposite the pub. Engine on."

Philip stopped the car, and Sara stepped out into what was a cool February night. The scent of fresh rain lingered in the air, although it was quickly overwhelmed by something that spoke to a more animalistic part of Sara's psyche. Blood.

Sara walked to the pub doors, occasionally sniffing the air, until she was close enough that the blood mixed with the contents of the large metal bins that sat along the side of the building. She looked down into the dark alleyway, took a deep breath, and followed the scent, expecting to find whichever unfortunate Dominik had decided looked at him funny.

She hadn't expected to find Dominik.

He lay up against the cold brick wall, a large rat edging nearer to his blood-drenched fingers. The rat sensed Sara a second too late, and she kicked it hard enough that when it hit the far wall, it made a noise signalling that it wasn't getting back up. Sara crouched down beside Dominik, who opened his eyes. Even in the darkness, Sara's vision was able to spot how pale the young man was. His shirt was covered in blood, and one hand rested against his side, which was similarly drenched.

"What happened?" Sara asked, moving Dominik's hand and peeling back the shirt to show several stab wounds. At least one had been deep enough to cause serious damage. Dominik wasn't getting back up from this one.

"Will I be okay?" he asked.

"No," Sara said, seeing little reason to lie to him. "You have been stabbed at least once in the liver. From the smell, they've perforated something else you need, too." She moved his shirt again. More stab wounds. "Someone really did a number on you."

"Three of them," he said almost dreamily. "I don't think they liked me. I don't want to die here."

Maybe you shouldn't have gotten stabbed then, Sara thought, but instead she removed her mobile and called Philip. "Get the tarp and put it over the back seats."

"I won't make it," Dominik said, sounding weaker by the moment. "You know that."

"Then your body will be taken to your father," Sara snapped.

"Turn me," Dominik said.

"Fuck no," Sara said, staring at the quickly dying Dominik. She stood and punched the wall, removing a chunk of brick from the force of the blow, and cutting open her knuckle in the process.

Vampire blood had revolutionised human medicine. It helped to alleviate pain, it aided in recovery after operations, and it helped make healing quicker. But vampire blood alone couldn't cure what was done to Dominik, and she *really* didn't want to do what it *would* take.

"Fuck," Sara shouted at no one in particular. She removed the phone from her pocket and called Henryk, who answered on the first ring.

"What happened to my son?" he asked, his Italian accent coming through, coupled with more than a little irritation.

"Dominik is going to die," Sara said. "He's asked me to turn him."

"Do it," Henryk said without hesitation and hung up.

Sara put the phone away and looked down at Dominik. What would Henryk do if he died? He'd be angry, unbearably so. He'd definitely take it out on those who killed his son. Their deaths would be long and arduous. Would he take it out on the vampire who couldn't save him? Probably not. He needed her. But that didn't matter. Sara would know that she had lied to one of the few people she trusted. It had been a trust hard earned over the years working together.

She gingerly picked Dominik up, carrying him in her arms as though he were a child to the waiting car, the rear door open wide so that he could be placed on the tarp-covered back seats.

"Home," she told Philip, who, true to his professionalism, didn't ask any questions. She moved into the back of the car and crouched down before the seats. "Fast."

Sara waited for the sound of the large engine to mask her words, then she whispered to Dominik, "This is going to take a long time, and it will *not* be fun. You are seriously injured, and to save you from death, you must drink my blood. I must take yours first, but I can't risk using my vampire side to cause the euphoria you'd normally feel from the bite. Can't risk you falling asleep, or your heart stopping."

Dominik blinked twice. "Do it."

Sara cursed everyone who had gotten her into this position, leaned into Dominik, and let her vampire side out. Her face became sunken, her eyes burning red, her fangs already out as if her body was waiting for what was about to happen. She sighed and sank her fangs into his neck. Dominik let out a little squeal of pain, which turned into a roar of agony, as she drank deeply for several seconds, before moving away, her vampire side now replaced with the more human appearance.

She raised her arm, and with one razor sharp talon, she slit her wrist, nicking the vein, and held it to Dominik's lips. Blood poured into Dominik's open mouth, and to his credit, he drank it down without trying to hold on when she pulled away.

"You will live," Sara said, her hand placed over the wound on her wrist as the bleeding stopped and it began to heal. "But your days as a human are done."

Philip pulled into the parking lot under Sara's home, turned off the engine, and sat still in the driver's seat.

"Do not help me," Sara said from behind Philip's ear. "You will wait for me to leave with Dominik, and then you will go home. You will mention nothing about what you saw here today. Do I make myself clear?"

"Yes, ma'am," Philip said, his eyes straight ahead.

Sara moved closer, her lips touching Philip's earlobe. "Do not fuck this up, Philip. I like you. I like that you have a family, a wife. Peter . . . am I clear?"

Philip gulped and nodded once.

Sara opened the Rolls's door and dragged the tarp and Dominik to the edge of the back seats so she could pick him up once again, this time with the bloody tarp wrapped around him. She carried him to the private lift a few steps away and up to her penthouse, where she placed the weakened man in the second bedroom, making sure the curtains were closed.

"Thank you," Dominik said.

"I will see you in one day," Sara said. "For the next ten days, you will slowly become a vampire. If you do what I say, when I say it, everything will be okay. If you do not, it won't. Am I clear?"

"Yes," Dominik said, now half asleep.

Sara stared at the young man in the bed and for the first time in a long while wondered what was going to happen next. He'd stopped bleeding, which was something, but his wounds would take several days to fully heal.

She closed the door, locked it, walked into the bathroom, and showered as the memories of who had stabbed Dominik flooded her brain. Ten days of having his memories in her head, and of hers in his, made her feel ill. When out of the shower, she poured herself a triple-sized scotch, the make of which she didn't care enough to check, knocked it back, and poured another. After the second one went down, she called Henryk.

"He alive?" he asked.

"For now," Sara said. "I've done all I can. It will take ten days. If he heals, and does as he's told, your son will be a vampire. If not . . . he might still die. It's possible he does everything right and still dies. Or, worst case scenario, becomes a desolate. And if that happens, he will have to be . . . dealt with."

There was a pause for several seconds. "Thank you. I know it will be hard for you. Does anyone else know?"

"My driver," Sara said. "He's not a problem. I trust him."

"If he blabs, it's on your head," Henryk said in a tone that left no doubt about the threat that was intended.

"He won't," Sara said firmly. "You should know, I saw the three men who attacked your son. His memories are all jumbled up at the moment, so it may take a few more days to get clearer pictures of their faces."

"We'll check for CCTV in the area," Henryk said. "We'll find them."

"Don't do anything until your son is healed," Sara said. "Vampires need to learn how to hunt."

Henryk laughed. "If my son survives, your debt is fulfilled."

It was Sara's turn to laugh, because they both knew that was never going to happen. Henryk needed her, and she in turn needed to work for someone she admired and trusted, if not always liked.

"Go sleep," Sara said. "I'll update you tomorrow."

Henryk ended the call, and Sara knocked back another drink before walking over to the far side of the room, next to the sliding glass doors that led to a large balcony where she'd started to plant flowers. To cultivate a place for herself. She crouched down and placed a hand on the floorboard between the windows, and pushed slightly on one side. There was a click, and the floorboard popped up, revealing a grey metal safe. She placed the pad of her thumb against the safe and it too clicked open.

Inside was a passport in a name that wasn't hers, fifty thousand pounds, the same again in dollars, and a phone. She removed the phone and switched it on, waiting for the old Nokia to power up. When done, she scrolled down the only menu on the black and green screen and selected *Messages.* She typed, *We have a potential problem,* hit *Send* to the only number stored in the phone, and waited.

The reply came quickly: *Explain.*

She did as she was asked and waited for a reply.

This needs to be monitored. Contact me after we know the outcome.

Sara knew that was the end of the conversation. She stared at the last message for several seconds, wondering just how bad things might get. She switched off the phone, replaced it back in the safe, and poured herself another drink.

CHAPTER TWO

The Fang and Fog was a jeweller in Soho, London, which had existed since the eighteenth century, or so the tale went. At one point, they'd been *the* aristocratic jeweller of choice, making bespoke and exceptionally expensive items, while being able to keep their mouths shut about who their clients were. Everyone wanted to believe that the upper classes had found the best hidden shop to make all of their finery, and so the Fang and Fog had done a roaring trade for decades.

No one had openly ever asked why it was called the Fang and Fog. No one had publicly ever wondered how the proprietor never appeared to age, or why they only opened at night. And that was exactly how the owner wanted it. Right up until the Blitz in 1941, when a German bomb fell in the street outside just as the owner was leaving. Even the most powerful vampires would have a hard time healing from several tons of explosives falling on their heads.

The name had remained, even if the owners had changed hands since, and the current human owners were the great-grandchildren of the young man the vampire owner had left everything to. The shop had moved away from catering almost exclusively to the aristocracy to become a shop that made vampire jewellery, such as the torc worn by all Arbiters.

One such Arbiter, Miles Watson, stood in the middle of the large bright shop as the March rain pelted down outside. The sun was setting, although considering how much it had rained all day, the sun had never bothered to get up in the first place. Not much of an issue for vampires, who, contrary to popular belief, could walk around in the daylight without fear of spontaneous combustion, so long as the UV index remained at zero. Maybe one or two at the most.

The shop had been open for an hour, and the owner—a forty-something-year-old human with a gaunt enough look that he could have passed for a vampire in one of the old horror films—and his three assistants were each going about their daily tasks.

Three customers had come in since the shop opened, all leaving with their new piece of jewellery while Miles pretended to study the lockets and charms that took up one of the dozen glass cases that littered the shop.

Miles was bored of looking at the same few objects, and he took a step to the right, where there was a collection of torcs in various styles, including one in bronze that gave the appearance of pieces of rope intertwined. It was almost identical to the one on his own wrist, which was covered by the sleeve of his long navy raincoat.

"You know, you could get some beads for that," one of the assistants told him.

Miles looked up at the young blonde woman who he guessed was no older than twenty-five. She was human, as all of the workers were, and had been keen to talk to the vampire Arbiter the moment Miles had entered the shop to have a private conversation with the owner.

This was day two of Miles's spending time in the shop. Like the day before, he was going to stay there for a while longer, before leaving to allow an ATO—Assault Team Officer—to take his place while he waited nearby.

Miles ran his hand through his shoulder-length brown hair, pushing it out of his face. "Beads for what?" Miles had been born near Stonehaven, Scotland, over four centuries earlier, and despite his worldly travels during his time as both human and vampire, the accent was always there.

"The beard," the woman said with a cheery smile. She removed a tray of brightly coloured beads from the tray in the glass case beside her and brought them over to him.

Miles ran a hand through his chest-length dark beard. "I've tried the bead thing before," he said with a smile of his own. "It's not for me, ta."

It was hard to explain that it wasn't for him because it brought back memories of his human time, when he was far from a model citizen. When he had done things that the current Miles was ashamed of.

"You sure?" she asked, masking any disappointment with another winning smile. She looked down at the torc on his wrist. "Why that one? We have golden, silver, I think we have some with diamonds inlaid. We did one a few years ago with emeralds in it."

"It's nae a statement piece," Miles said, and remembered the woman's name: Penelope. "It's my badge. Like a police officer's shield, although I hasten to add, I am nae anything close to a police officer."

"The vampire world has a lot of little details like that," she said. "Badges for the Houses, badges for the various offices and ranks. How do you remember them all?"

Miles shrugged. "You get used to it. How has today gone so far?"

"Sold a watch and a diamond ring to a vampire," she said. "We all know why you're here."

"Oh really?" he asked, leaning on the top of the glass case. "I assume Frank told you like I asked."

"Frank did confirm it, but we already knew. Why else is an Arbiter here after four vampire jewellers in London have been robbed in the last three weeks? We're human, not idiots."

Miles nodded. "I'm sorry. I didn't think any of you were idiots, I just thought it better coming from Frank than me."

"Are we safe?"

There was a touch of fear in her voice, which Miles would expect. The previous robberies were done at night, and were quick grabs by the assailants. Two humans got hit and one of those needed to be treated for a laceration to the face, but otherwise no one was seriously harmed. That had come later, when an Arbiter had been nearby on the last robbery, and one of the robbers had used a gun with incendiary ammo on them. It had resulted in third degree burns on the arm of the vampire. They would heal, but humans robbing vampire establishments using banned weapons was not something that could go unpunished.

There was no *if* when it came to the robbery happening. The Fang and Fog was the last of the jewellers that dealt in vampire items. If the robbers were smart, they'd leave the city while they still could, but Miles was pretty sure that brains weren't high in those who would steal from vampires to begin with.

"Aye," Miles said with confidence.

"Is the vampire who got hurt okay?"

Miles nodded. "I don't think she's best pleased, but she's okay."

Incendiary ammunition and other vampire combatting weapons were heavily regulated, and anyone found with them illegally was dealt with by the full force of the Assembly. Usually with either an ATO or an Arbiter turning up to make your day worse. Thankfully few humans wanted to play fuck around and find out with a bunch of highly trained vampires.

The bell on the door opened and three men rushed inside, all wearing balaclavas over their faces. They wore identical work overalls in black, and black boots. One of them carried a shotgun and the other two handguns, which they all waved around in a manner suggesting they had little idea what they were actually doing.

"On the fucking floor," one of the men shouted, while another switched off the interior lights and locked the front door.

"It'll be fine," Miles said to Penelope as everyone did as they were told and got face first onto the floor, with only Miles in an upright seated position against one of the cases.

"You," the man who had just spoken shouted, pointing at Frank with his handgun. "The safe, now."

Miles had discussed what to do when the robbery finally happened. He'd made sure that Frank told his staff too. You did what they said, when they said it, you didn't argue, you didn't get smart. Getting smart meant getting hurt. The object was to get out in one piece. The object was to get *everyone* out in one piece.

Frank nodded and got back to his feet.

"Beta, clear out the cases," the first man said as he moved through to the back room with Frank where a stairs led to the safe in the basement.

The previous victims had said they'd used Alpha, Beta, and Gamma, because being criminals didn't mean having to be original. The previous crimes had been done quickly, and within a few minutes they left with as much as they could carry.

"We told you to lay down," the criminal identified as Gamma said, pointing his shotgun at Miles.

"Mossberg 800 series," Miles said conversationally. "Specially designed to keep the incendiary shells inside cooled. It took them a long time to make work, so I hear. I prefer the Winchester lever action rifle for incendiary rounds—they managed to figure out how to make sure they leave the barrel at the same speed as a normal round."

Gamma's shotgun wavered slightly, but he kept it aimed at Miles.

"What you're holding there is a military-grade ATO weapon," he continued. "A weapon that the ATO—and I assume you know who they are—would be most aggrieved to discover is in the hands of a bunch of human thieves."

"What the fuck do you know?" Gamma said, his tone wavering slightly, despite the gruff edge he'd tried to put on it.

"I know you've committed several armed robberies in London over the last few weeks," Miles said, glancing over at Beta, who was continuing to go through the glass cases. Miles whistled.

"What the fuck was that?" Gamma asked.

"You should put the gun down," Miles said, pushing just a little at the edges of Gamma's psyche. He didn't have the power or style of House Umber to push into the criminal's mind, to corrupt it, to make him bend or break, but he, like all vampires powerful enough, could push *suggestions* onto the weaker minded. They didn't always work, and pushing too hard broke their mind like snapping a twig, but Miles got the impression it wasn't going to go that far. "You *should* open that door and walk out, hand yourselves over to the police, and regret every one of the choices you made that brought you to this moment."

Gamma's shotgun wavered a little more.

"What the *fuck* is that?" Beta shouted, fear dripping from every word, snapping Gamma out of his daze.

Gamma turned his head slightly to see what Beta had noticed, and Miles knew he was terrified of what he saw. The fear came off him in waves.

"That is a dog," Miles said. "Her name is Church. She is my dog."

"That's a fucking *horse*," Beta said, waving the gun toward a seated Church, who took up most of the doorway.

Miles stood in one fluid motion, and Gamma turned to look at him.

"*Don't*," Miles commanded, putting a lot more force into his voice than he would have otherwise.

Gamma paused, as though frozen in time.

"Church," Miles continued, stepping by the terrified Gamma, and removing the shotgun as he did, "is a Doberman pinscher. Or would have been had her mother not been genetically altered with vampire blood."

Church yawned, showing her large sharp teeth.

Beta's eyes had not left Church since she'd arrived, but he saw Miles move and swung toward him, gun coming toward the vampire. Miles moved faster, grabbing the man's hand and crushing the fingers around the trigger and grip before he could get off a shot.

He continued to crush them, forcing Beta to his knees. "You shouldn't have pointed your gun at my dog," Miles said, before driving his knee into the man's face, breaking his nose, jaw, and orbital bone in the process. He let Beta's unconscious body drop to the floor and turned back to Gamma, who had drawn a dagger and was holding it in one perpetually shaking hand.

"Fucking vampires," Gamma said. "You make it harder for the rest of us."

"How?" Miles asked casually.

"You just do," Gamma snapped.

"You're an idiot," Miles said as he took a step toward Gamma, who swiped with the dagger. Miles batted his hand aside and slapped him across the face hard enough to send him careening headfirst into the wall, where he fell and remained motionless.

Miles looked around, picked up the handgun that Beta still had clutched in his shattered hand, emptied both it and the shotgun, and opened the door, tossing the weapons out into the street next to Church. "Good girl," he said. "I won't be long."

Church's tail wagged enthusiastically, and Miles motioned for the two assistants to leave. "Church, take them to the ATOs."

Church barked once for yes.

Miles turned to the assistants. "Go with her. The ATOs are waiting up the street."

"Thank you," both of them said in unison as they ran out into the night, with the exceptionally large dog in the lead.

Miles turned back to the shop and walked across the darkened floor to the door at the far end, out of sight of the front door. He pushed it open and stepped inside. There was a small room to the left of the hallway beyond, which was where the staff ate lunch, and two bathrooms to the right, but in front of Miles was a staircase that went down to the basement and up to the roof. The former was Miles's destination, and he took the steps three at a time, bouncing from foot to foot as he made his way down the stairs as quickly as possible.

Upon reaching the door at the bottom, Miles pushed it open and stepped inside. It was a good-sized room used for storage on a number of metal shelving units or inside locked cabinets. At the far end of the maze of shelves was another door.

Miles heard the raised voice of Alpha the second he'd stepped inside the storage room. The final robber was screaming at Frank to hurry up, while Frank told him that the lock was on a timer that would only open every half hour. It was nonsense, and Miles hadn't told him to say anything of the sort, but Frank was buying time for everyone upstairs to get out safely.

Miles walked silently through the storage room, easily avoiding anything that might make a noise. He spotted Alpha through the open door, his back turned to the entrance as he screamed at a kneeling Frank to open the safe. The scent of blood reached Miles's nose, and he paused as Frank turned to look at the robber, giving Miles a chance to see the bleeding cut on his forehead.

Alpha turned, bringing his gun up to the storage room, as Miles stepped to the doorway of the small office. He grabbed the gun with one hand, wrenching it free of the robber's grip, while taking hold of the man's throat with his free hand.

With one hand, Miles lifted the robber off the ground and looked down at Frank. "You okay?" he asked.

"Been better," Frank said with a wry smile.

Pain laced through Miles's arm as Alpha stabbed him in the elbow, leaving the four-inch blade protruding from his flesh. Miles dropped the criminal, who ran out into the storeroom.

"That little shit stabbed me," Miles said, almost in disbelief that someone would dare. He pulled the blade free—it was a small kitchen knife, the type you'd use to cut an apple. Miles knew that the wound would bleed for a few seconds before it closed up.

"I'll be fine," Frank said, getting to his feet, reaching for a hanky in his pocket and placing it over his wound. "Don't you need to get him?"

"I think he's got bigger problems than me," Miles said as he helped a wobbly Frank through the storage room and up the stairs.

The shop above was empty, and apart from a few smashed cabinets, it didn't look as though it would be too much work to put everything back in working order. It would have been blissfully quiet if not for the screaming outside.

Miles walked to the door, where he found Church sitting atop the remaining robber. The man was screaming for help while two ATO officers, both in navy blue tactical gear, laughed at him.

"Good girl," Miles said, scratching Church behind one ear, her tail wagging, as the man beneath her whimpered.

A medic took Frank away to get treatment, and Miles crouched down beside the whimpering man. "Where'd you get the guns?" he asked.

"Get this fucking dog off me, please," the man said. "Please."

Miles looked up at the two ATO officers, both of whom had their sternest faces on, but he could see they were still trying not to snigger at what was happening to the idiot who had run away from an Arbiter straight into Church.

"Tell me, and Church will leave," Miles said softly. "Don't make me ask again."

Church let out a long, low growl.

"He calls himself the Wolf," the man said, his words spilling out.

"The Wolf?" Miles asked. "Seriously?"

The man did his best approximation of a nod, while trying not to make any movement that Church might consider to be threatening.

"Where do I meet this . . . Wolf?" Miles asked with a sigh. He removed the robber's balaclava, revealing a pale-skinned man who was no older than mid-twenties. He was clean shaven and had a tattoo of a bloody knife next to his right ear—it was about the size of a matchstick, and to Miles's eyes looked truly ridiculous.

"He has a place in Kensington," the man said. "Uxbridge Street, go all the way to the end, past Jameson. There's a grey door with *Wolf* written in capital letters."

"He's in a house?" Miles asked.

"Warehouse," the man said. "The whole street on that side is a bunch of garages and warehouses."

"If you're lying to me, there's nowhere you can hide now," Miles said. "You want to make sure you've told me everything?"

"Knock three times, wait to three, and knock twice more," the man said. "Armed guards?"

"There were always five or six guys with him when we went."

"Human or vampire?"

"Human, definitely human."

"The Wolf's real name?" Miles asked.

"No clue," the criminal said. "Can I go now?"

"Church, do you think he's told us enough?" Miles asked.

Church leaned down and sniffed the man's throat before getting off him. The criminal let out a long sigh of relief, as the two ATO agents arrested him.

"Remember, if you're lying, I know where you'll be," Miles told the young criminal as he was led away down the street toward a waiting van.

"Been a productive night," a man said from behind Miles.

Miles turned and shook the man's hand. His name was Jonathan Holt, an ATO commander who had been in charge of the agents used in the robbery investigation. It had been the first time Miles had worked with him, although his reputation of being a no-nonsense commander had been proven correct.

Jonathan was six foot four and built like a linebacker for an American football team, a sport that Jonathan spoke about often. He'd been born and raised in Tennessee, back when the Wild West was just everyday life. He had a bald head and shaved face and wore an expensive tailored suit, under the ATO-inscribed stab vest that all agents had to wear when on assignment. Knives were a lot more of a problem against vampires than guns for the most part.

"Three arrests," Jonathan said with a winning smile. "I assume you'll be writing in your report about how well my team and I operated?"

Miles laughed, although not because he found it funny. Jonathan appeared to have a bit of a need to constantly ensure he and his team got credit for anything they did, with an emphasis on *him*. Miles had no intention of leaving their contribution out. He knew that some Arbiters were less happy to share the credit, but that wasn't how he worked. Even so, he found Jonathan's need to get what was his a little bit grating. "Of course," Miles said. "I caught them with your help; the punishment portion of this investigation is yours. I still need to find out who's supplying the weapons."

"You need help, you know who to call," Jonathan said, that winning smile right back.

"Frank and his people okay?" Miles asked.

"They'll be fine," Jonathan said. "No one was really hurt, but they've been taken to the nearest human hospital as a precaution. I'll go with my people to interview our prisoners. See if we can figure out if more of those weapons are out there for public use. These idiots strike me as about as smart as a sack of rocks. I'm a little surprised they even figured out these were vampire businesses."

"Yeah, I've been thinking that myself," Miles said as two ATO agents went into the shop to continue their end of the investigation.

"Good hunting," Jonathan said with a wink and walked away.

Miles set off toward his car, parked a few streets over, and Church padded after him. She whined and nudged his hand with her huge face. They reached the car, a forest green Mercedes AMG GLE. It was a large car, but with Church, you needed the room.

He opened the rear door and let the dog jump in.

"What did you think of Jonathan?" he asked as Church lay down.

She let out a slight whine.

"Aye, I'm nae a fan either," Miles said.

Church barked once, agreeing with him.

Miles shut the rear passenger door, and after opening the driver's side door, got into the car and took a moment to relax. It was a long time until daylight.

"Shall we go hunt a Wolf?" Miles asked.

Church barked once again.

"Excellent choice," Miles said and started the engine.

CHAPTER THREE

Kensington and Chelsea was considered a posh part of London. It was probably the richest borough in the whole city, with a large number of wealthy residents who paid millions of pounds for their Victorian town houses.

Miles had worked in the borough a few times over the centuries, and witnessed the change from a rural idyll into the den of Land Rovers and Rolls-Royces it had become.

After parking the car a few streets over along Campden Hill Square, Miles and Church got out and looked around. It was still dark, it was cold, and it was quiet. The vast majority of buildings in the area were residential homes, and while the sounds of cars could be heard on the main roads a short distance away, it was fairly peaceful a little away from it.

"You ready?" Miles asked Church, who rubbed her head against his leg in response, letting Miles stroke her.

The pair walked along the quiet streets, appearing to anyone who might still be up and about as someone out walking their dog. Church took point, her head twitching toward anything she heard or smelled on the way. The animals of London's night stayed out of her way, although Miles had noticed over the years that the city foxes often came over to her to say hello.

Thankfully, on this occasion, nothing decided it was time for a social call, and the pair reached the start of Uxbridge Street without seeing another soul. Human or otherwise.

Miles crouched down next to Church. "You stay out front," he said. "Stay hidden, stay quiet. Anyone comes running out of there, let them go until I say otherwise. Okay?"

Church let out a soft whine.

"I know you want to come in with me," Miles said, feeling a little guilty about leaving her outside. "But I'm nae planning on going through the front door, and last time I checked, you can't scale buildings."

Church nudged him with her head, forcing Miles to rock back on his feet.

"It's nae my fault," Miles exclaimed. "Look, you stay here. If anyone runs who I want you to catch, I'll shout. Okay?"

Church looked down at the ground and huffed.

"Church," Miles said affectionately, "when this is done, we'll go back home, and you can go for a run in the forest. I'll even get you those biscuits you like. If she's not busy, maybe we'll even go and see Charlotte."

Church's head sprang back up, and she licked Miles's face.

Miles smiled. Church had taken a liking to Charlotte Henry, the First Counsel of House Venator, one of the five Great Vampire Houses. Miles had once been a member of the House himself, and First Librarian, but that had been a long time ago. He'd reconnected with the house the previous year, and had found that he missed the company of several of their members, chief among them Charlotte, who had formed a quick and strong bond with Church. It had warmed Miles's vampiric heart to see it.

With the matter settled, the pair walked along Uxbridge Street. There were several boutique shops, all closed, and a lot of expensive cars parked along the street itself. About halfway down Uxbridge street, the boutique shops turned into a terrace of workshops and small warehouses, all shut, with red graffiti covering many of the grey security doors. A little farther down, and the buildings changed again, this time to several at three storeys high, although the same grey security doors remained in place.

Miles and Church turned down into Jameson Street, which was adorned with terraced town houses, more expensive cars out front, and the sound of music somewhere in the distance. Hopefully if there was a party, it wasn't going to spill out into the street or annoy the neighbours enough to call the police. Miles didn't want anyone spooking the Wolf or his people.

Church sat in the shadow of a white transit van, her eyes on the building fifty feet in front of her, which was Miles's target.

"I'll shout, okay?" Miles reiterated.

Church lay down and placed a large paw over her face. She wasn't happy about being left out in the, quite literal, cold, while Miles got to go do what vampires in his job did, but Miles also knew she was only partially annoyed. If she'd been *really* irritated, she'd have just walked off and refused to come with him. Thankfully, that didn't happen often. Once Church decided not to cooperate, she was not one for having her mind easily changed.

Miles sighed and walked back up toward Uxbridge Street, crossing the road to stand outside of the building with the word *WOLF* painted in red across the grey security door. There was an approximation of a paw print next to the word, and the paint had dribbled down the door. It was, in Miles's artistic opinion, spectacularly shit.

He took a step back and looked up the red-bricked building. The criminal from earlier had said that it was a warehouse inside, and there was nothing on the exterior of the building that suggested he was lying. There were three windows, one directly above the other, with the final window just under the lip of the roof. Miles had checked the building on his phone before getting out of the car and discovered that there was a skylight atop the roof.

Miles scrambled up the outside face of the building, his nails becoming sharp talons that allowed him to grip the old brickwork with ease. He avoided the windows, and it took him only seconds to get to the roof, pulling himself up and taking a moment to look around as he moved to the skylight.

The skylight itself was halfway up the slope of the roof and was slightly ajar. It was big enough for a normal-sized person to get through without any problems.

Miles looked through the window to where it led inside the building. It was a twenty-foot drop to a bare wooden floor, and that was all he could see. Miles placed his hand under the window and pulled sharply. There was a crunch, and the hinges on the window snapped with a sound that he hoped anyone within hadn't heard.

After waiting for a few seconds to see if anyone might turn up, Miles dropped through the open skylight into the . . . empty loft conversion. The room was forty feet long and contained two dozen plastic, translucent tubs, piled in three sets of four at the end of the room. The opposite side had a door painted white. Miles ignored the tubs for a second and tried the door, which was unlocked.

Miles pushed the door open a short distance, revealing a corridor and set of stairs leading down. There were voices from somewhere below, but even with Miles's excellent vampiric hearing, they came through to him as muffled nonsense.

He returned to the room, closing the door behind him, and set about looking through the plastic tubs. Each one was three feet long by two feet wide, and a foot deep. The lids were held on with plastic clips, which after a little bit of frustration on Miles's part, soon came away without damaging the tubs themselves.

The contents sent a shiver up Miles's spine. Box after box of incendiary shells for shotguns, bullets for pistols, and rifle rounds. There were boxes of incendiary bullets designed to be used in machine guns, which was something Miles had never seen before. Thousands of rounds sat in the first half of the boxes, with the second half containing various shock and heat batons, and knives with electrical charges. All designed to hurt and kill vampires. All completely illegal in the hands of anyone not affiliated with the Assembly, who were meant to closely monitor such things.

Every box had *Templar International* stamped in black lettering over a traditional red Templar cross. What was Templar International, and why did they have so many vampire-killing bullets? And how did this Wolf character fit into it?

Miles took photos of the weaponry and used a search engine to check for the company they belonged to. According to their website, they were in security personnel and often did bodyguard work for the rich and famous. He replaced his phone in his pocket. He would take the evidence to the Assembly and let them figure it out. Or he'd go to the head office of Templar International, which was in London, and ask them himself. Either way, there would be answers that needed to be given.

Miles had finished replacing the last tub when he heard a creak outside of the room. He moved quickly back under the skylight and launched himself up and out, back onto the roof, where he stayed low and crouched as the door to the room was quickly pulled open and two men charged inside, both with their handguns out.

Unlike the three robbers whom Miles and Church had dealt with earlier, these two moved like people who knew what they were doing. Both were large men, wearing T-shirts and jeans, although one had a red baseball cap on his head, while the other had long hair up in a bun.

Miles watched as they walked farther into the room, torches in each hand, moving around, illuminating everything. They lowered their guns and stepped under the skylight.

"Nothing here," the one in the cap said.

"The motion sensor went off in the hall," the second one replied.

Miles cursed himself; he hadn't even seen a motion sensor.

"The boxes fell," the cap wearer said. "Maybe they fell and caused the sensor to trip slightly."

"You think that's likely? Everyone is down on the warehouse floor."

"Who was last up here?"

"Robin," Man Bun said.

"We need to have a word with him then," Cap Wearer said. "He didn't stack the tubs right. Maybe it was a rat that tripped the sensor."

"Don't even fucking joke," Man Bun said.

Cap Wearer laughed. "That's right, you don't like rats. Bet you used to watch *Roland Rat* as a kid and piss yourself."

"Fuck off," he snapped before mumbling, "Never liked that puppet."

Miles sighed. *Roland Rat* had been a children's television programme in the 1980s with an anthropomorphised rat as the title character. It had been a big success when it first came out. Miles had forgotten the show had existed.

Miles mentally shook the thought from his head as the two men holstered their guns. He gripped the edge of the skylight and felt his vampire side creep out. Violence was coming.

Man Bun looked up at the skylight and was about to speak when Miles launched himself through it. He dove down, grabbing him by the throat and driving him into the wooden floor with enough force to damage the floorboards, but not enough to do serious damage to the man himself. Miles spun, grabbed the cap wearer by one arm, and threw him across the room into the wall. He hit hard enough to drop straight to the ground and not move, plaster raining down over him like snow, but Miles heard the man's breathing, sensed his heartbeat. He was hurt, but he would live.

Miles walked over to the cap wearer, removed his gun, emptied it, and took a second to remove the slide, bending it enough to ensure it no longer functioned. He tossed the parts to opposite ends of the room before doing the same with Man Bun's gun. The man was groaning softly as he rolled onto his side.

"You'll live," Miles said, using his foot to push the man onto his back. "What happens next might change that."

"Vampire," Man Bun said breathlessly.

"I am," Miles said. "So this is how it's going to work. I'm going to ask questions, and you're going to answer them honestly. You have a weak mind; I can tell when you're not being honest." That wasn't entirely truthful. He couldn't tell if a human was lying by reading his mind, but he could push his own will into the mind of a human to compel them to tell the truth, or gauge if they were lying, even if he couldn't extract the real information himself.

"Okay," the man said.

"You only came up here because of the motion sensor? You're not making rounds?"

The man shook his head. "It's soundproofed up here; we only come up if the sensor goes."

"Why a motion sensor?" Miles asked, genuinely curious as to the reason behind it.

"The Wolf asked for it," the man said. "This room is far above the warehouse, and the Wolf didn't want any of us up with the merchandise all day. He has trust issues."

"Anyone other than you two who monitors the sensors?"

"Just us tonight."

"How many are there in the building?"

"Sixty."

Miles sighed, picked up Man Bun's hand, and snapped one of the fingers at the knuckle. Miles placed his own hand against Man Bun's mouth to stifle the scream. He crouched down beside Man Bun and whispered, "You have a lot of bones in your body, and I have only a few questions, so hopefully I won't have to break them all before you realise I'm nae playing games here. You've already told me that no one can hear us, so maybe think long and hard about your future here. If you like, I could just drink you dry and get the answers I need."

Miles didn't want to take any amount of blood from Man Bun. Vampires who drank from humans could see the life of the human, but the human could also see the life of the vampire, and Miles didn't want to have to kill the guard because he saw something he shouldn't have. Better to avoid the whole biting part than make a complex situation even worse.

"Four," Man Bun corrected quickly.

"The Wolf among them?"

"Yes, him and three others."

"They all armed like you two? Anti-vampire ammo?"

"Jerry carries a voltage baton and shotgun with incendiary rounds."

"The other two armed with anything that could hurt me?"

Man Bun nodded. "Voltage batons."

"Where'd he get the ammo and weapons?"

"He had a contact at the port, said some crates had fallen off the back of a lorry, if you know what I mean."

"The name of the contact?"

"Don't know it, man. Only the Wolf does."

"Do you ever feel stupid calling him the Wolf?"

"Every fucking time, man," the man said with an exhale that suggested he'd been sitting on that for a while. "He's a nerd, a fucking computer geek. He knows numbers; his dad used to be a bookie or something. He deals in stolen gear, normally just cars, he's got a chop shop in Whitechapel. He started to move into drugs a while back, got more cash from it, but this is the first time we got weapons. Never done this shit before, man. Never again."

"Because of me?" Miles asked.

"Nah, man, because the people who want that shit are fucking scary." The man's eyes were wide with fear; he meant every word. "I told the Wolf, you don't fuck about with vampire shit. You leave them alone, they leave you alone. He couldn't, though. Too much money in it for him to say no. Stupid fucking clown."

"You stay here, with your friend, and you behave," Miles told him, making sure to keep his tone soft, friendly, even if his face was still his vampire side. "You do that, I'm going to walk out of this room, and you'll never see me again. You come downstairs and help the Wolf, I'm going to make sure you have to relearn how to walk. Am I clear on that?"

The man nodded enthusiastically.

Miles turned back to his human appearance and stood upright. "Don't get up, don't try anything. Your guns won't work, and I'm in nae mood to fight nice with anyone who tries to attack me."

"I ain't doing shit," Man Bun said from his spot on the floor.

"Keep it that way," Miles said. "There a key for any doors?"

"No," Man Bun said.

"How many motion detectors?"

"Just the one in the hall. I assume you tripped it, yeah?"

Miles nodded. "Should have put one in the skylight."

"Was meant to," Man Bun said, moving slightly to look up at the ceiling. "But . . . well, no one wanted to get up on the roof to do it."

Miles snatched a set of cable ties from beside the boxes and looked down at Man Bun, who looked nervous, his fear coming off him in waves.

"You going to bite me?" Man Bun asked, obviously terrified. "You going to drain me and leave me a husk up here?"

"Absolutely not," Miles said, vaguely disgusted by the idea of drinking even a drop of Man Bun's blood. Miles turned the man onto his front and bound his hands and feet together, before pushing him onto his back again. He walked across the room and did the same to the now semiconscious cap wearer, but left him in a seated position, slumped against the side of a tub.

"He okay?" Man Bun asked, with genuine concern.

"He's not going to feel great when he comes around properly, but there's no head injury I can see, and his heart rate is strong," Miles said. "I wasn't trying to kill either of you. You both stay here—there will be an ambulance coming once I've spoken to your boss."

"I never hurt no one."

"But I bet your boss has someone who does. That it?"

Man Bun nodded. "Jerry."

"And Jerry is?"

"Psychotic."

Miles stared at Man Bun for a few seconds before he asked, "He human?"

"Yeah, the Wolf doesn't trust vampires. I don't think he trusts us half the time. He's paranoid, and thinks people are always out to steal from him. Also, he has a bit of a coke problem."

"Ah, that must help a whole bunch."

"It's best to go check on noises in the attic when he's on a bender."

"Like tonight?" Miles asked.

Man Bun nodded.

"You've been very helpful," Miles said. "I have some more questions. Where's the Wolf?"

"Bottom floor, at the back," Man Bun said. "The door is reinforced steel. There are four other rooms before then. Second floor has a kitchen and lounge area, where the Wolf takes clients. Bottom floor has a rear door, takes him out to an alleyway behind the building. Also reinforced steel. Both doors have UV lights on them."

Miles smiled as he exited the room. "So, he really doesn't like vampires. That's fine. I'm nae here to make friends."

CHAPTER FOUR

Miles stopped to look at the motion detector on the landing outside of the attic room. He was annoyed that he hadn't seen it, but it had worked out well in the end. He crept quietly down the staircase, pausing on the floor below to glance down the short corridor to the open door at the end.

He decided it was best to double-check that no one was about to creep up on him, then he walked into the dark room. There was a door inside, just to the right of the entrance, behind which was a small but smart kitchen. Other than that, it was a room of fifteen by ten feet, with a wooden table and four matching chairs in the middle. A large window sat at the end of the room, and Miles took a moment to look out of it, down onto a warehouse.

There were industrial metal shelving units all around the warehouse, giving it the look of a maze. The warehouse was well over a hundred feet long and forty feet wide and actually encompassed the buildings on either side of what Miles had thought were three separate places. There was a large office at the far end.

The shelving units had wooden crates stacked up to reach nearly forty feet high, and above those were the exposed metal beams of the building. The window had a latch, which Miles opened, climbing out onto the high beam and walking along with ease.

He was over sixty feet above the concrete floor, looking for the guards that Man Bun had said would be down here. The light in the warehouse came from a dozen black UFO-styled light fittings that were placed at intervals in threes along the building.

Miles stopped above a set of metal shelves, which had cardboard boxes instead of wooden ones, and dropped down onto it, making little noise.

He turned a fingernail on one hand into a razor-sharp talon and cut a hole in the corner, before retracting the talon and tearing down the side of the box. The contents of the cardboard boxes, each about a foot long and half as wide, spilled out over the metal shelves and down onto the floor, making an extraordinary amount of noise. Exactly the distraction he needed.

Miles was quickly back up onto the metal beam above, moving to the side of the warehouse into the shadows where he could watch whatever was about to unfold.

Two guards arrived quickly. Both wore the voltage batons that Miles had found in the tubs in the attic. They were both a little over six feet tall, of large build, with short dark hair. If it hadn't been for the fact that one of them had a goatee, Miles wasn't sure he'd have been able to easily tell them apart.

"What the fuck happened?" a shrill voice shouted from over at the far end of the warehouse.

The door to the office was open, and a short stocky man in a navy suit stood in the doorway, shouting at no one in particular as he stomped his way through the warehouse to the site of the mess. He was followed by, presumably, Jerry, who kept far enough back to watch as his boss shouted at the boxes on the ground.

"What the fuck happened?" the man Miles assumed was the Wolf yelled again.

"Don't know," one of the two men said.

"Looks like the box split," the other one said, looking up at the remains of the box above him.

"That is a cardboard box," the Wolf said, pointing at it, the disdain coming off him in waves. "Why is my shit in a cardboard box?"

Both men shrugged.

"Get it in a proper container," the Wolf said, sounding exasperated. "I'm trying to make a deal here, lads. I'd appreciate it if you all did as much as possible to not be utterly fucking useless."

Miles knew he could have taken them all there and then, but the distance between Jerry and the others was big enough that he would have to deal with at least one shotgun blast, and that meant someone getting seriously hurt. He didn't want that, if it could be helped.

He removed his phone and sent a message to the ATO group chat for the team he'd been working with on the robbery cases. He gave the address he was at and told them to be prepared for a long night going through a whole warehouse of stuff. Miles put the phone away before waiting for any replies.

Wolf and Jerry retreated back to the office, leaving the two guards to clear up the mess spilled all across the floor.

"Go get the lift," one of the two men said.

The other man sulked off toward the drivable orange scissor lift next to the entrance to the warehouse.

Miles moved back along the beams, until he was overhead of the man picking up boxes. He wondered if he could land quietly, decided it wasn't worth the risk, and continued on to the lift driver, who was fumbling with a set of keys.

Like most vampires, Miles had a bloodline gift—an ability passed through the bloodline of the vampires they belonged to—but also a secondary power. Miles's secondary power was telekinesis. Since the incident in Washington state, and the acquiring of his ability to turn into his beast form, Miles's other abilities and attributes had increased in power. Something that would come in useful now.

The guard eventually placed the correct key in the ignition of the lift, and Miles used his mind to pull it out, pushing it onto the floor and out of the cab.

"For the love of fuck," the man exclaimed, climbing down from the cab, as Miles dropped down silently onto one of the industrial shelving units, moved along it, and dropped down farther onto the stationary lift. He vaulted over the side of the lift, smashing his foot into the guard's face as he fell.

Catching the guard before he hit the ground, his face a bloody mess, Miles lowered him gently into the recovery position to make sure he didn't choke on his own blood. There hadn't been a noise. He moved along the shelving units, passing through one when there was a big enough gap, and continuing on until he was behind the second guard.

Miles grabbed the guard in a choke hold, using just enough strength to put him out without crushing his windpipe or breaking his neck. Both of which could have been done with the minimal amount of extra force.

He placed the unconscious man on the ground, picked up one of the crates, and opened it. A silver bar stared back at him. It had been placed inside a fitted piece of polystyrene so it didn't rattle or get damaged. Miles removed it and turned it over. No marks. No identifying features. It was a completely smooth piece of silver.

Miles opened a second and third crate and found all three to be the same. He moved to one of the nearby wooden crates and used a talon to cut open the plastic cord, keeping the lid tied to the rest of the box. He pushed open the lid and removed another small box, this one square in shape. Miles opened it and found dozens of bullet casings, all with a silver hollow-point tip. Were they making silver bullets? He took a handful and dropped them in his pocket.

After dropping the box back in the crate, Miles climbed the shelves again, got back up onto the beam, and moved across the warehouse at speed, sticking to the edges of the building in case Jerry decided to look up.

Miles crept around from the side of the warehouse and paused when he saw the UV lights hidden inside the doorframe.

There were no windows on the office, which Miles was pretty sure was a design flaw, and he'd seen no camera inside the warehouse itself. A little bit of a surprise that someone who had been described as paranoid had left any and all security measures to a lone man with a shotgun, and a few UV lights.

He took another step toward Jerry and froze. There was a camera. It was built into the office, directly above the door, and only noticeable when the lens zoomed out and back in. Miles looked around, a slight panic running through his head as he tried to see if he'd missed any cameras, anything that might give away his location, but there was nothing.

Miles quickly calmed himself and looked down at Jerry, who hadn't moved. He considered the best way of neutralizing him, without the Wolf inside the office catching wind and legging it out the back door. Miles would be able to hunt him with ease, but that wasn't the point. He wanted this to be contained; he didn't want to have to involve innocent people in the city, even in a short-lived way.

He moved across the beams that sat over the office, the roof of which had motion sensors crisscrossed over it, the red lines visible to Miles. He continued on until he sat over yet more metal shelving, where he paused, took some of the bullets out of his pocket, and tossed them all onto the roof of the office.

Alarms sounded from inside the office, and Jerry turned around, his shotgun pointed at the door as he opened it, stepped inside, and vanished from view.

Miles dropped down the sixty feet to the floor and hurried toward the office. He removed the final bullet from his pocket and used his telekinesis to throw it as hard as possible toward the exposed UV bulb in the doorway.

The bulb shattered, and Miles sprinted toward the door as Jerry came out, his shotgun already up. Miles grabbed the gun, aimed it up at the door behind him, and used his telekinesis again to pull the trigger, blowing apart the UV bulb that sat above it, setting fire to the wooden exterior of the door itself, and exposing the steel frame within.

Miles headbutted Jerry, shattering his nose, tore the gun out of his hands, and tossed it toward the Wolf, who had been trying to get something out of his pocket. The stock of the shotgun collided with the Wolf's face, and he went down with a whimpering noise that was decidedly un-wolflike.

Jerry's face was a mess of blood and broken bones, but he still took a swing at Miles, who stepped to the side faster than Jerry could have ever moved, and punched him in the stomach hard enough to drop the larger man to the floor with ease.

"The *Wolf*, I presume," Miles said, looking over at the wooden desk, under which cowered the man himself. A pile of cocaine had sat on top of the desk when Miles had entered. It now covered the desk and part of the black carpet, looking like the most expensive carpet cleaner in existence.

Opposite the desk, against the far wall, next to the door, was an old forest green sofa.

There was an explosion of noise as the Wolf fired a shotgun shell up through the side of his desk, directly where he expected Miles to be. Unfortunately for him, Miles had already moved to the side of the room, and was walking around to the back of it when the blast happened.

Miles flipped the desk over with one hand, feeling his anger flood into him. The Wolf's shotgun moved toward him, but Miles was on him in a flash, tearing the shotgun free and tossing it across the room as he grabbed the Wolf by the throat, lifting him off the ground.

The man's head bounced off the wall behind him as Miles held him in place.

"I am in nae mood to play silly games," Miles said angrily.

"Who are you?" the Wolf asked in a slight wheeze.

Miles released his grip, and the man fell to the floor. "You deal in drugs, guns, and cars. But I found a lot of silver out there, a lot of bullets, and no cars."

The Wolf was a man with pale skin, with long blond hair that fell over his shoulders, and a dark beard. He had a neck tattoo of a wolf howling at . . . Miles paused. "Why is that wolf howling at your ear?"

"It's not finished," the Wolf snapped back.

Miles pulled the man upright and sat him back in his leather office chair.

"What's your actual name?"

"The Wolf," the man said with what Miles assumed was meant to be menace.

Miles slapped him across the face, hard enough to hurt, but not hard enough to do serious damage.

"Noah," he said with a sob.

"Right, Noah, we have some things to discuss."

"I don't think so," Noah said.

Miles sighed and was about to speak when Jerry stirred. He went over to him, made sure he wasn't about to become an issue with his last zip tie, and turned back to Noah, who threw a grenade at him.

Miles pulled out the sofa with one hand and dove behind it as the room was bathed in UV light. "Fuck," Miles shouted, as the hand he'd used to cover the back of his head began to heal from the third degree burns it had sustained.

Noah was nowhere to be found, although his echoing footsteps told Miles that the little weasel had run out into the warehouse back toward the front of the building.

Two more grenades went off in the warehouse, and Miles ducked behind the wall of the office. The light was dozens of feet away, but it wasn't worth taking the risk.

"Oh, you little shite," Miles said as he left the office, feeling less anger at the fact that he'd been hurt, and more at the fact that Noah had run.

Miles walked through the warehouse, keeping an eye out for any more grenades that might come his way. He reached the end, next to the still-prone guard beside the lift, and opened the door to the hallway beyond. The front door was wide open, the darkness of the street just beyond showing Noah's running form farther down the road.

Miles jogged to the outside, where he found Church sitting on the ground, licking her paws.

"You let him go," Miles said.

Church continued to lick her paws.

"Church, you're mad you didn't come with me."

Church looked up at Miles and huffed.

"Seriously?" Miles asked. "Look, I'm sorry, but you can't climb walls. Besides, now you get to actually have fun. There was no fun in there."

Church stood and looked down the road toward Noah, who was a good hundred meters away.

"Fetch," Miles said.

Church set off at a full sprint, running down the road toward Noah like a furry rocket. Miles's hand was all but healed now, although it would be tender for a few days more. He leaned up against the wall and flexed his fingers, making them crack, as the sound of Noah swearing at Church wafted through the night. By the time Church had dragged the injured Noah halfway, he'd given up being angry and was now pleading with her to let him go.

Church ignored the criminal, and continued to drag him by the neck, as if he were a small puppy. She did this until she reached Miles, whereupon she dropped Noah on the floor and walked over his prone body to make sure he got the point about how she felt about him.

Church sat back on her hind legs and started to lick her paws again, occasionally giving a low growl toward Noah, who had wisely decided to keep his mouth closed.

"Templar International," Miles said as people opened their house windows to see what had caused such a racket. Occasionally someone would shout something, but it was London, and if something was happening early in the morning, and it didn't appear to need anyone from the emergency services, it was probably best to go back to bed. "You have a bunch of their stuff in your attic. You're going to tell me where you got it, who you sold it to, and anything else I ask."

"I don't know what you're talking about," Noah said.

Miles took hold of Noah's collar and dragged him back into the building, throwing him through the door at the end, where he collided with a box which turned out to be more solid than he was. Noah hit the ground hard.

"Watch him," Miles said to Church, and walked around the warehouse, dragging the unconscious and injured members of Noah's security over to one of the metal shelving units. He found some more zip ties and used one on each person to attach them to the metal shelves. When they eventually regained full consciousness, they weren't going anywhere.

Miles returned to Noah and Church. The latter stood in front of the former, growling low and menacing.

"What did you do to my dog?" Miles asked, dragging Noah to his feet.

"Your dog is psych—"

Miles punched him in the stomach, sending him back to the ground, gasping for air.

"Oh, get up, it was only a little punch," Miles said, dragging the human back to his feet. "Where'd you get the Templar International stuff from?"

"Vampires always think they're better than us lowly humans," Noah sneered. "You want to know, why don't you go ask Templar International?"

"I'm beginning to think you're not going to cooperate," Miles said, the sounds of cars pulling up outside reaching his ears. "So be it."

A few moments later five ATO members came into the warehouse, each one wearing the same tactical gear that they'd been in when Miles had seen them a few hours ago. Behind them swaggered Jonathan Holt.

"This is an ATO team," Miles said conversationally. "They're going to take you to an Assembly Inquisitor; do you know what that is?"

Noah's sneer vanished. He knew.

Inquisitors were, to Miles's mind, something that shouldn't need to exist. They operated adjacent to Arbiters like himself, but used much more . . . intense methods to get information from someone. That meant tearing into a person's mind with little regard for the damage it did, or maybe some light physical torture. Whatever it took. They were considered by some to be the last line of defence from the vampires just exercising control over the world, but in practise Miles felt that they were a group of people who enjoyed their jobs a bit too much.

As an Arbiter, Miles had very little oversight from the Assembly, beyond having to report on whatever investigation he was involved in. He wasn't even sure that the Inquisitors had that, and more than once he'd recently had to put down Inquisitors who'd decided to align themselves with people who didn't have the best interests of the Assembly, or vampires as a whole, in mind.

"You feel like talking now?" Miles asked.

"Fine," Noah snapped. "What do you want to know?"

CHAPTER FIVE

Noah had been quite forthcoming since the arrival of the ATOs. Miles sat with the unhappy human and asked everything he wanted to know, while the ATOs set about arresting the criminal's security guards and cataloguing everything inside the warehouse. They were going through his computer when they found spreadsheets with millions of pounds' worth of equipment listed, along with a list of buyers and dates for shipments.

"You've just put a target on my head," Noah snapped as an ATO gleefully showed Noah the lists.

"You did that when you started selling illegal tech to criminals," Miles said with no sympathy.

The pair had gone up to the room overlooking the warehouse itself, with Church having found a comfortable spot on the floor to lie down, while Noah was placed in a chair, his hands handcuffed behind his back.

"Oh look, human police," Miles said, pointing at the vast number of uniformed officers entering the warehouse.

"Fucking hell, man, you don't have to sound happy about it," Noah said glumly.

"It's a good day to be everyone but you," Miles pointed out. "Where'd you get the Templar International equipment?"

"Stole it from the docks," Noah said. "Got a phone call from a friend who says that Templar International has a warehouse down there, but they've undergone some personnel changes, taken their eye off the ball, so to speak. Was easy to get in, get out. Take a bunch of stuff. Which turned out to be not just weapons and ammunition, but silver bars."

"Did you melt the silver down to make bullets?"

"Thought we could sell them. People want to feel safe from vampires."

"So you're going to sell them silver bullets," Miles said slowly, as though he were talking to an idiot. "You know we're not werewolves, right? Silver's not really a big issue for us. Heat, decapitation, all things that will kill us. Sunlight can kill us, although it's nae the actual *light* part that's the issue. But silver is . . . well, it's nothing."

Noah stared at Miles for several seconds. "Seriously?"

Miles nodded. "You didnae know that?"

"How was I meant to know?" Noah almost shouted. "You mean I could have just been selling that silver? I wasted all that time and money for nothing?"

"You think some of the people you sold it to won't be too happy when they shoot a vampire who laughs at them?"

Noah paled.

"I'll take that as a *yes* then," Miles said with a smile. "Why keep anything in the attic?"

"We were transferring everything over to our own packaging," Noah said. "Didn't want it getting back to Templar. I heard rumours about them—I don't want no part of some mercenary organisation. I'll steal from them, but I don't want them to find out about it."

"Their website says they're a private military company," Miles said. "They run security for powerful people."

"And they send mercenary teams to deal with shit governments can't or won't touch," Noah said. "I know who they are. I did a lot of research."

"Before you decided to rob from the heavily connected, deeply dangerous mercenary company?" Miles finished for him.

"You make it sound like it was a bad idea."

Miles stared at Noah for a second. "Did ye get dropped on your head a lot as a kid?"

"I don't have to listen to this," Noah snapped.

"Aye, ye do," Miles told him. "How had Templar International taken their eye off the ball?"

"No idea, but my friend told me that there were maybe half the security personnel there had been a few months earlier," Noah said. He leaned toward Miles. "I think maybe the CEO had some kind of mental breakdown. And by breakdown, you know . . . they . . . *removed him.*"

"Killed?"

Noah nodded sagely.

"You think a multimillion-dollar company murdered their own CEO?" Miles asked, not bothering to keep the sarcasm out of his voice. "A security company that makes an ungodly amount of money murdered someone who is in charge of making them *more* money?"

Noah's expression faltered. "Maybe not *murdered*, but he hasn't been seen around. His head of security has been doing a lot of the work."

Miles brought up the company website on his phone, went to the personnel section, and showed the photos of the heads of the company to Noah. "Which one?"

"Sara Bakos," Noah said.

Miles tapped on the website where there should be a photo, except it was just a picture of the Templar International logo.

"You should know something—" Noah said, sounding cocky again.

"She's a vampire." Miles cut him off.

Noah's entire body appeared to deflate. "How'd you know?"

"There's no picture of her," Miles said. "Vampires can have their photos taken, but they don't like it. It's hard to pretend you're not a vampire when someone has a fifty-year-old photo of you and you haven't aged. Easier to avoid photos altogether. What do you know about her?"

"Nothing, no one knows a damn thing about her," Noah said. "Just that she hasn't been around as much the last few months. It used to be a watertight ship, and now it's sprung a few leaks."

Miles stood and stretched, looking down at the number of human and vampire law enforcement working together in the warehouse. "You tried to kill me," he said without looking back at the still-seated criminal.

"A vampire turns up to try and kill me, I figured you were with Templar," Noah said. "They're like an official partner of the Assembly; did you know that?"

Miles hadn't known that, although he didn't want to have to tell his prisoner that. Miles rapped his knuckles on the glass, and Jonathan looked up at him and waved. Miles motioned for Jonathan to head up, and the ATO Commander nodded.

"Templar is going to send someone after me," Noah said pleadingly. "They don't deal well with people who have tried to rob them. Their CEO, Henryk something or other, is not a man you cross."

Miles turned back to the exceptionally stupid idiot sitting at the table beside him. "How have you gotten this far in life?"

"I'm good at stealing cars," Noah said with a shrug.

Miles wondered how someone so self-absorbed as Noah had ever managed to live as long as he had with the lifestyle he led. "I'm going to pass you over to this ATO team, and you will almost certainly see a jail cell in your near future, and you'll almost certainly be placed on some kind of anti-vampire watch list.

"He's all yours," Miles told Jonathan and left the ATO to their job. Church joined him on his way out of the room, and the pair walked down the stairs and back out to the street. Judging from the number of people looking out of windows, there was some interest from nearby residents, but thankfully everything appeared to be calm.

Jonathan walked over and offered Miles his hand. "Thank you for the call."

"I'd rather you guys dealt with them than me," Miles said.

"That's two cases you've handed over in one night," Jonathan said, with a raised eyebrow. "No one is that altruistic."

"Not altruism," Miles pointed out. "Just not wanting to do any more paperwork than I need to. I'll write up my report and send it to Rosa."

Rosa Sanchez was his Arbiter handler. They changed from case to case, depending on their expertise of the country the Arbiter was operating in, knowledge of the crimes and criminal element, and whether or not the handler and Arbiter got on. The latter wasn't as important, but it was essential for an Arbiter to know that the handler had their back, and would run interference with local police, government, or anyone else. It was rare, but cases had fallen apart because of animosity between handler and Arbiter. Thankfully, he and Rosa worked well together.

"I'm going to owe you either way," Jonathan said. "What's the plan now?"

"I'm going to go to Templar International and have a chat with their security officer," Miles said.

"Now?" Jonathan asked. "It's early in the morning."

"She's a vampire. I think."

"They're Assembly accredited," Jonathan said. "You need to tread carefully."

Assembly accredited companies were allowed to deal in anything from weapons and intel to office supplies for all Assembly personnel, including Arbiters, handlers, ATOs, and anyone else they could think of. It was usually a long process to become accredited by the Assembly, so that those who made it through the process were loyal to the Assembly itself, and didn't work with the organisation just for their own profits.

"I always do," Miles said. "Have a good morning cataloguing all of that."

Jonathan looked back at the warehouse front door. "I'm beginning to think this isn't the boon I originally suspected."

Miles slapped him on the shoulder and walked off, Church beside him, until they reached the car. Miles opened the rear passenger door, and Church bounded in, making herself comfortable once again. He got into the driver's seat and used his phone to bring up the Templar International website. It all looked aboveboard, and looking through the various pages on the site showed an *Assembly Accredited* badge on one of the pages.

Templar International's address was Southbank Tower, nicknamed Templar Tower. The original thirty-storey building had undergone several redevelopments and now stood at forty-four storeys. The entire building was used by Templar International and its various subsidiaries. According to the blurb online, the floors were a mixture of offices, apartments for guests of the company, research labs for unidentified purposes—which Miles wasn't thrilled about—and probably a host of other things they didn't like to advertise. Three of the top four storeys were used by the company as meeting rooms and offices for their executive levels, with the final floor being used as a penthouse suite for its owner and CEO, Henryk Greger, and his family. Although details on said family were slight at best.

Miles scrolled through the numbers on his phone and called Rosa, who answered on the second ring. "I hear you've had a productive evening," she said. Rosa was originally from Puerto Rico, back when it was a Spanish colony. She'd been turned into a vampire just before the country was turned over to American hands, and had worked for the Assembly for almost the entirety of her vampire life of one hundred fifty years.

"You could say that," Miles said. "Jonathan Holt and his team will be happy that I've passed the jewellery robbers and a stolen weapons case to them."

"You know, if you keep letting others take the credit, it'll look like you're not doing any work." There was an obvious smile on her face when she spoke, but Miles knew there was some truth to her words, too.

"Low profile," Miles said. "That's all I'm doing right now."

Rosa chuckled. "You've never struck me as a man who does low profile before. This must all be new to you."

"I'm muddling through," Miles said.

The previous year, Miles had executed the House Umbra captain, Vedran Vinko. There had been a number of excellent reasons for this: Vedran was a murder, a sadistic bully, a man who allied himself with a group who wanted to exterminate vampires. But most of all, Miles executed him because Vedran hadn't deserved to keep living.

Miles and his allies had also killed a large contingent of Vedran's loyal personnel. And after it had all been done, Miles had been told to take a back seat for a bit. Don't give anyone an excuse to take an interest in him. Miles knew it was a good suggestion, but he couldn't just do nothing for a few years until members of the Assembly, or House Umbra, decided that he was no longer of interest. So, instead, he'd been doing the work and then giving the main credit over to any ATO teams he'd been working with. It couldn't last forever, though, and Miles could see an extended break in his near future to put a little distance between himself and those who might be looking for an excuse to keep a more *watchful* eye on him and his activities.

"Did you call because you missed me, or was there a more work-related reason?" Rosa asked.

"Templar International," Miles said, before explaining what he'd discovered.

"You know I can't tell you what to do and not to do," Rosa said after listening quietly to Miles's information. "But I will heavily suggest that you do not screw around with Assembly accredited companies without a lot of evidence that they've done something wrong. Especially ones that were given their accreditation in under six months."

"Six months?" Miles said, surprised. It normally took at least a year. "How?"

"No clue," Rosa said. "And by that, I mean I genuinely don't know. If you do decide to go poke this particular hornets' nest, which, let's be honest, we both know you're going to, tread *very* carefully. These people have deep pockets, long memories, and powerful allies. I've heard that there might be an open investigation into some members of their board, but it's only whispers of rumour at the moment."

"So you don't know who's heading up the investigation?"

"I don't, but I can find out. You want me to let you know?"

Miles considered it for a moment. It was probably best that he knew, simply so if he did find out something else, he knew if he could trust the person working on the Assembly's end. "Aye. Please."

"Will do. Be safe." Rosa hung up.

Miles used a USB wire to connect his phone to the car so that it would charge when he started the engine. He didn't want to lose battery power . . . just in case.

Church poked Miles's arm with her nose, and he raised it to give her some attention. "You think Rosa is on the level?"

Church barked softly.

"Me too," he agreed. Miles had worked with Rosa several times over the years, and he liked her immensely. She was competent, easy to share ideas with, and had the backs of her Arbiters a hundred percent. She was also exceptionally dangerous, and had once been spoken to by one of the Assembly Judges for breaking the jaw of an Inquisitor for making a comment that Rosa considered to be rude. That might have been the point that Miles decided he could trust her.

Miles started the car, used the car's infotainment system to find the playlist of thousands of songs on his phone, and started it. He took a moment to listen to B. B. King, then set off for the twenty-five-minute drive from where he was to Southbank Tower.

$\propto$ CHAPTER SIX $\propto$

Miles parked a short walk from his destination, and with Church beside him, they continued on to Southbank Tower on foot. They went through the still-open glass front door and into the large foyer, which had marble walls and floors, and a huge piece of granite serving as a desk for the two receptionists behind it.

There were two security guards standing over by the lifts, both of whom were large men, wearing black suits that suited their frame. Both had neat beards, short dark hair, and tattoos of black wolf silhouettes with crossed rifles beneath them, on the backs of their hands. Miles wondered if it had been a military unit badge, and if so, he wondered how many of the people who worked at Templar International had worked together for a long time. You can't buy that kind of loyalty.

Miles and Church stopped by the reception desk. The two receptionists, a blond man and woman who could have been siblings, looked over the granite block at Church.

"Is that a wolf?" the man asked.

"This is Church," Miles said. "Dog, not wolf."

Church sat and gave her best "I'm just a cute little doggy" expression, which Miles was certain wasn't fooling anyone.

"Can I stroke her?" the woman asked.

"Can she?" Miles asked Church, who padded over to the edge of the desk so she could get her attention.

"I'm here to see Sara Bakos," Miles told the remaining receptionist while Church was told that she was a good girl and fussed over.

"Do you have an appointment?" the man asked, tapping a few things on the computer that Miles couldn't see.

"No," Miles said, showing the bronze torc on his wrist. "I don't need one."

The receptionist stared at the torc for a moment. "You're an Arbiter."

"I am," Miles said with a smile. "If Sara isn't at work, I'll talk to whoever is still here. It's urgent that I speak to her. I assume there is someone available, because you're Assembly accredited, and that means you have to have staff twenty-four seven."

The man tapped a few more things into the computer. "Sara is in tonight. I can get her to come down and see you." He picked up a phone. "Your name?"

"Miles Watson. I think this is the kind of conversation that needs to be private."

The receptionist made a call. "Ms Bakos. It's reception. There's an Arbiter here to see you, name of Miles Watson. It's an urgent, private matter."

A pause.

"No, ma'am, he hasn't given any more information."

Another pause.

"Yes, ma'am, I'll have him sent up." The receptionist ended the call. "She said you can go on up." He removed a black lanyard with the Templar International logo adorning it and a blank badge from a drawer beside him, typed something into the computer, and handed the badge and lanyard to Miles. "You'll need this for security. Talk to one of the guards, and they'll accompany you to the correct floor."

"Thank you for your help," Miles said.

"Have a good visit, sir."

Miles nodded and looked at Church, who was clearly adoring all the attention.

"Sir," the male receptionist said, "your dog is more than happy to stay here. We can get her a bowl of water and maybe some food."

"I've got some roast chicken in the fridge," the female receptionist said.

Church looked pleadingly at Miles, who grinned. If anything untoward happened in Miles's absence, Miles was certain that Church could take care of herself. Besides, there was a good chance that taking her up with him would make people nervous about her presence, and right now he didn't want anyone more nervous than they might already be. "You want to stay for chicken?"

Church barked, the sound echoing around the room.

"I'll be back soon," Miles said to the two receptionists, before looking at Church. "Be good."

Miles left Church to her entertainment and approached the two guards. One had a small snake tattoo on his neck that was almost covered by the shirt and jacket collar. "I'm meant to get one of you to take me up to see Sara Bakos," he said, showing them the badge attached to the lanyard around his neck.

"This way, sir," the snake tattoo guard said, motioning for Miles to follow him around the corner to the nearby lifts.

There were twelve in total, six on either side of a long hallway. Miles was taken to the one at the far end, on the left-hand side. *Templar International* was written on a bronze plaque above the call button. The guard swiped his ID against the black panel under it, and the button glowed green.

Miles looked around and saw that the lifts on this side of the hall all had similar plaques, each with various names of companies on them. The opposite side lifts had no such plaques.

"These are for the offices," the guard said, as if he knew what Miles was thinking. "Those are for science and restricted floors. You can only get to certain floors with security credentials."

"Ah, so I can't get to one of these floors with this badge?" Miles asked.

"No," the guard said. "You can't use the restricted lifts either. It's all well-regulated and secure. The company paid a lot of money to own this place; they can't very well have just anyone coming and going."

The lift arrived and the doors opened, revealing a glass and bronze interior with a red carpeted floor. Miles stepped inside and saw that there was no button to press to go anywhere.

"Swipe your pass on the reader there, and it'll show you the options of available floors on the screen. Tap the one you want, and away you go."

Miles tapped his badge to the reader, and only one floor showed up on the screen: *PH.* He tapped the screen.

"Looks like your options are selected for you," the guard said.

"Thanks for your help," Miles said as the lift doors closed and he started his ascent up to the penthouse.

The doors opened a few seconds later, and Miles was met by a large man wearing jeans and a black T-shirt that showed off his muscular physique. He had a bald head and a face that looked as if it had been punched a lot;

his nose was crooked, and he had cauliflowering around both ears, along with a black eye and a cut on his cheek.

"You been to war or something?" Miles said. "That's a hell of a shiner."

The man touched his face and smiled. "Played a lot of rugby," he said, his accent pure West London. "Name's Furio Cappo. Everyone calls me Fury."

"You have the same wolf tattoo that the guys downstairs have," Miles said, stepping out of the lift into a foyer that had a polished wooden floor and a twenty-foot-long mirror that stretched the entirety of the room.

"Ah, a lot of us came from the same regiment back in the day," he said cheerfully. "You ever served?"

"A long time ago," Miles said. "I'm Miles, by the way."

"Yeah, I know," Fury said with a chuckle. "We don't get Arbiters very often."

Fury and Miles walked along the foyer, with Fury holding open the door for Miles to step through into a hallway with more polished floors, and pieces of art on either wall every few feet. Miles stopped by one of the pieces and looked over at Fury. "That's an Amico Corelli," he said, staring at the oil painting of a full moon night high above a small village. At first glance, it looked like just an exceptional painting, but Amico was a vampire painter—one of the finest in the world—and his art always held a little of the darkness that vampires were capable of. In this instance, a shadowy figure watching out of an alleyway.

"I see a new shadow pretty much every time I walk by," Fury said. "There's meant to be nine, but I can only find seven."

Miles spotted a few more shadows before forcing himself away and continuing on toward the set of double doors at the end of the hallway.

"Your boss likes expensive art," Miles said, as he walked by a second Amico painting, this one of what appeared to be a London street. It was next to a closed door that had been painted to resemble part of the wall.

"It's his weakness," Fury said. "Italian painters, mostly. I think he has pieces from most of the top vampire painters."

"Why vampires?"

Fury shrugged. "You'd have to ask him. Although I doubt you'll see him tonight."

Miles stopped by a metal door that had a six-inch blank security panel beside it. He tapped the panel, which came to life and showed that a facial scan was necessary.

"It's . . . a private vault," Fury said, tapping the panel. "The boss can't have everything out all at once."

"Understandable," Miles said as they continued on.

They reached the doors, and Fury pushed one of them open, beckoning Miles inside into a short hallway with coats hung up along one side, shoes under a rack on the floor, and a full-length mirror opposite. Apart from the main doors Miles had just walked through, there was one other door inside, which Fury opened, and they stepped into the penthouse itself.

Miles followed and immediately looked out through the windows that took up one entire side of the building, giving incredible views of the River Thames and surrounding cityscape. He spotted St Paul's Cathedral and several other landmarks.

"Impressive, isn't it?" Fury said.

"Yeah, it really is," Miles agreed, finally looking around the penthouse itself.

They stood in what Miles assumed was the living area. There were steps down into a sunken part of the room where a horseshoe couch sat, which was so big it could have easily housed actual horses. There was a TV on a wall halfway down the living area that Miles thought was actually of a reasonable size, not the gargantuan monstrosity he'd expected.

In fact, as he looked around, he found the whole place quite tasteful. There was a small bar at the far right of the suite, next to one of three doors, all of which were closed. He turned to look over to the left, where there were three more doors, one of which was open, revealing a large kitchen.

"Drink?" Fury asked.

"No, thank you," Miles said. "I expected more guards."

"Ah, well, guards don't normally stay up here," Fury said. "That room we passed by out in the hallway is a security room. Sara said it was okay that you knew that."

And to make me aware that there are guards nearby, Miles thought to himself.

"Please take a seat—Sara will be with you shortly," Fury said, directing Miles to the large sofa before walking away to the right of the room and exiting through the middle of the three doors.

Miles remained standing in the middle of the room. He walked over to the windows and looked out across the city of London. It wouldn't be sunrise for a few hours yet, but he knew that it was going to be getting busier soon. There was very little time when it wasn't busy.

"You must be Miles Watson," a woman's voice said from behind Miles.

Miles turned and smiled at the newcomer. She had dark, almost black hair, which was left to drop over her shoulders. She had several diamond earrings in each ear, and all of her fingers had at least one ring. She wore a white blouse with the sleeves rolled up, showing toned and muscular forearms. Black trousers and matching boots finished the outfit, along with a dagger in a sheath against her hip. She was a little shorter than him, and carried herself like someone who was confident with who, or what, they were.

"And you must be Sara Bakos," Miles said, offering his hand, which she shook. A firm handshake, not trying to crush his own hand or compensate for anything.

"I am," she said, motioning to the sofa. "Please sit. Did Fury offer you a drink?"

Miles nodded. "I'm fine, thank you. I don't want to keep you from what I'm sure is a busy role within a company of this size."

"I am always happy to be diverted for a few hours," Sara said in a slightly flirtatious tone, followed by a winning smile, which faltered for a moment. "I should let you know that I've already spoken to the Assembly about my murdered driver. I didn't expect them to send an Arbiter about it. Do I need to make a call to my lawyer, as they have the details?"

"No idea what you're talking about," Miles said.

"Oh," Sara said, clearly disarmed. "What is this about?"

"I came across a young gentleman tonight who has stolen a shipment of weapons and ammo from yourselves," Miles said, seeing no point in beating around the bush. "He was selling those weapons and ammunition to idiots who caught the attention of the wrong people."

"I assume you are the wrong people," Sara said.

It was Miles's turn to smile. "I've been called worse."

"Are you sure the merchandise was ours?"

Miles nodded. "Found the boxes, found the weapons and ammo. Found a large number of blank silver tablets."

Sara's movement was so slight that a human probably wouldn't have caught it, but at the mention of the silver, Miles noticed her shift uneasily. A microsecond of discomfort before the smile was brought back. "That is not good."

"No," Miles said. "No, it isn't."

"Do you know where the theft occurred? We've, worryingly, not had any reports of losses."

Miles gave her all of the details that he'd acquired, and Sara sat there and sighed.

"Not good?" Miles asked.

"We have been having issues with staffing over the last few months," Sara said. "We had a . . . family emergency within the organisation. Henryk's son, Dominik, was attacked in a bar in London, and he has needed a high level of care over the last few months. It has hit Henryk hard, and I have been trying to help out with some of the roles and duties that he would have taken. Unfortunately, it appears that those I placed in positions of trust within the organisation to help out have not been doing their jobs. We take our duty as an Assembly accredited company very seriously, Mister Watson. The people who have been lax will be punished for this transgression. It will not happen again."

The right-hand door on the left side of the room opened, and a man stepped through. He wore baby blue pyjama trousers and was barefoot. His chest was also naked, showing hardened muscle beneath a layer of thick dark hair. He was over six feet tall, with long, dark brown hair that looked wild and untamed, matching the expression on his bearded face. He reminded Miles of someone he'd once known who liked to walk out into the forest hoping to fight a bear.

Sara was immediately to her feet. "Henryk."

"Sara, I am informed we have company," he said, his accent Italian.

Miles got to his feet in preparation of an introduction, but Henryk walked over to the kitchen and disappeared from view for a moment, before returning with a crystal decanter in one hand. He removed the stopper, and the smell of blood reached the noses of the vampires in the room.

"Would you like a drink?" he asked.

"I'm good," Miles said.

Sara walked across the room and snatched the decanter from Henryk's hand, disappearing with it back into the kitchen.

Henryk looked perturbed. "She appears annoyed."

"You don't offer someone another vampire's blood without asking," Miles said. "It's a big thing."

"Ah," Henryk said. "I should really know that. I'm sorry, Sara."

"No harm," Sara said, in a tone that suggested a great deal of harm had been done. "It's been a hard few months, a lot of changes to get used to."

"I was sorry to hear about your son," Miles said. "Have the culprits been found?"

"Thank you," Henryk said, pouring himself a glass of whisky and knocking it back in one, before pouring another. "The correct authorities are dealing with the matter."

The correct authorities, Miles thought, fully aware that it meant Henryk was dealing with it privately.

Henryk walked over to Miles with a purpose that took Miles aback. "You're a hunter," Henryk said. "That's your job, yes?"

"Arbiters do hunt those who have wronged vampire kind, or human-kind for that matter, so in a way, aye, being a hunter is my job."

"You ever hunted an animal?"

This conversation was quickly heading to a weird place. "A long time ago, a particularly rich idiot purchased two Siberian tigers. They were kept in what was basically an open-air zoo, on his property."

"How long ago?" Henryk asked, taking a sip of whisky.

"Centuries," Miles said. "I was human at the time. We were in port, in Spain, I can't remember why. Anyway, these tigers attacked one another, one killed the other, escaped into the forest. Started killing people from a nearby village. I was asked to get a group together, find and kill it. Took three days, and two of the group were seriously hurt."

"But you killed it?" Henryk asked, his pupils wide with a mixture of intrigue and narcotics.

"Aye," Miles said. "I killed it. And then I found out that it had been abused by the rich idiot, who had used it for target practice."

Henryk's expression hardened. "What happened?"

Miles didn't break eye contact with the other man. "I dragged him through the village and let them have their justice for the deaths of their children. They stoned him to death. He deserved worse."

Henryk let out a short bark of a laugh. "Let me show you something." He knocked back the rest of the whisky and walked across the floor to the three doors on the right of the room, opening the left door and stepping through.

Miles looked over at Sara, who shrugged.

Henryk popped his head out of the doorway. "Come on."

By this point, Miles was more curious than anything else. He stepped into the room and wished he hadn't. It was a long, singular room, fifty feet in length and half as wide. There were photos adorning every wall, and glass cases, much like the ones that had been in the jeweller's earlier that night, sat in front of them.

The photos were all of Henryk, and the various animals he'd killed. Each one a picture of him smiling, blood on his arms, as he stood triumphantly over the body of an animal that had no defence against bullets, or arrows, or, in one photo, what looked like a goddamned battle-axe. Miles walked over to the first case, and saw the multitude of teeth and bones inside.

"I like to take something from my hunts," Henryk said.

"You killed a lion with a battle-axe," Miles said, looking at the photo again, still unable to comprehend *why* someone would do such a thing.

Henryk looked back at the twelve-by-twelve framed photo. "I did. It was a glorious hunt. They wanted me to use a rifle, but what kind of man kills such a majestic creature without looking it in the eye?"

"You used a rifle on that buffalo," Miles pointed out.

"Ah, that's an old photo. I was young and immature. I was . . . I needed to grow up. Anyway, these aren't why I brought you in here. This is." Henryk opened a case in the corner of the room and removed a photo, passing it over to Miles.

Miles stared at the photo of Henryk standing over the body of a desolate. There were a dozen more desolate dead behind him, and Henryk held the head of one creature by the hair. He'd used a two-handed claymore to kill them all, and the sword rested against his shoulder.

"You killed desolates," Miles said softly. "You hunted and killed these yourself?"

"I had a team," Henryk told him. "It took us a week to hunt these things until we finally found them. They'd made a nest inside a cave that ran under a disused factory. It was in Lithuania, not far from the Baltic Sea. We killed them all. I've never hunted anything like it."

When a human was turned into a vampire, sometimes it went wrong. Occasionally that meant the human died during the process, but sometimes you got a desolate.

The desolate were true monsters, and if they bit a human, they'd turn that human into a desolate. It always frightened Miles just how quickly you could go from having one desolate to a dozen, and on occasion a lot more. The desolate only care about rage, hate, and bloodlust, about infecting as many more as possible, and killing and devouring all in their path.

Then there were desolate royalty, a group so powerful that they could control their own kind, and until recently, Miles had assumed them to be the worst monster of all. In fact, that's exactly what he'd always been told. Turned out, that wasn't the whole truth. He'd met one a short time ago during his investigation in America who had been unlike any he'd met before. She had retained her humanity even while using the desolate to punish those who had wronged her. Miles occasionally found himself thinking about her, and he hoped that wherever Lauren was, she was safe and happy.

"You saved lives killing them," Miles said.

"I did," Henryk told him, his manner now cold as he stared at the photo. "We understand one another, you and me. We do what needs to be done. Thank you for coming tonight, for sharing your concerns about my business. I will ensure the problem you encountered does not happen again."

Miles wasn't entirely sure if he'd just been dismissed, but Henryk turned away, and Sara motioned Miles out of the room.

"He has been going through a lot," Sara explained as she walked Miles to the door. "I promise I will ensure no more shipments get into the wrong hands. Thank you for your time."

Miles left the penthouse and made his way back down to the foyer, wondering the whole time what had just transpired. Henryk was not only drunk, but almost certainly on something stronger, that much was obvious. The man was clearly hurting. Maybe that was his way of telling Miles that he would have those who hurt his son dealt with in his own way. It didn't much bother Miles; a bunch of humans brawling in a pub didn't factor as something he needed to be involved in.

Miles thanked the guards and receptionists, the latter taking a moment to say her own goodbyes to Church.

Miles and Church left the building and walked back toward where they'd parked their car. They were almost there when Miles's phone rang. He checked the name on the screen: *Megan*.

Megan Song was an ATO Commander, someone Miles had worked with on several occasions. They didn't always see eye to eye, but Miles found her to be excellent at her job. Megan's team had busted a large criminal gang that had been spiking blood bags with several different narcotics. Her team had been responsible for a lot of bad people losing a lot of money.

"Miss Song," Miles said, after answering the phone. "It's been an exceptionally long night, so please tell me you're calling to offer me a holiday somewhere."

"We need to talk," Megan said in her Welsh accent.

"Okay, when?"

"Now," Megan said as a black Ford Transit van pulled up next to Miles and Church. The panel door slid open, revealing Megan inside. The interior of the van had been converted to have two rows of comfortable sofa-like seats opposite one another. There was a small kitchenette at the end, and it looked for all the world like the sort of vehicle used by people who go camping every weekend.

"Hi, Megan," Miles said.

"Please get in the van," Megan said.

"Ladies first," Miles said to Church, who was only too happy to climb up into the van and lie down on the comfortable-looking rug between the two sofas.

Miles climbed in next, the panel door closed behind him by one of Megan's ATOs. He took a seat, and the van pulled away. "If I get a parking ticket for my car staying there, I'm nae paying it," he said.

Megan's smile was brief but warm. "We need to talk about how you've managed to insert yourself into my investigation."

"And which investigation would that be?" Miles asked, looking around at the other two ATOs in the rear of the van and nodding a hello to them.

"Dominik Greger," Megan said. "We need to talk about his killing spree."

Chapter Seven

Dominik is killing the people who attacked him in the bar?" Miles asked, looking around. "That's it, yes? Why does that concern the ATOs? Or me, for that matter?"

"It's not that simple," Megan said.

"It's never that simple," Miles pointed out. "So, where are we going?"

"Assembly Headquarters," Megan said. "There are some things I need you to see."

Miles looked around at the ATO agents in the rear of the van. "Megan, what am I walking into?"

Megan's expression softened. "Nothing like that, Miles, I promise. If I was going to drag you into a fight, I'd have made sure to give you fair warning. Especially with Church in here. Honestly, it's just a chat. But we need to show you some things, and I spoke to Rosa, and she recommended I . . ."

"You spoke to Rosa?"

"Yeah, she called me about your investigation," Megan said. "It was decided that I'd better get a hold of you before you involved yourself any further without knowing the full story."

"And you can't just tell me now, in the back of the van?"

"The data we've got is at the headquarters. I can run you through it all, but I want to see your impressions firsthand."

"Why?" Miles asked.

"Because we need to catch this asshole before he kills more people."

"How many people so far?"

"Sixteen," Megan said grimly. "In two weeks."

Miles settled back for the half-hour drive from Southbank to the headquarters in Highbury, Islington. There was an uneasy tension in the rear of the van that Miles attributed to the idea of someone killing sixteen people in two weeks, and still not being done. If it was Dominik, and Miles had nothing to suggest it wasn't, then he must have been set upon by the entire bloody pub.

He spent the time walking everyone through the conversation he'd had with Henryk and Sara, relaying everything about how Henryk had wanted to show him his hunting trophies. Which sounded even weirder to Miles when he said it out loud.

The van pulled onto the Highbury property, and Miles watched the huge iron gates slowly close behind him. A fifteen-foot wall encircled the front of the property, although having *Assembly Personnel Only* written on a warning sign on the gate usually deterred all but the most stupid or angry humanity had to offer. Usually both at the same time.

The van door opened, and Miles motioned for Church to leave first, which she was happy to do, sniffing the air as everyone else piled out. The van had been driven around to the small parking area at the side of the building. The front garden lifted up to let people gain access to the underground parking below, but it was used for dignitaries and high-ranking officials, and Miles was pretty sure neither he nor the ATOs fit into either of those categories.

The building had been built sometime in the late eighteenth century, and had a footprint four times the size of any other house on the street. It was only four storeys high, but there were another six underground. Of the aboveground floors, one contained a ballroom and another a gym complete with an Olympic-sized swimming pool. There was an entire floor of hotel rooms for when human guests came, along with a rooftop garden, three separate bars, one only catering to *exclusive* people—also not Miles—and two restaurants, one of which held three Michelin stars.

It was, to Miles's mind, a place that you probably never needed to leave, which is why so many of its residents lived in the belowground hotel rooms on a semipermanent basis.

The large oak doors were manned by a team of Assembly Guardians, whose entire job it was to protect the people who worked for the Assembly and the property itself. They were made up of vampires and human familiars, loyal to only the Assembly, so as to ensure a twenty-four-seven protection detail.

Human familiars were given a portion of the power of the vampire who changed them from human, giving them increased strength, healing, and several other abilities that made them an integral part of the vampire world. The six working the door—four inside, two out—all wore black suits, and openly carried a variety of firearms and bladed weapons.

Megan spoke to one of the Guardians, who opened the door and let everyone into the grandeur inside without any of them being checked. The floors were polished marble, the walls adorned with exquisite works of art, including a few Italian vampire painters that Miles was pretty sure Henryk would be unhappy to hear he couldn't possess. All in, the foyer, complete with a spiral staircase that led up to a second security check-point above, was quite the opening gambit in a game of *look at all of our stuff*.

A hallway just to the right of the staircase led down to the first bar inside the building, as well as taking people through to the well-maintained garden that had hosted royalty over the years. Vampires certainly knew how to throw a party, if nothing else.

Miles was taken off to the left, down the hallway, and through to a set of lifts, where Megan pressed the button and everyone stood and waited. No one had a security pass to get in, because you couldn't get in unless you were known to the establishment or had credentials they could check.

"You been here before?" Megan asked as the lift arrived, the doors opening to reveal an oversized interior.

"A few times," Miles said, stepping inside, with Church beside him.

Everyone else piled in, and the lift began its descent.

"You like it?" one of Megan's agents asked. Miles remembered his name was Sven, mostly because he tended to remember the names of people who towered over him.

"It was fine until some pompous ass complained that Church's paws were marking the floor," Miles said. "I wasn't sure I'd be allowed back."

Megan looked back at Miles with a grin. "Was that you?"

"Was what him?" a woman by the name of Claire asked.

"Miles punched out one of the Guardians," Megan said. "There was a big stink about it."

"I broke his jaw," Miles said. "He placed his hands on Church without asking. It was that or let Church rip his arm off—I did him a favour. Petty people should not be given power."

"Does the Guardian still work here?" Claire asked.

Megan shook her head. "Turns out that it was seen by one of the Assembly Justices, who did not take kindly to a Guardian shoving his weight around. You have friends in high places, Miles."

The lift stopped, and everyone stepped out into a hallway that almost mirrored the one they'd left. Megan took them to the right, stopping at the far end and opening the only door there, which had the letters *ATO* written in chalk on a slate hung beside it.

The room itself was big enough for a large table in the middle, a dozen chairs around it, and four blank whiteboards at the far end. A table sat nearby with a kettle and a number of cups piled high, a fridge on the floor next to it. A TV hung on the wall, with a green leather couch in front of it, but that was it.

There were two more people inside, and Miles was introduced to each in turn. They were all part of Megan's ATO team, totalling six, seven including her.

"So," Miles said as Church wandered off to find somewhere to put her head down and, no doubt, digest all the chicken she'd been fed, "I think it's time for you to tell me what's happening."

"I want you to look at some crime scene photos, and then we'll go from there," Megan said. "I want your completely objective view on this."

Miles looked around the group, all of whom appeared to have an expression of expectation on their face. *No pressure or anything.*

"Let's get this done, then," Miles said and followed Megan over to the first whiteboard, which she flipped over to reveal two dozen photos of CCTV showing the outside of a pub and its surrounding area. Miles took a moment to look through each photo in turn, before stepping back.

"You need me to tell you anything?" Megan asked.

The photos were in sequence, showing a man leaving the pub, followed by three other men and a woman. The woman remained outside the front door as a car pulled up. She walked over to the car, while the three men followed the first man around the corner. The last few photos were of the men running to and getting into the car.

"Do you not have video of this?" Miles asked.

"The video is shit," one of the ATO agents, who Miles remembered was called Jordan, said. "These are cleaned up as best we could, but the video took too long to try and make it not look like it was snowing."

"Great," Miles said. "These three followed that one and presumably beat the shit out of him. I'm guessing the first one was Dominik Gregor, and I'm guessing it was about that woman who stayed back."

"Why say that?" Claire asked.

"Because she's there," Miles said. "Dickheads pick fights for the stupidest of reasons, but since she was standing there, I'm guessing she was involved in why it happened."

"Dominik hit on her, repeatedly," Megan said. "After being asked to stop."

"Superb," Miles said. "And the rest."

"Those three men followed Dominik out of the bar and stabbed him," Megan said.

"Also repeatedly," Sven added.

"He didn't die," Miles said. "I assume you have that on camera, too."

Megan flipped the second board, which showed photos of a woman Miles couldn't quite identify carrying a clearly injured man over to a waiting car. The man's left hand was visible, as was the large tattoo of a snake that ran from the back of it, up his wrist.

"The woman?" Miles asked.

"We believe it's Sara Bakos," Megan said. "She does a lot of the day-to-day work that involves anything vampire related. If Dominik was in danger, Henryk would send Sara to deal with it."

"Yeah, I've met her," Miles said. "What do we know about her?"

"She's, we think, ex-KGB from the seventies and eighties," Sven said. "We have no date of birth, no records of her childhood, or her time in the military. She's of Polish origin, nothing else we could dig up."

"Not that old of a vampire, then," Miles said.

"We estimate her age at about sixty-five," Megan said. "Probably a vampire for about thirty of those years."

"I didn't get any sense of overwhelming levels of power when I met her," Miles said. "In fact, she was quite pleasant, which was unexpected. Henryk was . . . weird."

"We'll get to him," Megan said.

Miles considered something for a moment. "You're telling me that Sara turned someone who was dying into a vampire? That's dangerous on a number of levels. More likely to become a desolate, for one."

"We appear to have dodged that particular bullet," Claire said.

Megan tapped the wall of photos. "So, anything else about these?"

Miles's reply was instant. "Find the driver of the car."

"We did," Megan said, passing Miles a photo that she took from the table. "Or his body, at any rate."

Miles looked down at the burned-out husk of a car, the body of someone still in the driver's seat. "Rough way to go. Ah, this is who Sara was talking about. She said you'd spoken to her about it."

"We'll get to that," Megan said.

"So how'd he die?"

"His throat was slit to the bone before the car was set alight," Megan said.

"Why'd they kill him?" Miles asked.

"His name was Philip Toll," Megan said. "A month ago, he contacted the Assembly. We have a recording."

One of Megan's team opened a laptop and set a recording to play.

Is this the Assembly? Look, I don't know who to talk to about this. I don't know . . . goddamn it. Look, there's a vampire. He's . . . he's . . . he's . . . shit, I can't do this. They're going to kill me if they ever find out what I'm doing, but he turned up at my house. He sat with my wife and child, waiting for me to get home. He . . . he wanted me to know that he could get to me, whenever, wherever. Shit. I need help.

The message ended with Philip leaving a number to contact him.

"Is his family safe?" Miles asked.

"We moved them to a secure facility in Liverpool," Megan said. "They're safe. Philip wasn't so lucky. He said if he fled with his family, that they'd be hunted forever, so he stayed and worked for Henryk's company for two more weeks, hoping to get more information on the murders. Until this happened."

"You're thinking Dominik."

Everyone nodded.

"So, Sara illegally turns Dominik to save his life, and in turn, he becomes this psychopath?" Miles asked. "It was illegal, I assume?"

Megan nodded. "There's nothing anywhere to say that Dominik is even a vampire, so yes, I would say it was illegal."

Vampires needed permission from a House or the Assembly to turn a human into a vampire. It was mostly to ensure that the person becoming a vampire was someone who wanted to help vampires and offered something to the House or the Assembly that would be beneficial. One of two things happened to Vampires created illegally—they were either executed, along with whoever turned them, or they were monitored for several years to ensure that they weren't a danger to themselves, vampire kind, or humans.

Turning a human into a familiar—a human with the proportional power of the vampire who turned them—was more common and allowed by pretty much anyone powerful enough to do it. It was why a lot of new vampires started first as familiars, so that they could prove themselves to their House or the Assembly.

"What was he like as a human?" Miles asked.

"Officially, he was a well-behaved member of society," Sven said. "Unofficially, a lot of people were paid a lot of money to let things go. He was arrested multiple times for assault-related crimes. He once put a man's head through a window because he bumped into him in a bar."

"Sounds like the stabbing was karma catching him up," Miles said.

Megan moved the third whiteboard, showing crime scene photos of . . .

"Holy shit," Miles whispered, looking at the multitude of body parts in what appeared to be a living room. "That's a metric fuckload of blood."

"The victim, Jack, was at home with his wife and several members of her family," Megan said. "Eight people in total. All adults, thank Christ. Three had experience in amateur boxing before they left and decided that working for their dad in his gang was the better vocation. What I'm saying is, they were all tough bastards who knew how to fight. They all died hard, and they all died fast."

"This one?" Miles asked, looking at the picture of a small corner shop. Once again, it was awash with blood and body parts.

"A convenience store," Jordan said. "The two people were working when Billy and his three friends entered at three in the morning. All died. CCTV was torn apart, they took the drives with them, no cloud storage."

"We sure it's Dominik?" Miles asked.

Megan nodded and pointed to a photo of a man in a light grey hoodie taken from outside the shop, just after the murders.

"This is some guy in a hoodie," Miles said, getting a good look at the photo. The hoodie was covered in blood, which wasn't surprising considering the massacre that had just occurred.

"The snake tattoo," Megan said, pointing to his hand.

"Okay, evidence looks like it's Dominik," Miles said. "Or at least *could* be Dominik. So go get him."

"That is where the problems arise," Megan said. "While we're ninety-nine percent sure, Templar International is Assembly accredited, so we need more evidence than a photo of a tattoo before we go to his dad and ask awkward questions."

"He's killing everyone who tried to kill him," Miles said. "Not got them all yet, though. There was a woman, another man, and I assume a driver. Any details on their whereabouts?"

Megan flipped over the last whiteboard. A lone man lay in a field; his face was missing, along with his hands and feet. He'd been bisected.

"Fucking hell," Miles whispered.

"The getaway driver," Megan said. "Found two days ago."

"So, just the woman and last man?"

"Charlie Brook and Jennifer Fall. They're a couple," Megan said. "They've left their flat in North London, which has been turned over by someone searching for them. Charlie has no family in the country, and he worked for Jack's father-in-law. Jennifer has a mum and dad, who are both under protective watch from a secondary ATO team."

"Why haven't you brought in Sara?" Miles asked. "Surely you can question her about making an illegal vampire?"

"We did," Megan said. "As you know, we spoke to her about Philip, wanted to see what she knew. What she knew was to lawyer up pretty quickly, and being accredited means they have powerful friends within the Assembly. She was in our interview room for about thirty minutes. If we're going to nail all of these bastards, we need some ironclad evidence against them."

"She did ask if she needed her lawyer," Miles said. "She looked concerned about me arriving. When I told her about the shipments being stolen, she seemed to be a lot more interested in being helpful."

"She was probably on the phone to her lawyer the second you left," Megan said.

"But we need to stop Dominik from murdering people," Miles said. "I assume you get him to talk, all the dominoes fall. Lawyers or not."

"That's our thinking," Megan said. "We don't know who is and isn't on their side, but we know that until we have actual concrete evidence, we can't risk this investigation getting out."

"Do we have any idea *where* these two might have gone? Any connections in the UK? Anything?" Miles asked, looking around the room.

"Southampton," Claire said. "She went to university there ten years ago, has a friend who still lives there, name of Pearl Hallow, according to her social media. But neither of them are using social media at this moment, I assume because they're not stupid. We tracked Jennifer's phone to the area until it went dark, so we know she's there."

"Which means so might Dominik," Miles said.

"Yes, that's the fear," Megan admitted. "We have Pearl's address, and as soon as it gets dark again, we're going to go down there to speak to her. Two of my team were sent down earlier to make sure nothing happens before we turn up. I wanted to talk to you before we all went down there."

"So, what do we know about Pearl?" Miles asked.

Megan passed Miles a photo of a young woman with olive skin, long dark hair that flowed over slight shoulders, and an easygoing smile. "She's thirty-two, named after her grandmother, I would guess, considering they share the name. Divorced, no children. She works as a sales executive for a car dealership that has a specialty in high-end vehicles. Seems to be pretty good at it, considering how often she's gotten Employee of the Month, according to the website."

"Okay, so she's a salesperson," Miles said. "I wonder how much she knows about the danger she's in?"

"Even if she knows, I'm fairly sure she isn't prepared," Megan said.

"And you need my help because?" Miles asked.

"My people are running facial recognition software on the CCTV in the Southampton area," Megan said. "If, or when, we get a hit, I want to already be there to stop him."

There was a knock at the door, which opened before anyone could say anything, and Rosa Sanchez sauntered in. She was just over five feet tall and wore a tartan jacket of various shades of green, a matching skirt, and black high heels that clicked on the wooden floor as she walked. Her dark hair was pulled back in a ponytail, and she had an expression of someone who was less than happy to be in the position she found herself.

"Miles," she said with a smile.

"Rosa," Miles said with a smile of his own. "So, as I was asking, why am I here?"

"You asked me to find out who was investigating the company," Rosa said. "As I was looking into it, I saw that there had been an investigation into the murder of Sara's driver. I saw that Megan and her team had been involved, but that the investigation was considered no longer ATO priority. Figured I'd call them and see what was going on, just in case the murder and the missing weapons were somehow linked. Megan was only too happy to discuss it."

"No one has told me what they actually want me to do," Miles pointed out.

"You're an Arbiter," Megan said. "You can go places we can't, not without approval. You went into that building tonight like you owned the place. Sara calls a lawyer on an Arbiter and you have probable cause, you can just ignore them. No ATO is going to be doing that unless they like being yelled at by people well above our pay grade."

"You want me to be your battering ram for the investigation?" Miles asked, quite liking the sound of that.

Megan laughed. "No, I want you to find Dominik. Or work with us to. Yes, you're a battering ram. Church, too."

Church lifted her head, looked around, decided it wasn't worth her getting up, and promptly lay back down.

"But," Megan continued, "you turn up at someone's house, you have the authority of the Assembly behind you. Even the most ignorant of humans knows who the Assembly are. They've heard of Arbiters. Maybe they've heard you're the bogeyman, maybe they've heard a more accurate tale; either way, with you on our side, we have a higher choice of making sure that no one else has to die. Look, no offence to anyone on my team, but the ATOs aren't exactly known for turning up and asking questions. If we turn up in your life, it's probably going to be for a bad reason. Arbiters have a little more leeway. Also, and I don't understand it, but people like you."

"Why not tell me this on the way here?" Miles asked, managing to suppress a laugh.

"I needed you to see these crime scene photos firsthand," Megan said, pointing to the whiteboards. "I needed you to see what we're trying to stop. Words don't do this shit justice, Miles."

Miles glanced back over at the body of the getaway driver. Megan wasn't wrong there. "Okay, let's say that the Assembly stepped in because you were investigating Philip's murder. Why are they letting you get away with investigating Dominik? Surely if they knew about this, they'd shut you down, too."

"Officially, we are investigating the multiple murders," Megan said. "We've given no links to Dominik or Templar International. Until we actually accuse someone of something, those above us are being hands-off. I think they would like this to all be resolved without it being public. These murders are public knowledge, but the method of their deaths isn't. We don't need the humans to hear about vampires butchering them in their own homes.

Miles stared at the photos on the whiteboard again; he could feel the energy of everyone in the room. They were scared of this all getting worse before Dominik, or the ninety-nine percent chance it was him, continued his killing spree. "Are you *certain* it's Dominik?" he asked.

"Yes," Megan said.

"Could it be Sara?"

"You've met her," Sven said. "What do you think?"

Miles considered it for a moment. "She's smart. Smarter than whoever did this. This is pure rage and hate. Sara didn't strike me as someone who gives in to such things easily. Do we know her bloodline?"

Megan shook her head.

"Why hasn't Henryk or Sara stopped Dominik?" Miles asked. "Surely this is going to screw over their business if it gets out that the son of their CEO is a raving psychopath."

"We don't know that," Megan admitted. "The theory is that he was turned and escaped."

"That's certainly probable. We'll put a pin in it," Miles said and looked over to Rosa. "Any way you can look into Sara's bloodline? Handlers might be able to use routes that the ATOs can't. If it is Dominik, and it looks pretty clearly that it is, I want to know what I'm going to find."

Rosa considered it for a moment, before nodding. "If Dominik was made by Sara, he'll have the same bloodline ability. Maybe House Barbarous. They like their violence and bloodshed."

House Barbarous's bloodline gift was to be made stronger, faster, more resilient than pretty much any other vampire from another House. The flip side of that was that they needed to drink a lot more blood than other vampires. *A lot more.* And it was true that not all of them cared where that blood came from.

Miles had met several Barbarous vampires who were the exact opposite of that stereotype, but he had to admit that yes, there were many in House Barbarous who revelled in the violence and mayhem aspect of their vampire powers.

"Could be any House," Claire said. "The House rarely matters when it comes to being a raving psychopath. Especially if you were already a psychopath before you became a vampire."

"Very true," Miles said. "Dominik is only a few months old, so his bloodline ability might not have manifested yet, but just in case."

"Anything else?" Megan asked.

"This is your investigation," Miles told her. "I am not to be put on the report. At all. I don't want credit, I don't want acknowledgment. That's my one and only condition."

Several of the ATO agents shared confused glances. The idea of an Arbiter expressively asking for no credit at all in work that they'd done was not an everyday occurrence.

"Done," Megan said, offering Miles her hand, which he shook.

"I'll head to Southampton tomorrow. Send me everything you have."

"We'll be coming with you, although arriving separately," Megan said. "I've got a few people on the Greger household, too."

"What about Sara?" Rosa asked.

"She has a penthouse in Marylebone," Sven said. "We've been keeping an eye on it, but she's barely been back in the last few weeks."

"You had anyone get inside?" Miles asked.

"No," Megan said. "She works for an Assembly accredited company, I don't think that would go down well if we were caught. We're not Arbiters."

Miles laughed. "I don't think it would go down well if *I* was caught."

There was a knock on the door, and Sven walked over and opened it, followed by several seconds of him stammering and moving aside, bowing his head as he pulled the door open.

A middle-aged man walked into the room. He had dark skin, a bald head, and short beard. He wore a midnight blue suit and black shoes polished to a mirror shine. He carried a walking cane made from a dark mahogany, with a jade dragon's head atop it. He walked into the room, the cane tapping with his footsteps.

"Miles Watson," the newcomer said with a Spanish accent.

Miles stared at the man and sighed. Outwardly, he said, "Justice Mordecai Balderas, a pleasure as always." While inwardly, he thought, *Ah, bollocks.*

CHAPTER EIGHT

The Assembly Justices were, for all intents and purposes, thirteen of the most powerful vampires in the world, outside of the vampire House Lords and Ladies. Not necessarily in terms of raw, physical power, but certainly in terms of influence and position in vampire society.

The Justices got together once a month to discuss vampire law, any serious issues that might have arisen, and to generally just head off anything that might be an issue before it got serious. They arranged and monitored any disputes between the Houses, making sure that things didn't slip back into the way it had been done before the Assembly took charge.

The thirteen Justices were split into four groups. Of the four groups, each had three members—apart from the last, which had four. Each of the groups oversaw a different organisation within the Assembly: Arbiters, ATOs, and Inquisitors. Three of the groups came together to discuss internal security matters, and anything involving the Guardians or Administration—who were probably more responsible for getting things done in the Assembly than anyone else.

The final group were the four Justices who dealt with the Houses. As far as Miles was concerned, no one should have envied their job.

The thirteen Justices worked independently from one another, for the most part, only coming together for anything that required more than one Justice, or for the gathering of all of them. The latter of which occurred once a month.

Justices usually didn't come to talk to the ATOs or even the Arbiters personally. They preferred to leave it to the various underlings who existed as a buffer between the Justices and those they were in charge of. Although "in charge" was a loose term.

Everyone had left the room, except for Miles. Even Church had wandered out with Rosa and Megan, although it had been after Miles had told her to go. Considering she'd sat herself down directly between Miles and the Justice, showing no fear or even regard for the influential vampire, it was probably for the best. Justices weren't bad people, but a healthy attitude of trepidation and respect was always a good idea, and Church had neither.

"Your dog doesn't like me," Justice Balderas said as he took a seat at the table next to where Miles had previously stood.

"Church is always a little protective when I'm surprised," Miles said, sitting opposite the Justice. "And, to be frank, I'm always a little surprised to see a Justice."

Justice Balderas laughed. "I do like to make a habit of surprising people. Do you know why I'm here?"

"Got lost on your way to a poker game?"

Justice Balderas laughed again. "Drest always said that you had a smart mouth on you."

The fact that a Justice and Drest had been talking about him surprised Miles more than he wanted to let on.

"Yes, I know your old House Lord," Justice Balderas said. "We go back a long way. I knew him when I was human, all those centuries ago. He came to me when you decided you wanted to leave House Venator, said you would make an excellent Arbiter. Having seen your work these past decades, I'm liable to agree. You're not in trouble, Miles. I don't tend to make visits to people who are, unless they've wronged me personally, and very few people do that these days."

Miles relaxed a little, still confused as to why someone of Justice Balderas's stature would bother to come see him.

"Tonight, there were two crimes stopped in London," Justice Balderas said, almost wistfully. "One was a series of robberies in a number of jewellery shops that are friendly to vampires, and one was a local criminal, who was definitely not friendly to anyone. Both foiled before more harm could be done. Do you know why I know about these crimes, out of the hundreds that probably pass through my office in any given month?"

"I do not," Miles said.

"You see, I got a call from a friend of mine. You might know him—Frank, the owner of the Fang and Fog. He called to thank me personally for sending an Arbiter of such talent to deal with the issue. I explained that I hadn't sent anyone, that Arbiters are a law unto themselves, but he wanted to make sure that the person responsible for his staff walking away unscathed from tonight was commended. One Miles Watson."

Miles opened his mouth to say something.

"Don't speak, listen," Justice Balderas said in a tone that suggested he was not yet done. "After I heard your name, I remembered a few things. I remembered speaking to Drest about you. I remembered being impressed with your first few years here. I also remembered what happened in America. Where you killed the First Captain of House Umbra.

"Now, after I heard your name, I checked the file, and found out that the person in charge was ATO Commander Jonathan Holt. The same man who, mere hours later, put in a preliminary report for stopping an arms dealer from selling anti-vampire weaponry to people who should not have such things. Like the robbers of jewellery shops."

Miles remained silent, wondering where he was going with this.

"I contacted someone on his team I actually trust, because Jonathan Holt would turn up to the opening of an envelope if he thought he was getting something out of it, and you'll be so surprised to learn what I was told."

"I have no idea," Miles lied. He, unfortunately, had a pretty good idea.

"That you wanted no credit for your part in apprehending the thieves, nor in stopping the arms dealer," Justice Balderas said. "Now, I'm pretty sure I know why that is, but I wanted to hear it from you. I want to know why an Arbiter is actively telling people not to put his name anywhere near crimes he helped solve."

Miles remained silent for a moment as he tried to figure out how to say what he needed to say without causing himself any more trouble.

Justice Balderas decided to not wait out the silence. "You're keeping your head down."

Miles nodded.

"And you think that by passing over credit for everything you do, it might help alleviate any ill feeling harboured by the allies of a certain House Captain?"

"Can't hurt," Miles said. "I killed the First Captain of House Umbra, along with many of those working with him. Not all personally, but I was there when it happened. It was a legitimate kill. I'm nae worried about that. I just feel like maybe giving those allies who survived some time to get it out of their system might go a long way to no one doing anything stupid."

Justice Balderas stared at Miles for a few seconds. "You're not afraid for yourself."

Miles shook his head.

"You're worried that they'll come for you, and you'll be known as the person who eliminated not only a House First Captain but a large portion of their allies. Because if they come for you, you'll be walking away."

Miles nodded.

"That's very confident."

"I killed *the* Vedran Vinko," Miles said with a shrug. "He wasn't exactly a slouch in the vampire department. If they do manage to take me out, I'm going to do them a lot of damage first. I would rather just keep a low profile. I know that Vedran had allies in the Assembly. I know that when he died, their hope of whatever ludicrous thing he promised them died too. Wealth, power, whatever it was, he was making offers he probably had no way of fulfilling unless he also planned to kill a lot of Assembly Justices, Arbiters, and large numbers of ATOs and Inquisitors. Even the Administration would have been decimated. He wanted House Umbra for himself, and he would have culled those who opposed him, but going after the Assembly was going to take him a long time. He almost certainly made promises he never planned to keep, but I made sure he *couldn't* keep them."

"He was little more than a worthless bag of air," Justice Balderas said. "But it doesn't matter how long you wait, those allies of his are going to remain angry at you. They'll blame you no matter what the evidence said. They probably know Vedran was never going to do a damn thing he promised to do; he was all about Vedran. His death was not only completely legal, but warranted.

"He was responsible for the deaths of countless humans, multiple vampires, and the creation of several desolate. If you really wanted to get picky, you could blame the Desolate Queen on him, too—his stupidity led to her creation. A creation that killed several Inquisitors, all of whom had turned away from the Assembly. Probably a good thing they died—I don't think anyone would have wanted to take them alive. The embarrassment alone to know that our own Inquisitors betrayed us for the empty promises of power and wealth."

"You want me to stop letting others take the credit for my work," Miles said, wanting it spelled out so there was no doubt in his mind why Justice Balderas had visited.

"Yes," Justice Balderas said. "Not only that, but I also want you to understand that these people *will* eventually come for you. Not now—it's too fresh in people's minds, it would be far too big a deal should you be killed in mysterious circumstances. But eventually. And vampires have a *long* time to prepare these things."

"Do you know who they are?" Miles asked.

Justice Balderas shook his head. "Whoever they are, they're keeping quiet about it. I assume because they're not as stupid as Vedran was. No one wants our world to descend into the Dark Ages again, when the merest hint of a slight could end up with someone trying to assassinate another. We're meant to be above all of that."

Miles laughed. "I'm nae sure that's true."

Justice Balderas sighed. "Probably right, but let's at least *pretend* we're above it. Anyway, I'm here because I needed to relay to you that no matter *what* you do, these people are going to want your head. Also, I wanted to expressly tell you to stop giving Jonathan Holt any credit for things he hasn't done. That man does not need more excuses to have an inflated ego."

"Can I ask you something that is unrelated to this?"

Justice Balderas nodded once.

"Who approved the accreditation of Templar International?"

"I have no idea," Justice Balderas said with a shrug. "Am I meant to know?"

"They were given it after only six months."

"Six months?" Justice Balderas asked with a hint of surprise. "That's fast. I guess it does happen, but it's unusual."

"I've never heard of it before," Miles said.

"I don't see why you would have," the Justice said. "I didn't recall when we were meant to inform the Arbiters of our decisions."

"Fair enough," Miles said.

"As a less flippant answer, it depends on what they're offering as a service to the Assembly, or to the vampire community," Justice Balderas said. "Anyone with a good record of conduct can suggest an accreditation. And anyone can put forth an argument for an accreditation to be accelerated. It would need someone to make the initial suggestion, and there would need to be evidence given of the company showing a good standing when it came to vampire dealings. It would go to the Administration branch of the Assembly for oversight, and then to at least one of the four branches of the Justices for final sign off."

"Did it?"

"Your handler can find out that information," Justice Balderas said. "Whoever it went to, it wasn't the Arbiter branch of the Justices. But I'll tell you this—if it went to another branch, watch what you say. Don't go accusing an entire branch of Justices of being on the payroll of a human company, or anything else deeply offensive. If this company got through the accreditation, it was because they were proven to be in good standing. They would have to show they've cultivated relationships with vampires, with the Assembly, with ATO teams. They would need to be ATO members who had been given positive write-ups, Arbiters, too, in most cases. Are you suggesting they aren't in good standing?"

Miles shook his head. "Officially, there's nothing wrong with anything they've done, but they were lax at a warehouse in London, which caused vampire-killing weapons to get into the hands of people like the arms dealer, and then those jewellery thieves. That should be enough to get their accreditation looked into, even normally, but with such a quick signing off . . . " Miles let the sentence trail off.

"The arms dealer from tonight?"

Miles nodded.

"I will look into it," Justice Balderas told Miles. "Something will need to be done to ensure it doesn't happen again."

Miles had considered telling Justice Balderas about Dominik. About the possibility that he'd been turned into a vampire and set off murdering sixteen people, with more still to be hunted down. He'd been all set to state everything, but something stopped him. Megan had kept this investigation secret until Rosa had phoned her, in part because of Templar's accreditation and how quickly Megan's team were shut down from interviewing Sara. They needed solid, airtight evidence before taking it to the Justices.

It wasn't that he didn't trust Justice Balderas per se, but the fewer people who knew about a murderous vampire with ties to a powerful organisation who itself had ties to the Assembly, the better.

Justice Balderas removed a white card from his pocket and passed it to Miles, who glanced down at the name and phone number. He turned the card over, but there was nothing written on the back. "Should you ever need to contact me directly," Justice Balderas said.

Miles put the contact details in his phone and sent a text message to the number. The Justice removed his own phone from his pocket and smiled.

"Your actual number," Miles said. "I expected an assistant."

Justice Balderas removed a second card, this one blue, with the exact same layout but a different phone number. "My assistant. Her name is Karine. If you can't get ahold of me, contact her."

Miles put Karine's number into his phone. "Thank you."

"I will look into this matter," the Justice said. "We cannot have bad people making our lives more difficult. When I've found something, I'll let you know. I'll be at my home in Bourges on and off for the rest of the year, so should you need to get in contact with me by any means other than phone, call Karine. She will know what to do."

Justice Balderas said nothing for a short while, but he turned toward the door and back to Miles. "Your dog, she is who I think she is? Who she belonged to?"

Miles nodded. Church's owner had been a vampire geneticist who had done experiments on Church's mother to try and give her vampire genes to ensure the dog's extended life. Unfortunately, Church's mother had died, leaving two surviving pups. One being Church. The other was . . . well, no one knew. Miles hoped wherever they were, they were happy.

"That was a hard time for a lot of vampires," the Justice continued. "He was a good man. Or at least, I thought he was a good man."

"Me too," Miles said softly.

Justice Balderas offered Miles his hand, which Miles shook. "Thank you for your time. I hope the next time we speak, it will be under more pleasant circumstances."

"Thank you for coming to speak to me," Miles said. "I'll make sure to stop trying to keep my head low."

Justice Balderas nodded once. "Just be ready when they come. Because they will eventually."

Miles's smile was tight, and he watched the Justice leave the room, with Rosa and Megan entering a few seconds later, followed by Church, who bounded by them to be by Miles's side.

"That was weird," Rosa said.

"When was the last time a Justice came by to have a chat?" Megan asked.

Miles couldn't disagree. "He says I need to stop letting others take the credit for my work, so I guess my name needs to be in the reports."

"That's it?" Megan asked.

"He's also going to look into Templar International, considering they were pretty lax about keeping dangerous weapons under lock and key," Miles said, unable to shake the uneasy feeling inside him.

"Anything else?" Rosa asked.

Miles shook his head. There was a moment at the end, when they spoke about Church and the man who had created her, that Miles thought the Justice was going to say more, but it was fleeting and he was gone soon after. Miles dismissed it as a sad thought from someone who had once been friendly with someone who had turned out to be a disappointment to everyone who knew him. He'd felt the same way about him for a long time.

Church laid her head on Miles's lap, and received the attention she was after.

"We're off to Southampton," Miles said.

Church looked up and licked Miles's face.

"Send me everything you have on our two lovebirds," Miles said. "I'm going to take a room while I'm here, have a drink, and rest until the evening."

Rosa checked her phone for the weather forecast. "We already have a room set up. You'll need to sign in at reception and get your key. UV level is one from about two in the afternoon. Overcast and drizzling for most of the day, pretty much everywhere along the south coast. Do you want a car and driver?"

"What happened to the car I was driving earlier?" Miles asked.

"We've retrieved it," Rosa said. "We can have it cleaned and ready for you by this evening."

"I wish I had a handler," Megan said, looking between Rosa and Miles.

"She also yells at me when I do something stupid," Miles said. "It's nae all car delivery and checking the weather for me."

"I yell a lot," Rosa said.

"A lot?" Megan asked.

"*A lot,*" Rosa said.

"You do that many stupid things?" Megan asked Miles with a smile.

"Yes," Rosa said before Miles could answer. "Yes, he does."

"I'm going to bed," Miles told them both. "Thank you for arranging everything, Rosa. And thank you, Megan, for making my life much more complicated than it was a few hours ago. Really appreciate it."

"My pleasure," Megan said with a warm smile.

After finding his room key from the receptionist and getting into his room, Miles showered, while Church ate the bowl of food that had been thoughtfully arranged for her. Someone had brought a change of clothes—a black T-shirt and faded blue jeans, along with clean underwear and socks, both still in their packaging—and had placed them in the room. Assembly premises often had a lot of clean clothes waiting to be used by vampires who got covered in blood, or turned into their beast form and destroyed whatever clothes they were wearing.

The room was underground, so no need to worry about blackout curtains, or curtains of any kind, and was basically a queen bed, a lamp and phone on a bedside table, a leather armchair in the corner, a TV on the wall opposite, and a well-stocked fridge. There was fresh blood on delivery should it be needed. It was synthetic; Miles had been here several times over the decades and found that the taste had improved.

He used the phone to order a real blood pouch, and it was delivered a few minutes later by a woman in the same navy blue uniform as all the staff members in the building wore. The blood pouch was inside a wooden box, which sat on a silver tray.

Miles thanked the woman, took the box, and went back to the armchair. He opened the box and read the note inside, which described the details of the blood; where it had come from, what it was meant to taste like, the aroma. No details of *who* had donated it, because that could have been dangerous, but it was enough to get the gist of the age and lifestyle of the person. Miles always thought it was a little like reading a wine list, which, considering a lot of vampires liked comparing humans to wine, Miles figured was probably apt.

Synthetic blood had a similar list, although they also posted details of the lab it had been created in. Personally, he liked knowing that it was from a good laboratory and of good quality, which the Assembly-served synthetic was. No Assembly premises would serve cheap synthetic blood.

In this instance, Miles wanted the real thing, though. It had been a few weeks since his last drink, and it had been a long day.

Miles tore the top off the pouch and drank the half pint of blood down in three swigs. While synthetic blood was best served chilled, actual blood was better after sitting at room temperature for a short time. The bag was warm to the touch, and after Miles removed the cap, he took a smell of the contents. It smelled good. It had been something which had taken him a long time to get used to. Actually *enjoying* the smell of blood, not just the taste.

Miles used his little finger to take a taste of the blood, before having another long drink. The sense of calm that washed through him was almost euphoric. There were some bloods that really riled up the emotions, the *need.* Whatever that *need* was changed from vampire to vampire, but the synthetic stuff didn't really have that same kick.

Three swigs of the pouch, and the blood was gone. Miles sat in the chair and sighed deeply, contentedly. It was a glorious thing in that moment after drinking blood, although very different from drinking it from a living person. Drinking from a person gave the vampire and human a glimpse into each other's minds and heightened their emotions, which could mean a wonderful euphoria or nightmares for weeks. Drinking real blood from a pouch was considerably safer for all involved.

After a few minutes, he tossed the empty pouch into a hazard waste bin in the bathroom and lay on the comfortable bed as he felt the sun begin to rise outside. He was asleep within seconds.

CHAPTER NINE

Miles woke to the combined sounds of the air-conditioning unit and Church's gentle snoring. He rolled over and checked his phone. The screen said two in the afternoon with a UV index showing currently a three outside. He had a few hours to wait for it to drop to safe levels.

He could survive outside in a level three for several minutes, but those would be excruciatingly painful minutes, and having done it before, he was not keen to repeat the process. Best to wait for it to drop to a one, or better yet a zero.

Miles flicked through to the weather app on his phone—sunset was just before eight PM, although it would be safe outside from about six onwards. Plenty of time to get down to Southampton and begin the hunt for the two missing people.

Church made a noise that sounded like she was less than thrilled to have been woken up, and she jumped up onto the bed next to Miles, lying beside him, her head on his chest as Miles stroked her neck.

"Long day today," Miles told her. "I say we get ready and go up to the restaurant for some food. You feel like a burger?"

Church barked. Miles was never exactly sure why Church *adored* a good burger, cheese and all, and Miles had originally been concerned about what to feed a dog with vampiric DNA. Turned out, she could eat pretty much everything she wanted with zero side effects, much like a vampire.

Miles gave Church a little push, and the dog rolled over to give him room to get up. She remained on the bed as Miles dressed in the jeans and T-shirt supplied by the Assembly, which fit him perfectly.

Once ready, he put his dirty clothes inside the bag that the clean had arrived in, checked he hadn't forgotten anything, and left the room with

Church behind him. They headed up to the reception area, where a Guardian stood next to the door which led onto that floor and to the floors above. Behind the wooden reception desk sat a woman with blonde hair and a smile so full of cheer, Miles imagined it could have been seen from space. Miles figured that like most of the humans working in Assembly buildings, she was a familiar.

"Hello, Mister Watson," the lady said, getting to her feet and looking down at Church. "And who's the best girl in all the world?"

Church barked once.

"That's right," the receptionist said, before looking back up at Miles. "She's so lovely."

"She is," Miles agreed, scratching Church behind one ear. "I was wondering who I needed to thank for the change of clothes."

"Oh, that was Megan," the receptionist said, moving enough that Miles could now see the name tag on her lapel: *Star*. "She hoped she got the fit right."

"They're fine, thank you," Miles said.

"Would you like to use our free cleaning service?" Star asked. "We'll have your clothes laundered and ready to go by the time you leave. I assume you'll be staying until the UV drops."

"Thank you," Miles repeated, and passed her his bag of clothes when she motioned for them. "Rosa said she had my car all sorted, but I'm going to need a place to stay in Southampton, too."

"I believe Rosa has arranged it all," Star said. "She told us to say that she will meet you in the non-executive restaurant at six PM. The restaurant is on the second floor. Please keep your torc on at all times, else you be considered a security risk."

Miles smiled and risked a glance at the Guardian, who hadn't moved a muscle. "Not my first time here," he said. "But thank you for the warning."

"Please do stay off the top floor for the time being—it's being used by several *exclusive* guests."

Miles noticed the tiny fraction of unease in Star's eyes.

"*Exclusive?*" he asked. "I'm pretty sure there's nowhere in this building I can't go if I have cause to. Must be some pretty important people up there."

"Mister Watson," Star said, followed by a long sigh. "Rosa asked me to tell you to keep off that floor. She said I should try saying please if you become irritated at being told what to do. So, *please* stay off that floor."

Miles took a chance. "It's fine, I'll stay off that floor. I assume the allies of Vedran Venko will afford me the same privilege."

Star opened her mouth, closed it, shook her head, and chuckled. "You don't know anything, do you? You're just guessing and hope that I say something to confirm it."

"Sorry," Miles said. "Old habit. But, *should* it be House Umbra, and *should* they be people who might have an issue with my being here, I will make sure to keep out of their way."

Any act of unprovoked physical violence against a vampire on Assembly grounds, without express permission for such an event to take place, would be met with the Guardians intervening. And they didn't usually intervene in a good way. It would also mean the attacker's expulsion from the building, and probably a visit from an Arbiter or Inquisitor. You played nice in an Assembly building, or you got your life turned upside down.

"Are you allowed to tell me who the Umbra resident is?" Miles asked.

"Sorry, that's not allowed," Star said. "You understand."

"Do they know I'm here?" Miles asked. "Whoever it is?"

"They do," Star said slowly. "They saw you coming in with the ATO team. They were . . . well, they were not happy about it. Rosa said it should be fine, but even so, please enjoy the second floor's amenities, and the apologies of the Assembly for any undue stress this causes."

"It's nae bother," Miles assured her.

Miles and Church left the reception and took the stairs to the second floor, pausing occasionally for Miles to take a look at a piece of art he liked. Heavy curtains hung in front of every window, blocking out any hint of daylight outside.

Miles arrived at the second floor and walked down the hallway toward the restaurant and bar, passing several doorways that led to rooms he'd never been in before. No vampire stayed above ground in an Assembly building, but any human assistants needed to stay somewhere, so why not stick them in a room fifty feet away from a bar that never closed?

Miles arrived at the restaurant and bar and looked around. The two places were separated by a wall that stretched the length of the room, ending at a set of windows that, like all others, were hidden by curtains. The bar was playing an eighties power ballad, although Miles couldn't have named the performer with a dozen guesses.

The bar had soft blue lighting, with a dance floor and space for a band on a raised area beside it. There were booths down one side and a staircase that led up to a balcony overlooking the establishment. You could easily fit a hundred people in there, probably double that.

The restaurant had a similar aesthetic with the lighting and also several booths, although the music was more blues. Miles took the few steps down to the restaurant, where he was met by a young man wearing a charcoal suit and burgundy red tie, with multiple piercings in each ear and an easy smile.

"Sir," the man said, "my name is Brandon. How can I help you?"

"A booth please," Miles said. "For me and Church."

Brandon looked over at Church as she smiled. "What a lovely dog you have," he said, although Miles got the impression the compliment was slightly wary on his part. "We have several booths open; will you be here for the evening?"

"I plan on having food and staying here until sunset," Miles said. "Church will need feeding, too. Normal food, nothing you don't already serve. Is that okay?"

"Of course," Brandon said. "We are always happy to serve dogs here. Please follow me."

Miles and Church did as they were told, and Brandon led them to a booth at the far end of the room, next to where there would have been a good view of the area if the curtains hadn't been closed.

"Perfect," Miles said as he sat on the red leather seats, giving him a view of the restaurant entrance, while Church lay on the floor under the table.

"I will bring over your menus. Would you like a drink?"

"Can we get a bowl of water for Church?" Miles asked. "I'll have some orange juice and a large cappuccino."

"Chocolate on top?" Brandon asked.

"Please," Miles said, and watched Brandon leave. "He seems nice."

Church snorted from under the table.

"You're just annoyed he didn't tell you how amazing you are," Miles said, struggling to keep the mocking from his tone.

Church snorted again.

"You know you're amazing," Miles told her.

Church looked up at Miles and smiled, before lying back down again.

After the drinks arrived, Miles ordered a steak—blue—with peppercorn sauce and chips, and got Church a bacon double cheeseburger with extra cheese.

It was a myth that suggested vampires couldn't eat food. They could eat pretty much anything they wanted to, although it was true that some vampires found that food they'd loved as humans now repulsed them. While a blue steak was probably stereotyping his own people, it was also true in Miles's mind that the best steak should be eaten in the way that best suited the cut. Besides, anything more than rare was just ruining it.

Church finished before Miles was even halfway through, and Miles asked the waiter if he could get someone to take her outside to have a little run and enjoy the sunshine. Despite her physiology, UV rays had very little detriment on Church, although she didn't like it during the summer months when they could reach much higher numbers.

Brandon looked confused, then concerned, and finally agreed to find someone. That someone ended up being Star, who was all too happy to let Church out into the garden at the rear of the property. The pair walked off, leaving Miles alone to finish his meal.

It wasn't five minutes later when someone joined him, remaining on the opposite side of the table to where he continued to eat. Miles made a point of ignoring the newcomer and continued enjoying his steak.

"It's rude to just keep eating," the man said. He had pale skin, long dark hair that was tied back with a red ribbon, and a Russian accent. There were black tattoos of skulls on the backs of his hands, and he wore a black suit, white shirt, and black tie. On his lapel was a badge consisting of a white background with a charcoal grey skull on it that appeared to be fading the further down the skull you went. The House Umbra badge.

"It's rude to interrupt me when I'm enjoying my food," Miles said before eating another piece of steak. He looked up and took a long drink of water before using a napkin to dab his mouth. "House Umbra, yes?"

The man nodded. "You are Miles Watson."

Miles placed his knife and fork on his plate and sighed. "And you are?"

"Vladimir Petrov," he said.

"Good for you," Miles told him. "I'd like to finish my food now."

"You murdered my House First Captain," Vladimir said, although there was no anger in his tone. He said it in the way someone might say that the sun was hot, or water was wet.

"Murder implies it was unlawful," Miles said. "It was not."

"'Assassinated' a better word?"

"Not really," Miles said. "First Captain Vedran Vinko was a traitor to his own House. A murderer, a crook, a thief, a charlatan, and probably some other things I can't remember right now. He died because he thought he was better than everyone else. Specifically, he thought he was better than me. Turned out, he was wrong. So I'd advise you to fuck off and leave me alone."

Vladimir slammed the palm of his hand onto the table. "Vedran's *assassination* will be avenged. You only won through cheating; let's see how you do when you have to win a straight-up fight."

"We're really sticking with the word *assassination* here?" Miles sighed. Vampire House bullshit was so exhausting. There was no point in telling Vladimir that he'd beaten Vedran in a fair fight, it was just that his First Captain had been overconfident in his own abilities. "We both know that you're not going to do anything in here. You can puff out your wee chest and shout about avenging people, but you lay a hand on me and you get expelled. Actually, first, you lose your hand."

"I just like to look a man in the eye before I kill him," Vladimir said. "I will come for you. I will make sure that you know how it feels to be beaten."

Miles stared at Vladimir for a few moments. "Vlad, can I call you Vlad?" No response.

"Look, Vlad," Miles continued, "I don't know anything about you, and it's pretty clear you don't know *anything* about me. You're full of piss and vinegar, and you want to make a name for yourself, so you come and threaten an Arbiter. Which means you're either unbearably stupid, or . . . well, no, just that. You come after an Arbiter, and you kill me, then you've got the Assembly after you. Or you die by my hand. Doesn't sound like a win either way."

"They may kill me," Vlad said. "But I will have you beg for your life first."

"You do know that I'm an Arbiter?" Miles asked, showing his torc. "You did hear me say that? So, you must know that you're threatening one right now?"

Vlad stood and opened his mouth to speak as another voice bellowed from the entrance of the restaurant. "What in all the *hells* do you think you're doing?"

Miles craned his head to one side as Justice Balderas entered the room and walked over to them.

"I think you may have fucked up there, lad," Miles said with a smile.

Vlad moved away from the booth but continued to stare daggers at Miles, who went back to eating his chips.

"You were told to leave this man alone," Justice Balderas said, poking Vlad in the chest with his finger. "You were *told* to conduct yourself as an adult. Yet I find you here, threatening an active Arbiter in a place of safety. Have you lost your mind?"

"I merely wanted to get a feel for a murderer," Vlad said without looking away from Miles.

"You've been told it was a legitimate kill, *boy*," Justice Balderas said, furious at the Russian vampire.

"By Assembly law," Vlad almost spat. "My House will decide on what is and isn't legitimate. *Old man*."

Miles ignored the argument and finished his meal, before taking his time to drink the rest of the jug of water that was on the table. When done, he looked over at Vlad and Justice Balderas, the latter of whom was almost vibrating with anger. Miles got to his feet, stretched, and watched the two men as they both turned toward him.

"Vlad," Miles said softly, "you came to me to threaten and intimidate, but it's pretty clear you don't know who I am. I killed your First Captain because he needed killing. He brought the fight to me; he betrayed his House and his people for power and wealth. Actually, not even that, for the *promise* of power and wealth. I'd rather it ended there, I'd rather we all went about our lives, but if you really need to come for me, get it signed off as a legal challenge from one vampire to another, and I'll meet you wherever you wish."

"I will do just that," Vlad snapped, turning on his heel and storming out of the restaurant.

Justice Balderas sighed and rubbed his hand over his face. "I am sorry. I didn't know any House Umbra were in the building until you'd already gone to sleep."

"It's fine," Miles said. "Thank you for coming to talk to him. It seems clear that there's nothing to discuss. He has set his mind to trying to kill me. It will not end well for him."

"I will talk to his House, see if we can smooth this over before it goes further." Justice Balderas offered Miles his hand, which he shook. "Thank you for remaining calm about it."

Star entered the restaurant with Church beside her, who ran back to Miles. He checked his watch and found that it was a little after five PM. He still had a few hours to kill. He thanked everyone for their help and left the restaurant to go to the library on the first floor, where he found a quiet corner and a good book, and hoped no one else was going to try and kill him. At least for the next few hours.

Chapter Ten

While Miles had wanted to just read, he'd instead looked up his would-be combatant in Vladimir Petrov, who was, according to the information he could find in the vampire Assembly database, only a hundred fifty years old. The database didn't have photos, or anything beyond a name, date of birth, and date of rebirth, and was only really there in the same way that a census is used to see who is and isn't alive. Being able to know how many official vampires there were in the world was a useful tool. Tracking the unofficial ones, that was a slightly larger problem.

Star found him before he left and apologised for any trouble, offering a complimentary suite within the building the next time he stayed, which Miles was thankful for. The moment the UV index dropped to one, Miles and Church were in the car and ready to go.

Miles was happy to be out on the road, although that happiness was dampened somewhat by the time he reached the M25. While motorways were designed to make it quicker to get from point A to point B, the M25 took a different approach. It basically took his drive to a crawl for close to half an hour. Still, Church was happy to sprawl across the back seats of the Mercedes. The boot contained Miles's clean clothes and a full tactical kit, including an MP5 submachine gun with suppressor.

After the M25, Miles took the M3 south, where traffic was lighter, and continued on to the M27. He followed the instructions on the satnav as he left the motorway and drove through Southampton's still-busy city centre to Ocean Village. He parked the car in an underground parking lot, on top of which sat a twelve-storey building, got out, and grabbed an overnight bag from the rear seats, as Church jumped down and stretched.

The flat organised for him was the penthouse, which Miles had to admit was nice. The Assembly owned buildings and accommodations all over the globe. Not every city had an Assembly building like the one in Islington, as they were usually only kept for the vampire-controlled areas, which Southampton—despite being a major port—had never been.

Miles and Church took the lift up to the only penthouse suite on the top floor, using the key that had been in the car waiting for them. The suite was spacious, with a view of the nearby marina and River Itchen. There was a large, well-stocked kitchen, two double bedrooms—each with their own ensuite—and a huge balcony that stretched the length of the accommodation, but Miles wasn't planning on staying there for long enough to enjoy it. He dropped his bag in one of the bedrooms and, with Church behind him, exited the patio door which led to a rooftop garden, complete with a good-sized lawn and several flower beds. Church went off to do what Church did in such situations, and Miles took a seat on one of the chairs that were around a glass-topped garden table. He placed his laptop on the table, opened it, and made a video call to Rosa, who answered a few seconds later.

"I've been expecting you," she said with a smile.

"That should make the next few minutes easier," Miles said. "So, do we know where Jennifer or Charlie are hiding out?"

"Jennifer's friend Pearl lives a few minutes' walk away from where you are," Rosa said. "Megan and her team are en route. They said they'll see you there. They got a hit on the facial recognition. Looks like Dominik drove over Itchen Bridge toward Woolston on the other side of the river early this morning, when we were still in London. Photos are taken of every single car, apparently. I'll send you the photo."

Miles's phone vibrated and he looked down at the remarkably good quality photo. There was very little of Dominik's face, as despite it being night, he wore a hoodie and sunglasses, but the snake tattoo was clear.

"I assume Megan's team all know," Miles said to Rosa.

"They're waiting for you," Rosa said.

"Do we know where he's staying?"

"Not a clue," Rosa said. "I'll send you the address where to meet the team."

Miles's phone pinged again, this time with a message showing the address in question, as well as a map showing the best route to walk there. "Oxford Street," Miles said. "Looks like a lot of bars and restaurants down there. It's nae even midnight, it's going to be busy. Judging from the previous murders, the more the merrier for Dominik." He hoped that whatever happened tonight, the extra people nearby weren't going to give their quarry extra targets if things went in a less than ideal fashion.

"Megan and her people are some of the best," Rosa said. "I'm sure they'll have considered it."

Valid point, Miles thought.

"Megan asked for you to meet her and her team at midnight. They're keeping watch until then, but they want the bars to have closed before they move in. That good for you?" Rosa asked.

Miles checked his watch; he had a little time yet. "Yeah, that's fine."

There was a pause for a few seconds before Rosa said, "You okay?"

"I'm good," Miles said and explained his run-in with Vladimir.

"That motherfucker," Rosa snapped. "I'll make sure he never tries that shit again. With one of my Arbiters? Who the fuck does he think he is?"

"Justice Balderas dealt with it."

"You think he'll be a problem?"

"Vlad?" Miles asked, with a laugh. "No, I think he's a punk ass dickhead, with more pride than common sense. He'll either try to make it official, in which case he'll get badly hurt, or he'll try to come after me without anything saying he can, which will get him killed. There's no good ending for Vlad. But he's probably not the only one who wants to take out the man who removed the Vedran money tree. Hopefully whatever bullshit they've got festering in their minds will wait until after the Dominik thing, but I figured it was worth mentioning to you."

"I'll keep my ear to the ground," Rosa said. "Be safe tonight."

Rosa ended the call, and Miles sat where he was, looking across the River Itchen at the multitude of homes, of businesses, of people going about their lives. None knew that not far from where they stood could well be a serial murderer, a psychopath who seemingly cared little for the lives of anyone. If you were in his hunting ground, you were fair game.

Miles went back into the penthouse and changed into a pair of jeans, a black T-shirt, and an old pair of trainers that were comfortable but disposable should they become ruined. He pulled on a black hoodie and checked his watch: *11:40 PM.*

"Time to go," Miles said, and Church followed him out of the penthouse, back down to the ground floor, and out onto the fairly quiet streets.

The pair walked through Ocean Village, which had undergone an injection of wealth over the years, which had turned what was once a bit of rundown area of the city into a mass of town houses, apartment buildings, and a high-end hotel that sat against the river.

The occasional person walked by the pair, giving Church a wide berth in the process, until they'd reached the entrance to Oxford Street, where a large group of revellers was busy being ejected from a soon-to-be closed pub.

Miles walked through the group, ignoring the stench of alcohol and cigarettes. One man bumped into him, turned, and snarled something in Miles's direction, but after one look at Church reconsidered his life choices and backed away quickly.

There were a dozen bars in Oxford Street, and they all closed at roughly the same time, so the whole area became awash with drunken idiots. According to the news, which Miles had been reading on his wait to leave, there had been a running battle between groups of people in the street a few years back. Chairs and tables had been thrown, and the police had been called. Miles had thought it was pretty funny, not just because idiots were throwing chairs at one another, which was always comical, but because some people thought vampires were the big bad monsters lurking in the dark, when humans were quite content to be their own biggest problems.

Halfway up, Oxford Street changed from bars and restaurants to a series of three-storey town houses in a terrace configuration. There was a side street, down which sat newly built town houses that used to be more bars. A dozen cars were parked outside of the houses, one of which, a grey Ford Transit van, had taxi plates on the front, and someone sat behind the steering wheel. Miles assumed it was probably waiting for one of the drunken revellers and continued on. A hundred meters later, the road ended at a junction, next to which, in a parking bay, was Megan's vehicle from London.

The door opened, and Megan smiled. "You ready?"

Miles nodded. "What do you want me to do?"

"I think you should go knock on the door and ask to speak to Pearl," Megan said. "Explain who you are and why you're here. My two team members said that no one has left that house all day, and no one has arrived there, but the rear conservatory door has been opened a few times so someone who matches Jennifer's description can go have a smoke. We know she's there—once we get her and Pearl out of there safely, we wait for Dominik to turn up."

"I saw the photo," Miles said. "He's in the city."

Megan nodded. "We don't know where. But presume he's on his way here."

"You armed?" Claire asked from the driver's seat.

Miles shook his head. "No need to be. I'm just here to talk, remember?"

Megan looked down at Church. "Can she stay here?"

Church let out a snort that told everyone what she thought about that.

"Not because you're not helpful," Megan said. "It's just some people are scared of dogs."

Miles rubbed Church's head. "You want to stay here or come with me?"

Megan picked up a tub and opened the lid, revealing the smell of bacon. "I made bacon rolls."

Church looked between the bacon and Miles. She whined and used her pitiful *I've never been fed* look which all dogs seemed to have perfected.

"Okay, fine, go eat. *Again*," Miles said as Church licked his hand, and Megan gave her a slice of back bacon.

"Hey," Megan said after Miles had walked away a few steps.

Miles stopped and turned back to her.

"Don't scare this woman unless you have to," Megan said. "We know Jennifer is in there, but we don't know what Pearl has actually been told."

"I'll be nice," Miles promised, crossing over his heart.

He continued on down the street as the revellers from earlier walked up toward him on the opposite side of the street.

"Where's your big doggy now?" one of the men shouted.

Miles ignored him and continued on for two steps before he heard the whistle of an empty bottle being thrown at him. He snapped toward the missile and caught it in mid-air, letting his vampire side show the second he did. He stared at the terrified humans across the street, who practically fell over themselves to get away.

Returning his features to human, Miles placed the bottle on the pavement.

He continued on to the address and stood at the bottom of a set of three steps. There were five-foot-high metal railings on either side. The steps led up to a white front door, with a metal number *27* just above a peephole.

A camera doorbell sat to the right of the door. There was a window below street level, looking up through the grate next to the steps. Most of these old town houses had basements, which in Miles's case just meant there were more places for people to hide. Or try to.

Miles pressed the button for the doorbell, which let out a loud chime, followed a few seconds later by, "Yes?"

Miles let out a slight sigh of relief. It had occurred to him that as humans, they may well have gone to bed. Vampires sometimes forgot that not everyone was a night owl. He was glad that the concern was unfounded.

"My name is Miles Watson," he said into the microphone just below the doorbell. He raised his hand to show the torc to the camera. "I'm an Arbiter. We need to talk, right now."

"I have nothing to say to you," the voice said.

"Pearl," Miles said softly, "I need to speak to Jennifer. I know she's there. I know she's in danger. I want to help her. I'm nae here to hurt or arrest anyone, but a bad person is looking for her, and if I don't stop him people are going to get hurt."

There was silence for a few seconds, before the door unlocked and was opened cautiously, revealing the woman from the photo Megan had shown him, although that woman hadn't been so obviously terrified.

"Dominik," she said softly. She wore jeans and a T-shirt, and looked as if she hadn't slept in some time.

"You know him?" Miles asked.

Pearl shook her head and held the door open for Miles to step inside. "Sorry, do I need to invite you?"

Miles took a step into the house. "No," he said. "One of many myths that I'd hoped would have gone away by now, but seems to have taken hold."

The hallway had three doors and a set of stairs leading to the floor above. Of the three doors, the one at the far end, opposite the front door, was open, revealing a tidy living room.

"Follow me," Pearl said and took the lead down the hallway.

Miles stopped by the first door and opened it, revealing a long kitchen diner, with patio doors at the far end of the room.

"What are you doing?" Pearl asked from the doorway, fear laced through every word.

Miles had walked halfway across the long room, into the kitchen. He ignored her and continued on to the sliding patio doors, looking outside into the small but tidy garden. There were no sheds, no trees, nowhere for someone to hide.

"I asked you a question," Pearl said, her fear replaced with anger.

Miles turned back to her. "Checking this isn't going to be an exceptionally silly ambush."

"I . . . no," Pearl stammered. "No, I'm not going to ambush you."

"Not you, but your friends," Miles said. "You do know they would get hurt if they tried. So, if there's anyone in this house that shouldn't be, they need to come out. Now. I'm really not in the mood to play silly fuckers."

Pearl opened her mouth to argue and then closed it.

"Where is Jennifer?" Miles asked, his tone hard.

Pearl visibly straightened. "You cannot threaten me, Mister Watson."

"I'm not," Miles pointed out. "I'm here to make sure that you and Jennifer don't end up like the others Dominik has killed. Do you know about that?"

Pearl nodded.

"Do you know what he did to those people?"

"Charlie said he tore them apart," Pearl said softly.

"Did he say that Dominik also killed *anyone* who was with his target? Family, friends, strangers, it doesn't matter. Charlie and Jennifer have put your life in serious danger by coming here. I understand you want to help your friends, I do, but I know that Jennifer is here. My friends saw her going out for a smoke earlier. We also tracked her phone here. If I know, there's a good chance Dominik knows. If Dominik turns up, and I'm not here to help you, I don't want to think of the horror he's going to inflict on you all."

Miles had considered sugarcoating it, not making Pearl afraid of what was almost certainly coming for her friends, and by extension her. He'd quickly discarded the idea; there was no time to use kid gloves in this situation.

"Vampires don't scare me," Pearl said, although her voice wavered a little.

"We fucking well should," Miles snapped. "Goddamn it, Pearl. Where are they? Dominik is going to kill everything and anything in his way. All he wants is vengeance for what they did to him."

Pearl's expression faltered just a moment. "What?"

"Missed out the bit where Charlie stabbed him to death, did they?"

"I don't . . ." Pearl took a breath, letting it out slowly. "I don't know Charlie. I know Jennifer. Or knew her. We stayed in touch over the years, mostly getting together for a drink here and there. I think she's scared of him."

"Where is she?"

"In the basement," Pearl admitted.

"Go get her, bring her here," Miles said. "I don't want to hurt her, or Charlie, I just need to make sure they're safe. I need to stop more bodies from piling up. Please."

Pearl nodded and walked off, leaving Miles alone in the room.

"I'll make some tea," Miles called after her to no reply.

He put the kettle on, found three mugs, and took a few seconds to find tea, which was in a container helpfully marked as such. Right next to one marked *sugar*. The kettle was still boiling when Pearl returned with a woman who looked like Jennifer, albeit a Jennifer who hadn't slept or eaten in several days. She wore grey jogging bottoms and a navy blue hoodie and stood in the doorway, hugging her arms around her chest.

"I thought tea might help," Miles said to Jennifer.

"Milk, one sugar," she said softly, almost a whisper.

"I'll get it," Pearl told Miles. "Please go easy."

Miles nodded and looked over at the woman in the doorway. "You want to go sit down and talk?"

Jennifer nodded and walked back out into the hallway, with Miles following her into the living room. Jennifer sat on a three-seater, light grey fabric sofa and pulled her legs up to her chest, resting her chin on her knees.

Miles sat on a deep brown leather armchair next to the opposite side of the sofa to where Jennifer sat, staring at the floor.

"Anything you want to tell me before we start?" Miles asked.

"Charlie was going to kill Dominik the second he walked into the bar," Jennifer said sadly.

CHAPTER ELEVEN

W hat do you mean by that?" Miles asked.

"We were in that bar when Dominik came in," Jennifer said. "It's not a local or anything, but we've been there a few times. Bill, one of Charlie's mates, recognised Dominik as someone who had attacked a friend of his a few weeks earlier. Said that Dominik was some rich asshole who got his daddy's goons to batter him, left him in hospital. Charlie said maybe we should repay the favour.

"I was to start up a conversation with Dominik, to get him to go outside so that Charlie and the others could follow. But Dominik started pawing at me, grabbing at me, I shoved him away, and he shouted at me, just as the barman was about to shout last call. Dominik grabbed me by the hair, called me names, threatened me. Charlie stepped in, and he got his wish. Dominik said to meet him outside, but Charlie wasn't going to fight him, he was going to use his knife. He told me that the second Dominik placed his hand on me, he planned to kill him."

"So, you were already in the bar?" Miles asked. "It wasn't until Dominik walked in, that Charlie was going to kick off, and all of this was going to happen because Dominik attacked some friends of Bill's?"

Jennifer nodded.

"Charlie killed people before?"

Jennifer nodded, looking grey.

"Works for bad people?"

Another nod.

"And you?"

"I . . . I'm not allowed a job," she said softly. "He gives me an allowance every month. I'm only allowed contact with people Charlie okays."

"Like his boys?"

Jennifer nodded again.

"Any of them ever cross Charlie when it comes to you?"

Tears ran down Jennifer's cheeks.

"Okay," Miles said, wondering if he should just let Charlie die anyway, considering he sounded like a piece of shit. "Where is Charlie?"

"I don't know," Jennifer said. "He told me he was going to hunt for Dominik. Said he had a friend who lived in town. He was going to stay with him, and then they were going to find Dominik."

"How long since you last saw him?"

"Since lunch, so maybe twelve hours," Jennifer said.

Pearl arrived with a tray and three mugs of hot tea. She placed the tray on the glass coffee table in the centre of the room and passed one to Miles, who nodded appreciatively before quickly placing the hot drink on a coaster on the table.

"Too hot?" Pearl asked with what Miles thought was genuine concern.

"It's okay, I prefer my tea lukewarm," he said with a smile.

Pearl passed Jennifer a mug, who smiled weakly as she took it, mouthing *thanks*.

"You must be good friends to let her stay here after all this time," Miles said. "You said you stayed in touch over the years, but letting someone you chatted with a few times on social media crash at your house because a deranged vampire is after her is a bit more than just online friends."

"I may have undersold it," Pearl said, sitting beside Jennifer.

"I have a secret account," Jennifer said. "I'm allowed an online account because Charlie can keep an eye on it, but he doesn't know about the other one."

"Have you ever tried to run before?" Miles asked.

Jennifer nodded. "Once. He caught us."

"Us?"

"His name was Peter," Jennifer said. "He was a friend. He tried to get me out of the house, to get me to safety. Charlie's friends beat him into a coma in front of me. Told me if I ever ran again, he'd make me watch as he killed anyone I was with."

"Where's Peter now?" Miles asked.

"He moved away, blocked me on anything I could have contacted him on."

"Charlie is a bad guy," Miles said. "You know that, right?"

Jennifer nodded.

Miles looked over to Pearl. "*You* know that too, aye?"

"Fuck yeah," Pearl said. "Frankly, I hope Dominik and he kill each other."

"*Pearl*," Jennifer exclaimed. "I don't want him dead. There are times he's sweet and caring, and a good man."

Of course there are, Miles thought to himself.

A phone rang, and Jennifer picked it out of her pocket. "Charlie," she said, sounding happy.

"On speaker phone," Miles said.

Jennifer nodded and answered the call. "Charlie?" she asked.

"Hello, Jennifer," said a voice that sounded like someone gargling with gravel.

"Dominik," Jennifer said with obvious fear.

"I have your *boy*," he said. "They thought they could hunt me. *Me!* I'm a vampire, for fuck's sake. Unfortunately, his friends got a little . . . damaged."

"What did you do to Charlie?" she asked.

"Charlie, say hello to your woman," Dominik said, followed by an ear-splitting scream of pain.

"Charlie!" Jennifer shouted at the phone.

"Oh, he's a little bit busy for talking," Dominik said. "We started playing a game of 'This Little Piggy,' and right now he's lost three piggies."

There was another scream, and a man pleading for it to stop, followed by a snapping noise and more screaming.

"Four piggies," Dominik said.

"What do you want?" Jennifer shouted.

"You," Dominik said. "You were part of what they did to me."

"I didn't know they were going to try and kill you."

"I don't care," Dominik said. "Oh, and hi to the Assembly vampire standing beside you."

"Hello, Dominik," Miles said, texting Megan the phone number to track. "How do you know I'm here?"

"Oh, well, I may have been watching your ATO friends arrive," Dominik said. "I was going to grab Jennifer last night, but there's an ATO team watching, and so I thought I'd just enjoy my time with Charlie and his friends. I saw you and that dog of yours. You're not going to stop me."

"Why not come and say hi?" Miles asked, the hairs on the back of his neck standing up at the idea of being watched and not noticing. And even stranger, of Church not noticing. It was an unnerving thought, until something occurred to him. "You put a camera watching this house."

Dominik laughed. "Smart vampire. Smarter than the ones my father employs. I wanted to see who was going to turn up. I'm honoured that it's so many Assembly vampires."

"I am an Arbiter," Miles said. "Do you know what that is?"

"Executioner," Dominik said, sounding almost envious.

"I'm not," Miles said, without adding *but for you, I'll make an exception.*

"I didn't want to leave Charlie all alone," Dominik said, followed by a yell of pain from somewhere close to him. "I just want you to know that I know you're there. I honestly think I might enjoy the challenge."

"I guarantee you won't," Miles said, his voice low, full of anger. "Just give up. We can do this quickly and no one else gets hurt."

"Oh someone is going to get hurt," Dominik said. "But I want Jennifer. So, Jen, you come to me, or I hurt people to get to you. In fact, I won't even kill that Pearl friend of yours. Hi, Pearl."

"That's not happening," Miles said before either Jennifer or Pearl could answer. "You hand yourself in, or I come find you."

"Is that a threat?" Dominik asked, the grin on his face obvious.

"Aye, it is."

"I don't care," Dominik said, as if waving away Miles's involvement. "You were there, Jen, you were part of it. You get to suffer for your sins. You come to me, you give yourself up, and I'll let Pearl live."

"Just leave us alone," Pearl said. "You have Charlie. He's the one who stabbed you."

"I know," Dominik said, his voice low and angry. "But I need more than just him. I need *vengeance.* I deserve it. Do you know what it feels like to be stabbed over and over? Do you know that pain? Do you have any idea what it's like to feel your body's life slipping away, only for it to be wrenched back as a vampire? The pain of the transformation is not something I would have considered before it happened to me. Apparently, it's because I was so close to death myself. I feel like I need to show others what I've gone through because of your boyfriend and his friends. So here's the deal. You come to me, I won't hunt you, I won't kill Pearl, and I'll make your death quick. I know where you live, Pearl. I could take you both at any time, but I think it would be easier for everyone if I didn't have to leave my new friend. I won't even make you watch what I do to Charlie. He's going to take a long time to die."

"You know the Assembly isn't going to allow this," Miles said.

"I know," Dominik said. "But if you don't, I'm going to try and turn Charlie into even more of a monster. Maybe he'll become a desolate. I could release him into the city. Or maybe, I just start going door to door around here and massacre anyone I feel like. So many blocks of flats that house innocent, unsuspecting families. I wonder how many I could kill by dawn. I have such a lovely view, maybe I'll go across the river and start at the expensive houses there? I think that might be fun."

"Where do I need to go?" Jennifer asked.

"The other side of Itchen Bridge," Dominik said, before giving an address. "No Assembly. No Arbiters. No dogs. You come alone, and let yourself be taken, or I start tearing the limbs of children. You understand, Arbiter?"

"I understand," Miles said through clenched teeth.

"One hour," Dominik said. "That's enough to say your goodbyes. It's a half-hour walk, so don't take too long. If you're a minute late, I start leaving a lot of innocent bodies in my wake. And then, I come for you both anyway. And Jennifer, I'll make you watch as I flay your friend."

The call ended.

"You can't possibly go alone," Pearl said.

"He's going to murder people," Jennifer said.

Miles took the piece of paper from Pearl's hand as Jennifer wept. He put the address into his map app and found the best way to get there. The address was a large supermarket which had hundreds of houses around it, and several blocks of flats, too. A thirty-six-minute walk, according to the app.

Miles studied the map on his phone. "Dominik said he had a lovely view," he said. "Where's a good view around here?"

Pearl looked at the phone screen, pointing to several places. "All of these have a good view of the river. You can see Ocean Village from there."

"Right. You're both coming with me and going to an ATO team," Miles said. "You're not safe here until Dominik has been dealt with."

"I have to go," Jennifer said. "He's going to start killing people."

"He's going to kill people no matter what you do," Miles said. "We'll go to this area and start searching. We either find him, and we're very good at finding people, or we spook him. Either way, no one else is dying tonight."

"Do you think Charlie is okay?" Jennifer asked, seemingly ignoring his words.

Miles and Pearl shared an expression. They both knew that Charlie was anything other than *okay.*

"Why don't you both go upstairs and get some stuff to take with you," Miles said.

"Will we be safe with the ATOs?" Pearl asked.

Miles nodded. "Megan and her people are the best."

Pearl hurried Jennifer out of the room.

Miles sighed. Things were getting messy. He called Megan and explained everything that had happened.

"We got a ping off the phone," she said. "It's a block of flats near that supermarket. I've sent you a photo. Doesn't mean he's still there, but it's worth a start. Maybe Church can get a scent and we'll go from there."

"Sounds like a plan to me," Miles agreed, checking his phone and looking at the aerial photo Megan had sent. The block of twelve-storey flats overlooked the River Itchen and was out of the way of the main road. If Dominik was there, he was either an idiot for not realising he was going to be traced, or he didn't care. And from what Miles had seen of the killer so far, it was the second. He'd considered leaving Church with Pearl and Jennifer, but he was pretty sure that he was going to need Church to find their prey.

"I'll leave two of my team with Pearl and Jennifer," Megan said. "That way, we can go with you."

"Fair enough," Miles said. A couple of highly trained ATOs keeping an eye on Pearl and Jennifer was probably the best option.

"We'll be ready to go when you are," Megan said and ended the call.

Miles went to the bottom of the stairs and called up. "You're both staying here. The ATOs are going to send some of their people to keep an eye on you."

Pearl arrived at the top of the stairs. "Probably for the best," she said. "Jen is . . . she's had a hard time."

Miles nodded that he understood and went to the front door. He hadn't quite reached it when there was the sound of squealing tyres outside, followed almost immediately by gunfire. Miles practically wrenched the door open as more gunshots echoed around the street. Four shots in total. Miles quickly pinpointed the sound as having come from where Megan and her team were.

He jumped down the few steps and sprinted to Megan and her team, fear pounding in his chest as the screams of residents and revellers shattered the quiet neighbourhood.

"Church!" Miles shouted, the large dog bounding over to him. He dropped to his knees and checked her. "Are you okay?"

"We're fine," Megan said.

Miles looked up at Megan. "Sorry, I . . ."

"You thought Church was hurt," Megan said, motioning for her people to go calm the humans who had witnessed the attack. "Mostly it's just our egos."

"What's going on?" Miles asked, getting to his feet and immediately seeing the problem. Someone had shot out the tyres on the van.

"Grey van, taxi plates," Megan said, fury slipping through her words.

"It had been parked down there," Miles said, pointing to the street he'd seen it in.

"They were all masked up, no idea who they were, but everyone is okay."

Miles looked over the van, which had bullet holes in the tyres, and Sven stood in front of it swearing repeatedly in Norwegian. He stared at the bullet hole in the panel of the van, and then down at Church. His anger bubbled up inside of him.

"Miles," Megan said softly.

Miles opened the passenger door on the van, and removed his hoodie and T-shirt.

"Why are you taking your clothes off?" Claire asked.

"Fed up of losing clothes," Miles told her, removing his shoes and socks and placing them in the footwell. Wearing only a pair of black shorts, he turned back to Megan. "Catch up to me."

Megan nodded. "Be safe."

Miles looked down at Church. "Let's go get them."

Church barked and set off at a run through the dark Southampton streets. Miles ran a few steps as he turned into his vampiric beast form.

The first time it had happened, Miles had felt pure agony tear through his body, and while the white hot pain was still there, as his body broke and healed almost instantly, it was fleeting. When it was done, Miles's arms were longer, his hands and fingers elongating even further than in his vampire form. Fur had grown over his body, and two black wings tore out of his back. Each wing was longer than he was tall.

Miles knew from experience that his face, while still vampiric in appearance, had changed. His jaw jutting out, his ears now long and pointy. His eyes now blazing red pools with black centres. Hardened ridges of bone sat over each eye, and his cheeks were sunken. His fangs were now accompanied by razor-sharp, sharklike teeth, along with two more fangs on the bottom row.

He beat his wings once and tore into the sky at speed.

Miles soon caught up to Church, who was bounding toward the Itchen Bridge, a near kilometer-long structure that sat over the River Itchen. As they both reached the bridge, Miles noticed the van about halfway over, having had to go the long way around the roads to reach the same place.

Miles swooped down toward Church, motioning for her to stop as the van reached the apex of the bridge and started down the side toward Woolston and the address that Jennifer had been given by Dominik.

Miles landed next to Church. "Stay back," he said. "Follow when it's safe."

Church growled.

"I know, just keep back."

Church huffed in response but made a nodding motion.

Miles ruffled her fur, ran to the side of the bridge, and leapt over it.

The bridge was only a hundred feet above the water, which was only a few meters deep, even at its deepest point. Miles fell for a second, before his wings beat again, and he flew across the river, his hands almost touching the water. Every beat of his wings peppered him with water spray, and he couldn't help but smile for a moment, before he remembered what those people in the van had done. They had *shot* at Church.

The smile vanished, and a cold, dark anger settled inside of him.

He beat his wings and took off straight up, until he was a few hundred feet above the river. He caught sight of the van as it turned off the bridge, avoiding the tollbooths at the end. He followed the van as it turned down the road, ignoring any traffic lights, and continued on along Woolston's main shopping street, which was little more than a few charity shops, a couple of newsagents, and from what Miles had found out when looking into the area, a particularly good bakery.

Miles flew toward where he'd seen the van and caught sight of it heading toward the address that Jennifer had been given before someone had decided to shoot their petty human weapons at Church.

The van continued on by the supermarket toward the block of flats where Dominik had used Charlie's phone. The address was one of four buildings in the area. There were two of similar height, one next to the other, and a third was set a little way away from the other two. The third was only six storeys tall, and wrapped around the whole area. It had apartments above and shops and business premises on the ground floor. Miles landed on the block of flats next to the one he was interested in. Where Dominik was. Or at least, where Dominik had told Jennifer to go.

The grey van pulled up outside of the building, and six people got out. They all wore military-style clothing with bulletproof vests and black helmets, along with similarly coloured masks. They all carried submachine guns, although Miles couldn't tell, and didn't care, what the makes were. They had shot at Church. They could be holding miniature nukes, for all he cared.

Miles studied the target building. There was a lot of scaffolding around it, and several of the floors didn't have windows or anything inside them. The top two floors did, although even with his excellent vision, Miles couldn't see through them. If Dominik was in there, he was going to be on one of those floors.

Miles unfurled his wings and took off into the sky again, until he was a few hundred feet above the van and soldiers below. He needed to make sure they didn't go anywhere. Megan and her team could do cleanup and deal with anyone who had shot at them when they finally arrived. They needed to be alive for that. But they didn't need to be in *good* condition. He wrapped his wings around him, and let himself fall.

He hit the top of the van with an almighty crunch, having used his wings to steady his descent enough to ensure he didn't go right through the roof at high speed. One of the tyres on the van didn't like the impact and popped loudly as Miles stepped off the top of the van, his wings vanishing as he stopped his beast form.

The six soldiers had turned to Miles the second he'd hit their van. Their weapons were trained on him, the stench of fear coming off them in waves.

Miles looked between each of the soldiers in turn, as the anger inside of him threatened to take over. He didn't care that he was almost completely naked. His face changed to its vampire side. Violence was coming.

"So, which one of you *cunts* shot at my dog?"

CHAPTER TWELVE

One of the soldiers stepped forward to speak, but Miles was well beyond discussion and kicked him in the chest, sending him crashing back into the pack behind him. The soldiers fell about the ground, most of them losing their grip on whatever weapons they were holding.

Miles darted toward the one soldier who hadn't been bowled over, grabbing his rifle in one hand and wrenching it free, tossing it toward the masked face of another soldier. The butt of the gun struck him clean in the face, snapping the plastic mask and dropping the soldier to the ground.

Miles caught a punch from the soldier he'd just disarmed and snapped his elbow, pushing him to the side as he charged into the remaining soldiers, who were all getting back to their feet.

Miles grabbed one soldier by the throat and threw him back into the side panel of their van with a loud thud. He heard the sound of someone picking their gun off the floor, and turned to see Church barrel into the soldier, biting down on his arm and swinging him around. The loud snap and scream of pain as the soldier's arm was broken ended the fight quickly for him.

Three soldiers left.

"Stop!" one of them shouted, raising his hands up in surrender. "We weren't going to hurt your fucking dog."

Miles grabbed the soldier by the throat and lifted him off the ground, his feet dangling above the concrete. "You *shot* at my dog," he all but snarled, before dropping the soldier to the floor. "You're lucky none of you are dead."

Church sat beside one of the still conscious and relatively healthy soldiers, who were trying to get off the ground, and let out a long, low growl. The soldier lay back down and gave Church a thumbs-up.

"My people need first aid," the soldier said.

"Your *people* are lucky they're still breathing," Miles told him. "Broken bones heal, so if you want to help them, talk fast. Looking at your gear, I'm guessing you work for Templar International, yes?"

The soldier nodded.

"You're going to need to explain why you're here," Miles said, crouching down beside the soldier. "And do it quickly."

The soldier stared at Miles for a few seconds. "We were put in charge of Dominik's security while he adapted to his new vampire life. He escaped—we were told to get him and not come back without him. We knew he'd come for Charlie and Jennifer, so we remotely hacked their phones. Decided to listen in on their conversations. We knew they were both in Southampton, so we came here to watch and wait."

"Why not GPS tag him or track his phone?"

"He binned the phone," the soldier said. "We did put a GPS tracker inside him. He tore it out and placed it outside the house of the first set of victims."

"You knew this was where Dominik called from," Miles said, the realisation of how they knew dawning on him. "You traced Charlie's call just like we did."

The soldier nodded.

"How did you think this was going to go?" Miles asked. "You shot at an ATO team. Was that on the list of things to do?"

"We've been here since we knew that Jennifer and Charlie would come this way. We knew we just had to sit and wait for Dominik to make his move. Didn't expect Charlie and a bunch of his idiot friends to go out like nothing was wrong. Once Charlie didn't come back, we knew Dominik would have them. Knew he was in the area, but had to wait for him to move again before we could pinpoint him."

"You could have just gone quietly," Miles said. "You'd have had time. You didnae need to start shooting."

"We thought we'd been made," the soldier said. "Couldn't go back and say we'd lost him again. Couldn't let him fall into the hands of the Assembly. He's an illegal vampire, for God's sake. At the very least, he'd be arrested on the spot, along with Sara. Possibly Henryk, too, if he knew about it or had ordered her to make his son a vampire."

"That probably wouldn't be good for his business," Miles said. "How'd you know for sure he's even here?"

"He's up there," the soldier said. "He's not running, he's not interested in hiding. He'll wait for the ATOs to come, and he'll try to kill them all. I know Dominik, or did when he was human. The top floors of the building are still under construction. That's where he'll be. Waiting. He thinks he's invincible."

"Life has taught him otherwise," Miles pointed out.

"Yeah, and now he's a vampire," the soldier said. "I guarantee you he believes he'll just kill anyone who comes for him and go finish his delusional mission."

The sounds of footsteps coming toward them caught Miles's attention. He got up and looked over at the nearby street as four ATOs and Megan ran toward him.

In the distance was a siren, presumably because some of the residents in the nearby flats called the police. Miles couldn't say he'd blame them for that. He looked up at the flat where Dominik was hiding. The element of surprise was well and truly over, but thankfully the building backed onto the river, so Dominik's means of escape were limited. He wasn't anywhere near old enough to turn into whatever his vampire beast form would be, so he either sat tight and waited, went through the ATOs out front, or swam. Miles figured Dominik wasn't about to make it easy and would wait for people to come to him.

"Miles," Megan said with barely a hint that she'd been running anywhere. Vampire physiology in action. She took in the carnage around Miles and tossed him a bag full of his clothes. "You do all this?"

"No one is dead, just hurt," Miles assured her as he pulled on his jeans. "Although that one over there that Church got hold of probably needs an ambulance. Actually, a few of them probably need an ambulance. Dominik is on that top floor. I'm going to go up, subdue him, and bring him down."

"And we're going with you," Megan said.

"Actually, I figured it better that you all wait here and around the back of the building should he decide to leg it after all. The soldier doesn't think he will, and I think if the ATOs go in there, someone is more likely to get seriously hurt. He's a new vampire, and he's out for vengeance, and doesn't care who's in his way. If I go in there alone, I might be able to flush him out, then you can subdue him down here. At the very least, I'll be able to make sure the only person getting hurt is me, and I'm pretty sure I can take a newly turned vampire."

Miles looked up at the scaffolding around the building. It would be difficult for Church to get up to the top floor without using the stairs inside, and Miles wanted to make sure they were free in case Dominik did decide to make a run for it. "Church, stay with Megan. If Dominik does leg it, take him down. Fast and hard, okay?"

Church barked once.

"Don't do anything stupid," Megan said.

Miles smiled and ran up to the building, launching himself up to the scaffolding. He grabbed the first bar that was twenty feet off the ground, pulled himself up, and began climbing up the outside of the metal and wooden structure. About halfway up, the smell of blood became increasingly prevalent, even with the strong wind that constantly blew from the river.

Miles stopped on the eleventh floor. He realised that the windows were dark not because the curtains had been pulled, but because they'd been blacked out from the inside with tarpaulin. He tore through the tarp and looked inside at a shell of a floor. Exposed wiring hung from the ceiling like stalactites, and while some of the walls were boarded up, most were just the skeletal frame.

It was easy to see all the way through the floor, and he saw nothing out of the ordinary, so he continued up the scaffolding as the sounds of police sirens got closer. The smell of blood was almost overpowering. No matter what happened inside this building, it was turning into an exceptionally long night.

Miles tore the tarpaulin apart and stepped inside the dark floor beyond. Like below, it was clearly unfinished, with partially exposed walls and fittings all around, but unlike below, it was at least set into the configuration of something close to liveable.

The smell of blood from deeper inside the shell of the flat started a *need* inside of Miles. He hadn't fed that long ago, but fresh blood was always preferable to prepackaged. He pushed the feeling down and ignored it, something he'd had plenty of practice doing over the centuries.

Miles stepped through the doorway into what he assumed was meant to be the hallway beyond. There were four more open doorways, one small with a bathtub and toilet, neither of which were connected, one that was a slightly smaller version of the one he'd entered into, and a third, which was a *box* room. A room small enough that it wasn't comfortable enough to actually *be* a bedroom, but big enough that it could still be *called* a bedroom by estate agents.

The last doorway took Miles out into a large space that he assumed was meant to be the living and dining area. A closed door, the only one he'd actually seen, sat to his left, and the start of a kitchen was directly in front of him. It was looking like a pleasant place to live. Although whoever lived here would probably want to get rid of the stench of blood and death first.

Charlie sat tied to a chair in the centre of the room, the sheet plastic beneath his feet covered in blood, all in various stages of congealing. A thick rope had been placed around his neck and looped up and over the exposed concrete beam above his head.

Miles walked over to Charlie. He was still barefoot, but stepping on blood didn't bother him. You didn't get to be a vampire and be squeamish about bodily fluids. Even so, Miles avoided a large pool of black ichor, and he moved Charlie's head back, revealing the rope burn around his neck. What had been a white T-shirt and jeans were bathed in red. He was missing all ten toes and six fingers, and he had a multitude of cuts all over his body. Charlie had not died easy.

The door to the flat opened, and Miles looked up as a man stepped inside, closing it behind him. He wore bloodstained white Nikes, ripped and tattered jeans, and a black *Evil Dead* T-shirt that had seen better days. His hair was shoulder length and looked greasy and unwashed. To Miles, it looked as if Dominik, because that was definitely who it was, hadn't taken care of himself for several weeks. He was dirty, grimy, and gaunt.

"You a cop?" the man asked.

"Dominik, I assume," Miles said, not really needing the confirmation, but wanting him to know that Miles *knew.*

Dominik nodded and brushed the long hair out of his face. "You must be the Arbiter. I figured my threat might have had an effect on you."

Miles shook his head. "You told Jennifer where to go to meet you. Figured you'd be nearby, but your dad's friends were nice enough to lead us right here. They knew you would just wait. You didn't think we'd track the phone, I assume."

"Didn't care," Dominik said. "I'm a vampire now. A powerful one. I can hold my own against anyone else."

"Fan of the film?" Miles asked, unsure where to start this particular conversation, but not wanting to antagonise him further.

Dominik looked down as if seeing his T-shirt for the first time. "No, don't like horror. I stole this from a laundrette in London. I think it's an original. Probably worth something. Maybe the blood adds to the value." He cackled at his own joke.

"You killed Charlie then," Miles said, motioning toward the body.

Dominik nodded sadly. "I *really* wanted to keep him alive, but my need to hurt him got the better of me. I was actually surprised he lived through me tearing his toes and fingers off. Can I assume that Jennifer isn't coming?"

"That's a good assumption," Miles said.

"Shame," Dominik said. "I'm going to have to make her watch as I skin her friend."

Miles laughed. It was the only thing he could do in the face of such outright delusion.

"You think that's funny?" Dominik asked, a little anger in his tone for the first time.

Miles nodded. "You're not killing anyone else. Your options here are twofold. Either you come with me quietly, and I pass you over to the ATO team for transport to a vampire prison, after which you'll be assessed by the Assembly and dealt with however they see fit."

"I don't think so," Dominik said. "What's option two?"

Miles kept Dominik's eye contact. "Trust me, you won't like option two."

"You think you can beat me in a fight?" There was a hint of entertainment to his body language.

Miles raised his wrist, showing the torc. "You know what this is?"

Dominik laughed again. It was an unpleasant noise, almost a rattling in his chest. "I don't care that you're an Arbiter. If you kill me, my dad will kill you, and if you take me in, my dad will get me out. Benefits of being part of an important company like my dad's."

"I think you vastly overestimate how important your dad is."

"I won't be taken," Dominik said. "I just won't. My family would never live it down. My father would never live it down. I'll make him proud, and if that means going out fighting, then so be it."

"You don't have to do this," Miles said, heaving a sigh. If it came to it, he would kill the young vampire and that would be that, but he knew of too many Arbiters who were all too happy to take the executioner part of their job too quickly, when other avenues were available.

"I watched you fly here," Dominik said. "You can't do that again for a while, can you? Sara told me that vampire beast forms are really powerful, but can only be used for a short time, and then you have to wait to use it again. Shame, I think I'd have enjoyed killing you in that form."

"You'll just have to settle for this one," Miles said with a resigned feeling inside of him.

Dominik rushed forward without another word, his face taking on a sneer as he let his vampire self out. Miles avoided a swipe with Dominik's now talon-like nails on his elongated fingers, and slapped Dominik across the face with enough force to send the younger vampire to his knees.

Miles moved around toward the doorway that led to the hallway and bedrooms. He didn't want to give Dominik a lot of room to move around, and he also didn't want to have to fight where there was a possibility of slipping on the bloody floor.

Dominik snarled as he got to his feet.

"Last chance," Miles said, noticing the bloodstained footprints that he'd left on the floor. He was going to need a long shower when this was all done.

"Fuck you!" Dominik shouted and ran at Miles, who stepped to the side, caught the younger man by his lapel, and kicked out his knee, sending him headfirst into, and through, the wall next to the hallway.

The crash of plasterboard mixed with a howl of pain and rage from Dominik as he landed inside the empty box room beyond. Miles ignored him and continued on down to the end bedroom, walking back into the room he'd first entered.

Miles reached the torn tarpaulin and shouted down, "Come get him!"

Megan gave a thumbs-up, and Miles turned to see Dominik walk through the wall separating the two bedrooms. It was as if he'd glitched, his whole body flickering in and out as turquoise bolts of what looked like lightning flickered across his body.

"What the hell?" Miles asked.

Dominik grinned the smile of a predator and darted forward. Miles went to block the blow, but Dominik's arms went through his, reforming inside his block, and striking him in the chest hard enough to force him to take a few steps back.

"What the fuck are you?" Miles asked.

"Your better," Dominik said.

Miles kicked out at Dominik's knee, but the younger vampire ghosted through it, tackling Miles to the floor, his hands around his throat, his nails shorter so they could dig into Miles's throat.

"I'm going to rip you apart," Dominik said, spittle flying out of his face.

Miles channelled his bloodline gift and slammed his palm into Dominik's chest. The effect was immediate as all strength was sapped out of the murderous vampire.

Miles pushed Dominik off him with one hand, sending him flying across the room into the wall adjacent to the window.

"What did you do to me?" Dominik screamed, looking all too human.

"*My* bloodline gift," Miles said. "I can separate the vampire from the human. I'd like to say the next few minutes won't hurt, but I'd be lying."

Dominik roared and charged at Miles, who hit him in the stomach hard enough to take the other vampire off his feet and dump him back on the ground.

While Miles's bloodline gift did separate the vampire from the human, how long it lasted depended on how powerful the vampire was. With someone as young and new to it all as Dominik, even with his glitching power, it was going to take him a good half hour before he'd be able to reconnect with the vampire side.

Dominik pulled himself up by the window ledge, pulling the tarpaulin down from where it was attached. "You took it from me," he cried out.

"Don't make this harder than it needs to be," Miles said. "Surrender."

"Fuck you," Dominik said, climbing out of the window, onto the scaffolding.

Miles took a tentative step forward, and Dominik smiled. "I'll not be cowed by you or anyone else. See you in hell."

Miles couldn't reach Dominik in time to stop the young vampire from launching himself over the side of the scaffolding. He watched as Dominik hit the van belonging to his father's security people headfirst, disappearing through the roof of the vehicle.

Miles climbed out onto the scaffolding and looked down at the small group of police, Templar International security, and ATOs. He wondered if Dominik would survive such a fall while so young and having had his vampire side nullified.

One of the ATOs opened the side panel of the van, and a head rolled onto the ground beside them. Screams sounded out from several of the flats around the area who had balconies overlooking the scene below.

"Well, that answered that," Miles said to himself as Dominik's head was hastily put back into the van.

PART TWO

Chapter Thirteen

Eight Months Later

Megan Song sat in the back of an unmarked black Ford Transit van, a cup of coffee in one hand, the steam from the reusable metal cup a constant reminder of just how cold it was. It wasn't quite freezing outside, but November in Lithuania wasn't far off. The Baltic Sea was a few miles to the west of where Megan and her team were working, but considering the strength of the wind whipping outside the van, she'd have been surprised if it would have been much worse right next to it.

The last nine months had been hard on Megan and her team. After Dominik had taken a decapitating swan dive out of a twelfth-storey window, her team had been stood down pending an investigation. Everything had been aboveboard, and along with Miles, all had been cleared of any wrongdoing. In fact, Templar International had lost its accredited status and been forced to have an investigation of its own.

It was ruled that the murderous Dominik had died from his own actions. He'd chosen to jump a hundred twenty-seven feet to his death, and probably would have survived had he not hit the van roof at such an angle to remove his head. The fact that he didn't have access to his vampire side because of Miles's bloodline gift had no bearing on it. Decapitation was death for a vampire; the age didn't much matter.

After four months of investigation, Megan and her team had been allowed back out into the field, albeit under supervised conditions. Those conditions had been lifted a month ago, and it had been back to normal ever since.

One of Megan's team, Sven, had brought intel to them about a gang working out of Lithuania who had been splicing various narcotics into vampire blood without any kind of regulation. An unsuspecting vampire had taken a blood bag and ended up losing her mind, killing three people before she was finally stopped. While she was taken alive, her mind had all but broken, both from whatever it was she'd taken and from what she'd done after.

Megan's team investigated further and discovered that the bad blood was possibly linked to a gang who had been shipping spliced narcotic blood all across Europe. Megan had hoped that when they'd raided the London address with Miles a year back that the drugs would stop, but the gang had just found new avenues to exploit. She was going to track down whoever was behind it and end it before more people died.

Megan and her people had set about looking into it and discovered that the gang were running their operation out of a small abandoned village inside Lithuania. Hopefully Megan would get answers from whoever they found.

The village had twenty-six four-bedroom, detached houses, each one with a front and back garden and driveway. The properties were all built on one road, which curved up and around a gentle hill, with a final twenty-seventh building at the top of the hill. That one had twelve bedrooms and was clearly some sort of mansion, although the team hadn't been able to find any blueprints of the property.

The project had seemingly lost or run out of funding and had sat unused for several months, which was probably why a gang of drug-dealing morons had taken up residency. Megan had sent her people in two groups to scout the village, while Megan sat in the relative warmth of the van and listened to them doing their jobs.

There was a knock on the van door, which slid open revealing Sven and Jordan, both in tactical gear, including stab-proof vests with *ATO* written in big yellow letters.

"You're going to want to see this," Sven said. "It's weird."

Megan put her coffee down and sighed, swinging her legs out of the van and making sure she had her weapons with her: a shock baton and a Mossberg 800 series with incendiary rounds. She'd have rather taken the gang alive, and she wasn't sure if they were human or vampire, but either way, an incendiary round was going to give them a bad day if they didn't behave.

"Show me," Megan said, and followed Sven and Jordan from where they'd parked, in a lay-by just outside of the turnoff for the village. They continued along the road for several minutes until reaching the remaining six members of Megan's eight-member team.

"Boss," Claire said, "this is weird."

"Weird how?" Megan asked.

"The village is empty," she said.

Megan frowned. "Seriously?"

"No lights, no activity, no nothing," Sven said. "We haven't gone all the way through yet, but we swept through a few of the houses, and all of them have the same layout. All with nothing suggesting anyone lived there. They've built the houses, but if anyone lives in them, they're the most minimalist houses of all time."

"And the mansion?" Megan asked, considering what was going on.

"We didn't check," Sven said. "Came back to get you after sweeping the outer buildings. If there's a gang in there, they're hiding so well that vampires can't find them, or they're not there."

They group continued on to the entrance of the village, which had a large sign on the front stating *Homes for the Future*, written in a yellow font beside a happy-looking couple standing in front of a house as their children played in the garden.

"The lawns are well maintained," Megan said, looking across the houses.

"Tidy and dust-free inside, too," Sven said.

"Okay, so someone is keeping this place neat and tidy," Megan said. "If you were in a gang, and you came here to hide out and run your little money-making scheme, would you stay in a house or a mansion?"

"Mansion," all eight of her people said at once.

"Me too," Megan said. "Okay, Sven, Jordan, take Bill and Dean and head left. Claire, Terri, Viktor, and Koby, with me. We'll head right and meet up at the top of that hill outside of the mansion. Do not enter without backup. If you see any activity in one of the houses, let us know; otherwise, we do this slow and quiet."

"Got it," everyone said, and the teams split into two.

Megan's team moved through the well-maintained rear gardens of several empty homes, vaulting over the short fences with barely a sound. They made good time and were soon at the houses around the curved part of the single road, the mansion looming up ahead.

They continued on until leaving the garden of the final house, but had seen no signs of anyone. They met up with the rest of the team and remained outside of the mansion as Megan studied the property. It had a twenty-foot-tall black iron fence, with two large gates in the centre. There was a large gravel drive beyond, which could have easily doubled as a parking area for the whole village. A dozen steps led up to the double doors that were the entrance to the building. There were no lights on, no scents of people, no nothing. Just a vast empty building that imposed itself on the neighbourhood.

"It's not exactly inviting, is it?" Claire said.

"How are we getting inside?" Jordan asked. "You want me to try the gates?"

"Go take a look," Megan said, and Jordan set off to the front gates as everyone else kept lookout.

Jordan pushed one of the gates, which swung open. He looked back at Megan and shrugged.

"Sven, take your team around the perimeter of the building," Megan said. "We don't want any surprises. Everyone else, we're going to look at gaining entry. We do this quietly, and maybe we can shut this all down before anyone knows we're here."

"Front door?" Claire asked.

Megan nodded. "Sven, if the perimeter is clear, head back to the front and provide cover."

Sven nodded. "Will do, boss."

"Something feels *off* about this," Megan said. "Everyone keep your heads straight and watch out for traps. I've got a hot mug of coffee I need to finish. Let's go."

The team headed onto the gravel, which crunched loudly in the still night. The teams split into two, with Claire and Koby moving to the front door, while Megan and Jordan remained back, keeping an eye out for anything that would look untoward.

Koby picked the lock and pushed the front door open, revealing a dark and empty foyer. Like the houses below, there were no furnishings inside. Who would go to all this effort to build places to live but not actually live there?

Megan and her team entered the building, listening for any signs of nearby trouble, but the house was as quiet and devoid of life as the rest of the village.

They moved as a group, checking and clearing room by room, finding nothing but empty dark spaces, although the feeling that something wasn't quite right grew inside of Megan. They completed the circuit of the rooms on the ground floor and ended back at the foyer.

"Nothing," Claire said. "Did we get wrong intel?"

"We got the wrong *something*," Koby said. "You want to check upstairs?"

"We'll wait for the others," Megan said.

"It takes a lot to be creepy for vampires," Claire said. "But this whole place is weird. They went to a lot of effort and cost to build these places, just to keep them empty."

Megan said nothing as the door opened and the other half of her team entered the room. Jordan was last, and as the door began to close, Megan thought she caught a smell of something. "Wait," she called out, and Jordan held the door open.

"What's up?" Sven asked.

Megan sniffed the air. "You smell that?"

"I don't smell anything," Sven said.

Megan left the house and stood on the gravel driveway looking down at the empty village. Claire came to stand beside her, the house door held open by Jordan.

"What did you smell?" she asked.

Megan took a long inhale of the air, letting it out slowly, but found nothing. A vampire's senses were stronger than those of a human, certainly where the scent of blood was concerned, but whatever it was Megan thought she could smell, it had gone.

"Maybe it was just something from the woods around there," she said. "Pine, or sap, or something. I don't know. It's gone now. It was almost a perfume smell. Just for a moment."

Claire raised her rifle and looked through the scope at the village, moving across to the woods.

"See anything?" Megan asked.

Claire shook her head. "No . . . wait." She paused. "Ma . . . "

Claire's head vanished in a plume of blood and gore.

"Claire!" Koby screamed from the doorway, raising his own rifle, only to receive a bullet to his head, which had a similar effect to that of Claire's. Koby's body toppled out of the mansion and down the stairs, as lights lit up from all around the ground, having been partially covered by the gravel.

Megan was already sprinting back to the house, pulling the door closed behind her as another bullet smashed into the brick nearby, showering her with dust and brick shrapnel.

"What the fuck?" Sven shouted, moving toward the window and staying to the side as more explosive rounds hit the front of the mansion.

"How did we not smell them?" Viktor asked.

"Back of the house!" Megan shouted. The how this happened could wait until they were all safe.

The team moved as one, keeping low and heading toward the rear of the mansion, through to the kitchen. It was sixty feet from the door to the woodland, although there was a large metal shed between them and what Megan hoped was their way out. If these people were smart enough to hide from vampires, they were smart enough to completely surround the mansion.

"Boss," Sven said, "any ideas?"

"We could wait them out," Bill suggested.

Megan shook her head. "Too many places they can gain entry. Too many places they can just firebomb us. We can't stay here and keep every entry point secure."

"We can't leave Koby and Claire," Jordan said.

"You want to go get them?" Bill snapped.

"Hey," Megan said, raising her voice. "Let's get out of here and figure out what's going on. No one is being left, but we can't exactly carry their bodies through a firefight. One thing at a time."

An arrow came through the kitchen window, smashed into the tile on the opposite wall, and exploded, showering the wall with fire.

"Everyone out!" Megan screamed as flames engulfed the room, the smell of accelerant burning her nose.

Everyone ran out of the room and back through the building toward the foyer, where explosions rang out, shaking the floor of the house.

"We need to get out of here," Sven said.

The fire from the kitchen had taken hold of the doorway and hall beyond, the wooden frame of the house acting like kindling for the flames. It wouldn't be long before the whole structure was burning beyond saving.

The remaining members of the team ran through to the rear right-hand side of the mansion, with Sven putting rounds from his own rifle through the window. "Contact!" he shouted.

Someone cried out from outside.

"Cover me," Megan said and jumped through the window, landing next to the wounded man, who was dragging himself away, leaving a bloody trail in his wake.

Bullets tore out of the room the rest of the team was in, as Megan grabbed hold of the man by his belt and threw him back across the side of the house, toward the nearest tree. She sprinted after him, picking him up by his hair and throwing him up against the tree fifty feet away from the mansion.

Sven and Terri jumped out of the mansion as more rounds were fired into it from the shadows of the rear of the property. They'd just reached Megan when there was a terrible explosion from the room where the rest of Megan's team was. A fireball erupted out of the room, destroying all of the windows, flames leaping out to touch the side of the mansion. Megan felt the heat of the explosion across her face, as she stared in horror, and knew that no one could have survived it.

Sven and Terri had thrown themselves onto the soft ground and were getting back to their feet when an arrow smashed into Sven's leg, just above the ankle. It exploded, tearing his leg off at the knee, his screams of pain silenced by a second arrow to his head.

Terri turned into her vampire side and roared in defiance as another arrow hit her in the throat, exploding and taking her head with it.

Megan cried out in pain, her momentary lapse of concentration giving the man at her feet time to stab her in the thigh with a blade. She lashed out with the back of her fist, crushing the man's face with the force of the blow.

She moved farther into the woods, narrowly missing an arrow which hit one of the large trees and exploded, tearing the trunk apart and forcing it to collapse, which in turn took out several more trees.

Megan continued to move, not daring to slow down, ignoring the pain in her thigh. She was several hundred meters into the woodland, her vampire night vision taking control, making sure she didn't accidentally run into a low-hanging branch as she kept a good pace. Putting as much distance as possible between herself and their assailants. Then she would find out who it was and why. Vengeance came after that.

There were shouts behind her, and the sounds of gunfire. She pushed her House Barbarous bloodline gift to make her faster, to ignore the pain, but every few steps a searing agony tore through her thigh. She stopped behind a large tree and took a look at the wound. It wasn't too deep, and the bleeding had stopped, but it smelled noxious. Great, she'd been poisoned, or infected with something. She was sure her vampire physiology would get rid of it eventually, but that wasn't going to do much help in the middle of some woods. There was no point in circling back around to the car; it was either destroyed or being watched.

Megan removed her phone from her pocket. No signal. *Just great.*

She was about to continue on when she spotted someone walking through the woods toward her. They wore a long black coat over jeans and a black hoodie, with a hockey mask covering their face, which they removed to reveal the features of Sara Bakos.

"You killed my people," Megan said. "My friends."

"We did," she said without any hint of remorse.

"So what now, we're going to fight in the woods?" Megan asked in a mocking tone.

Sara shook her head. "Fury," Sara said.

Megan turned as the shock baton struck her in the side of the head, her entire body collapsing to the floor, her consciousness wavering. She moaned in pain and tried to move as Fury hit her again and again, each time sending waves of electrical pain through her body, until he broke the baton across her skull and had to fetch another.

After what felt like an eternity, Sara stopped him and stood over the battered and bloody Megan. "Not out yet?"

Megan didn't bother to say anything, but she saw the dozen people leave the woods. All wore camouflage or ghillie suits. She looked up at Fury, who wore a beret with a badge on it: a wolf of some kind. She looked around and discovered that more than one of the people surrounding her wore a similar beret and badge. The whole thing had been a setup. Her people had died for nothing.

"Don't worry," Sara said, kneeling down beside Megan. "We're going to have a lot to talk about during our time together."

"You killed my friends," Megan said. "This was a trap."

Sara nodded. "Vampires can't smell those who hide six feet under the ground. The tunnels are all around this place. You walked right into our trap. Because of your arrogance, your people died. But you get to be lucky, little ATO worm, you get to see what happens to those who cross us. You get to watch as your world burns. You were responsible for taking everything from me. So first you die, then that Arbiter bastard."

Megan made a sound that was meant to be a laugh, but sounded like something rattling inside her throat.

"That funny?" Fury asked.

Megan shook her head, and showed the armed and ready incendiary explosive she had in her hand. "This is."

Sara and Fury dove away as the device went off, rolling down the hill, far enough out of the blast radius, as the explosive bathed everything around it in napalm. Heat tore through Megan, and she had one last thought of being glad she had gone out on her terms, and not as the tortured captive of some psychotic arseholes.

❧ Chapter Fourteen ❧

Østmarka nature reserve in Norway was, according to the brochure, eighteen square kilometers of unparalleled beauty and mostly untouched wilderness. The word "mostly" was the one that stood out in Miles's mind as he walked onto the decking of the five-star accommodation known as the Vampyr Retreat.

The retreat was approximately an hour's drive from Oslo, and south of the small village of Flateby, Norway. It took a drive upon what Miles assumed was ironically labelled a road—where he hoped the suspension of the four-wheel-drive taxi was going to cope—to arrive at the retreat.

The whole place was one of relaxation, at least in theory. After the Dominik situation, the investigation had found that Miles and the ATO teams had acted within reason and cleared them of any suspected wrongdoing.

Miles had been informed that he was clear to return to active duty, but he'd kept pushing for answers about Dominik's strange glitching ability, and it hadn't gone down well. To be able to become almost ethereal was not anything Miles had ever heard of, but no one else seemed to think it was a big deal.

"There are always bloodline gifts, or secondary powers, that are rare," one of the Justices had said, before Justice Balderas took Miles aside and made a less than subtle suggestion that Miles stop talking about vampires becoming ethereal. That it was a long-lost bloodline, and that was it.

Miles knew that Sara had turned Dominik, and must have therefore been a part of some long-lost bloodline who could walk through walls and glitch out. But Sara had gone missing after Dominik's death, and no one had been able to find her. Partly because of what happened, and partly because he'd vowed vengeance upon Miles, Henryk had been questioned, and monitored for some time, but to no avail. He'd been ousted as CEO of his company, which had officially undergone a *restructuring*, and then he'd also gone missing. The Templar building in London had only a skeleton crew of people working there. It was assumed that Henryk and Sara had vanished and would, at some point, resurface either dead or alive. As had been explained to him several times, there were arrest warrants out for Henryk and Sara, and they were being dealt with. Miles's job in the whole fiasco was done.

Even so, something about the way the Justices had all closed ranks around it didn't sit well with him. Miles had looked through the Assembly archives but found nothing linking a bloodline gift of being able to glitch with any known vampiric powers. He'd used their libraries in London and Prague, but again, nothing. After five months of this, Justice Balderas had said that he should take some time off. Go on holiday, see friends. He'd also suggested that Miles's "obsession" with this bloodline gift was making people nervous and he needed to "just let it go."

Miles had always wanted to try the retreat in Norway; he'd been told several times by people over the years that it was an excellent way for a vampire to relax and get away from it all. No humans allowed. Apparently, according to Jonathan Holt, who'd recommended it to him, what happened in that forest stayed in that forest. So Miles had booked his holiday for a month later, and taken time off to spend at home, while finding himself looking forward to his trip.

The hotel was surrounded by vast woodlands, and was a three-hundred-foot-long, three-storey building, with a large glass front that showed off the foyer and reception area well. The warm lights were inviting, and the people pleasant and happy to help. Each room had a king-sized bed, television, enough storage for someone to pack away their whole life, and an en suite bathroom with a bath big enough for three people. Church had practically claimed it as her own the second she'd seen it.

The room also came with a balcony, which looked over the nearby fast-moving river, the name of which Miles couldn't remember, although he was told that it was bitterly cold all year round.

Miles was resting in a hammock, next to a sheer drop into the forest. The decking stretched the length of the hotel, with an outside restaurant and bar at one end, and enough space for people to come and be one with nature. The restaurant and bar were separated by a large wooden wall, giving the people there privacy from those on the decking.

According to the staff, the entire hotel was fully booked, and had been for several weeks, although Miles had only seen a fraction of the inhabitants of the two-hundred-room capacity. Apparently, the vast majority were vampires on some kind of research trip into the forest. Miles had met a few of them, but none had been particularly chatty, and they had been out in the forest doing whatever it was research people did.

The bad weather was fine with Miles, and the lack of guests just added to the relaxation. He'd have been perfectly fine if he, along with Church, had been the only guests.

He looked out across the forest. The small lights that had been strategically placed by the hotel lit up parts of it and gave a comforting feeling. The rain had started up again.

"Sir," a young man said as he approached Miles, who was considering what he was going to be eating tonight. The hotel had fresh blood should it be needed, and several of those who worked the hotel were human, and quite willing to spend time with the vampires after their shifts.

Miles looked over at the young man. He was in his mid-twenties with a rugged appearance; he hadn't shaved in several days, and his hair looked tousled. Miles imagined it took a lot for such an appearance to appear unkempt when it was anything but. "Sorry," he said. "What's up?"

"You have a call in the private lounge, sir," the young man said with a smile that even in the darkness sparkled. The resort had excellent Wi-Fi, but the private lounge used a satellite connection, giving it greater security and constant connection. Miles wasn't concerned about bugs in the room, considering the amount of money spent to come to the retreat and the standing its owners had in the vampire community.

"Thank you," Miles said, trying to remember the man's name. "William, isn't it?"

William nodded. "It is, sir. Have you been enjoying your stay?"

Miles swung his legs off the hammock and stepped onto the deck. "It's been very peaceful and relaxing. And I had the roast duck last night, it was excellent."

William's smile broadened as he walked with Miles back to the hotel. "Have you had a chance to partake in our blood stores yet?"

"Not yet," Miles said.

"Well, if you ever need any assistance, please let me know," William said with a slight bow of his head as Church ran up. "And you too, Church."

Church wagged her tail and barked once.

"You're being spoiled," Miles said to Church as they walked through the open foyer, past the large pool with a water feature in the centre. The pool was surrounded by a three-foot-high pale brick wall, and inside the pool were several stone animals that each had water coming out of their mouths. Miles had liked the feature on first entering; the sound of the cascading water was soothing. There was a sign at the rear of the pond that stated that it was five feet deep and was not for swimming. Miles wondered how many people tried before the sign had been necessary. No time to enjoy the tranquillity as he continued on to the room at the side marked *Private Lounge*. He nodded to two female members of staff, who also had winning smiles. Apparently, it was something they were taught.

Church barked again.

Miles pushed the wooden door open and stepped into the lounge. It was considered private because it was where people went if they needed some time to talk business. There was a burgundy leather sofa that could have sat five people comfortably, a glass coffee table, and a coffee machine on a sideboard in the corner. A large TV screen sat on the wall, which had the face of Charlotte Henry on it.

"Miles," she said with a French accent.

Charlotte had pale skin with long dark hair that she had pulled back into a ponytail, and she wore a plain forest green T-shirt. She had several rings on her fingers and a number of bracelets. She was, in Miles's opinion, one of the most elegant people he'd ever met. She could have worn a burlap sack and still looked radiant.

Charlotte Henry was the First Counsel of the House Venator, and an excellent lawyer, with a sharp mind that wandered occasionally into *devious,* another of the things Miles liked about her. When Miles had been part of House Venator all those years ago, she was probably the person he trusted the most. It was why when he'd arranged to come to Norway—he'd called her to ask if she could do him a favour.

"So," Charlotte said, "how is the decadent lifestyle treating you?"

"Not exactly decadent," Miles said.

"Hello, Church," Charlotte said with a wave as Church jumped up onto the sofa.

Church barked and whined.

"She misses me," Charlotte said. "You should come to Scotland and see us all again."

"I will," Miles said.

Church nudged him in the chest and whined again.

"I *will*," Miles promised her. "Did you find anything without having to involve Gideon?"

Gideon was the First Librarian of House Venator, and someone who disliked Miles intensely, although if Miles was honest, the feeling was more than mutual. Miles had been hopeful that the information he'd asked Charlotte about would have been achievable without the use of Gideon and the little kingdom he'd created for himself within House Venator.

"No," Gideon said with a frown, appearing next to Charlotte.

"Tada," Charlotte said.

Gideon was a tall, thin man with dark wispy hair and an almost continuous facial expression of smug superiority. He wore a purple velvet suit with a black and red bowtie, making him look a bit like someone who was about to start pulling rabbits out of hats. Miles stifled the laughter that threatened to bubble up inside.

"I was on a *date*," Gideon said, seemingly aware that his attire was somewhat more formal than a video call with Miles required.

"Apologies to your date," Miles said, satisfied with the double meaning that he knew Gideon would mentally dissect later.

"I've been informed that you have already been to the libraries in London and Prague," Gideon said. "But not New York, Milan, or any of the other two dozen around the world. Why stop at those two?"

"Because all the others contain pretty much copies of everything I found in those first two," Miles said. "Besides, after Prague, I was told to stop looking. I thought I was being subtle, but apparently not."

"Why do you think we can help then?" Gideon asked.

Miles had dreaded this bit. He knew it was coming, but giving Gideon praise was not something that Miles had ever really enjoyed. "Gideon, when I was First Librarian of House Venator, we had one of the best libraries of vampire knowledge in the world. Seeing how you are probably one of the foremost experts on House lineage, I assume that collection has only grown."

Gideon smiled and let out a long sigh. He picked up a mobile phone and pressed a button, listening to Miles's words again. "That is going to be a thing of beauty for years to come."

"Gideon," Charlotte warned. She didn't like to put up with his nonsense any more than Miles did, although she was considerably better at hiding it.

"Fine," Gideon said. "I've done a preliminary search and found nothing. No bloodline has anyone glitching, or becoming ghostly. Nothing of the sort. Are you sure you weren't high?"

Miles counted to ten. "No," he said eventually. "I know what I saw, Gideon. Dominik was able to turn ethereal. It was like he was glitching."

"You watch too much anime," Gideon said. "Or superhero films. No one *glitches*. No vampires can turn to ghosts. Hey, there you go, maybe he was a ghost."

"Not a ghost," Miles said. "I hit him with my own bloodline gift and it turned him human. Any chance it's from one of the no longer used Houses?"

"You mean the dead bloodlines," Charlotte said. "There aren't many Vampire Houses where their bloodline isn't around anymore. There are a few expunged bloodlines, though."

"The expunged bloodlines are not researchable," Gideon said sternly. "If this was one of them, that would explain why you were told to drop it."

"Would Drest talk to you about it?" Miles asked.

Gideon sighed. "I will continue to research, but don't expect me to find anything. It's almost certainly not an expunged bloodline. Those bloodlines are extinct, Miles. Everyone who has the blood of one is long dead. There hasn't been an expunged house in over six hundred years. Whatever you saw was an aberration. Maybe his secondary power."

"He was, *at most*, a few months old," Miles almost snapped. "Not a secondary power."

"Well, I'm going to go and see if I can find a way to save my love life," Gideon said, getting to his feet. "You both have a good evening." He walked away, the sounds of Miles's recorded praise easy to hear from his phone.

Charlotte watched the librarian leave before speaking. "I'll make sure he keeps looking. You say this vampire turned ghostly. You want me to ask Drest?"

Drest was the First Lord of House Venator, and the vampire who had turned Miles several centuries earlier. He was the closest thing Miles had ever known to a second father.

"Probably not," Miles said. "If you tell him, and it actually is a thing, he's going to be involved, and then that brings questions about me asking a House for aid. Unless necessary, let's just leave him be."

"You know, I should already be putting this forward as a cross Assembly/House investigation," Charlotte said. "But I won't, because I like you. And I told Gideon that if he did, I would make him watch as I went into his computer and deleted the book he was writing."

"Harsh," Miles said. "Also, he's writing a book?"

"They say that everyone has a book in them," Charlotte said.

"And sometimes that's where a book should stay," Miles replied.

Charlotte laughed. "Be careful, Miles. Take care of Church. We'll talk soon."

"Take care," he said, with Church barking beside him, and the screen went dark. Miles sat there for a short while before speaking again. "Maybe I'm just barking up the wrong tree."

Church pawed him in the chest.

Miles chuckled. "Sorry, I wasn't mocking."

Church whined and got down from the sofa.

"Oh, come on, I wasn't mocking ya," Miles said.

Church turned back and snorted, but barked a moment later and wagged her tail. Miles got up and gave her a scratch behind one ear.

"Why can't I let this go?" he asked.

Church whined and licked Miles's face.

"I'm glad ya believe in me, girl," Miles said with a smile.

The pair left the private lounge and found William waiting outside. "Everything okay, sir?" he asked.

Miles nodded. "Thanks for that. If anyone contacts me again, please let me know."

"I shall," William said with a bow of his head.

A group of people were standing in front of the receptionist's desk, all talking at once. "What's going on?" Miles asked.

"Ah, we've had a Wi-Fi issue," William said as he walked with Miles and Church back toward the decking area. "It started just before you left the room where you had your call—it seems that no one can connect using their cell service either. It's probably just the tower nearby—we've had some bad weather recently and it occasionally needs someone to go check it, but both the Wi-Fi and cell connections being out is somewhat of an inconvenience."

Miles looked back at the rapidly increasing guests in front of the receptionists. Many vampires might be centuries old, but the vast number of them still relied on modern society's ability to be constantly connected, usually while lamenting that modern society is constantly connected.

"Any idea how long it'll be down?" Miles asked.

William held the door open for Miles to step out onto the decking. "Unfortunately not," he said. "Could be an hour, could be until tomorrow. People can use the private lounge should they need to, or one of the emergency satellite phones, should it become necessary. It's barely two AM, so I'm hoping that it'll be fixed before dawn. Is there anything I can get for you?"

Miles shook his head. "No, thank you. I might go for a walk in the woods, stretch my legs."

William nodded. "You know where I am, should you need me."

Miles walked to the edge of the decking and looked down to the right, where one of three staircases led from the deck to the forest. "You know, how about a run?" he asked Church, who barked enthusiastically.

"I'll go change, you stay here," he said as Church lay down and stared out at the forest, barely able to keep her excitement in check.

"I'll tell you what," Miles said. "Why don't you start without me, and you can come find me when I start."

Church barked, leapt to her feet, and ran down the decking to the stairs, practically bounding down them with a level of enthusiasm that Miles envied. "Have fun," he called after her, receiving a bark in response.

Miles nodded hello to several guests as he made his way back toward the hotel entrance. He entered the hotel and made his way through to his room, where he got changed into a pair of black shorts and white T-shirt, along with his navy blue Adidas running shoes. He grabbed a black hoodie, too.

Miles had been in his room for five minutes, maybe less, when he heard the sound of someone screaming outside. He opened his balcony door just as something landed on it. Two grenades, one standard and one UV. Using his telekinesis, he quickly picked up the grenades and tossed them over the side of the wooden balcony. The UV grenade exploded first, the balcony shielding Miles from the worst of the rays as he dove to the floor. The standard grenade exploded only a fraction of a second later, tearing through the wood that had been a shield only moments earlier. Miles moved to get back into the room when the balcony collapsed beneath his feet.

CHAPTER FIFTEEN

Miles landed on the partially destroyed balcony for the room directly below him, hitting it hard and rolling to his side, onto what remained of the glass window and door to the room. Miles cursed and got to his feet, removing an inch-long shard of glass from his palm.

The glass in the room crunched under Miles's feet, and he was grateful he had shoes on and wasn't going to spend the rest of the waking hours recreating *Die Hard*.

The room was empty, which was probably for the best, although there were enough bags and clothes in the room for it to be obvious that someone was staying here. Miles removed his phone from his pocket. No service. No reception. No nothing. The attack coming when comms were down couldn't possibly be a coincidence.

Miles walked across the room, stopped at the door, and listened. He heard nothing, but checked the peephole anyway, seeing only an empty hallway beyond. He opened the door and stepped out, letting it shut behind him as another explosion sounded from somewhere inside the hotel. They were under attack. Miles had a brief thought about Church, but knew she would be fine—certainly she was in a better position than he'd been, and could take care of herself in even the most dangerous situations.

He ran to the end of the hallway, going past the lifts and continuing on to the stairs around the corner. He placed his hand on the door to open it as the echoes of gunfire reached him. If you were going to launch an assault on a vampire hotel in the middle of nowhere, you would need to be either exceptionally stupid or exceptionally confident in your ability to get out alive. Miles hoped it was the former.

Miles pushed the door open just as someone jabbed a shock baton up toward his face. He dodged back, kicking out at the door as it swung shut, smashing his assailant in the face in the process. Miles pushed open the door to find a young vampire prone on the stairwell. He looked up at Miles with hatred, which was compounded by the fact that his face was covered in blood.

"Getting hit in the face with a door doesn't feel great," Miles said from the top of the stairwell, looking down on the man. "You want to tell me what's going on?"

The man deftly swung his legs to the side, planted his hand on the step, and sprang back, down the stairs to the section below. He snarled, his face turning to his vampire side, and leapt up at Miles, who stepped back and caught the younger vampire with a kick to the stomach, which sent him back down the stairs.

"I don't have time for this," Miles said, jumping down the stairs and landing on the younger man's chest, pinning him to the ground.

"I'll tear your face off!" the man screamed.

Miles punched him in the throat with enough force to make the man's eyes bulge as he fought for breath.

"New vampire, I see," Miles said. "It sucks when we can't breathe, but those of us who have been around a bit tend not to panic so much. It's a very human reaction, though, so it takes a while to get used to. You'll be fine in a few seconds, just calm yourself."

As Miles had said, a few seconds later, the young man could breathe again, although each breath was raspy and pained.

"You're going to tell me everything I want to know," Miles said. "Or not breathing is something you're going to deal with on a more permanent basis."

The man snarled at Miles, but something had gone from the look in his eyes. His rage and fury, his hate, replaced with fear. It's hard to snarl at someone at the best of times, but even more difficult when your heart isn't in it.

Miles picked the man up by the top of his bulletproof vest and threw him across the landing they were on. The man collided with the wall head-first, and slumped to the ground, leaving a trail of blood along the wall.

Before the younger man could move, Miles was on him, pinning him to the floor, his breath warm by the man's ear. "You tell me, or I take what I need from your mind. You won't like what you see in my brain, but I promise you won't be alive long enough for it to be a long-term problem."

He didn't want to drink from the vampire, didn't want to see his memories. For a start, there was no way to be certain that Miles would see what he wanted to see. Instead of information about the attack, he might see images of the man as a child, or a time something horrible happened to him, a memory that stayed with him for a long time, or his most recent shopping trip. He might see nothing. There was no guarantee you'd see what you were looking for, and unless you had House Umbra's bloodline gift, or you were telepathic yourself, no way to tear through the mind of a vampire to find a specific memory. If he had to do it because there was no other choice, he would, but he wouldn't be happy about it.

"You are Miles Watson," the man said. "We are here to kill you, kill your dog, and kill anyone who stops us. You do not deserve to live."

"Good job they sent idiots like you, then," Miles said, kneeling down on the man's back and patting his pockets for anything that might show identification. He had nothing. He tried to figure out who might have sent people to kill him. He'd made a lot of enemies over the years, but recently the only person he could think of was Dominik, and he was dead. Dominik's father, Henryk? Maybe.

"You do not deserve to live," the man repeated.

"Cool story. Who sent you? Do you work for Henryk?"

"Those of you who cross us will become ash on the wind," the man said as if reciting something from memory.

"Nice," Miles replied. "Who said that?"

"My death will only bring about your ruin," the man continued as if Miles hadn't spoken. "My life will be given to bring you pain."

"Cool," Miles said and placed his hand against the man's neck. "Tell me. How would you like to die a human?"

The man turned his neck to the side, and the fear from earlier was now outright terror. "No, I am a vampire. I am one of the children of the night."

"Well, in about five seconds, you're going to be human again, and then I'm going to use you as a meat shield when I go down to kill all of your friends. You'll be very helpful, I promise. One."

"My death will only bring about your ruin," the man repeated.

"Two," Miles said.

"I am . . . my life will be given to bring you pain," the man almost cried.

"Three," Miles said and winked at the man when he turned to look up at him.

"I don't know!" the man shouted.

"Four," Miles said softly.

"Megan Song," the man snapped.

Miles paused. "What about Megan?"

"She was one of the targets tonight," the man said. "Two teams, one went after her, one came for you. We've been here a few days now. Waiting."

"Wait," Miles said. "You're the *researchers*. The ones who make up most of the guests. Why not kill me in my sleep?"

"Had to make sure the attacks happened together. No one in this hotel leaves. No witnesses."

"No hostages?" Miles asked.

"Only if we can't carry out our primary mission."

"Which is killing me?"

The man nodded.

"You cut the communications," Miles said, pressing down on the man's throat when he didn't answer.

"Yes," he said. "We disabled the comms, the emergency call button. We've made sure you can't contact anyone. No one is coming to help you. You're all going to die here."

"Who do you work for?" Miles asked, feeling a hot rage burn inside of him.

Miles heard the footsteps beyond the door below, and was already moving when it opened and the stairwell became a shower of bullets. Several struck the young vampire in the head, setting his hair on fire. The vampire's screams were short lived as the bullets burned him from the inside out.

As the gun was reloading, Miles sprang forward, picking up the remains of the vampire and hurling them at the gunman at the door. Miles followed the body a second later, as the gunman desperately tried to reload his weapon and avoid the incoming corpse.

He managed to complete one of those actions, but his gun clattered to the ground when the feet of the dead vampire smashed into his face, stunning him and sending him staggering back. Miles was on him a fraction of a second later, taking him by the throat and smashing the back of his head into the stairwell wall. There was an awful crunch as the man's skull shattered from the impact, leaving a hole in the concrete, along with bits of what should have stayed inside the attacker's head.

Miles let the man drop to the ground, and checked him for ID. Nothing. He picked up the Uzi he'd been using, which explained the vast amount of bullets that had been sprayed up the stairwell, and checked the magazine. Normal bullets. So not all of them were incendiary, that was good to know. Probably. Miles figured it was just a better idea to avoid being shot at all.

He removed the slide of the gun, which was warped slightly from the heat of the incendiary round being fired, and tossed it down the stairs. More screams and explosions rang out from inside the hotel. The attack was still ongoing. They might have been there to kill Miles and Church, but they were going to make sure to kill as many more as possible.

It was weird that a vampire and a human were working together to kill vampires in what should have been a vampire safe zone. Miles had angered a lot of people over the years, and he'd had many threaten him with various forms of death and torture, but he couldn't imagine many of them would go to the extreme of killing innocent vampires just because he happened to be there, too. Killing an Arbiter was going to bring the Assembly down on whoever was responsible, but killing an Arbiter and a bunch of other vampires who were staying in what was meant to be a safe area? That was going to put a large number on their head, and on the heads of everyone who helped. Who wanted that kind of heat? Who could afford it? Questions for after he'd found Church and stopped people getting hurt.

Miles opened the door the attacker had come through, finding the first-floor hotel rooms beyond. There were bullet holes in the wall and the prone body of a man halfway down, a dagger protruding from his head. Miles ran over, but whoever the victim had been, he was dead. The dagger had a shock component, which from the smell alone told Miles his brain had been cooked.

He ran back to the stairwell and continued down one more flight of stairs, where he paused by the door and pushed it open a fraction. There were two dead bodies, both missing their heads, by the reception desk. A man and a woman. Miles left the stairwell and crossed over toward the deck, but didn't recognise either body. The man's face looked up at Miles as he vaulted over the desk; he'd turned into his vampire form before being killed, but it hadn't saved him.

Behind the desk was a young woman with two bullet holes in her head. She hadn't been a vampire. She'd been kind and helpful, and the need to hurt the people responsible for this massacre intensified inside Miles by the second.

An arrow lay on the ground beside the receptionist, and Miles picked it up. There was a small device attached to the shaft, just behind the arrowhead. Miles tapped the device, and an electrical pulse went through the metal barb. He wondered if the device changed how the arrow flew, but quickly decided that was another question for later.

Miles tossed the arrow away and moved along the receptionist desk, where he could see across the whole entrance of the hotel, as well as through the broken glass windows to the front of the building. There was no one else in the foyer.

The front of the hotel had several cars ablaze and a dozen people in armour carrying bows, walking around. Miles didn't see any guns, although bows with the ability to shock was a problem in and of itself. Several bodies lay among the wreckage of the vehicles, most of whom wore the security uniform for the hotel. He could just go that way, eliminate the killers, and make the exit free, but that would mean potentially leaving hostages for these attackers to kill in an effort to get to Miles.

Between the reception desk and the decking were several overturned tables, but after that it was twenty feet of open space. Miles looked behind the desk at the security room and rushed inside, keeping the door closed as he moved to the still-active computer showing the CCTV. He flicked from screen to screen and spotted several hostages in the restaurant area—at least eighteen, along with six hostage takers. The latter were all armed with bows and bladed weapons.

He continued through the screens and spotted more attackers in the floors above, all with various guns. They were going door to door, placing sticky UV lights to the outside of doors. Anyone inside getting out was going to get badly burned at the very least. Miles wanted to go up, to kill them all, but he had to get the people out of the restaurant first.

Miles flicked through to his floor and saw the scorch marks in the hallway. Two armed guards came out of Miles's room, followed a few seconds later by flames. More people to deal with.

After he'd gone through everything, he counted eight more attackers spread around the hotel. A few seemed to have met with resistance, and there were several dead attackers who had run into vampires who were unwilling to go quietly. Unfortunately, they were outnumbered and being hunted through the upper floors. He hoped they'd be able to take care of themselves for now.

The majority of the attackers not out the front entrance or at the restaurant moved in pairs, and acted as if they'd been trained. Miles wondered if the two in the stairwell were meant to be moving as a partnership.

He moved to the computer beside the monitor and accessed the hotel security commands. There should have been shutters on the front and decking entrances, and the lights could be put in an emergency state, making everything dark red. Someone had come in and disabled the shutters, the sirens, any outside communication. Like the vampire had said, they'd disabled the emergency broadcast before the attack had begun. No one was coming to help. They were on their own.

Miles activated the emergency lighting, but nothing happened. *Superb.* Still, at least he knew how many people he had to deal with. He was about to click through to another screen when everything switched off, and the hotel was bathed in darkness. The lights came back on in their emergency form. Had it done it anyway? Had someone else done it?

Miles looked around the security room. There was an old couch at the far end, next to a water dispenser. A wooden table in front of the couch had seen better days. A set of metal shelves sat behind the door. *Not a lot of places to hide and wait.*

Loud voices could be heard from outside, and Miles moved up the metal shelves to the top, hidden from view as the door opened and a man walked inside. The door closed behind him, and he muttered obscenities to himself as he accessed the computer. Miles silently dropped to the ground and snapped forward, grabbing the man's arm and breaking it at the wrist and elbow, before smashing his forehead into the desk, obliterating the keyboard. It wasn't quiet, but it stopped him from yelling out in pain.

"Vampire," Miles said, dragging the man away, disarming him of his shock baton and dagger and throwing him onto the sofa. "You came to kill me."

The man radiated hate as blood poured out of his broken nose and down over his long beard.

"You're very bad at your job," Miles said. "Why kill these people?"

"They prop up an obscene institution," the man said, in an accent that Miles couldn't quite place. Eastern European, maybe Lithuanian. "You all should be ashamed of what you have done to the world."

"You're a vampire," Miles said. "You don't think the Assembly helps us?"

"We are a new kind of vampire," the man said, his face now showing his vampire side. "We will bring about a new way of doing things. A new world for us all. No more corruption, no more sycophantic oligarchs taking everything they want without consequences. We are the consequences."

"Nice speech," Miles said. "One of your friends recited poetry to me earlier. Or maybe it was song lyrics."

"Those of you who cross us will become ash on the wind," the vampire said.

Miles picked up the dagger, turning the electricity switch on and listening to the purr of the volts as they coursed through the metal. "That's the one. It's nae very catchy."

"A new world," the vampire said.

"I heard," Miles told him. "You've been here for several days, planning, getting into position. It must have been hell for you to see me walking around."

"The prey that takes patience is all the sweeter for the kill."

Miles laughed. "Okay, so you're the idiot of the group. Can I assume you won't tell me who you're working for?"

"Your previous victim never mentioned it?" the man asked with a gleam in his dark eyes.

"No, but I'll get the answer eventually," Miles said, crossing the room, dagger in hand. The vampire sprang to his feet in an attempt to defend himself, but Miles pushed his good arm aside, broke his knee with a stamp, and drove the dagger up under the vampire's chin, into his brain. He activated the electrical current and stepped away, letting the vampire fall to the floor in silent agony. Miles wasn't sure if the vampire would die from having his brain cooked. If he was young enough, then more than likely, but an older vampire might heal given time. He brushed the thought aside. No matter his age, the vampire had made his decision.

Miles went back to the screen and checked the front of the hotel again. No difference in the number of attackers. Same at the restaurant, although there were fewer people searching the floors and more out on the decking area now. He flicked to the basement level, where there were cameras monitoring the outside of the door to, according to the camera name, the *Electrical Room*, which Miles assumed meant the place where the circuit breakers and such would be. He wondered who had switched off the power, so he rewound the live footage to see if anyone had entered the room around the time of the power outage.

It didn't take long to find two vampires, a man and woman, both entering the room and both leaving after the power went out. *Good job, guys.*

There was a loud buzzing noise, before a voice went over the internal speaker system. "Miles Watson," the voice said. It was a deep voice, with a Russian accent. "I assume you can hear me."

Miles flicked through the monitor until he found the restaurant, outside the front of which knelt the man and woman he'd just seen on the monitor. Both were pleading with two armed men, and both looked as if they'd taken a beating. Another female attacker held a bow, pointing an nocked arrow at the back of the head of the male vampire, while the woman looked between her captors, pleading with them.

"You're probably out there looking for these," the voice on the speaker said, and one of the armed men on screen lifted a satellite phone from a box on the floor.

"Bollocks," Miles whispered.

"These two thought that shutting off the power would aid their escape," the man said, speaking into a wall-mounted phone that could be used to patch into the speakers across the floor. He was tall and broad, and held himself like someone who was used to people following his orders. "They were wrong."

On screen, the woman with the bow wavered between the man and woman, before eventually firing the arrow through the skull of the female vampire. The explosive attached to the arrow obliterated the vampire's head, as the man beside her screamed. He got up, tried to run, and was shot in the leg by one of the other armed men.

The man went down hard, blood pouring out of the wound on his leg. The woman with the bow calmly drew another arrow, nocked it, walked over to the crawling vampire, and fired it into his head as he looked up at her. The arrow hit its target and exploded. Two dead vampires in less than five seconds.

"After two minutes," the man in charge said over the speakers, "I will kill another hostage. And then another every sixty seconds until you appear before us. See you soon."

🙠 Chapter Sixteen 🙢

The execution of two unarmed vampires had changed Miles's priorities. He was always going to have to get the hostages away from their captors. He was always going to have to deal with those who had attacked the hotel, but now he was on a timer. Two minutes was not long to formulate a working plan that didn't get anyone else killed. There was no point in going over to the restaurant and handing himself in—that would end with his and everyone else's deaths.

Miles wondered how many incendiary bullet rounds they had. Probably not many, hence the bows. Explosive and shock-tipped arrows weren't a new thing to Miles, but once you got hit with one, you definitely didn't want to get hit again. He'd had a shock-tipped arrow strike his shoulder many years previously, and it had definitely left an impression.

He got up to leave and thought about Megan. Was this part of an Assembly-wide attack on ATOs and Arbiters? Was Megan okay?

Miles looked back at the screen. Thirty seconds down. *Damn it.* He walked over to the vampire with the dagger in his throat and removed the blade, cleaning it on the trouser leg of the dead man. Turned out the vampire hadn't been old enough to survive. Miles removed two UV grenades, along with one incendiary grenade, putting them in his hoodie pockets, before removing the dagger sheath on the man's hip and placing it around his own. The UV grenades were spherical in shape, and you had to twist the top and bottom separately to cause the grenade to activate. Then you had six seconds to run like hell.

UV grenades gave off a level ten UV light for three seconds, easily enough to kill any vampire unlucky enough to be within the six-foot blast radius. If you were within a few dozen feet, you got a nasty dose of UV, which Miles had seen firsthand set vampires alight. It wasn't pleasant, but it was effective.

The incendiary grenade was a stick about the size and shape of a flare. You pulled the pin out of the top and threw it like a flare, too, although once the fire burned through the outer casing and made contact with the flammable liquid capsule inside, it exploded. Like the UV grenade, it wasn't an elegant way to remove a problem, but it too was effective.

The man didn't carry a gun, which was fine because Miles didn't want to have to use one unless necessary. And there were better ways to kill vampires.

Miles checked the camera in the restaurant again; all of the hostages were positioned together at the rear of the establishment, next to the doors that led to the outside dining area. The doors had a thick chain wrapped around them, which Miles imagined would take even the stronger vampire a few seconds to deal with. A few seconds for an arrow to go through your neck.

Apart from the Russian and three hostage takers who had killed the posh vampire couple, there were two more patrolling around the restaurant. Both had bows and a number of sheathed knives about their person. *Great.*

"Forty-five seconds," the voice said, accompanied by a high-pitched yell. "Tell him your name."

"Da—Danny," the man said in an American accent.

"Do you work here, Danny?" the Russian asked.

"Y—ye—yes," the man stammered with fear. "I—I'm a . . ."

Miles left the room and heard a noise that he knew too well. Danny had been hit.

"Stop snivelling, you little shit!" the Russian screamed. "Answer the question."

"I'm a waiter," Danny said. "Just a waiter."

"A human?" the man asked.

"Yes," Danny said. "Just a human. I'm not a threat to anyone."

"Did you hear that?" the Russian asked. "Just a human. You know what, we've got about twelve seconds left, but I'm an impatient man."

Miles stood and started to walk as a shot rang out. Miles stopped halfway, fifty, maybe sixty feet between the hotel entrance and the restaurant, crouching down beside the wall of the pond.

"Sixty seconds until we play again," the Russian said. "Unless I get impatient."

These people were going to kill the hostages no matter what Miles did. They were there as a stick to beat him with. A way to get him to hand himself over only for him to be forced to watch while they were executed. No one in this hotel was going to be permitted to leave. Better to think of the hostages as already dead. Miles sighed. He couldn't think like that. They were innocent in all of this. These attackers had come to Oslo to kill Miles, kill innocent people . . . to kill Church. That was not going to happen.

Miles had been someone for whom the use of violence had been as easy as breathing. Back when he'd been a human, he was almost certainly responsible for the deaths of people who didn't deserve it, who were in the wrong place at the wrong time.

Becoming a vampire had, in a way, saved his life. It had certainly saved his soul. Miles wasn't religious; he didn't believe in heaven or hell, despite— or because of—his grandparents trying to beat it into him. But he did believe that everyone had a soul. A part of them that was the essence of who the person was. Miles's soul had needed a long time to balance the scales after he'd become a vampire.

Seeing people murdered with such callous disregard for their lives brought back memories of a time Miles had long since put behind him. Miles had been lucky that Drest had decided to train him, to make him a better man, instead of just killing him and being done with it. Drest was a good man, a man of honour and principles, who wanted to give people a second chance if he saw that they could do some good with it. Miles occasionally wished he was more like Drest, because Miles did not give people a second chance.

"Thirty seconds," the Russian said. "Are you human?"

"Yes," a woman said, her voice shaky.

Miles stood and walked toward the restaurant.

"Where are you from . . . Fiona?" the Russian asked.

"Denver," Fiona said.

"Colorado?" the Russian asked in mock interest. "I've heard it's a beautiful place. You're a long way from home. Have you told your parents you loved them recently?"

Fiona started to cry.

Miles continued at a steady pace until the bow-using woman spotted him and aimed her bow. "Halt," she said, the same accent as the Russian.

Miles halted. He looked beyond the attacker at the large Russian who stood beside a much smaller woman. The woman wore the outfit of the waiting staff in the restaurant, a burgundy polo shirt and dark trousers.

"You okay, Fiona?" Miles asked, keeping his tone conversational.

"You talk to *me*," the Russian said, gripping Fiona around the back of the neck and pushing her forward a step.

The Russian was easily six and a half feet tall, and probably weighed close to three hundred pounds, which from the size of his arms Miles assumed was all muscle. He wore a dark green beret, like the kind worn in the military, with a badge in the centre above his forehead that Miles didn't recognise—a silver wolf standing in front of a red star, with gold trim encircling it.

Miles held his hands behind his back, making sure the UV grenade was still hanging from the back of his shorts, a feat he was not exactly thrilled about.

"Hands," the woman said, her bow never wavering.

Miles brought out his hands. "Nice badge," he said, pointing to the cap. "Don't recognise it. Russian special forces? KGB?"

"Something like that," the man said, pushing Fiona another step.

"Why don't you let all of these people go?" Miles said, looking down at the two dead vampires he'd seen executed and the young waiter he'd seen around since arriving. "Didn't need to do that."

"You tell me what I do and don't need to do?" the Russian asked.

The two armed men who stood beside the Russian stepped out of the mouth of the restaurant and took up positions to Miles's right. He looked over at them, noticed their AK-47s, and looked back at the Russian. "Little bit of a stereotype, isn't it? The AK, I mean. I figured you'd want something that's a bit more reliable with incendiary ammo. Although that one guy had an Uzi, so maybe you're going for an eighties bad guy kind of vibe?"

"You think you are funny?" the Russian asked.

"I *think* I'm a delight," Miles said. "I *know* I'm funny."

"I think I'm funny, too," the Russian said, lifting Fiona off the ground with one hand, her feet dangling as she tried to undo his grip on her neck.

"Fiona," Miles said conversationally, putting his hands behind his back again. "I'm *really* glad you're not a vampire."

"What?" the Russian asked.

Miles unhooked the UV grenade, and with his hands still behind him, twisted the top and bottom to activate it. He dropped it to the ground and kicked it toward the Russian and the bow woman before diving back, putting as much power into his legs as he could to propel himself as far away as possible. He hit the ground hard, rolled to the side, and dove into the pond as the grenade went off.

Miles hit the bottom of the pond and propelled himself along, coming up at the far side and pulling himself out. He caught sight of the attackers at the front of the hotel, moving aside as a large truck backed up to the hotel front doors. No time to wonder what was going on as the screams of whoever had been unlucky enough to be blasted by UV rays rang out.

Running around to where the attackers were, one of the humans raised his AK-47 at Miles, but a blast of telekinesis sent the gun aiming up toward the ceiling. Miles, now in his vampire form, used his talons to slice through the throat of the human, moving on to the second, who was screaming at the fact he had pieces of the bow woman on him and was currently on fire himself. The Russian had fallen back after dragging another vampire into his path. The unfortunate vampire had been hit by the UV, setting him on fire. Miles picked him up, ignoring the flames licking up at his arm, removed the dagger from the sheath on the man's chest, and drove it into his eye, dropping him back to the floor.

The bow woman was sitting on the floor looking at where her arms should have been. The UV blast had turned them to charcoal. She was no threat in that state, so Miles moved into the kitchen, where one of the attackers barrelled into him. Or tried to, anyway. Miles moved too fast for his would-be attacker and slashed through his throat, pushing him away as he bled out on the floor.

Miles moved on through the restaurant, where two vampires leapt onto the tables, their fangs showing as they screamed at him. He kicked out at the table that one of the vampires stood on, sending the table careening back into the restaurant, as the vampire lost his footing and fell back.

"New vampires," Miles said disdainfully as the second vampire jumped toward Miles, who slammed his hand toward the attacker, using his telekinesis to send him spinning back, through an intricately decorated wooden partition.

The second vampire got to his feet and charged, but Miles was too fast, too strong, and the vampire was dead a moment later, the electric dagger buried in his eye, the current turned on. Miles stepped around to the first vampire, who was looking a bit as though he regretted his life choices but had no option about continuing on. He tried to rake his talons across Miles's face, but he was easy to dodge, and even easier for Miles to drive his own talons into the vampire's throat, tearing them out the side and practically decapitating him as he fell to the floor. Miles placed one foot on the spine of the vampire, grabbed the head, and pulled, finishing the decapitation. He carried the bloody head through to the hostages, where the final attacker was.

The Russian, now sporting a nasty cut that ran from his temple across his nose to his mouth, held a gun to the head of a waiter. "I will kill him," he said.

"And then you die," Miles said, tossing the head of his companion at him. "You have two choices. You either surrender peacefully, or I kill you. If any hostages die, I kill you. If you use harsh language with me, I kill you. I think you're getting the idea?"

The Russian vampire looked down at the head of his ally and pushed the hostage away, putting his hands up to show he surrendered. He placed the pistol on the table beside him and got down on his knees, his hands still in the air. "I surrender," he said. "I heard the screams from the front. Everyone else there is dead?"

"Aye," Miles said. "UV grenade at point-blank range. You're all new vampires. Not one of you is older than a few years. That about right?"

The vampire nodded. "Most are eight months since they were turned. These were all turned by an old mercenary," he said. "Eighteen in total."

"I've killed six vampires and three humans, and I have you," Miles said. "Makes a fair few more vampires still alive. They all in the hotel?"

"No, only a few are," the vampire said. "The rest are busy elsewhere."

"Megan," Miles said grimly.

The Russian vampire smiled, although nothing about it was pleasant.

"You're older, right? UV grenade should have turned you to dust, too."

He nodded. "I'm much older. I was turned during the nineties by Sara Bakos."

Miles stared at the vampire. "The Head of Security at Templar International?"

The vampire nodded. "She *really* hates you. You took everything from her. Her job, her wealth, her status, everything. She's been planning this ever since. We've all been planning this."

"I did wonder where she'd gone," Miles said. "Why not come after me herself?"

"There's someone she hates more than even you," the Russian said with a chuckle.

"A lot of moving parts to get all of this done in nine months," Miles said, walking past the Russian and pushing open the rear restaurant doors.

Miles looked over at the huddling two dozen or so hostages. Most were human staff, and even young vampires were dangerous to them. "All of you, out of that door onto the decking at the end of the restaurant. Stay low, stay quiet, and no one on the decking will see you. You get down off that decking and into the forest. You run for the nearest town. You do not stop. Not for anything. Anyone unable to do that, just hide in the forest."

"What are you going to do?" Fiona said from behind Miles.

Miles turned to regard her, noticing the haunted look in her eyes. "I'm going to find my dog, kill anyone who stops me, and if there's anyone left after, I'm going to kill them, too."

He motioned for everyone to come to him, and watched them leave quietly, several of them patting him on the shoulder as a thank-you.

Miles went back to the Russian attacker. "You can put your arms down."

He did as he was told.

"What's with the truck backing up to the front of the hotel?"

"Truck?" the man asked, looking surprised. "You're sure you saw a truck backing up?"

Miles nodded. "Big white thing, the kind of truck you see on the motorway carrying food to big supermarkets."

"No, no, no," the man said, panic written clearly across his face. "It's not time yet. We're meant to be out of here."

"What?" Miles asked.

"You need to close the restaurant shutters," the man pleaded. "Please. That truck is going to . . ."

There was a crash of glass from out in the foyer, and Miles ran over to the restaurant entrance, looking out across the foyer. He moved out, keeping low, and noticed that the bow woman from earlier was no longer

conscious. He kept moving until he reached the edge of the decking windows, and spotted several dead outside, but no more guards. *Odd.*

The truck had driven right through the front door of the hotel, lodging
itself there like the world's worst parking job.

Miles took a step back as the smell of rotting flesh and blood reached
his nose. There was a small explosion at the end of the truck, and the two
doors swung open. Miles was already moving back toward the restaurant as
the Russian prisoner was in the doorway, slamming his hand on the button to close the shutters. The shutters were loud and slow, and Miles easily
ducked under them, dragging the unconscious bow woman with him. He
didn't care if she lived or died, but he was damned if he was going to leave
her out there for what was coming.

"Oh good, you made it," the Russian vampire said. "I was worried."

Miles punched him in the face, knocking him to the floor. "Be quiet."

The man lay on the ground, his nose busted open as the windowed
shutters finished their descent with a loud clunk. Miles stared out of the
thick glass windows on the shutters as the part of the contents of the truck
crept around the pond, sniffing the air. They saw the dead human, the
blood all across the area, and descended as a pack.

"You brought desolates with you," Miles said, incredulous that anyone
would do something so dangerous and stupid. "Goddamn you all."

CHAPTER SEVENTEEN

Twenty-five desolates screeched and clawed at the outer shutter of the restaurant, baying with bloodlust as they tried to get to the only living things they could smell. The shutters throughout the hotel were designed to stop vampires from tearing through them, one of the many security benefits that the website for the hotel had lauded. Miles was thankful that it hadn't been hyperbolic.

Some of the desolates rolled around in the blood outside, causing a fight between several, which ended with one desolate death as it was torn apart by the others.

"Now if the rest could just do that," Miles said.

The prisoner was standing by the large window to the right of the restaurant. Beyond the window was a wooden wall, and then the decking area. An explosive arrow hit the wooden wall, tearing a huge chunk out of it, allowing the five attackers on the decking a good view of the restaurant interior, or at least the part where Miles was. Miles had forced the Russian to stay there, hoping that these people weren't going to sacrifice their own friend to get inside.

Miles knew he could leave the same way the hostages left, but he also knew that doing so could lead the remaining attackers to him, and in turn lead them right to the people he had been trying to get as far away from them as possible.

One of the hostage takers peered through the remains of the wall, pointed at Miles, and laughed.

"Fuck you, chuckles," Miles said, flipping him off, which caused the man's expression to change to one of anger almost instantly.

Miles checked his phone, and there was still no reception. *Goddamn it.*

"They're going to kill you eventually," the Russian said. "I will watch as you are gutted and hung from a post, a warning for those to never cross us."

"Where is Henryk as all of this happens?" Miles asked. "Is he behind it all?"

The large man shrugged. "No clue, I haven't seen him in months. Since you *murdered* his son."

Miles ignored him and turned to the bar; he wasn't concerned about having his back to the larger man, since they both knew how that fight would end. Miles leaned over the bar and grabbed a bottle of whisky, several rags, and a pack of matches. He wasn't quite sure where this was all going yet, but he figured he might as well be productive, especially considering he was going to have to kill the desolate at some point. He couldn't just leave them out there, and he doubted there was a Desolate Royal nearby to control them. Miles paused. He *really* hoped there wasn't a Desolate Royal nearby. He got the feeling that the one good one he'd met was the exception, not the rule.

"Why did you bring desolates here?" Miles shouted at the Russian.

The Russian still looked concerned about how close he was to a bunch of monsters who would happily tear him limb from limb, just like anyone else. The desolate without a King or Queen to lead them knew no allies other than their fellow desolate.

Miles clicked his fingers in quick succession. "Hey, over here."

"They're here to clean up," the Russian said.

"You're going to make it look like a desolate outbreak," Miles said. "You all get away scot-free in the process."

An explosion behind Miles was big enough to throw him over the bar, where he collided with the floor, and half a dozen bottles rained down on him. Pain laced through his arms and back as he shielded his head from anything knocking him silly. He might heal fast, but he got the feeling he was going to need his wits about him.

His ears rang from the blast, and his sight darkened. He blinked several times, hoping his body would get the healing bit done as soon as possible.

The floor was slick with various types of alcohol and the remains of the bottles that they'd once belonged inside of. Miles glanced behind him and saw that there was a lot less glass there due to the lack of bottles stacked at that end. He shuffled back toward the far end of the bar, his vision returning to normal by the time he was there, his ears no longer ringing. He smelled blood, which he assumed was due to whatever had happened to the Russian vampire, but he didn't want to put his head up over the bar to find out.

He bumped into the end of the bar and moved until he was sitting up against it.

"He's mine," the familiar sound of the Russian said.

Oh good, he's alive, Miles thought to himself.

"Your arm is fucked," a voice Miles didn't know said, although he had a similar accent.

"I don't need both arms," the Russian snapped.

Miles removed the incendiary grenade and held it down by his leg as the Russian's head loomed above. "Hey," Miles said with a little wave.

"Fucker is alive," the Russian said with glee, and jumped up onto the wooden bar top.

Miles noticed that the Russian's arm hung uselessly and was bleeding a lot. "You get caught in the blast?" he asked.

The Russian looked down at the steady stream of blood that fell from his hand. "It'll not stop me from killing you."

"I didn't expect them to blow you up," Miles said. "I assume you didn't either."

"The mission is more important," the vampire said, dropping down into the working area of the bar.

Miles nodded.

"We've got him," the voice from somewhere near the broken window said. "We'll clean up after. We'll sort out the rest; you going to be able to do this?"

The Russian looked over. "Yeah, go, we'll spend some time getting to know each other."

"You're not going to enjoy getting to know me," Miles said softly.

The Russian smiled and looked down at Miles. "You might have beaten me before, but you're in no position to be a threat now."

There was a low growl from somewhere outside, and Miles smiled. The growl was soon followed by a muffled cry and a horrible crunch.

"What the hell was . . . " the Russian said, looking over at the window as Church barrelled into him, clamping her jaws around his face and taking him to the ground, crushing the front of his skull as she did. She let go and moved back toward Miles, who got to his feet and stroked her.

"Good timing," Miles said, looking outside at the body of one attacker. He replaced the incendiary grenade on his belt and glanced down at the Russian.

The Russian was still alive, bubbles of blood popping out of his mouth with every breath. Miles vaulted over the bar and walked over to the ruined window. He removed his incendiary grenade, made sure that Church had left, activated it, and tossed it over the bar. The whoosh of fire was immediate and terrifying. The unconscious female vampire would be killed in the resulting fire, too, but Miles had used up all of his kindness making sure the desolate hadn't eaten her.

"Thanks for the timely assist," Miles said to Church, who rubbed her face against his hand. Her face was wet, and Miles's hand came away stained with blood.

The pair stopped by the dead body, which Miles searched, although he didn't find anything of note. No ID, which he'd expected, but apart from the bow, several more explosive arrows, and a dagger, there was nothing of interest.

Church growled and Miles looked up as a man walked around the corner of the decking. He spotted them both and drew an arrow, nocking it, but he never got further than that, as a bullet smashed into his skull and he crumbled to the ground.

"What the fuck?" Miles asked.

Miles ran to the dead man and narrowly avoided an arrow, which sailed over the edge of the decking, exploding as it went, taking a chunk of the wooden deck with it. A second bullet was fired, and Miles dropped to the ground. A lot of shouting came from those at the front of the hotel, most of it around trying to find out who was shooting them from the forest.

"Church, find out who has that rifle," Miles said. "If they're friendly, make sure they stay safe."

Church looked down at the dead attacker and back up at Miles. She whined.

"I'll be fine," he said as the shouting grew louder. As a woman walked into view, she was quickly caught in the head with a bullet.

Church barked and ran down the nearby staircase and into the forest. Miles turned into his vampire form and sprinted forward, around to the corner of the hotel, ignoring any bodies there. He grabbed an attacker with an assault rifle as they walked around the corner themselves, tearing it out of his hands and throwing it like a javelin at another man who walked around the corner at the wrong time. He tore out the throat of the first man and continued moving toward the second, who was on his feet, now in his vampire form.

The vampire charged and was caught by a bullet before he'd taken two steps. Miles drove his talons into his skull, making sure he wasn't going to be getting back up.

The front of the hotel had several attackers, who were now all hunkered down behind various vehicles, which wasn't going to stop them getting shot, but made it harder.

Miles pointed up toward the sky and hoped his unknown friend was watching. Wings tore out of his back, but pain ripped through them as an arrow went through the back of one wing membrane and exploded next to him.

The force of the blast threw Miles back, and only using his telekinesis to pull up one of the bodies beside him kept him from being seriously hurt. But while he was mostly uninjured, the membrane in his wing was shredded, forcing him to cast his beast side away as he turned to see who had shot the arrow at him. Blood poured down Miles's back as he retracted his wings. He was going to need some time to heal when this was all done.

Miles turned to whoever had hurt him and found one of the attackers holding an arrow in his only hand, the other having turned to charcoal and partially collapsed in the fire. Half of the man's face was a mess of melted flesh, his clothes seemingly grafted into his cooked skin. Miles wasn't even sure how he was still alive.

The man brought back his arm and threw an arrow like a spear, using a surprising amount of force given his condition of shambling melted candle. It hit the ground near Miles and exploded again, but Miles was already sprinting toward the attacker. He collided with the barely alive vampire, tackling him off his feet. Unfortunately, the man had already grabbed another arrow, and the impact of the tackle made him throw it up toward the glass windows dividing the decking from the hotel. The hotel where the desolate were gathered expectantly, like lions in a zoo just waiting for someone stupid enough to break the glass.

The explosion broke the glass.

Miles rolled away from the dying vampire as the desolate began to pound at the shattered window, easily breaking the reinforced glass open.

But because the hole wasn't big enough to fit all of them at once, they got stuck. Miles would have laughed at the whole thing if it hadn't been so damn terrifying.

Miles removed his last UV grenade, primed it, and threw it at the hotel where all of the desolate were still trying to get free. He was going to make sure he removed the problem before it even started. The UV grenade landed in front of the desolate and bounced, just as the seriously injured vampire stabbed his last explosive arrow into the decking between himself and Miles.

Miles threw himself back, having intended to dive over the edge of the decking to avoid the UV blast, but the explosion from the arrow washed over him, throwing him off balance, so he spun back over the edge.

Miles spiralled down the hundred feet into the forest below, smashing into what felt like every branch on every tree in his way, until he finally hit the ground, breaking an unknown number of bones in the process. He lay on the hard cold ground for several seconds before letting out a long, pained moan. Followed by several shorter moans as his body started to fix itself. His ribs had broken, his right wrist was fractured, his right knee was dislocated, and he'd broken several bones in both feet. He would need blood before long.

After what felt like an age, but was probably only a few minutes, he heard shouts from deeper in the woods. He forced himself upright and leaned against the nearby tree for support for a few seconds until he saw lights, too. He was being hunted, and he was in no condition to fight off however many of them were left. Not if they had their array of arrows and explosives. Time to find Church and his rifle-using friend and figure out how to stop the desolate from spreading. At the very least, putting some distance between himself and whoever was still after him would give Miles some time for his body to heal up.

Miles took a step, and pain laced up his leg. He looked down at the six-inch piece of tree sticking out of his foot. Sucking in a big breath, Miles grabbed the branch and pulled it out, wishing he'd put something in his mouth to bite on beforehand. The wound bled freely, which wasn't going to be great in aiding him to escape if any of the remaining people who attacked the hotel were vampires.

Pushing the thought aside, Miles moved as quickly as he could through the dark forest, trying to ignore the shouts from somewhere to the right. He knew that the shots from whoever was helping him had come from the side of the hotel with the decking, and that they had to be up on high elevation. That meant on the other side of the river. There was a small bridge connecting the two parts, which was Miles's destination. Get across the bridge, get up high, and hopefully Church would find him and whoever was helping them. Deal with the desolate and remaining attackers. It wasn't a great plan, but it was all he had right now.

He trudged on through the forest, moving as fast as his multitude of injuries would allow him. After a few minutes, his foot stopped hurting, something in his shoulder popped, and he let out a little moan of pain. He hadn't even realised there was something wrong with his shoulder, but he felt much better after it happened and quickened his pace.

The sound of fast running water reached Miles's ears, and he hastened his pace just as an arrow smashed into the tree beside him and exploded, throwing him back and peppering his body with tiny shards of wood.

Miles scrambled back to his feet, feeling more than a little irritated that as a centuries-old vampire, he was left to avoid people with bows and arrows in the middle of a forest. He ducked down behind a large tree and waited for his ears to stop ringing for the second time in only a few minutes. This holiday was not turning out to be as relaxing as he had been led to believe.

About to move away, Miles heard someone nearby and shifted, easily avoiding the knife of his new attacker. Miles used his own talons to open the human man's throat, and took a moment to drink deeply from the blood as it spurted out of the large wound where the man's neck should be. Having not bitten the man, Miles didn't take the memories of his attacker, but he didn't need to see the awful things his food had done; he just needed the blood for his body to hasten its healing.

Miles let the body drop to the floor, feeling refreshed and a little light-headed. Still in his vampire form, he looked out among the trees and saw movement deeper in the forest. With his body still healing itself, he turned and sprinted into the forest, running as fast as he could toward the bridge. It wasn't going to be a safe crossing; the bridge was two hundred feet long, and there was nowhere to hide once on it, but diving into the water was out of the question—the current was too fast, and he had no way of telling where he'd be able to get out.

He considered hunting the rest of those who'd hunted him, but it would take too long, and he had no idea if there were more people now chasing after whoever had the rifle. Which meant Church was a target. The thought spurred Miles on, and he ran flat out for several hundred meters until he heard the rushing water in front of him. Unfortunately, his need to get to Church, and his concentration on where he was heading, meant he was a fraction too slow to react to the sound of the arrow as it buzzed toward him, striking a nearby rock and exploding.

Miles banked to his right, putting himself directly into the path of a second arrow, which punctured through his shoulder. A massive electrical current tore through Miles's body, and he staggered forward, tripped, and hit the ground hard, snapping the end of the arrow off, but continuing on over and over, down the hill toward the river.

Miles tried to find purchase, tried to stop the inevitable, but his talons found only loose ground, his body seemingly destined to continue on. He smashed into a rock at high speed, his ribs snapping again from the impact, as he was thrown up and over it, leaving claw marks in the terrain as he tried to use it to slow down. He hit the ground hard and skidded off the end of the hill, into the water below.

While vampires like the cold a lot more than the heat, the freezing temperature of the water took Miles's breath away, and the speed of the water grabbed hold and dragged him under, slamming him into a rock, before practically spitting him back up to the surface.

Miles didn't know where he was, and as he looked around to try to figure it out, he was dragged under again, the strong current mixing with Miles's myriad of not quite healed injuries to make the worst of a bad situation. His left arm was useless, the arrow having punctured through his shoulder blade, the fibreglass shaft still protruding from his back.

Using his talons to try to get purchase on any of the rocks was a fruitless endeavour, and he only succeeded in breaking his index finger. No matter how strong he was on land, in the water, with only one hand, there was only one direction he was going. And that was wherever the water wanted him to go.

Having seen a bank farther down, he stopped fighting the current and tried to gradually move toward the side of the river. He'd only been in the water for a few hundred feet, but it felt like miles. He kicked out with every bit of strength he had, and kept kicking, using his one good arm to drag himself out of the centre of the water. Eventually, the river did the work for him, and after he hit yet another rock, he was deposited on the soft muddy bank.

Miles felt jaws around the back of his clothes, dragging him farther up the bank, away from the fast-flowing water. Church lay down beside Miles and licked his face.

"Thanks, girl," Miles said, patting the dog and wincing as he remembered his finger was still broken. He rolled onto his back and flexed his fingers, feeling the digit snap back into place. It still felt hot and painful, but it could fight for first place among all of the other injuries he had. The blood from the attacker had helped, but hadn't been enough to fix him.

Miles got to his knees and looked up at more forest. "We need to go," he said.

Church barked and let Miles use her to get to his feet. She barked again, and Miles followed her into the forest. They moved at a decent pace considering Miles's condition, and were soon up on top of the cliff overlooking the river from the opposite side from where Miles had entered. He looked out over the trees on the side he'd been running through not long ago, to the hotel in the distance. The fire had taken hold, and the entire restaurant and decking was ablaze. He hoped that no one else was in there.

Miles followed Church's barking again, and he climbed up a steep spot, reaching a plateau where a familiar face greeted him.

"Rosa," Miles said. "You are a sight for sore eyes."

Rosa, who wore a ghillie suit and held a large sniper rifle, the barrel resting against her shoulder, looked Miles up and down. "Well, you look like absolute shit."

CHAPTER EIGHTEEN

Rosa quickly explained that they couldn't actually leave the forest until it was deemed certain that every single desolate in the hotel was dead. A job Miles had to agree was probably more important than leaving to have a lie-down after drinking a bottle of whisky.

Most of the desolate had been destroyed by the UV grenade, but a few remained inside the hotel.

So, two hours later, Miles found himself still at the hotel, having changed into a new pair of jeans and a plain black sweatshirt. There were three helicopters, two of which were modified Chinooks, both of which landed in what remained of the hotel parking area after the third helicopter, an Apache, had obliterated it.

Miles had watched the attack from the safety of the hill as Rosa scanned the hotel for anything still alive and deemed a threat. When she got the all clear, she told Miles, and along with Church, the three of them made their way back down the hill to the bridge that Miles had *meant* to cross. It was a considerably easier journey back to the hotel than the one he'd had leaving it.

Miles had assumed it was the ATOs taking control of the hotel, but upon arriving at the decking to see several people putting out the fire that had all but destroyed the restaurant, he realised he'd been wrong.

"You didn't contact the ATOs?" Miles asked as they walked along the decking.

The windows separating the decking area from the hotel were all destroyed, and water hoses had been dragged through the centre of the hotel, making the floor wet and slippery as Miles followed Rosa.

"I will," Rosa said by way of explanation. "There are Assembly people here who were killed. It looks like the attackers actually made up most of the guests, just waiting for the signal to commence trying to kill you. I need to know who to trust, though."

A few people waved in Miles's direction, and it dawned on him who everyone was. "You called House Venator?" he half whispered.

"I trusted they were the only people who I could be certain didn't want to kill you," Rosa said.

Church barked, agreeing with her.

"That might change," a woman said as she stepped into the hotel reception area, several others bowing in reverence as she walked by. She was six and a half feet tall, with dark brown hair plaited down her back, ending at her waist, and olive skin. She wore the same black tactical gear as everyone else, and carried herself with an air of confidence that only came with someone who was supremely aware of her abilities and place within the world.

Miles had once heard someone suggest that if Wonder Woman was real, she'd look like Halime, and that was a fair representation of the First Captain of House Venator. Although Miles was pretty sure she wouldn't be caught dead out in public in Wonder Woman's outfit.

Miles walked over to Halime and hugged the taller woman, noticing her three-person Blood Guard close by, all keeping an eye on their principal. "Good to see you," he said.

All vampire First ranks had access to a three-person Blood Guard, although some vampires, like Charlotte, didn't bother using them. They were, for the most part, vampires who knew their principal well, who were well liked and trusted by their House as a whole.

Halime bent down and gave Church some fuss. "Wish I could say it was good to see you both, but this is a shit show. You can't even go on vacation without someone trying to murder you."

"I'm a people person," Miles said.

Halime laughed, the audible equivalent of warm honey.

"So, does anyone want to tell me how you got here so fast?" Miles asked, looking between Rosa and Halime.

"We need to talk," Rosa said in a tone that did not suggest it was an option. They went into the security room, and once Miles, Halime, and Church were all inside, Rosa closed the door.

"Right, well, the last few hours haven't been great," Rosa said, leaning up against the table on the wall opposite the door, while Halime and

Miles took their seats and Church lay on the ground beside them. "After Miles spoke to Gideon and Charlotte, the latter contacted me concerned that she couldn't get back through to you. She tried several times to contact the hotel, and you, but got nothing. She contacted me and asked if I would be willing to check on you. I'm your handler, so of course I was willing to. On the way here, the helicopter took fire from someone at the hotel, so I got the pilot to land nearby and decided to go through the forest. There was little point in arriving at the front door and getting shot at."

"With a sniper rifle," Miles said.

"I like to be prepared for any eventuality," Rosa said with a smile. "Also, it was onboard, as was the suit. Once we were attacked, I contacted Charlotte, who sent people to help."

"Okay," Halime said. "Why not contact the Assembly, get ATOs here?"

"Two reasons," Rosa said. "One, I wasn't sure who the people attacking were. I knew they weren't House Venator, so that was why you were on top of my list. But two, Megan and her entire ATO team went missing a few hours ago. They were last in contact in Lithuania, where they'd gone for a mission to deal with a vampire gang. All routine, all very normal, but all of them are missing. I assume you haven't had any contact?"

Miles shook his head. "No phone reception for the last few hours."

"We're working on that," Rosa said. "Whoever did this made sure people couldn't get out."

"The Assembly have sent more ATOs to Lithuania to investigate," Rosa said. "No idea whose team it was, but if something has happened to Megan, I hope they're okay. Megan and her team are no pushovers."

"We've found a group of vampires and humans to the south of here, running through the forest," Halime said, gaining Miles's attention. "They told us that they were sent out by a vampire who rescued them. That you?"

Miles nodded. "Yeah, needed them out of the way before I dealt with the attackers. They unleashed a group of desolate on the hotel. Hence the fire. I assume the people you found were all okay."

"They're a bit roughed up, and some are going to have a fair few therapy sessions, but they're okay," Halime said. "The desolate are done, thankfully. We found a few surviving guests hiding in rooms upstairs, but we found a fair few dead, too. Whoever these attackers were, they came prepared to kill vampires. A lot of vampires."

"Templar International," Miles said. "That's who sent them. Well, Sara Bakos. I assume this is vengeance for what happened to Dominik. I also assume Henryk is involved."

"You sure?" Rosa asked. "Templar International shut up operations in London, moved to Paris. The Tour First building. They renamed it Tour International. It didn't go down well. We kept an eye on the company, and whatever else is happening, the Paris branch has done everything it can to distance itself from Henryk, and anyone else who worked at the London branch."

"The London branch is still open, though," Miles said.

Rosa nodded. "We sent an ATO team to go look around the place, and they reported back that it was a few dozen security and IT people, but that was it. It's mostly just guards patrolling the building while the actual bulk of the staff, and anyone involved with the running of the company, left. You think the London branch is still operational?"

Miles shrugged. "I've been trying very hard not to pay attention to anything to do with the Dominik case for the last few months. Henryk screamed vengeance about me, so I heard, but people want vengeance on me all the time. I'm an Arbiter, it comes with the life. And then the next I'd heard, Henryk vanished without a trace."

"If this is Henryk, it looks like he's finally decided to show himself," Halime said. "What are you doing about Megan and her team?"

"The Assembly is looking into it," Rosa said. "It's outside of my remit, and officially I'm not even allowed to nudge people about it, but Justice Balderas kindly said he would keep his ear to the ground and let me know."

"How did anyone know you were here?" Halime asked Miles.

"I didn't exactly make a secret of it," Miles said. "Told Charlotte, Rosa, spoke to several other Arbiters who all recommended it as a place to stay. I didn't switch my phone off either. This wasn't a big secret, this was just me trying to get some rest for a few weeks."

"That didn't work out well," Halime said with a gentle slap on the back of Miles's shoulder, which made him wince. "Good thing you have people looking out for you. You still hurt?"

"They shot through my wing membrane," Miles said. "Also, I think I broke more than a few bones. It'll take me a while to heal up. I could do with a feed."

"We've got synthetic blood," Halime said. "Good shit, too, not the over-the-counter emporium crap."

Miles laughed, which hurt, and he ended up coughing instead, which also hurt. It had been a bad few hours. He glanced over at the monitor, which showed as a static screen, the CCTV camera in the restaurant presumably destroyed in the fire. He thought back to how the vampire had managed to survive a fire that should have killed him, seeing how young he was. He'd died eventually, and hard, but even a few decades old should have died after the first UV grenade.

"What?" Halime asked, glancing at the monitor.

Miles walked over and rewound the footage from the CCTV, until he found the spot where he'd started the fire. He used the nearby joystick to zoom onto the bar area and watched as the fire engulfed the area.

"Holy shit," Halime said. "You did that?"

Miles nodded. "Not a lot of good opt—" He paused. "Did you see that?"

"Is that a glitch?" Halime asked.

Miles rewound the footage again, and sure enough, the Russian vampire he'd killed shortly after the fire had started was walking through the flames. He would turn ethereal, manage a few steps, and have to reform. It was evident to see that every time he turned back from being ethereal, or *glitched*, the fire consumed him, only for him to go ethereal again. He repeated the same thing over and over. Each time the fire was put out, he restarted as he moved. The agony must have been unbearable. Eventually, he collapsed and died, but he'd managed to make it a long way before that happened.

"Oh shit," Rosa said. "Like Dominik."

"Someone else did that weird . . . whatever the hell that is?" Halime asked.

Miles nodded. "That vampire said he was turned by Sara Bakos. Which means she's the official link between these vampires and whoever turned Dominik."

"You know something?" Halime said, pointing at the screen. "I do recall something about a ghostly bloodline power. I don't remember why, but yeah, there's definitely something there. You should speak to Drest, he'll know more."

"We need to get this footage to the Assembly," Rosa said. "This proves that Dominik and this attack are probably linked. Chances are that either Sara turned them both, or whoever turned Sara did."

"None of the other vampires here showed the ability to do that," Miles said. "And they weren't that old, either. The guy on fire said that there were a bunch of new vampires turned by a mercenary. You know of any groups that do vampire creation on the sly?"

"Yes," they both said at the same time.

"There are always groups who will turn people into vampires for enough money," Halime said. "But these people all look like professionals themselves, so I'm assuming whoever they got in to do it wasn't a slouch."

"It happened eight months ago," Miles said. "Just after Dominik died. Weirdly, I didn't think Henryk would burn his own company for revenge."

"Grief can mess with someone," Rosa said.

Miles nodded but was unable to put his finger on what it was that bothered him. "Can you contact whoever is working on what happened to Megan and her team? They could be in serious trouble."

"Any chance the phones are working?" Rosa asked.

Everyone checked their phone at the same time. Miles had one bar, but no Wi-Fi signal still. He told everyone his phone's status.

"One bar here, too," Rosa said.

"I got three bars," Halime said excitedly. "Which isn't something I should be proud of. When did technology take over our world?"

"Probably with the Romans," Miles said.

"The bastards," Halime said, passing Rosa her phone. "Go make your call."

Rosa left the room, and Miles sat back in the chair, rubbing his neck.

"Go get your drink," Halime said, practically lifting Miles out of his seat. "Come on."

Miles followed his old friend through the busy hotel, where most of the House Venator troops were still making sure that everything was safe. There were patrols being sent out into the forest, just in case a desolate got free. It was unlikely, but even one could cause havoc across the region if it started to attack people.

They'd been brought to the hotel to destroy evidence, to make the attack look like the desolate had done it all. Miles doubted the story would add up once looked at with any scrutiny, but it would definitely have given the Assembly personnel arriving pause. Enough time for the attackers to go wherever they were going next. In Miles's opinion, it all felt a little too slap-dash for Henryk. He struck Miles as someone who liked a plan, which, to be fair, so had Sara. So what had changed? Apart from grief, but to Miles's mind, grief would have made people even more determined to get the job done right the first time.

They left the hotel, and Halime pointed Miles toward the Chinook helicopter, where a middle-aged man with a red cross on his stab vest stood. Even vampires needed medics, although usually it was for the people the vampires had been dealing with.

"Halime said to get some blood," Miles said. "The good stuff, apparently."

The man laughed. "We've got a lot of good stuff, my man." He sounded a bit stoned.

The medic removed a blood pouch from a cooler onboard and passed it to Miles, who tore it open and took a long drink. Halime was right, it was the good stuff.

"See?" the medic said with a knowing smile and nod.

"You got something for her?" Miles asked, nodding to Church as he finished off the blood pouch.

"Ah, we've got something in here," the medic said, clambering back inside and coming out with a bag of jerky. "You like jerky?"

Church barked and sat as the medic opened the bag and placed it in front of her.

Miles noticed Halime wave him over, and he left Church alone to finish her snack.

"Drest wants a word," she said to Miles and mouthed *sorry*.

Miles took the phone.

"You okay?" Drest asked as Miles held the phone to his ear.

"I've been better," he said. "Been worse, too, so let's call it a mediocre evening."

Drest chuckled. Considering how large and imposing Drest was in real life, his laugh sounded like something that could have easily come from a bear. "Halime filled me in on everything," he said, any trace of humour replaced with concern. "Someone attacked a vampire resort. A safe space, Miles. And they used desolate to do it."

Miles considered how he was going to respond. There was a tone in Drest's voice that he knew well was the *I'm one word away from losing my shit* tone. Miles didn't fear Drest losing his temper, but it would mean someone else would have to deal with his wrath, and he didn't really want to be responsible for that.

"Templar International," Miles said. "At least, I think so. The vampire I spoke to said he was turned by their security officer, and I get the feeling he wasn't lying."

"The same people as you dealt with earlier this year?"

Miles nodded, remembered Drest couldn't see him, and sighed. "Yeah. Sounds like they went after an ATO team, too, in Lithuania. You got any friends over there you can speak to?"

"No," Drest said. "I can make enquiries, though. I assume Rosa contacted us because she doesn't know who to trust. Is that still the case?"

"Templar were an accredited company," Miles said, looking out across the forest as the first rays of dawn threatened the horizon. It had been a *long* night. "They've hit an ATO team and an Arbiter in the same night. They either don't care about repercussions because they have someone to help them, or they've gone full rogue and are happy to watch their world burn. I'm on the way to Scotland now, and we need to talk about something else. A bloodline gift that lets the vampire glitch."

"Glitch?" Drest asked. "What does that mean?"

"They can walk through walls; they sort of turn ghostly," Miles said. "I've never heard of it before, and no one seems to have any clue what House their vampire would belong to. I figured it might be one of the expunged bloodlines, but I haven't had a chance to look into that side of it yet."

There was a long pause from Drest. "Come to Scotland and we'll talk," he said. "Tell Halime to bring Rosa, too, if she's working with you on this."

Miles blinked, but Drest had aready hung up before he had a chance to question him further.

Miles passed the phone back to Halime.

"You don't look thrilled," she said, pocketing her phone.

"Looks like a Glen Affric visit," Miles told her. "Drest wants to talk to us. Rosa and you, too. He was as informative as ever."

Halime looked surprised for just a moment, before her usual calm expression returned. "This whole thing has just gotten a lot more interesting, I assume."

"You say interesting, I say shit," Miles said. "These people used the desolate as a weapon, Halime. They had to have a bunch of desolate kept somewhere to use when the time was right."

"You think they're hoarding a . . . well, a literal horde of desolate?"

"They brought them in the back of a truck." Miles pointed to the partially destroyed vehicle that had been dragged out of the hotel front window. "That one, in fact. They can't have made them in there. So, they're collecting them from somewhere."

Halime looked out at the forest before turning back to Miles. "I don't like the idea that there's someone willing to use a literal monster to send against us. Makes you wonder what else they'll do."

"Let's get to Scotland, find these people, and put a stop to them before they can continue," Miles said, while he wondered exactly how many more people were going to have to die before those behind the attack were stopped.

CHAPTER NINETEEN

Within an hour, dawn was threatening, as the sky lit up in shades of red and purple. The vampires among the House Venator team had either returned to the Chinooks or moved into the hotel so that they could continue their work of making the place safe. A hotel the size of the Vampyr Retreat had a lot of little nooks and crannies where someone could hide, and the whole place needed to be checked.

Miles, Rosa, and Church were all inside one of the Chinooks. The rear passenger area was separated from the flight crew, who were always, as Miles knew, human. There were vampire pilots, especially after the advances in glass not allowing UV rays through, but it was just safer for everyone if pilots didn't burst into flames should a window's protection fail.

The two small windows in the rear of the helicopter were both UV protected, and heavily tinted on both ends, meaning it was hard to look out of, or into. There were warm lights both above the two benches facing one another, with a large gap in between where gear could be stowed as well as placed into the metal floor. The whole area was somewhat cavernous and could easily sit twenty-five people, with room to spare for the various things that needed to be transported. There was a near constant smell of oil and grease, and it wasn't even close to the most comfortable ride in the world, but Miles had been in considerably worse aircraft in his life.

On this occasion, there were only fourteen people aboard, most of whom Miles had never met before. A few of House Venator who'd been there when he had been First Librarian waved or said hi, and they made small talk for a short time, but most of the people were new to him.

Halime climbed aboard and took a seat next to Miles, putting on her headset like everyone else. Vampire hearing was phenomenal, but even the most powerful of vampires would have a hard time making out full conversations with the sound the Chinook made as it flew. "Humans are staying back," she said. "We've contacted the Assembly; they're going to send a team to help, but I'd rather our own people did the handover. Just in case."

"In case of what?" Rosa asked.

"In case you were right not to trust them," Halime said with no semblance of feeling on the matter one way or another.

Miles stroked Church, who had taken up position under the benches, her head sticking out between Miles and Rosa, so that she could get attention from both.

The engines in the Chinook started up, and even all of the sound dampening in the rear did little to stop the noise from reverberating about the cabin. A few seconds later, and they were off. They landed at the Oslo airport, where they swapped to a private jet that would take them the rest of the way. Only a short time after landing, they were flying across Norway toward the North Sea, and eventually Scotland. Miles had taken the trip by boat several times during his life, and with the advent of being able to fly, made sure he never had to go by boat again. It was not a fun journey.

It took roughly five hours to fly from Oslo to Inverness, so Miles imagined that it was roughly the same time to get to the newly built private airfield close to Glen Affric. Maybe a little more, depending on the conditions. The airfield was strictly for House Venator personnel, so the fact that they were landing there instead of Inverness meant everyone was taking the threat seriously.

Miles had been lucky that Rosa had contacted House Venator the moment she'd been unable to get in touch with him. Luckier still that they had listened, although he guessed that was more out of the knowledge that if he was in trouble, it was probably worth getting involved to find out what was on fire before that fire became out of control.

"The resort might not open again," Halime said after a short period of nothing but the noise of the flight.

"It was a nice place to stay," Miles said. "Church enjoyed it."

Church rubbed her head against Miles's leg in agreement.

"Do you think it's safe to fly?" Rosa asked. "Just wondering about what these people will do to actually get Miles."

"We're good," Halime said with confidence. "We're safer in here than we were on the ground. Although I do think that if they attacked a resort with innocent vampires and humans staying there, there's no telling what they'll be willing to do in future."

"Either of you heard anything from Lithuania?" Miles asked.

Rosa shook her head. "No, it's going to be a while before I hear anything back. Probably by the time we land. Speaking of which, do I need to sign any confidentiality waivers?"

Halime laughed. "No, it's fine. You contacted House Venator instead of going through normal channels; I'm pretty sure whatever you see or hear won't matter much."

Rosa sighed. "I think I'm going to be having a chat with the Inquisition."

"You'll be fine," Miles assured her. "You did what you thought was best at the time, and there's still no evidence that the Assembly weren't helping Templar. Until we find something that proves their guilt or innocence, you've done nothing but aid your Arbiter. You did your job. Well, I might add."

The conversation forward went in starts and stops, with no one seemingly interested in having a good talk about anything in particular. Miles was fine with that, as it gave him time to consider what he'd seen and done in the last few hours. What he'd learned. He thought about Megan and her team. If something happened to them, either death or capture, he hoped they made it hard for their attackers.

"Penny for your thoughts?" Halime asked.

"If Megan and her team were ambushed like I was," Miles said, "I hope they're okay. I only got away due to dumb luck."

"That doesn't bode well for Megan and her team," Rosa said.

"I know," Miles said, wishing he could say quite literally anything else. "I just think we should prepare for the fact that whatever has happened to them was bad. If they've taken Megan and her team, we need to find them, and fast. These people do not care about playing by whatever rules we think we have in place in modern society."

"We'll find them," Rosa said.

"And then we'll find whoever did this and stop them," Halime continued. "I'm all in on this now. Drest himself couldn't stop me. These people need to be stopped."

"Thank you," Miles said.

"I think most of the Houses will be enraged about this," Halime said. "The political motions of the Houses might not move quickly enough to help you stop them, but I think it's safe to say that once word gets out that a vampire safe hotel was attacked, none of them are going to just sit back and take that."

A few hours later, there was an announcement by the pilots that they'd be descending to the private airport close to House Venator estate. The last time Miles had been to the estate, he'd had to land at a public airport and be driven the rest of the way, but at the time House Venator was hosting the Gathering of Houses—where everyone from the Assembly was scrutinised before arrival—so he understood that there were protocols to observe.

Miles felt the plane drop slowly and closed his eyes, focusing on his breathing as the aircraft got closer to its destination. He wasn't scared to fly, or land, but he didn't want to go into a meeting with Drest, and whoever else might be there, without a clear head.

There was a slight bump as the plane touched down, but everyone remained in their seats and waited as the engine noise faded to nothing. Halime was the first up, opening the door and motioning for everyone to get out, before congratulating her people on a difficult job. First Captain was a hard role to do well. Too many people used it as a way to create their own mini army, but Miles had always known that wasn't quite what the job entailed. At least it wasn't for those who didn't have one eye on the position of First Lord. It meant being a general *and* a soldier *and* security consultant *and* any other role that dealt with looking after the people within the House. It also meant knowing when to go from one to the other. And Halime had always been good at knowing exactly what hat to wear for what occasion. These were *her* people, and Miles was pretty sure there wasn't a force on earth that could harm them without Halime arriving at your doorstep looking for blood.

Miles checked the UV level, which said *zero,* not uncommon for this time of year. It was also drizzling. Also not uncommon. According to the weather forecast, the entire British Isles were going to be inundated with rain for the next few days. Once again, Miles thought, not uncommon. At least it meant he didn't have to worry about himself or those with him as they walked around in what was going to pass for daylight.

"Her people respect her," Rosa said when she and Miles had exited the Chinook and walked away to the side of the landing zone, which gave great views of the vast amount of land that surrounded the estate.

Loch Affric was nearby, and there were trails in the hills that Miles had spent time running and hunting over the centuries that he'd lived here. It was a place he found peaceful, despite also having gone through difficult times while living there.

"Her people *adore* her," Miles said. "It's something Drest has mentioned before."

"Because you shouldn't love your commanding officer?" Rosa asked.

"Because the House comes first," Miles said. "She knows it, they know it. They adore her, but every one of them would throw it all away if Drest commanded it."

"Before the Assembly was created, just having the Houses, must have been a period of chaos."

"And fear," Miles said. "There were no checks, no balances. Only those imposed by the First Lords. So, if you had a benevolent lord, you probably did okay. But if you had the vampire equivalent of Caligula, you probably lived day to day not knowing when you were going to say or do the wrong thing."

"You two done?" Halime called as the second Chinook began its descent from the sky, Church by her side having sat and watched everyone leave.

Rosa and Miles followed Halime through the estate, with Church stopping to sniff everything on the way. The landing zone was a ten-minute walk to the main house, although it soon became apparent that they weren't heading that way.

"Where are we going?" Miles asked.

"Library," Halime said without looking back. "Drest's orders."

Miles looked over at the buildings set out in a horseshoe a short distance from the main estate. There had been a number of vampires from the Great Houses there only a short time ago, and now there would be all but a skeleton crew of staff to make sure it remained clean and tidy for future Assembly visits. The Assembly picked one Great House a year to host them and members of the other Great Houses for a period of time. It was called the Gathering of Houses.

The current gathering was being hosted in New York, by House Phalanx, which Miles was certain was going to be one of the most tedious periods of time in the lives of everyone who attended. Members of the House Phalanx were not exactly known for their warm and welcoming demeanours to outsiders. The First Lords and Ladies were required to attend the gatherings for the first week, but afterwards, they were allowed to go about their usual lives. That usually meant that the rest of the First members of a House stopped attending, too, unless they had business that required them to be there.

Miles's mind drifted back from his previous visit to the estate to more immediate matters as the group reached the vast House Venator library, probably Miles's favourite place on the estate. A three-storey building of white stone, with a slate grey roof, it had huge windows around all sides, with imposing dark wooden double doors. The library, like all House libraries, contained a history of their House, their bloodline. Even most of the Minor Houses had a library with its own history, with the Assembly having libraries that were meant to overlap between Houses. Meant to ensure that nothing was omitted from a House's past.

Under Miles's stewardship as First Librarian, he'd quickly discovered that the House Venator library had a lot of books, scrolls, parchments, and various other forms of recordkeeping that they were never meant to have. The histories of other Houses, other First Lords and Ladies, other dangerous people who had left their Houses, some who tried to assassinate their own First Lords. Some who failed. Some who succeeded. None of which was meant to be in House Venator's library.

Drest had told Miles that it was their duty to be keepers of the truth of the vampire world. That there had been too many times when a House, Minor or Great, would destroy or hide information that would show them in a bad light. House Venator had, before the Assembly had taken control, been the vampire House used to hunt other vampire Houses. They were not dubbed the House of Justice for nothing. Although Miles had heard them dubbed several other, much less kind, things over the centuries.

Gideon opened the doors to the library and beckoned everyone inside. It had started to drizzle since they'd landed, and Gideon was already whinging about getting water on his polished floors. Miles sighed. Complaining about the rain and drizzle during a Scottish winter was like complaining about the heat in the Bahamas. You dealt with it, or you moved.

Miles looked up at the interior of the library, the roof of which sat three storeys above him, the second and third storeys being circular rings with a large opening in the middle, looking down on the entrance. The roof had large specially designed panels all along it that cast rainbows of colour all around the wooden interior, bouncing off strategically placed polished surfaces. The panels stopped actual light from outside from entering the library. Books and vampires shared a dislike of being in natural light for too long. Maybe that was why Miles liked being First Librarian for so long, although he had to admit that the view inside the library definitely helped.

Thousands of books sat inside the hall of the library, detailing thousands of years of vampire and human history. Not always pleasant, not always harmonious. At least, not until the Assembly took control and things got better, if not all together easier.

Drest sat at a wooden table designed for four people a short distance from the front door, reading a book. He looked up and smiled.

While Drest appeared to be a man of about fifty, with long grey hair that fell over his shoulders, he was one of the oldest vampires Miles had ever met. He'd been turned when Scotland was ruled by the Picts, which made him well over fifteen hundred years old, maybe closer to two thousand. No one really knew, and Drest was in no hurry to tell anyone. He had a long beard that reached his chest, which as always was plaited down the centre with a golden ring just beyond his chin, and silver ringlets further down. He had piercing blue eyes, and his enormous muscular hands were missing the little finger on one and the top of his index finger on the other. No one knew why. Another in a long line of mysteries about the First Lord of House Venator.

Drest got to his feet, the smile remaining in place. He was taller than Miles, and about as broad in the shoulders, and had silver cross earrings hanging from both ears, as well as several gold and silver bracelets on both wrists. His fingers were adorned with golden, brass, and copper rings, some lined with precious gems, but most plain, or covered in Gaelic writing.

"Glad you came," he said, giving Miles a hug, the smile never wavering.

"Thank you for sending people to help in Norway," Miles replied.

"Ah, I cannae have you get killed," he said with a chuckle. "I'd never hear the end of it. Thank you for bringing them, Halime."

Halime bowed her head. "I have other duties to attend to, if I may."

"Of course," Drest said.

"It was a pleasure, Rosa," Halime said, hugging the smaller woman.

"Yeah, you too," Rosa said.

Halime turned to Miles. "Try to stay out of trouble for a few days."

"I don't think I can promise anything," he said.

Halime laughed. "I have missed you. Do not take so long to see me next time." She slapped Miles on the shoulder, bent down to kiss Church on top of her head, and left the library.

"Shall we?" Drest asked, motioning for Rosa and Miles to follow. "Church, would you like to rest in the corner over there? I have prepared food and water for you."

Miles looked over at where Drest was pointing, and spotted the large comfortable-looking bed that if Church wasn't going to use, he might.

Church licked the back of Miles's hand, barked once, the sound echoing around the library, and hurried over to the food.

"She knows how to live her best life," Rosa said.

Drest continued on to the rear of the building, where he removed a key from his pocket and placed it into a slot against the wall, next to a bookshelf. The bookshelf rumbled to the side, revealing a door behind it.

"Did you know that was there?" Rosa asked.

Miles nodded. "Never had to use it much, though."

"Before we go farther, I need some assurances," Drest said, turning back to Miles and Rosa, any hint of the smiling First Lord from earlier gone, replaced with a stern expression.

"What kind of assurances?" Rosa asked.

"He wants us to promise we will never reveal what we see down there," Miles said. "I've worked here for a long time, Drest. I've never told anyone about the information you have down there. Never will."

"What kind of information?" Rosa asked. "What am I getting into? Is it legal?"

"Information on other Houses," Miles said. "Stuff some of them would rather not see the light of day. Some that might hurt any relationships between them and other Houses, or them and humans. When we hunted a vampire who killed humans, back before the Assembly was what it is now, we made sure we wrote about who they were, their bloodline, their secondary gifts, and anything else we got out of them."

"You never handed it over to the Assembly?" Rosa asked, looking between Miles and Drest.

"It would not have ended well for many people," Drest said. "Some things are better left buried. But Miles is right, it is information that you may see. Information that is to stay within these walls. I need assurances that you will not speak of anything you see here."

"On pain of death?" Rosa asked and laughed, before seeing Drest's face.

"Aye, that about sums it up," he said.

"You'll kill me?" she almost shouted.

"Not *your* death," Miles told her. "There are things down there that should they come to light, Houses might decide to settle old scores. It's why the Assembly was never given them. But they're important to keep a record of. Should we ever need them. Like now, I assume."

"I will never mention anything of what I'm about to see," Rosa said. "I don't want to start a war here, just want to find out why someone else does."

Drest didn't move.

Rosa sighed. "Fine, you have my word. Whatever I'm about to see, I keep to myself. Unless you have Bigfoot, and then I'm telling everyone."

Drest glanced over at Miles.

"Do you have a fucking Bigfoot?" Rosa asked.

Drest smiled. "No, of course not. Be weird if I just kept one under my library." He turned and unlocked the door, revealing a black iron spiral staircase beyond. A single bare bulb hung in the ceiling above the staircase, illuminating a fraction of the stairs going down.

"That the only light?" Rosa asked.

"You're a vampire," Drest pointed out.

"Still like lights," Rosa replied in a whisper. "How far down is this?"

"About a hundred feet," Miles said as the three of them started their descent.

CHAPTER TWENTY

The only noise in the stairwell was the echo of their footsteps. As Drest had said, there were no lights apart from the bulb at the top, and within a few feet of the entrance, the stairwell was bathed in darkness.

The bottom of the stairwell had another light, illuminating a metal and wooden door, which Drest opened with the same key from above. There were, as far as Miles knew, only three of those keys in the world. Gideon and Drest would each have one, and a third was kept under wraps in a vault under the main house. A place used for storing anything too important to have lying around.

With the door pushed open, the room beyond was revealed. It was a cavernous place with stacks of books on pale grey stone tables, and even more on the multitude of shelves. The shelves were made of five levels, each with twenty compartments. Each compartment was separated from the others and had a plexiglass front with a label on it stating pertinent information. Some of the compartments were filled to the brim with scrolls, and Miles had an unfortunate flashback to the numerous times when he'd had to remove one that had created a domino effect of several dozen of the things coming with it.

A staircase sat at the side of the room, leading up to a floor above, the balconies of which looked down on the stone floor that the three now walked along. There were lights everywhere, illuminating the whole place even more so than the library floor above.

"This place is insane," Rosa said looking around, her mouth occasionally agape. "There are thousands of scrolls here."

"Scrolls, journals, even some papyrus," Drest said. "Leatherbound books, a few books bound in things that aren't really worth thinking about.

There's a room back there where the most dangerous or valuable items are concealed in little safety deposit boxes cut into the stone walls, like a bank."

"Do you know what all of this is?" Rosa asked.

"No one does," Drest said. "I imagine even Miles, who worked here a long time, never got through all of this. It's the product of thousands of years of information. The stuff on the floor above us, by those balconies, is older than I am. A few items are in languages I've never even heard of. When people say the vampires have always been here, they mean it."

"So, one of these scrolls is going to help us figure out who's behind the attack?" Rosa asked.

"Maybe, but probably not," Drest said as the three of them reached a wooden door at the rear of the cavern. "But we're far enough away from prying eyes and ears."

Drest pushed open the door, motioning for Miles and Rosa to step into the room beyond. Inside was a long wooden table, ten leather chairs around it, and a large American-style double fridge, which Miles thought was both new and a little weird to see down here.

"People spent hours and hours down here," Gideon explained. "They needed sustenance." He sat in one of the chairs at the table, a glass of water in front of him. Beads of condensation had formed a small puddle atop the coaster he was using.

Charlotte was already waiting downstairs, sitting at the far end of the table, several feet away from Gideon. "There's a bathroom upstairs now, too."

"The miracle of modern life," Miles said. "What's with all the cloak and dagger?"

"Sit, please," Drest said, and both Miles and Rosa took their seats opposite Gideon, with Drest sitting at the end opposite Charlotte.

"This is nice," Miles said. "So cosy."

"Rosa, this is Charlotte and Gideon," Drest introduced. "First Counsel and First Librarian. They're here in an official capacity."

"I have some documents for you both to sign," Charlotte said, removing some from her bag and passing them over. "They state that neither of you will reveal whatever it is Drest tells you. And no, I don't currently know what that is, so we're all going to be *really* lucky to find out together."

Miles looked down at the paper, and up at Charlotte, as a pen skidded across the desk. The piece of paper had a lot of legal stuff about not *divulging secrets* and *punished with the severity of the law* written on it, but Miles signed it anyway. Anything to get all of the cloak and dagger stuff finished with.

Rosa signed her paper, and both were sent back to Charlotte.

"This had better be some of the best information I've ever heard," Rosa said. "You better have a Bigfoot now."

Gideon removed a large leatherbound book from a bag beside him and placed it on the table with a slightly overly exaggerated thud. The book was old, the pages stiff and stained with age. The leather was burgundy, and the book creaked as it opened.

Miles clapped. "The performance art is magnificent."

"There's a way to do things," Gideon said snidely.

"Make them faster," Miles retorted.

Gideon sighed and turned the book around, passing it across the desk to Miles, who looked down at the writing and tried to read the squiggles that someone had decided to use as handwriting. He looked over at Drest.

"That book is the last record of a Great House," Drest said. "House Divinus. Ever heard of them?"

Miles nodded tentatively, passing the book over to Rosa, who started to read. "Aye, I think so. They're a story told to new vampires about what happens to those who go against the Houses."

"Yeah, I remember that one," Rosa said, looking up. "Although I don't remember it being House Divinus. I remember it being about a group of vampires who thought they were above the rules of the Houses and were punished for it. But this here says they were expunged. What actually happened? What did they do?"

"Before anyone else in this room was born, and when the Assembly was nothing more than a bunch of loose ideas, we had five Great Houses still," Drest said. "Always been five. Not always the same Houses. House Phalanx is the newest of the Great Houses, having been promoted when House Bane lost its position. Houses used to come and go all the time. Or they did at least once a century. Some would have their First members assassinated, some had House-contained civil wars. Some just collapsed under their own incompetence. House Divinus was one of only three Houses to be expunged."

"Expunged means something a lot worse than just the bloodline dying out, doesn't it?" Rosa asked.

"They're *removed* from the vampire world," Drest said. "It's a House death sentence. Anyone with that bloodline was to be hunted and their line destroyed so none of them could ever sire new vampires."

"Fucking hell," Charlotte said in a whisper. "Are you seriously talking genocide?"

Drest nodded. "Only ever been used three times in all of recorded history, and not since Divinus."

"You know, I *really* would have liked a heads-up about that," Charlotte said. "I'm meant to protect you in a legal sense, Drest."

"There's nothing here that I need protecting from," Drest said with a shrug.

"What did they do?" Miles asked.

"They built a city in what is now northern Lithuania, close to the Baltic Sea. And for several years they welcomed humans, said it was a safe haven for humanity and vampires to coexist. You remember what happened in Maine in the 1980s?"

Maine had been a vampire city that to some acted as a warning about what could happen when vampires were allowed to rule. While outwardly it was all fine, it was later discovered that vampires had been experimenting on humans who were dying, and ended up creating hundreds of desolate. Desolate that they then experimented on to try and figure out how to control them. It did not go well.

The desolate escaped and overran the state in a matter of weeks. It cost thousands of human and vampire lives, as the desolate not only took over Maine, but spread to New Brunswick. Eventually, the desolate were stopped, and those in charge who weren't killed during the outbreak were hunted down and executed.

In the aftermath, a wall was built around parts of Maine and New Brunswick, and large military installations were put in place around the edges of the two areas, with Nova Scotia becoming a land of refugees and military personnel for many years.

There were still vampire towns in Maine, and humans still lived there, too, but the vast majority of the state had become a lawless place. Some vampires saw going to the site of the initial outbreak as a pilgrimage. Miles had been once since it happened, and hoped he'd never have to go back again.

"Vampires experimenting on humans?" Miles said, the memories of that time flashing across his mind, and bringing with them a feeling of unease. "A plague of desolate. A lot of dead people. Basically all the bad parts of the apocalypse in one place."

"Yeah, well, this was worse," Drest said. "They used that city as a base of operations to raid human settlements all across what is now Eastern Europe. They killed a lot of people, and framed other vampires for it. They didn't kill those people for food, not for any need to defend themselves, just because they could. Those attacks led more and more refugees who had escaped the attacks to come to the gates of their city. They thought they were running from vicious murderers, they thought they would be safe. Instead, they ran right into the spider's web. The city of Pax was the jewel of vampires and humanity together. Until the doors were locked one night, and twenty-five thousand people were slaughtered over a period of a few weeks."

"Oh shit," Rosa said.

"The rest of the Great Houses discovered and were, *mostly*, outraged," Drest continued.

"Really?" Miles asked. "Outraged. I've met some of the people who would have been around then. Outraged isn't the word I'd have used to describe what they think of the murders of humans."

"That's why I used the word *mostly.* House Divinus brought the rest of the vampire Houses into serious danger," Drest said. "Lone vampires out in Eastern Europe were murdered by villagers who were terrified of us. Tales were told, fear was stoked, and House Divinus sat daring us to do something about it. They wanted to start a war against the humans. They wanted the vampires to be the *only* ruling class of people on this planet. No human cities, just human cattle. Bred to be food for their vampire masters. The massacre at Pax was their first step to test the waters and see what the reaction would be from the rest of us."

"Nothing good, I assume," Rosa said.

"A delegation of the other Houses were sent to Pax," Drest said. "I walked through those bloodstained gates and into a city of fear and death. Any humans still breathing were only alive because they were being used for sport. We were taken to the First Lord of House Divinus. He sat there all puffed out and self-important, next to his First Captain and First Authority. Told us that we were to join him, join his war against the humans."

Drest closed his eyes and took a deep breath.

"You killed him," Miles said.

Drest nodded. "Eventually. We left the city, the Houses united, went back to our people, and we waged war on House Divinus. We eradicated everything in that city, and when it was done, we burned that city to the ground, and hunted for the First Lord, who had fled. We expunged them all. Not a single vampire was allowed to live who had been part of that evil. And then we expunged their bloodline from our world, made having it a death sentence. After it happened, we let the vampire world know the punishment for anyone committing such an atrocity. House Divinus was a relatively small House, so it didn't take long for us to decimate their number. But, as with anything, over time, the tale of House Divinus went from something approximating the truth to a cautionary tale told to new vampires. Those of us from the Houses who carried out the death of the House Divinus bloodline allowed the story and the mythology of the tale to mix together. Even a hundred years later, what was truth and what was fiction were hard to tell apart. All that mattered was what happened to House Divinus was etched into the minds of new vampires. Don't fuck with the Houses."

"Okay—great history lesson," said Rosa. "But I'm presuming there's something here that connects this story to our case?"

Miles smirked at the lack of deference.

Drest heaved a sigh. "The bloodline gift for House Divinus was quite unique. They were able to turn themselves incorporeal. It only lasted moments for the youngest vampires—but for those who were older, they could phase in and out of reality with ease and precision."

"Jesus, Drest," Miles snarled. "So basically glitching. Which means Sara—and therefore Dominik—have some kind of link to a long-extinct vampire house?"

"That about sums it up," Drest said. "We spent years hunting anyone who was linked to what Divinus did in Pax. While humans might not have known what really happened back then, it took us centuries for them to stop fearing us just by hearing the word *vampire*. We're still not done on that part. It was also one of the points in vampire history that led to the full creation of the Assembly. We knew we needed to have someone who was keeping an eye on the Houses, that we couldn't just keep policing ourselves."

"Okay, so what does this all have to do with how I find Sara and stop her before she kills someone else?" Miles asked. "Or find Megan and her team? I assume you still haven't heard anything?"

The last sentence was said to Rosa, who checked her phone and shook her head sadly. "It's not looking good, though, is it?"

"You said northern Lithuania," Miles said. "That's where Megan's people were when they went missing."

"Coincidence?" Rosa asked.

"Or something more sinister?" Drest asked.

"I think heading to Lithuania when we don't actually know what we're getting into is a recipe for disaster," Miles said. "We need more information about Sara, about whoever she was working with. I'd say it's about time to search her house."

"What if they're expecting you?" Charlotte said. "What if Sara has booby-trapped her entire apartment in wait for someone to come look around?"

"Won't know until we try," Miles said.

"I don't disagree," Charlotte replied. "I also don't want you to rush over there."

"We have two issues," Drest interjected. "We have someone who has tried to take the lives of an Arbiter and an ATO team. They're unaccounted for. Miles survived his attack, so the likelihood is that they will try again. The second issue is that you can't keep just surviving attacks, and you can't just let them keep attacking either. At some point they're going to do something that brings a lot of attention their way, even more so than what happened in Oslo."

"They clearly don't care about innocent bystanders," Miles said. "They used desolate in the attack. Whatever their link to hundreds of years old atrocities, it's secondary to our need to stop them now."

Gideon scooped the book back across the table and returned it to his bag.

"Anything else?" Rosa asked. "I get the feeling there's something else."

"The Assembly," Miles said. "Look, we've all heard the tale about the vampire Houses that were destroyed because they committed a crime that was too big to allow them to continue, but does the Assembly know the truth?"

"Several of the Justices do, aye," Drest said. "It was made sure that they were on the panel who looked into Dominik's death. The story of House Divinus being expunged for committing horrific crimes loses its impact quite a bit if it turns out that we didn't quite do a good enough job to remove them all to begin with. Besides, humanity is finally on something of an upward trajectory when it comes to vampire relations; we would rather not have the whole tale of *why* House Divinus was expunged getting out. Maine was bad enough; let's not continuously remind humanity where they really sit in the food chain."

"Wait, the Justices are keeping the exact details of what happened to House Divinus from the larger Assembly personnel?" Rosa asked.

"Of course," Drest said. "The Justices don't share everything with those who work within the Assembly. They've been vampires for a long time, some almost as long as I have. A few were around when this all happened. They know where most of the skeletons are buried. Not all of them. Maybe a third. At most."

"A third of the skeletons, or a third of the Justices?" Rosa asked.

"Little of both, I think," Drest said.

"Where is Justice Balderas?" Miles asked.

"At his home in Bourges," Drest said.

"You trust him?" Miles asked.

"As much as I trust any of the Justices," Drest said. "He's a good man. I can say that much."

"Does he know what happened in Oslo?" Miles asked. "I haven't contacted him or anyone else yet. I wasn't sure who was behind the attack, and right now that's all it is. An attack on me and on Megan and her team. The Assembly is already looking into the latter."

"I've contacted him," Drest said. "I'll be sharing everything we know. He might want to see you once he learns what happened."

"Good idea," Miles said. "We can always go to see him after we've been to Sara's house. What are the other vampire Houses doing about this bloodline business?"

"Nothing yet," Drest said. "I'll talk to my allies and see if we can get some vampires from several Houses working together. We'll get you to London. We'll keep looking into trying to figure out just who turned Sara. Halime and her team will be on standby just in case you need her, although obviously if you're several hours of flight time away, you're going to be on your own for a while."

"Any chance House Divinus had something to do with Maine?" Rosa asked. "Just to make sure they haven't been around for hundreds of years doing evil shit and no one noticed."

Everyone remained quiet.

"So, that's a yes, then," Rosa said.

"It's a . . . possibility," Drest admitted. "We have no evidence to suggest they were involved in any aspect of what happened there. We thought this whole bloodline was done."

"Leaving aside something that we do not want to get involved in," Charlotte said, "do you actually have a plan after you've searched Sara's home? I assume you know the address?"

"It's in the official reports of the investigation," Miles said. "Marylebone, if memory serves."

"I'm coming with you," Charlotte said.

"Charlotte," Drest said.

"No," Charlotte replied. "Not as your First Counsel—as Miles's friend. He's going to need a few to watch his back. Rosa's, too. Even if I stay with you to look through Sara's home, it's an extra pair of eyes. After that, we'll figure out what to do. I won't be involved in anything involving Divinus itself, just helping a friend to ensure that he works by the letter of the law when searching the home of a possible terrorist."

"We're labelling them terrorists now?" Miles asked.

"They attacked a hotel," Gideon said. "They murdered innocent people. They are doing this for personal reasons, but it's completely possible there are wider political machinations involved here. We just don't know. Besides, should this all blow up in everyone's face, and we say we were helping track down a possible terrorist organisation, I think the Assembly would be a lot more inclined to look the other way."

"Man makes a point," Rosa said.

"Any chance your attacker lied about Sara's involvement?" Charlotte asked. "For unknown reasons?"

Miles shook his head. "I doubt it very much. As far as I'm concerned, she's our prime suspect until we figure out different. But right now, we need proof, and until we have it, we don't know who is and isn't involved."

"We have a lot of questions to get answers to," Drest said, standing. "Time to get to work."

Miles, Rosa, and Charlotte were joined by Church as they left the library. Charlotte had, it seemed, prepared a bag to take with her, having already decided to join Miles on his trip south. Drest didn't bother trying to stop her. Short of commanding her to stay, she wouldn't. And commanding Charlotte to do anything she didn't want to do would put a wedge between the pair, which no one wanted.

"Miles," Drest said, motioning for him to come over as Gideon made his excuses and walked away without another word.

"I'll catch up," Miles said, and went over to the First Lord of House Venator. "If you're about to tell me to keep Charlotte safe, I'm going to tell her, and she's going to yell at you."

"Charlotte can take care of herself, as you well know," Drest said with no humour in his voice.

"Can I assume she still hasn't bothered to elect a Blood Guard?" Miles asked.

"Of course not," Drest said, with the tone of someone who has experience of that exact conversation. Repeatedly. "I expect you, Church, and Rosa to keep Charlotte in one piece."

"She'll be fine," Miles told him. "Although I'd quite like her to keep me in one piece, too."

Drest smiled, although it only lasted a second. "Look, this *has* to stay out of public human knowledge. These people can't be handed over to anything close to the human authorities."

"Aye, I figured that bit out on my own," Miles said.

"Do you know what that means?"

"They will be dealt with, Drest," Miles said. "I know how to do my job."

"Aye, but how many people who work for the Assembly would sell these secrets to the human press?" Drest asked. "You know what needs to be done."

"Wherever these people are, they've hurt people I like. On top of that, they went after me. They killed innocent people. And more importantly, they tried to hurt Church. I'm going to find out where they are and stop them. Permanently. But I won't kill innocent people just in case the past gets out and humans might be scared of us again."

Drest nodded once as if understanding. "Be careful, Miles."

Miles forced a smile and walked back to the others, who were all waiting at the private airfield they'd arrived at. This time they were using a Chinook, albeit one with an extended fuel tank to ensure they could get to London without the need to refuel. The rotors on the Chinook were already spinning, and Miles briefly wondered how many of the vehicles Drest currently had. He pushed the thought aside, climbed aboard, and placed his headset on. Church came over and sat beside him, her head on his leg.

"Did he tell you to keep me safe?" Charlotte asked as the helicopter lifted off.

Miles looked over at Rosa, who with no headset had her eyes closed, getting a few hours of well-earned rest. He shook his head. "He wanted me to understand that this whole thing needs to stay out of humanity's view."

"Yeah, I don't really think that's going to be a problem," Charlotte said. "We can deal with all this without it becoming front page news. Vampires don't need more negative headlines."

"It would have been helpful if the Houses had just been open and honest with everyone back in the day," Miles said. "Might have given humanity less of a reason to be terrified of us if they knew that we'd gone out and removed the vampires who had killed them."

"You're preaching to the choir here, my friend," Charlotte said. "They even keep secrets from their own Firsts. Can you imagine the nonsense they must have gotten up to before the Assembly came along? The parts that aren't censored are bad enough, how bad must the rest of it be?"

"It's bad," Rosa said.

Miles looked over to see that Rosa had put on her headset. "I'm sorry you've been dragged into this."

Rosa shrugged. "The Assembly keeps its secrets, too. Lots of secrets in the vampire world. Lots of people who hold grudges over centuries, lots of people who would use what First Lord Drest told us as a way to show the Houses were always corrupt. There are people in the Assembly who want the Houses dissolved. Who want *only* the Assembly. I don't need to tell anyone how bad that idea would be. The police policing themselves never works."

"Doesn't the Inquisition police the Assembly?" Charlotte asked.

Rosa nodded. "And look how well that worked out with what happened in Seattle last year."

Miles remembered all too well. How some of the Inquisition had been in bed with Vedran and his allies. How many of them had been willing to sacrifice their own people for more power and wealth. He wasn't sure if he'd ever really trusted the Inquisition, but now he was pretty sure they were to be kept at arm's length if possible.

The conversation drifted off after that. Miles had to admit that the Assembly was less than perfect. Quite a lot less. But it was also considerably better than *not* having it. The Houses were not capable or trustworthy enough to police themselves, let alone one another. Miles closed his eyes and tried to rest, soon falling asleep.

❧ Chapter Twenty-One ❧

Miles had previously had dreams which had been close to prophetic, a swirl of nightmares given subconscious form. He had seen death and destruction, and had been unable to stop the future from ending up that way. The fact that the death and destruction came in the form of his enemies decimated before him gave him some solace about the dreams.

This time it was a forest, a burning forest. Everything was ablaze, and Miles was unable to withstand the heat as he walked close to it. He held up his hands to shield himself and saw the flickering embers of people within the inferno.

The heat disappeared in an instant, although the flames remained. Miles couldn't stop himself from taking a step into the flames. They felt cool to the touch, and he watched as they danced over his flesh, never burning him.

The flames extinguished with a gust of wind, quickly replaced by a freezing fog and snow. Miles was peppered with shards of ice, several of them leaving small cuts in his arms and hands, which healed immediately and hadn't even hurt to begin with.

The fire started to dissipate, revealing a stone mausoleum that Miles had never seen before. It was a large structure, with a sloping green tiled roof and stone gargoyles carved into the pale brick walls. The fire stopped at the door of the mausoleum, which opened, revealing a crypt. In the centre of which was a large stone sarcophagus, the lid firmly in place.

Miles found himself standing in front of the sarcophagus, the multitude of torches that sat around the crypt bursting to life. He looked around, finding himself on a mound of skulls. Thousands and thousands of skulls, the sarcophagus resting on top of them.

The wind and ice returned, twirling around him, gathering speed until a piece of ice whipped across Miles's face, leaving a thin line of blood across his cheek. "Enough!" Miles shouted.

The ice and snow immediately stopped, although the wind and fog remained mercifully just outside of the pile of skulls and sarcophagus.

"You should speak to Drest," a voice said from beyond the veil of fog. "He will tell you what you need to know."

"He told me everything I needed to know." Miles said.

The wind abruptly stopped, and a cloaked figure walked toward Miles. He carried no obvious weapon, but the level of power that flooded out of him made Miles take a step back, almost losing his footing on the skulls in the process.

"Ah, but did he tell you about me?" the figure said, and vanished in a flock of bats.

Miles woke and sat bolt upright. "What the fuck?" he said, looking around at the concern on the faces of those seated in the Chinook with him.

Charlotte pointed to the headset next to Miles, and after he'd put it on, she said, "You okay?"

Miles wasn't entirely sure what to say to that, so went with, "I don't know. Weird dreams."

"Prophetic?" Charlotte asked with more than a little concern.

"Maybe. I honestly don't know. It told me to talk to Drest."

"That's not helpful," she said.

"Maybe it's nothing," Miles told her, not entirely sure he believed it.

The Chinook landed at one of two helipads at London City Airport, and the four passengers disembarked. The weather was cold and overcast, but thankfully the rain held off. Charlotte spoke to the pilot and told them to wait until she returned. They could refuel while they waited.

Charlotte, Miles, Rosa, and Church left the airport using a private exit, where a BMW SUV waited for them. Charlotte drove the hour through London to Marylebone, and by the time they'd reached their destination, what had been a grey day was replaced with dark clouds and the opening salvo of rain.

Miles checked his phone. "Sunset is in three hours."

Rosa looked up as they walked toward the building where Sara's flat was. "I don't think it's going to make much difference. I like this time of year."

"The rain?" Charlotte asked.

"No, just being able to walk around during the day. Not worrying about UV levels and whether or not I'm going to burn. Can't do that during the summer, even a summer in the UK."

Charlotte and Rosa continued on to the building as Miles stood outside, looking up. The building had one three-bedroom penthouse, with an outside garden and a nice view of the surrounding areas, and the other four floors were made up of either one three-bedroom or a combination of two- and one-bedroom flats. Someone had made a lot of money buying the old building, renovating it, and selling it on as flats.

"Hey, Miles, what's up?" Rosa called out.

Miles raised a hand to say give him a second, and looked around. It was a busy neighbourhood, which summed up most of central London, but he'd noticed that Sara had picked a London borough with no vampire control.

"You okay?" Charlotte asked as she joined Miles.

"Just looking around," he said, studying the people passing by.

"You think she's watching us?" Charlotte asked.

"I doubt Sara herself is," he said. "She must have paid an absolute fortune for this place. She probably cleared out pretty quickly, but if I'd paid the asking price for this place, I'd probably want someone keeping an eye on it, just in case."

There were hundreds of people in the area, all walking around, doing completely normal-looking things, even as it rained. No one appeared to give Miles or his companions a second look. Maybe he was getting paranoid.

"Okay, let's go," he said, and followed Charlotte back over to a waiting Rosa.

Church rubbed her head against Miles's hand.

The group entered through the front entrance of the building, where they were stopped by a security guard who asked why they were there.

"I'll meet you up there," Miles whispered to Charlotte as she began to spout a lot of legalese at the unfortunate man.

"You okay?" Rosa asked.

"Got a plan," Miles said, before turning to Church. "Go with them."

Church barked as Miles left the building and walked around to the back, where there was an alleyway between the block of flats where Sara lived and a smaller two-storey building. The alleyway contained several large metal bins on wheels. Each one with a number for the corresponding apartment. Miles ignored the sounds of scurrying and looked up at the gap between the two buildings. He considered using his wings to fly up there, but it was still daylight and with the nearby population, he didn't want to have to bring any undue attention to himself. Quickly climbing up a few walls was one thing; flying up a near sixty-foot building in daylight was going to get noticed by someone. Besides, he hadn't checked his wings to see how they'd healed up.

Miles turned into his vampire side and quickly climbed the larger building, pulling himself up and over the penthouse's garden safety wall. He landed quietly on the roof and brushed himself down. He hadn't changed since the clean clothes he'd been given by Halime's people, and now he was covered in grey brick dust and grime.

The rooftop garden was spacious and meticulously tidy. There was patio furniture just outside of the windows that ran the length of the penthouse. Flower beds sat empty, waiting for the spring or summer to come to life, and there was a built-in barbecue which sat next to a white wooden cupboard.

Miles went over to the barbecue and opened the cupboard, revealing the gas canisters inside. He closed the cupboard and looked over the side of the building down on the city of London. High enough up that the wind would block out a lot of noise, especially on days like the one they were currently having. The wind whipped across the garden as the rain intensified.

He walked over to the sliding glass doors and tried the handle; locked. Miles had expected as much. He looked through the glass at the tidy living area, the spacious kitchen-dining area, and the closed doors that he presumed led to bathrooms, bedrooms, and the like. At first glance, everything appeared to be perfectly normal. He tapped the glass, which gave off a slightly odd sound. It was thick, certainly thicker than the kind of double glazing you saw on houses.

After a quick glance around, Miles grabbed the handle on the sliding door and pulled it. The door didn't move. He tried again, and once again the door didn't budge. The locks, and he was pretty sure it was more than one, were stronger than Miles. Sara had been keen on insuring that vampires couldn't get into her home.

He considered breaking the glass but didn't want to set off an alarm, so he searched the rest of the garden and waited the few minutes until the front door opened. Church ran up to the patio door, barking at it, as if annoyed it barred her.

Rosa and Charlotte walked over to the door, with Rosa brandishing a security card, which she pressed against the side of the sliding door, and pulled the door open.

"Ta-da," she said with a flourish.

Miles stepped inside the building, scratched Church behind her ear, and thanked Rosa.

"This whole floor has a bunch of security systems installed," Charlotte said. "The very nice man in the foyer pointed out to us that we'd need a security card to get in here. Apparently, it's company policy to not give one out unless accompanied by a warrant."

"Or by a Great House First Counsel," Rosa said.

"You threatened him with something," Miles said, walking around the open space and getting a feel for it. There was a smell of lavender that he found came from a plug-in air freshener.

"Many things," Charlotte said. "This place has a cleaning staff that comes once a week. They have a key. Now I have a key. Maybe you should have stayed with us."

"Maybe," Miles admitted. "Didn't know the door was vampire proof."

"There are four locks in here," Rosa said as she stared at the patio door. "The frame is some kind of metal, and the glass is . . . wait, is it bulletproof?"

"Maybe," Miles said. "The plug-in air freshener was replaced recently; it's still nearly full. I assume the cleaning staff."

"I would assume so," Charlotte said. "I'll take that door there."

"I'll take the other one," Rosa said.

Both women left Miles to search through the cupboards and drawers in the living and dining areas. He found nothing, and even Church let out a frustrated whine when she couldn't get a scent.

"This place has been scrubbed clean," Charlotte said from the doorway. "Going to look at the other bedrooms and come back."

"Nothing here, either," Rosa said. "No one has lived here in weeks, maybe longer."

Miles nodded as he closed a sideboard drawer. He dropped to his knees and looked under it, tapping the bottom of the sideboard, not expecting to find anything, but still coming away disappointed when there was nothing to find.

"This has been a waste of time," Rosa said.

"We now know that Sara hasn't been here in a while," Miles said. "We can cross this place off as somewhere important to the investigation."

Charlotte reappeared in the doorway. "Found something."

Church practically ran over to her, and Miles and Rosa followed into the last bedroom, which was little more than the size of a single bed. It was completely empty of anything except the same blinds used throughout the penthouse. Charlotte pointed up to an attic hatch above the bedroom doorway, in the dark hall they'd just walked down.

"This place has an attic?" Miles asked.

"I guess so," Charlotte said and jumped up to the hatch, unfastening it and landing back on the ground as the wooden hatch flopped down above her.

"Who wants to go first?" Rosa asked.

Miles jumped up, grabbed the entrance to the attic, and pulled himself up into the space. "Give me a second," he called down as his eyes quickly adjusted to the darkness. The attic space stretched the length of the hallway below and across the bedrooms to the right of where Miles crouched. Someone had brought up thick wooden planks and turned the attic into a small room. Albeit a room with uncomfortably low ceilings and a generally musky odour.

A small spotlight sat in the middle of the room, which Miles turned on, revealing the myriad of cobwebs all around the attic. At the end of the attic was a pale wooden cupboard about three feet tall and the same wide. Miles pulled open the two doors, revealing a number of ring-bound books. He pulled one at random and discovered it was a journal.

"Something good?" Charlotte asked from the hatch.

"Journals," Miles called back, taking one from the bottom row, and finding it was dated only a few months ago. He read the final entry and turned to Charlotte. "Sara liked to journal."

Charlotte took the journal, opened it at the space Miles pointed to, and read. "She knew she was going to give Dominik her bloodline gift."

Miles nodded.

"She *really* didn't want to do that," Charlotte said, passing the book over to Rosa as she joined them.

"*Dominik is already a monster,*" Rosa read. "*I know what I am, I know what my bloodline means, and at some point Dominik will bring the Assembly down on me. I had to turn him, I know that, he would have died, and I owe Henryk so much, but as I watch his son turn slowly into a vampire, I know that he will bring ruin down upon us all."*

"The rest of it doesn't sound any better," Miles said. "She didn't want to turn Dominik but did it anyway. And now she's turned a bunch of others into vampires and sent them after me. Didn't sound like she cared much about Dominik. Why so mad he died?"

Miles picked out another journal and flicked through it. "This one is from a few years ago," he said. "She's talking about how Henryk has a lab."

"What?" Charlotte asked.

Miles read, *"The Accreditation was a success. The Assembly wants to see more of what we can do. Henryk took that to mean spend more time up there in his lab."*

"There are labs in the Templar building," Charlotte said. "A whole bunch of them underground."

"What was he doing in there?" Miles asked, remembering he'd been told about the lower-level labs on his last visit. "Whatever it is, it has to do with the accreditation. Maybe someone who works there still knows more? Wait, if these labs are underground, why did she write *up there*?"

"A lab higher up in the building?" Charlotte asked. "You see one on your last visit?"

Miles thought back to the door with the facial scanner on the top floor. "Aye, although I'm unsure how we're getting in without Henryk."

"Ummm, we may have a problem," Rosa said, still reading from the most recent journal. "That wasn't the last entry. There's one a few weeks old."

"What does it say?" Charlotte asked.

"It's all a bit squiggly," Rosa said, squinting at the book. "I can't even tell if it's still Sara writing this, but here goes. *Why am I so angry? So consumed with rage and hate? I want to break it all. I want to break their faces, to hurt them for looking down on me. For thinking less of me. They took him from me. They took everything. I tried to fix it, tried to make it better, but now I'm broken. I'm going to break them all for what they've done."*

"That's not good," Miles said.

"Several of the words are written in caps, several are underlined," Rosa said, flipping a few more pages. "Oh. Oh dear."

"Is it worse?" Charlotte asked.

"Break them. Break them. Break them. Burn them. Hurt them. Pain, death, pain, death," Rosa read and looked up at Miles and Charlotte. "It goes on like that for a while until the last bit; *Blood for blood. Dozens dead. Dozens will die."*

"That it?" Miles asked.

Rosa nodded and passed the journal to Charlotte as though it was tainted with evil. All three of them remained quiet for a long moment as Charlotte flicked through the journal.

"Miles," Charlotte said, passing him the journal.

Miles looked down at the jumbled mass of hate written down on the page. "This doesn't feel like the Sara I met," he said eventually. "She was put together. She didn't strike me as someone who would write *blood for blood* fifty times and circle the words."

"You sure it's Sara?" Rosa asked. "Could be someone else. Maybe Dominik stayed here, maybe he wrote it all, Sara hid it, didn't want people to know what kind of vampire she'd just created."

Miles took photos of all the pages, and of the cupboard, before placing it all back inside and closing the doors, while Charlotte and Rosa took photos of the other journals.

When it was all done, and everything was back in its place, they left the attic, putting the hatch back. They all took a moment to stand quietly in the hallway as Miles stroked a confused Church, who licked his face and buried her head in his arms.

"If that's Dominik," Miles said eventually, "he killed a lot of people, but it sounded like he had no intention of stopping with those who tried to kill him."

"Could Sara be finishing the job?" Charlotte asked.

"Rosa, do we know where the two women we found in Southampton are?" Miles asked. "Jennifer and Pearl?"

"They went back to Southampton," Rosa said. "I think the ATO team stood down about a month ago. There was nothing out of the ordinary, but I can look into it."

"Can you look into them both, discreetly?" Miles said.

"Can do," Rosa said as she started looking on her phone, accessing the Assembly database to find out what she needed.

The four of them remained inside Sara's penthouse until they'd finished. "Both in Southampton," Rosa said first. "Same address. At least that's where they're both registered. So far nothing out of the ordinary. I've requested an ATO team head down there to check it out."

"You think that maybe they might want some backup?" Charlotte asked, getting to her feet, phone in hand.

"Can't hurt," Miles said.

Charlotte left to the rooftop, returning a short time later. "Done," she said. "Drest has some people in the South of England who can check. They're going to be a few hours, but they're good people. Halime's people."

"So, where to now?" Rosa asked, looking between Miles and Charlotte.

"Templar International," Miles said. "Rosa, can you look into who investigated the place last? I want to know if they went down to the labs."

"Anything else?" Rosa asked.

"Yeah, no need to be quiet about it," he said with a wry smile. "Let's see if we can shake some trees and see what falls out."

Chapter Twenty-Two

They took some time to go grab some food before going to Templar International. The sandwiches were overly expensive and decidedly unfulfilling, but it gave the three of them some time to sit and discuss how they were going to deal with Templar International should Henryk or Sara be there.

"You think it's likely that they'll be there?" Rosa asked as she finished her coffee and threw the cup in an arc, which ended as it landed in the bin twenty feet away, without touching the sides. She raised her arms in mock victory.

"I think it's less likely than you hitting that shot," Charlotte said, offering Rosa a fist bump, which was reciprocated.

The rain, which had thankfully held off for the few hours after they'd left Sara's penthouse, was beginning to make its comeback.

"Shall we?" Miles asked.

No one responded, but everyone got to their feet and walked back toward the parked car, where Charlotte took up driving duties again, and headed through London to the Southbank Tower. The traffic was still fairly heavy, and it took nearly an hour to make the five-mile-long journey, but Miles took the time to sit back in the car and figure out what he was going to say.

"Do you have a plan?" Rosa asked as the tower loomed into view ahead. "Any of you? I include Church in this."

Church barked.

Miles turned in his seat to look at Church, who barked again. "What's the plan?" he asked her.

Church grinned, showing her large, sharp teeth.

"We're not biting anyone," Miles said.

Church whimpered.

"Okay, we're not biting anyone as a first response," he corrected.

Church barked again, and Rosa laughed as Charlotte shook her head and smiled.

"There's a good chance you're going to get to bite someone at some point, Church," Miles said. "Probably soon."

Charlotte parked the car and everyone got out, the rain having started to come down heavier the longer they'd been in the dry.

"So, how do we do this?" Charlotte asked.

"We go in," Miles said. "I'll figure the rest out once there."

"That does not fill me with confidence," Charlotte pointed out.

"As his most recent handler for UK operations, I feel like this is how he always seems to work," Rosa said. "It has caused drama."

"Yeah, Miles and drama are old friends," Charlotte said with a chuckle.

"Didn't you threaten to cut the balls of a House Barbarous vampire who got a little bit too interested in being your friend?" Miles asked.

"He did not respect my personal space," Charlotte said. "Not drama."

"It was at a party for the Firsts of the Great Houses," Miles said. "If I remember correctly, it definitely caused a little drama."

"Okay, a little drama," Charlotte admitted. "It was worth it."

They walked into the foyer of the Templar International building, which had one young man sitting behind reception, reading something in front of him, his head low. Miles didn't recognise him from the last time he'd been here, but the lack of people, especially security, made him wonder what was happening.

Miles stopped at the desk. "Hi, I'm Miles, I'd like to . . . "

"Top floor," the receptionist said, finally looking up. He had blond hair, blue eyes, and the expression of someone who was already bored with whatever you were about to say.

"What?" Miles asked.

"You're wearing an Arbiter's torc," the man said, passing Miles a pass. "I've been told to tell anyone who comes who has one on and gives their name as Miles to go to the top floor. It's all been locked down for weeks. As of the last two days, there's only me. There was a skeleton crew, about fifty people. Guards, IT people, scientists, and then a week ago they all left. I got here in the morning, and there was no one else in the building. So I get to sit here for twelve hours a day and do nothing. This is the most boring job on earth."

"At least no one has tried to eat you," Charlotte said.

The man's expression became concerned. "Eat me? I came from an agency. Are you telling me I might get eaten?"

Charlotte moved her hand from side to side.

The man's eyes widened when he saw Church. "By that?"

"No, that's Church," Miles said. "She only eats people I tell her to."

Church barked, the noise echoing around the room.

"You should go home now," Charlotte said. "Leave the keys, we'll lock up."

"They left a note," the man said, suddenly very nervous. "Told me to sit here, keep quiet, and not explore the building under any circumstances. If a Miles arrives, you're to be told to go up to the penthouse."

"How do I get into the security vault?" Miles asked.

"The what?"

"The sealed room on the penthouse floor."

The man removed an envelope from beneath the desk and passed it to Miles, who opened it, revealing a six-digit code. Miles turned the paper over, but the code was all that it contained.

"Just told to give that to you," he said.

"Anything else?" Rosa asked.

"No one else is allowed in or out. I'm meant to tell people that there's some kind of bacterial infection in the floors above. Stop people going up. Except you, apparently."

"Go home," Miles said. "Pretend none of this happened."

The man practically leapt over the desk, throwing the keys behind him, and ran to the exit.

"Nice guy," Rosa said. "Little highly strung."

Miles tossed her the keys, and Rosa went to lock up. The four of them walked to the lifts, switching off the lights in the reception area as they went. The lift arrived, and Miles used the keycard to go up to the floor he'd been on before. Where he'd first met Sara and Henryk.

"This is clearly a trap," Charlotte said.

"Aye, it is," Miles said. "Rosa, when we're done here, can you find out which ATO team was on this building, and why they didn't bother mentioning that the entire building was empty apart from one highly strung receptionist?"

"Already on it," Rosa said, tapping away on her phone.

The doors opened, and the smell of death and blood poured into the lift. Church let out a low growl, and Rosa's fangs extended.

Miles, still looking human, exited the lift first, with Charlotte behind him. "You okay?" he asked Rosa, who was breathing deeply.

She gave him a thumbs-up as her fangs retracted, and she stepped out into the dark hallway beyond. "Wasn't expecting the shock to the system."

"Church, you take the lead," Miles said, and Church wordlessly moved forward, with Miles just behind, and Charlotte and Rosa a few steps behind them. They didn't stop to look at the destroyed works of art, the bloody handprints all across them, with more than a few pieces missing entirely. Church occasionally changed her movement slightly to avoid broken glass on the floor, but otherwise they made it to the end of the hallway without incident.

The smell of blood and death had increased exponentially the closer they got to the security door. Miles stopped and looked back at Rosa and Charlotte, who both looked prepared for whatever was about to happen. "Whatever we find behind here is going to be bad."

"Do it," Charlotte said.

Miles tapped the screen, which flickered to life. He tapped a button on the screen, which took him to a digital readout and a numeric pad. He inputted the six-digit code and pressed *Enter*, and the air locks on the door disengaged, letting Miles push the door open.

Church ran in and stopped a few feet inside the room as everyone else followed her. Miles had expected bad. He'd expected blood and dead bodies, but he hadn't expected . . . "What the actual fuck?" he whispered.

There was a large dark wooden table in the centre of a large open room. All the pieces of furniture—tables, chairs, a desk, and quite a lot of smaller items like beakers and microscopes—had been pushed to the sides. Around the table sat eight seats, half of which were filled by the decapitated bodies of people in tactical gear. Two more bodies, both missing their heads, were hung from hooks above each end of the table, the ends of the hooks puncturing out through their chests. All of the heads were piled in the centre of the table. Unpleasant things crawled around the mass of blood and gore, and black flies buzzed around.

"I . . . " Charlotte began and shrugged.

"You ever seen anything like this?" Rosa asked.

Miles had to admit that, aye, he'd seen some pretty awful stuff. The worst humanity and vampires had to offer, but all of what sat before him . . . that was new. "I guess we know what happened to the people Henryk sent to find Dominik," he said, recognising the faces of two of them.

"These were the people in Southampton who shot at Church?" Rosa asked.

Church growled.

Miles nodded and stroked the back of Church's head. "I know, girl," he said softly as he looked over to a wooden door on the far side of the room, next to a glass staircase that led down to the floor below.

Church whined as Miles continued to look around the room.

"She okay?" Rosa asked.

"There's too much blood," he said, looking over at the entrance to the labs and wondering exactly why Henryk would need his own lab. "It's everywhere. It's screwing with her sense of smell. Mine, too, for that matter, but hers is much more sensitive."

"You want me to take her out?" Rosa asked.

Miles looked down at Church. "You want to go back to the hallway?" he asked her.

Church shook her head, but rubbed her nose with her paw.

"We'll leave soon," Miles promised. "Let's see what we've been left."

"These people have been dead for a few days," Charlotte said, picking up one of the cups that lay on the table and sniffing the remaining contents. "Just before the attack on Miles and Megan's team, I would guess. These people were human. I think they were drugged—I can smell something off in the drink. They were murdered. And then they were displayed. Whoever did this is not someone who should be left to their own devices."

Miles crossed the room and pushed open the door, revealing a small cupboard full of medical equipment and scientific implements.

"Anything interesting?" Rosa asked.

"Drugs, a centrifuge, quite a lot of test tubes, and gloves, and masks, and nothing out of the ordinary," Miles said. "Go downstairs, I guess?"

"After you," Rosa said with a smile.

Miles descended the stairs and pushed open the metal door, which wasn't locked. The room beyond was fifty feet long, with six doors along one side, each one resembling the kind you'd find on a ship.

On the opposite side of the room were several computers on two separate desks, with each computer having three screens, none of which were currently on. Rosa immediately made a beeline for them, turning the computers on and waiting for them to boot up.

The room itself had a black and white tiled floor, along with bare walls, and a high ceiling. At the far end of the room were four large metal doors, one of which had dents in it the size of Miles's head. The side of the door was missing a few rivets.

"What the hell did that?" Charlotte asked.

"Nothing I want to meet."

"I found something," Rosa called. "I found *a lot* of somethings."

Miles and Charlotte hurried back to Rosa, who enlarged the video she'd been watching until it filled the entire thirty-two-inch screen, and pressed play.

"That's Henryk," Miles said as the missing man came into view. He was wearing green hospital scrubs, and paced up and down in front of the camera.

"This is day one," Henryk said, taking a seat in front of the computer. "I lost my boy; they took my accreditation. Well, I'm going to show them all. I'm going to finish the work the Assembly wanted me to do. I'm going to sell it to the highest bidder, and fuck those vampire pieces of shit." Henryk sighed. He looked tired and mentally exhausted.

"What did the Assembly want him to do?" Miles asked.

Rosa shrugged. "No clue, but it sounds like it was what got him the accreditation so quickly."

"Are there any more?" Charlotte asked.

Rosa minimised the video as it continued to play, showing the hundreds of videos in the file. "A few, yes."

"Try the last one," Miles said.

Rosa opened the video with the date of four months earlier, showing a considerably more haggard-looking Henryk, although he was still wearing his scrubs.

"The desolate are strange and terrifying creatures," Henryk said. "But they're also hardy, and when coupled with a Desolate Royal, capable of being used without fear of injury. The desolate never turn on their royal masters; they do as they are told; they protect their King or Queen without question.

"They can survive for weeks without sustenance, creating cocoons of their own body fluids to live in, a sort of hibernation until disturbed. But we've also found that if left in one of those cocoons for too long, they can metamorphose. They can grow larger and stronger. For years, we at Templar International have strived to make a device that would ensure that the desolate would no longer be a threat. That they could be controlled. That they are . . . oh, fuck it, I forgot the line. Sara, if you please."

Sara came into view wearing a black trouser suit. She had a smile on her face and an easygoing demeanour to her. "That they are something that can be used as a weapon of defence, and not just something to fear."

Henryk looked back at Sara. "That's right." He let out a deep breath. "I'll figure out the speech later. Let's do the active test, and then we can use the footage to hopefully make a lot of money."

"The Assembly will regret ever removing our accreditation," Sara said.

Henryk's smile was short lived. He stood and took Sara's hands in his. "Thank you for all of your help. I know Dominik's death was difficult for you, as he was one of your blood."

"I'm sorry I couldn't save him," Sara said softly.

"He facilitated his own demise," Henryk said sadly. "There's blame enough to go around. Maybe if I'd sent better people to find him, he'd still be alive. I heard the evidence from that Arbiter about what happened. I heard the evidence from that ATO commander, Megan. I wanted to hate them for it, but Dominik was always going to end up with a bullet in his head for killing or hurting the wrong person."

"I mean to contact Megan and her team," Sara said. "I've been thinking about them a lot. About what they found at the crime scenes before Dominik was stopped. I feel like I should reach out, apologise."

"You should if it'll help," Henryk said.

"The video is still on," Sara said, pointing to the computer.

"Oh for fuck's sake," Henryk said with a slight chuckle. "I'll fix it in editing."

Sara laughed.

"Are you ready to do this?" Henryk asked her, picking up a remote control from the desk and clicking a button, which turned the camera to an overhead one.

Miles looked up at the camera in the corner of the room. Did it feed outside of the lab? Were they being watched, right now?

"Right," Henryk said, opening a drawer on the desk and removing a small device that looked to Miles a bit like a black crown, with a circular metal part at the front. He showed it to the camera, before placing it around his forehead, attaching each end to one of his ears. "We're performing test number two six one. This will be a live test. Are we ready, Sara?"

"Yes, boss," Sara called out.

Henryk walked to the middle of the room, took a deep breath, and started talking. "I am currently wearing a desolate control device." He pointed to the circular metal object on his forehead, which started to pulse a bright red. "Now, to use this safely, we've installed a receiver in the skull of the desolate we use. The receiver needs to have the same frequency that the Desolate Royalty have, which gives them their control. It's a bit like telepathy, but it requires more scientific equipment to get right. The main thing is that this doesn't work on vampires. We are in the process of having this device used by vampires, but it doesn't quite work yet. Sara, release the test subject."

Sara moved over to the computer and clicked on the screen, which in turn activated the ship-like doors. A yellow light flashed above one door. The door hissed loudly as it opened, moving to the side by itself.

Miles watched as the desolate stepped out of the darkness of its cell and into the light. He stared at Henryk, before looking over to Sara and hissing loudly. The desolate wore no clothes, its sunken frame a mass of wiry muscle. Its face and long, spindly hands were caked in blood. It looked emaciated, but Miles knew from experience that it wasn't.

"How old do you think that desolate is?" Charlotte asked.

"Months at least," Miles said, as he watched the desolate make a tentative step toward Henryk.

"As you can see," Henryk continued, his concentration squarely on the desolate, "this desolate has been regularly fed. The cells here have a false back, where we can get behind and put food in for them. We want them healthy, or as healthy as the shambling dead can be."

The desolate took a step toward Henryk.

"Stop," Henryk commanded.

The desolate stopped, its head jerking from side to side as if it wasn't entirely sure why it was stopping.

"Kneel," Henryk said.

The desolate dropped to one knee.

"Stand," Henryk continued, now clearly in his element of showman.

The desolate once again did as it was told.

"As you can see," Henryk said, "the desolate is completely under my control. Release the next one, Sara."

Another of the doors slid open and a second desolate stepped out, before screaming in incandescent fury. It looked much like the first one, although this still had some remnants of black hair atop its head.

"Stop," Henryk said, and the second desolate did as it was told. "Sit."

The desolate sat.

"Stand," Henryk commanded.

This time both desolates stood.

"Superb," Henryk exclaimed, before an almighty smash as something pounded its fists against the metal doors at the end of the room and caught his attention. "Sit."

The desolates sat.

Henryk looked over at Sara. "Goddamn it, can you sort it out?"

"On it," Sara said. "She clicked something on the computer, accompanied by a muffled shriek of pain from behind one of the doors.

The desolates stood.

Henryk's gaze snapped back to the two desolates. "Sit," he commanded once again.

The desolates sat.

There was another series of muffled slams behind the metal door. Henryk walked over to the door, just as there was the sound of tearing metal and a loud *ping*. Henryk's head violently snapped to the side, the device on his head flying across the room.

The two desolates dove on Henryk in a heartbeat as the pounding behind the door continued unabated.

Henryk screamed as one of the desolates sank its fangs into his forearm, tearing free a chunk of flesh, while the other went for his stomach. Sara dove over the table, slamming into the nearest desolate, and throwing it back across the room, as she tried to help Henryk.

She grabbed the second desolate, who pushed her away with enough force that she flew back into the desk behind her. The desolate sank its fangs down in Henryk's exposed throat as the second leapt across the room.

Sara grabbed the device from the floor, put it on, and screamed, "Stop!"

The desolates stopped trying to tear Henryk to pieces and turned to Sara. They didn't look happy.

"Move over there," Sara commanded, pointing to the far wall.

The desolates did as they were told, although they never turned away from Sara, who dropped to her knees by a bleeding-out Henryk. The expression on Sara's face said all anyone would need to know about his condition.

One of the desolates stepped toward Sara—she heard the noise and spun toward them. "Kill yourself!" she screamed at them.

Both desolates roared at her in defiance.

"Kill . . ." Sara screamed in agony, her face contorted in pain as she dropped to the ground, clawing at her own face as she threw the device across the room. She was quickly in her vampire form as she writhed around the floor, but as soon as it had started, it ended. Sara leapt across the room at one of the desolates, sinking her fangs into its throat and taking a long drink, before smashing its head against the frame of their cell door over and over again, until what was left could no longer be called a head.

She screamed something unintelligible at the second desolate, who bowed its head and shuffled back into the cell. Sara stood alone in the room. She walked back over to Henryk, who was pretty clearly dead. She screamed in rage, looked over at the dead desolate, and tore it to pieces, drinking more of its blood.

"What the fuck?" Charlotte said.

"Oh this is bad," Miles said. "This is so bad."

The video ended with a blood-drenched Sara, standing in front of the computer. "Test failed," she said, and the screen went to black.

CHAPTER TWENTY-THREE

Church pawed at the back of Miles's leg as he, Rosa, and Charlotte stared at the computer screen.

"What the fuck did we just watch?" Charlotte asked quietly.

"I don't even know," Rosa said, looking through the drawers and finding a USB drive. She inserted it into the computer and started copying the files over. "Henryk was killed by desolates."

Miles nodded.

"Sara drank from a desolate," Charlotte said. "Fucking hell, Miles. Why would she do that?"

Vampires could not drink the blood of a desolate because it would link the mind of the desolate and the vampire, doing potentially untold damage to the psyche of the vampire. To drink as much as Sara had was unheard of.

"She'd be unhinged," Rosa said. "Right?"

Miles nodded. "I think it's worse than that. You saw what happened when she put that device on. It doesn't work for vampires. I think she . . ."

Church whined beside him.

The door to the room slammed shut and the lights switched off, replacing them with dark red emergency lighting.

"So, this would be the trap portion of the visit," Rosa said.

Miles looked over at the camera and flipped it off. "We need to figure out how to . . ."

There were several loud beeps as the large metal doors at the end of the room slowly slid open.

"Off the leash," Miles shouted at Church as Charlotte ran over to the entrance door and tried to pry it open.

"It's not budging right now," Charlotte called back.

"I'll see if there's a way in the computer," Rosa said.

Church dropped low, her hackles raised, her teeth bared for what was about to come.

Miles took two steps away from the computers when the first desolate almost fell into the room. Followed by another, and another, all looking around as if just woken from a deep slumber.

"Got a plan?" Charlotte asked as more desolate entered the room.

"Kill everything, don't die," Miles said as the desolate screamed.

A flood of death poured out from all four of the rooms opposite from where Miles, Charlotte, and Church stood. The snarling mass of corruption scrambled over one another to get to the vampires. All of them held their nerve; all of them waited until the desolate reached them. Sticking together was their only choice.

"Give me some time," Rosa said, turning away from the computer and sitting cross-legged on the ground as the sounds of the desolate filled the air.

"What the fuck?" Charlotte said. "Now isn't the time."

"Trust me," Rosa said, took a deep breath and let it out in one go.

"Church, keep Rosa safe," Miles said as the first desolates managed to untangle themselves from the horde and rushed toward him. He took hold of the office chairs beside him with his telekinesis and threw them at the desolates, knocking several of them back into others, and sending them sprawling once again.

Miles easily avoided the lunge of one desolate, slashing the creature across the face with his talons as he stepped by, removing a chunk of the monster's face and head in the process. Killing desolates was hard, bloody work, but while they were easier to kill than vampires, their sheer numbers usually overpowered a lone vampire attacker.

"Goddamn it," Charlotte said just before one desolate smashed into the nearest wall, leaving a bloody smear as it fell to the floor.

"You good?" Miles asked without risking a glance Charlotte's way.

"Fabuleux," she snapped, before reeling off a stream of obscenities in French. "I cannot do this all day."

Miles had been forced farther and farther to the side of the room, toward the ship-like doors. He grabbed a desolate by the throat, avoiding the snapping jaws of the creature, and used it as a javelin, throwing it back into the throng, before narrowly avoiding another desolate as it leapt toward him.

He rolled to the side and tore the face off one desolate with his talons. It wasn't going to kill it, and in fact the creature barely seemed to notice, only pausing for a second, but that was all Miles needed to telekinetically blast it back into the far end of the room, giving him some room to move.

Church moved from desolate to desolate, tearing out the backs of their legs and crushing their skulls as they fell. She moved fast, bouncing from one attack to another, never stopping, never slowing down.

Rosa was still on the floor, her head touching the ground as the air above her shimmered.

"What in the heavenly fuck is she doing?" Charlotte asked, using her secondary ability to telepathically turn off the minds of individual desolates. It didn't work for long, but long enough for her to kill those who fell without fear of being overwhelmed.

Miles knew that Rosa was from House Nix, the House of Demons. Their bloodline power allowed them to conjure entities. House Nix said they were Conjurations, small two-foot-high red creatures who were both sentient and intelligent enough to carry out whatever the vampire needed. They helped with defence and attacking, too, and Miles had seen a few of the little creatures scurry into battle at their master's order, protecting their vampires with their lives. He wasn't entirely sure how one little Conjuration was going to help against what was a seemingly never-ending mass of desolate. They must have been crammed into the rooms tight, before they were locked in. Dozens lay dead on the ground, but dozens more continued on, uninterested in their deceased brethren.

Miles was about to unleash his beast form, the lack of room to fly around be damned. The added strength and speed would be an asset against the desolate.

Before he could do it, Rosa said, "Bring them to ruin." Despite the fact that her words were a whisper, they bounced around the room. "Charlotte, Miles, get over here now. Church, you too."

Miles ran across the room, avoiding the desolate, completely unaware of whatever Rosa had planned, but trusting that she knew what she was doing.

Rosa had hold of Church, keeping her close, and Charlotte dove toward them as the air in the room shimmered, and there was a sound like the tearing of fabric.

"What the fuck?" Charlotte asked as something terrible stood before them. The creature was eight feet tall, with burned red skin and cloven hooves. It looked exactly how Miles had seen demons drawn, even with a long tail and huge black horns. It looked down toward Rosa, its face resembling a black skull, with burning orange in its eye sockets and the holes where it would have had a nose. It opened its mouth, and more orange spilled out.

It all took less than a second, but Miles just sat dumbfounded, unable to figure out what he was actually seeing as the creature moved its arm and a sword that was more lump of steel than actual blade appeared in his hand. It swung the blade through the desolate, who hadn't paused despite the newcomer's clear and obvious danger. The sword cleaved through the mass of creatures like cutting through paper, leaving the smell of burning flesh behind.

It swung the weapon as though it weighed nothing, moving with a grace and speed that Miles thought made it even more terrifying an opponent. The sword went through three more desolates, and the creature continued the swing, cutting through the walls of the room themselves, to bring it around to more desolate. Part of the ceiling collapsed, as the creature spun the sword back, cleaving through the locked door.

The creature moved around the crouched vampires, swinging the sword in all directions, tearing the desolate apart. Occasionally one would get close, and the creature would grab the desolate by the head, incinerating it, and tossing its body aside as it tumbled to ash.

As more and more of the normal desolates were killed, a larger one exited the room. This desolate was nearly eight feet tall, with huge clawed hands and glowing red eyes. It saw the demon and charged.

It wasn't so much a fight as a slaughter. The large desolate was utterly destroyed in moments, and by the time it was over, only a few stragglers remained. They too were soon more piles of ash. When it was done, the sword vanished, and the creature turned back to Rosa, who stood before it. The creature dropped to one knee, and Rosa placed her hand on its head, wincing as the heat from the skull burned her flesh.

"You are free to rest," she said.

"As my lady commands," the creature said in a deep booming voice before vanishing.

Charlotte and Miles stared at each other for a few seconds before looking over at Rosa, who had her hand clenched in a fist.

"What the hell?" Miles asked.

"House Nix make those cute little demon things," Charlotte said. "You know, the little, happy, bouncy things. House Nix does not make a fucking demon from the depths of hell."

"Same things," Rosa said.

"Bollocks," Miles said, getting to his feet. "You're telling me that those helpful little demons are the same as the . . . whatever that was?"

"A Greater Conjuration," Rosa said. "Yes, they are the same species. Just that mine is much, much older."

"Can all of House Nix do that?" Charlotte asked.

"No," Rosa said. "Just a few of us. And we're not exactly looked upon with envy and excitement. We're feared. It's why I work for the Assembly. Less judgment."

"Wait, House Nix isn't happy that there are people who can conjure a Greater Conjuration?" Miles asked. "Because I'll tell you, if I could do that, I'd have one with us all the time. Would you like your own Greater Conjuration, Church?"

Church looked around and shook her head.

"Dog makes a valid point," Charlotte said.

"We are considered to be too dangerous to keep around," Rosa said. "It takes us a long time to get used to bringing forth our entity. There have been incidents when someone brings one out at the wrong time, and it all goes a bit awful. It's a whole internal politics thing. Those of us who could do this were linked directly via bloodline to the old First Lord, and when she died, the new First Lord, who wasn't linked directly, decided that we were a link he would rather not have repeatedly shown in his face."

"That sucks," Miles said.

"It wasn't a great time for our House, or me personally. He's right about us being dangerous, though. I have to concentrate all the time to keep it under control. If I lose control, you've got thirty to sixty seconds of an unstoppable monster rampaging through wherever it is."

"Oh," Charlotte said.

"Yeah, it's not good," Rosa said. "Also, it talks to me when I sleep. Tells me to allow it freedom, tells me it can eliminate my enemies. Only really happens when I'm stressed or upset, though. Once a year, I have to let it out. Without control. Only way to keep it from trying to force its way out."

"This sounds worse and worse," Miles said. "Are you okay?"

Rosa nodded, although it didn't look particularly convincing. "I can't do that again now for about a month."

"That's a hell of a cooldown," Charlotte said.

Miles looked over at her. "Cooldown?"

"The council members have a D&D club; we get together once a month and defeat evil while rolling dice and drinking," Charlotte said by way of explanation.

"We should get out of here," Charlotte said.

"That big desolate," Rosa said as the group climbed over the remnants of the door and started up the stairs beyond. "I assume it's from a desolate who stayed in the cocoon?"

"That's my guess," Miles said, hoping he never had to meet one of those when there wasn't a House Nix Greater Conjuration around to deal with it.

"So, who locked us in?" Charlotte asked.

"Receptionist," they all said at once, with Church agreeing by way of bark.

They left the labs and ended up back in the blood-smelling hallway, continuing on to the penthouse suite, which Miles opened with a swift kick, breaking the lock. He was well beyond anything close to caring about someone else's property at that point.

The scene inside explained why the smell of death was so prevalent in the hallway. Henryk's decomposing corpse was lying on the couch, a dagger stuck up into his throat.

"Sara stopped him becoming desolate," Charlotte said.

Miles removed his phone from his pocket and called Justice Balderas, who answered quickly.

"Miles," he said, putting the phone on loudspeaker. "I assume you're not calling because of anything good."

"House Divinus," Miles said.

Justice Balderas was quiet for a few seconds, before he said, "Who else is there with you?"

Charlotte placed a finger to her lips.

"Rosa Sanchez," she said.

"Your handler," Justice Balderas said. "I assume this is to do with the attack on you and on Megan's team."

"Sara Bakos," Miles said. "She's of House Divinus bloodline. As was Dominik, despite people telling me to drop it and suggesting I didn't see what I saw."

"Can I assume you've spoken to Drest?"

"Aye," Miles said. "He told us what happened to House Divinus, but this isn't about them. We just watched a video about Henryk's death at the hands of some desolate, and Sara drinking their blood."

"Oh," Justice Balderas said. "That's not good at all."

"They'd been trying to control the desolate with a device. Sara put it on and started screaming," Miles said. "I think it doesn't work for vampires because there's some kind of feedback on it. It scrambled her brain, the vampire side figured *I need blood to heal*, and she went after the first bit of blood she needed to tear into."

"The desolate," Rosa said.

"They'd just killed Henryk," Miles said. "Sara isn't very old, and instinct driven by pure rage took over. Even if she'd figured out what she was doing, the second she linked minds with a desolate, she was screwed."

"It's that fast?" Rosa asked.

"You drink from a desolate, you take part of that mind into yours," Justice Balderas said. "It'll drive you insane. Over time. But once it starts, there's no stopping it."

"She had her faculties long enough to stop Henryk becoming one," Miles said, removing the dagger from Henryk's throat to check it. "Killed him with a heat-dagger. Probably barred anyone from coming up here, got as many people out as she could. Sara was functioning on rage and hate, but she knew at some point we'd come here to look for her. Set her trap a few days ago, probably just in case I survived and went hunting. Justice, this device to control the desolate, it's pretty similar to research that was being done in Maine."

There was silence for several seconds. "You think Henryk got hold of information from there?"

"I'm just saying it's a big coincidence," Miles said. "They were doing experiments on desolate, trying to make them controllable, trying to figure out if they could stop them from happening. If we hadn't come along, and those desolate had eventually been found by a bunch of human cops, we'd have had a repeat of Maine on our hands. Except in the middle of London."

"We'll look into it," the Justice said. "If there's any link, *at all*, we'll find it."

"Why go after Megan first?" Rosa asked after the obvious tension had started to evaporate from the conversation.

"Her brain is no longer Sara's," Miles said. "Whatever feelings and emotions she had beforehand are going to be turned up to eleven with no rhyme or reason. She was upset about Dominik's death, mostly it seemed because he'd been turned by her. She was thinking about Megan before Henryk died, before she drank from the desolate. I think that's why she went after her. Her brain turned the need to reach out and talk to someone into something dark and ugly. She's more desolate than vampire now. She needs finding and stopping before anyone else is hurt."

"You should know," Justice Balderas said, "we found the bodies of Megan's team in a burned-out van parked near a beach in Lithuania. I'm sorry."

"I didn't think it was going to have a happy ending," Miles said sadly.

Justice Balderas said nothing for a few seconds. "I'll get a cleanup team there as soon as possible. Are the desolate all dead?"

"Oh aye," Miles said, remembering the piles of ash after the Nix demon had finished. "Don't think you're going to find much left."

"What about the people who worked in the building?"

"I'd check with their other offices for missing employees," Miles said. "But I think most of the desolates will be people Sara had a grudge against. Maybe parts of the gang that the Wolf worked for."

"We can check into that. It boils down to an executive of Templar International turned a bunch of humans into desolates, on purpose, and left them in central London to use as a weapon against Assembly personnel," Justice Balderas said, speaking slowly, purposefully. The answer came through the phone speaker like a blunt weapon.

"Aye," Miles said, his own anger at what had happened, what *could* have happened, still a pit inside his stomach.

"Can you get to me in Bourges?" Justice Balderas asked. "We've been working to get intel on whatever happened in Lithuania, but after talking to Drest, I figured it's better to let you do your thing. Now, I think we need to figure out our next step, and I think it's going to involve you going to Lithuania."

"I'm beginning to get the same impression," Miles said.

"Take the Eurotrain," Balderas said. "Should be one running regularly through the night. Let me know when you're on board, and I'll have my people meet you at the station. And Miles, Rosa, be careful. Someone who will use the desolate like this, they don't have a limit to what they'll do."

"Why not a private jet?" Rosa asked. "We'd be there quicker."

"The European Assembly private jets are all in use," Balderas said. "Unless you wish to fly commercial in the morning, the train is the quickest way."

"Okay. See you soon," Miles said and ended the call.

"I'll stay here, coordinate things with the Assembly when they arrive," Charlotte said. "You really think Sara left those desolate for us?"

"I think they've been there for a while," Miles said. "But specifically, I think she's been cultivating desolate to use as weapons."

"Can we stop the vampire and desolate parts of Sara from merging further?" Charlotte asked.

"No," Miles said. "It's nae a repairable thing. Maybe House Umbra could make her comfortable, but it can't stop the dreams. That's where the big problem comes in. All of Sara's dreams will be about her. The old her. Screaming to be let out as she dies slowly every night, for months and months, until at the end, she just has an echo of who she used to be come to her every time she rests. It'll shatter her mind. She probably had a few months with moments of lucidity, and even now she'll have time when she's her old self, but she's not long before she's just a mass of jabbering nonsense. I've heard of a few who drank from a desolate who took their own lives. Walked out into the sunshine on a warm day, or walked into a fire. The vampire mind, it isn't meant to have this kind of stress put on it."

"That is so much worse than I thought," Charlotte said. "So whoever *that* is, it's not Sara."

"Not anymore," Miles said. "That's a fucked up mess of Sara and a desolate. Her already fractured psyche has turned into the world's most fucked up kaleidoscope. She needs me dead, because she thinks it'll bring her some comfort. It won't. Just like killing Megan didn't. And with Megan dead, I am now the focus of her wrath."

"She's dangerous," Charlotte said. "More so than I could have possibly imagined."

"I guess we know why the accreditation was done so quickly," Miles said. "If these people found a way to control the desolate, that would be worth the Assembly getting involved."

"We have no proof of that," Rosa said. "Although I've gotten everything I could from the computer, so maybe there's something on there. If there is, it would explain the speed of their accreditation, yes. That kind of tech could save lives . . . if used correctly."

"I'm going to Bourges, and get Justice Balderas to send a task force with us to find her," Miles said. "Before she decides to recreate this desolate weapon on a much bigger scale."

No one said anything for several moments. The idea of using the desolate as a weapon in a town or city was horrific, and would result in the deaths of countless innocent people.

"You think she will?" Rosa asked.

Miles shrugged. "I think right now, I'm her focus. I think we should keep it that way. She'll be hunting us. She doesn't care how I die, or who kills me, so long as I do."

"You are notoriously hard to kill," Charlotte said.

Miles allowed himself a smile. "Let's hope that stays true. Let Drest know what's going on. Once we're in Paris, we get out of that city quickly, too. Let's not give Sara any more options for chaos."

The four of them left the penthouse and took the lift down to the reception area, which was completely empty, the receptionist having run for it. Hopefully karma would catch up with him, because Miles had bigger things to worry about.

They decided to wait for a few minutes for the Assembly personnel to arrive so that they could explain what was going on. In the meantime, Charlotte took a call from Drest, giving her an excuse to be outside when the ATOs turned up.

Jonathan Holt and his team were the first on the scene, with Jonathan walking into reception and ordering his people to head upstairs, going floor by floor, to secure the whole building. Two more ATO teams turned up shortly after, followed by two Arbiters who both nodded Miles's way but didn't stay around to talk.

"You having a rough day?" Jonathan asked Miles and Rosa.

"That's one way of looking at it," Rosa said. "Thanks for coming so quickly."

"We were at an Assembly safe house, got the call to head over," Jonathan said, looking outside at the dark street beyond, before turning back to Miles and Rosa. "You don't need to be asked twice when the desolate are involved. We'll sweep it all, get everything tagged and bagged, and make this whole place look like no one was ever here. You staying to help? Could use the extra hand."

"Can't," Miles said. "Got a lead on who decided to use the desolate as a jack-in-the-box. Can't wait around."

"Hey, sorry about what happened in Oslo," Jonathan said. "If I'd known that there was going to be some kind of assault on a hotel, I'd have recommended somewhere else."

Miles knew that Jonathan was just trying to loosen the tension in the air, but the joke didn't quite land. "Been a long few days."

Jonathan patted Miles on the shoulder. "Okay, man, go get your bad guy. We'll get this lot dealt with."

Miles thanked him as Jonathan shook Rosa's hand. "You heading with Miles?"

Rosa nodded.

"Be careful, too," Jonathan said. "Sounds like you've gotten yourself into something dangerous."

Rosa smiled, and with Church beside her, they and Miles left the reception area and found Charlotte around the corner.

"I'm coming with you," Charlotte said. "Halime's people found the two women in Southampton. No indication that anything is amiss with them, but our people took them into protective custody. They're going to be taken to the estate. Nowhere safer."

"Good," Miles said as they all walked back to their car. "I thought you couldn't come with us."

Once everyone was inside the car, Charlotte said, "Like you said, this is bigger than just keeping a secret. I'll come with you to Justice Balderas's place, and hopefully together we can figure out how to find and stop Sara. Besides, if I went back now, I'd only worry about you all." She looked behind her and gave Church a stroke behind her ear. "You especially."

Church licked Charlotte's face.

"See?" Charlotte said. "I'm her favourite."

Church barked once and sat back in the seat.

Miles looked back at Church. "You say that now, but just wait until she's not here and you want a bath."

Church whined and laid her head on Rosa's lap, who started to stroke her. "He's such a meanie," Rosa said sympathetically.

"So, we're going to need another train ticket?" Miles asked.

"Nope," Charlotte said. "I'm flying. You're getting the train. I'm going to drive back to the airport and head back to Drest. I'm hoping that Gideon might know of something in his library about what we're dealing with, regarding Sara's mind."

"Good luck with that," Miles said.

Charlotte smiled. "Even so, I should probably be in France not long after you get there. Besides, you know you're being followed, yes? Figured you might want to have a chat with them before you left."

Miles tried his hardest not to look over at the parked BMW M3 on a nearby road, where four men sat inside, all watching the tower. He nodded. "Aye, I clocked them when we left."

"Any idea who it is?" Rosa asked.

Miles nodded. "Unfortunately. Can you drop us off at St Pancras station?"

"I can," Charlotte said, starting the engine and driving off toward a situation that Miles hoped he could defuse without having to kill anyone else.

Chapter Twenty-Four

St Pancras train station sat directly across the road from King's Cross train station, sharing a common underground. It was a beautiful red-bricked building that took up a large footprint, and the inside was just as impressive from an architectural point of view.

Charlotte pulled up outside the main entrance, and everyone else got out. Miles looked up at the clock high above him: nearly three AM. With the time difference for France, and the length of time it would take to get there, it was going to be dawn in Paris by the time they arrived. Miles checked the weather forecast on his phone and found that it was going to be a UV index of zero with long periods of heavy rain throughout most of the day.

"Vampire weather," Rosa said as Miles showed her his phone.

"I could do without the rain," Charlotte said. "Get enough while I'm here."

"Let me know when you're on the way," Miles said. "We all need to keep in contact here, just in case Sara decides to take another swipe at us while we're on the way."

Miles noticed the BMW pull up farther down the road.

"Is it going to be a problem?" Rosa asked.

Miles shook his head. "How long till the train?"

"Thirty minutes," Rosa said. "Enough time to get a coffee in their executive lounge, which is vampire friendly, according to the website. I've never caught this train before, so this is all new to me."

"It's two and a bit hours, and a large chunk of that is under the sea," Miles said. "Done it a few times. Charlotte, take care, see you in a few hours."

Charlotte said goodbye to Church, got back in the car, and headed off.

Church, Rosa, and Miles headed into the terminus, and with Rosa leading the way showing the tickets, the three of them were allowed through into an impressive lounge area. While the floor was slate grey, all of the furnishings were either cream or mahogany in colour.

The three of them sat at the far end of the long, narrow room, next to a spiral staircase that led up to the floor above. Miles and Rosa took the cream couch, and Church the red and white floor rug. They were all offered free food and drink, with both Miles and Rosa opting for a blood pouch, which was brought to them, as well as Church getting a bowl of water and a second, smaller bowl of shredded beef.

Miles's phone vibrated in his pocket. He removed it, reading the text from Charlotte: *At the helicopter.*

He replied, *Waiting for the train. See you soon,* and put the phone back in his pocket.

"We should have booked a later train," Rosa said. "We don't have time to try all of their freshly cooked food."

Miles finished his blood pouch and placed it beside Rosa's also empty pouch on the nearby table, both of which were quickly picked up by the staff.

When there were only ten minutes to go, the three of them continued on to the train, and quickly found their seats in the Business Premier section at the front. The train itself was navy blue and grey, with yellow highlights. It was a long train, capable of holding up to nine hundred people. Several of the coaches were vampire friendly, with the Business Premier section having tinted windows and blackout curtains. While Miles doubted many vampires used the service during the day, he had to admit it was nice that they considered vampires while designing it.

The seats in the Business Premier section were made from blue leather, and Miles sat opposite Rosa, facing the front of the train, with a table between them. Church lay under the table, her head poking out one end as she managed to squeeze herself into something approximating comfort. Miles was always impressed that despite her size, Church managed to squeeze herself into much smaller spaces than he would have thought possible.

A short time later, the train began to move out of the station, and Miles felt a little relief that the confrontation he assumed was going to happen didn't. There had been enough violence and pain for the last few days, and adding more to it wasn't something he wished for.

Miles closed his eyes for a moment, and his mind went back to the dream of standing in front of the sarcophagus, the crypt, the torches. The thousands of skulls.

"You okay?" Rosa asked.

Miles blinked and looked over at her. "Sorry," he said, glad he'd been woken up properly before the dream could take him fully. "Off in my own little world. I'm fine. The blood back in the lounge helped perk me up. How about you?"

Rosa considered the question for a moment before answering. "I don't know. This is the most death I've seen inflicted in . . . well, maybe ever. The hotel, the London office, it's all quite a lot to take in. I like being a handler mostly because I get to help while not actually being targeted myself."

"Sensible," Miles said.

Rosa smiled. "You'd think so, wouldn't you? How do you do it?"

"The killing, and running, and fighting, and generally living inches from someone trying to murder me?" he asked.

Rosa nodded. "That about sums it up. How?"

Miles exhaled. "I've fought my whole life. In one way or another. I was a soldier, a gang member, an assassin, a particularly unpleasant human, a librarian, a hunter, an investigator. Probably a few other things I can't remember, but they always involved fighting, or stopping others from fighting, or hunting down people who had been fighting. Sadly, you get used to the death and violence. Being a vampire actually makes it easier. I don't feel about it the way I might do as a human. The longer you're a vampire, the less it feels like something to worry about. That's what Drest told me."

"That's quite sad," Rosa said.

Miles looked out of the window at the darkness as the train moved through London, out into the English countryside, and on toward the Channel Tunnel in Folkestone. An hour and a half before going through the tunnel. He turned back to Rosa and nodded. "I guess it is. You know, after the whole bullshit with House Umbra and Vedran, I spent six whole months without having to kill anyone. Vampire or human. A whole six months, before those arseholes at the jewellery shop put me on a path to this mess."

"You ever think about taking time off?" Rosa asked as a member of the waiting staff came over with complimentary champagne and menus to pick which food they'd like.

The sigh that left Miles sounded as if it had been waiting for a chance to escape for a long time. "I tried that in Oslo, and it didn't exactly work out."

"So, that's it, you give up on the idea?" Rosa asked.

Miles chuckled. "When this is over, I think I'm going to take some time off. Just me and Church and the Scottish Highlands, and peace. It's going to be amazing."

Rosa knocked back her champagne in one swig. "Needed that."

Miles pushed his own champagne flute across the table. "Be my guest."

"Not a champagne drinker?" Rosa asked, taking a more measured drink of this one.

"Don't like fizzy alcohol," Miles said. "Or fizzy water for that matter. It's weird that someone thought making a drink fizzy was the way to go."

Rosa laughed. "That's quite the hill to die on."

"Ah, I have many hills which I can sacrifice myself upon," Miles said. "Fizzy alcohol is probably the smallest of them."

They both settled in for a comfortable ride, and having been placed at the front of the lengthy train, they could get out of the station in Paris first, too.

After ten minutes, the waiting staff collected their food order: cheese omelette for Rosa, and bacon sandwich for Miles, along with a pot of their strongest coffee to be shared between the two of them. A few minutes later, the food was delivered, along with a second bowl of water and some treats for Church, which she was eager to sample before going back to sleep.

"Nearly at the tunnel," Rosa said as the pair finished their food. "How long does it last under the sea?"

"About thirty minutes," Miles said. "If I remember correctly."

Rosa looked about the carriage. "We're the only ones here."

"Probably not a lot of people wanting a Channel crossing at four in the morning," Miles pointed out. "I can't even imagine many vampires use it. Bit too close to dawn."

"UV is still zero in Paris. Still lots of rain, even more in Bourges."

"Probably a good thing, otherwise we wouldn't be going via train."

The countryside outside changed to darkness as the train entered the tunnel.

Rosa and Miles sat in silence for a few minutes before Rosa said, "I think I recognise that man."

Miles looked behind him as Vlad walked into the carriage. "Oh, for fuck's sake, man," he said, having hoped that he wasn't going to have to put up with any more nonsense from the Umbra House's resident idiot.

Vlad wore a tailored black suit with a burgundy shirt. He sat on the opposite side of the aisle to where Rosa sat, staring at Miles.

"Can we talk?" he asked.

"No," Miles said, pouring himself a cup of coffee. "I've had a long few days. I'd like to sit here, drink my coffee, and not have to deal with anyone who thinks that fighting me is a good idea."

"The carriage beyond here is quiet," Vlad said, getting to his feet and brushing down his jacket. "You can either come with me to talk there, or I can move you."

Rosa looked up at Vlad and laughed. "Much as I'd love to watch you try, I'll tell you what, Vlad. I'll go take Church for a walk, and you sit here and talk to Miles."

"It's okay," Miles said, getting to his feet. "I could use the walk myself. You got your friends back there to help?"

"They are not a part of this," Vlad said. "They are only here to watch me in my triumph."

Rosa laughed again, placing her hand over her mouth to try and stop the sound. "I'm so sorry," she managed as Vlad glared at her. "It's just, I don't get to witness the last words of many people."

Vlad looked up at Miles, his chest puffed out, his hair immaculate. "Did you get dressed up for me?" Miles asked.

"The occasion needs to be dealt with accordingly," Vlad said.

"That's a really nice suit," Miles said as Vlad walked by him toward the end of the carriage.

Church looked up, snorted, and went back to sleep.

Miles left Rosa and Church and walked through the carriage to the one attached to it. It was also Business Premier, and it was also empty, except for the three men sitting around one table halfway down. They all wore navy suits and white shirts, and they all looked as if they were going to business school or the world's most boring party.

"They can stay there," Miles said, taking a seat next to the carriage door so he could keep an eye on them.

Vlad looked down at Miles and over to his backup. "They are not to interfere."

"You three vampires?" Miles asked.

One of the men, who had a shaved head and tattoo of a snake on his neck, nodded.

"You stay there," Miles said. "You move, it ends badly for you."

The man with the snake tattoo laughed, but his friend beside him locked eyes with Miles, and elbowed snake tattoo in the ribs, whispering for him to shut up.

"Do they know who I am?" Miles asked, rubbing his wrist where the torc sat in clear view.

"Arbiter and murderer," Vlad said, finally sitting down. "I am here for judgment."

"You're an idiot," Miles told him. "Have you got it officially sanctioned that you can come for an Arbiter?"

Vlad removed a piece of paper and placed it on the table. "All done."

Miles picked it up, read the form, which was legal, and saw the signature, which was stamped by Justice Balderas. In the wrong place.

"You stole the stamp of a Justice to do this?" Miles asked, looking over at the three idiots farther down the carriage. "Wow. Which one of you numpties did this? Do you know the punishment for forging the stamp of a Justice?"

Vlad's eyes showed the concern at having been found out.

"Yeah, you knew, you fuckin' idiot," Miles snapped, rolling the paper up into a ball and bouncing it off Vlad's head. "Look, you little bawbag, I am done playing with you. I'm nae here to make you feel better. Your hero was a murderer, a psychopath, and a monster. He died because of it. He died because he did so many stupid things that I actually lost count. He was partly responsible for the creation of a Desolate Queen. And at least several dozen desolates. He allied himself with people who want us dead, because he thought he could use them to further his own bullshit. I cannot stress enough how fucking idiotic this is. Go home, grow up, and find a hobby, because you don't want to fight me, Vlad."

Vlad stood, smoothed down his jacket, looked back at his friends, and threw a punch at Miles.

Miles had been expecting the attack, although the audacity of Vlad's assault was still a bit of a shock. Miles defected the blow, standing up, and elbowed Vlad in the stomach with enough power to send the younger vampire to the floor of the carriage.

Miles looked down on Vlad and up at his friends. "You move, you die. We clear?"

The snake tattoo guy nodded last, but the other two made up for it by looking as though they were trying to give themselves whiplash.

Vlad got back to his feet and shrugged off his jacket.

"Vlad," Miles said, trying for the last time to stop something stupid from happening, "I don't want to throw you headfirst through that window into the Channel Tunnel. I will. I just don't want to. Go home, lad."

Vlad turned to his vampire side and threw another punch, which Miles easily deflected. He moved toward his opponent, burying his fist in Vlad's stomach. The younger vampire dropped to his knees, and Miles kicked him onto his back. Placing one foot on the chest of the House Umbra vampire, pushing down hard enough to make the vampire wince, but not hard enough to crush his chest.

"I will have my vengeance," Vlad said.

"You're a persistent little idiot, I'll give you that," Miles said, before looking up to his friends. "You get him to the back of this train, and when we reach Paris, you take him home. Am I clear on this?"

No response.

"I asked you a fucking question," Miles shouted, making one of the three jump.

"Yes, sir," the vampire sat next to the snake tattoo said meekly.

Miles looked down at Vlad. "We're done here."

"We're never going to be done while you live," Vlad said, and Miles saw the knife in his hand as it flicked out of his pocket.

Miles stopped the knife with a telekinesis blast, took his foot off Vlad, and struck him in the chest with his bloodline gift, severing the vampire and the man. Vlad blinked twice as Miles lifted him to his feet, slapping him across the face, and splitting his lip.

"You understand now?" Miles asked.

"This won't stop me," Vlad said.

"For fuck's sake, Vlad!" one of the three friends shouted. "Just let it go."

"Never!" Vlad screamed, staring into Miles's eyes with unyielding hatred. "I will hunt you on the streets of Paris. You will never be safe."

"How'd you find out I was in Templar International?" Miles asked no one in particular.

"One of the Assembly Team agents called us," the vampire next to snake tattoo said. He was clearly the one of the three most uncomfortable with what was happening.

Vlad tried to headbutt Miles, who slapped him again. This time he used a lot more force than he had before, breaking Vlad's nose and jaw, and sending him to the ground with a thud as blood poured out of his ruined face.

"We're done here," Miles said. "I see any of you again in the next twenty-four hours, I kill all of you. Clear?"

Only Vlad didn't nod that time, although Miles realised that was because he was unconscious.

"Get out of my sight," Miles said, turning on his heel and leaving the carriage as the three young vampires helped move their hurt and unconscious friend.

"He going to live?" Rosa asked, having watched the events unfold from the other side of the partially frosted glass door dividing the carriages.

Miles nodded. "Hopefully, I never see him again. Or at least next time he realises the error of his ways and decides to find something more productive to do."

"That likely?" Rosa asked.

Miles looked back down the train as the four men disappeared from sight when the carriage door closed behind them. "No, he's not done. Too much anger, too much of a need to prove himself. But hopefully he's done for now. I doubt we'll be seeing him in Paris or Bourges. His friends value their lives a lot more than he does his, apparently."

The darkness of the tunnel outside turned into light as they exited on the French side of the line, where they were greeted by whatever storm currently sat over the area. Miles looked down at his hand. There was a smear of blood on his palm, presumably where he'd slapped Vlad. A lot of blood had been shed in only a few days, and he wanted this all over as quickly as possible. Thankfully, it wasn't long to go before they reached their destination. And from there, hopefully they would find a way to stop Sara and her allies before a lot more blood stained Miles's hands.

CHAPTER TWENTY-FIVE

The Paris Gare du Nord station was a beautiful building, and had Miles the time and energy, he may have considered looking around the exterior a little more. Instead, they hurried through the station, showing their IDs at the separate exit from anyone needing customs. One of the good things about being a vampire that few people considered was the lack of having to queue up when entering a new country. It was a small thing, but it always made Miles a little happy.

The three of them exited the station, where they were met by a young man in a snappy black suit and chauffeur cap. He walked over to them and smiled warmly, although he didn't offer a handshake. "Miles, Rosa, and Church, yes?" he asked in French. "Justice Balderas sent me. My name is George."

"Lead on, George," Rosa said in French, accompanied with a warm smile of her own.

The three followed George up the road to a private parking area, where Miles and Church got into the back of a black Audi Q7, with Rosa and George in the front. Even the short walk from the station was enough to get Church wet, and Miles knew she was dying to shake herself dry, but would wait until they were at their destination.

Considering that was a few hours away, it felt cruel to make her wait. "Go ahead," Miles said.

Church licked his hand and gave herself a shake, spraying a fine mist of water all over the leather seats and Miles.

"I'm sorry for the rain," George said. "It's been terrible here for days. I hope your visit isn't impacted by it."

"I've been in worse weather," Miles said, keeping to French himself.

He was fluent in several languages, and could get by in a few more. When he'd been human, he'd only known English, French, and Portuguese, but becoming a vampire had seemingly made it easier for him to learn languages. He still had to work at it, but it quickly felt more natural.

George drove through Paris at speed. The car had an Assembly diplomatic mark on the rear, just under the large window—a black A in a vermillion circle—so Miles knew that they wouldn't be disturbed by the local law once they saw it.

It was meant to be close to a three-hour drive from the station to Bourges, although they finally hit traffic as they were leaving the city, when they reached the point where they needed to cross the Seine.

"We were making good time, too," George said, slightly annoyed at having what Miles assumed was an everyday rush hour occurrence in Paris.

"Is it just the Justice at his home?" Miles asked.

"No, sir," George said, glancing back in the rearview mirror before aggressively changing lanes as they moved to get onto the A6b, practically cutting up another car in the process. "Justice Balderas has a full staff at his home. And Karine is always there. The Justice says he wouldn't be able to run his own life without her."

"She's important to the Justice then," Miles said, finding the amount of car horns that were being simultaneously beeped to be overkill. No one was going anywhere; he wasn't sure how beeping the horn was going to help.

"To us all," George said. "We've all worked for the Justice a long time, but she's been with him for even longer. Longer than I've been alive."

"How much do you know about why we're here?" Rosa asked.

George didn't answer for a few seconds as he navigated getting into the right lane. The traffic thinned out, and they were back to driving at high speed. "Not much at all," he said finally. "The Justice doesn't really inform us of his work. Except for Karine, obviously. I'm only his driver. He told me to meet you at the station, so I met you there. I drive you to his home. I don't ask questions about anything to do with work. I learned a long time ago that Assembly business is none of mine. You can both rest, we'll be there quickly."

The windows of the car were all tinted black, and Miles knew that even if the weather had been considerably warmer, he was perfectly safe in the back of the Q7 driving through the day, but he also knew *resting* was not currently an option.

The drive was pleasant, and once they were well outside of Paris, relatively free of other traffic. Church went to sleep on the floor of the Audi, and Rosa asked George if she could put the radio on, which was met with a thumbs-up. She flicked through the channels until she found one that, according to the display, played seventies hits, and settled back.

"A seventies music fan?" Miles asked.

"Music peaked in the seventies," Rosa said without looking back.

Miles wasn't really sure he agreed or disagreed, but he settled back as the sounds of a variety of genres accompanied the drive.

"Almost there," George said after a few hours.

Miles looked around at the empty countryside. "Where are we?" he asked.

"You'll soon see," George repeated with a hint of a smile. A few minutes later, he turned off down a side road populated with large evergreen trees on either side, casting a permanent shadow over the road. A minute after that, they turned a corner, the house coming into view ahead.

"Holy shit," Rosa said.

"*That* is where Justice Balderas lives?" Miles asked.

"Impressive, isn't it?" George said.

Impressive was underselling it. The property was huge, and consisted of one large château directly in front, and eight smaller buildings forming a circle around a patch of greenery in the centre, with the driveway sitting between the buildings and the green.

"Is all of this just for one man and his staff?" Rosa asked. "Because I'm *obviously* in the wrong job."

"The main house is straight ahead," George said as they started to drive around the green centre of the property, parking up outside the steps that led up to the house. He pointed to a long building next to the entrance. "That's the stables, and the two-storey building next to it is one of two guest houses. The other being on the opposite end of the property behind us."

Miles turned to look behind the car at the identical building. "What are the others for? There are two towers next to the main building."

"Guard stations," George said. "The building next to the guest house behind us is used by Assembly personnel when they come. It's usually staffed with ATOs whenever the Justice is here. The buildings on either side of the entrance are garages, and that small hut building next to one of them is a chapel, although I think it's only there because of historical significance."

"Where do you all live?" Rosa asked.

"We live in the wings of the main house," George said, pointing to the wings on either side of the large central building. "When it's just the staff, we tend to stay out of the main building unless we're preparing it or tidying up, but the amenities are all ours to use as we wish."

"Amenities?" Miles asked as a woman exited the building and walked down the stairs to the car.

"Swimming pool, sauna, tennis courts, that kind of thing," George said as the door beside Miles was opened.

"Miles Watson, I assume?" the woman asked in English, her French accent prominent.

Miles nodded. "This is Church and Rosa," he told her.

The woman smiled. She was of average height and build, with auburn hair and pale skin. She wore a diamond bracelet on one wrist and a plain golden ring on the other. She was dressed in a royal purple suit with black and red heels, and had the aura of someone who was used to people doing exactly what she told them to do. "My name is Karine Beaumont," she said in English.

"Pleasure to meet you, Karine," Miles said in French. "English isn't necessary."

"You all speak French?" Karine asked with notable happiness. "Apologies, but my English was never great. We all have those things we never quite pick up, no matter how hard we try."

"Golf," Rosa said, coming around the car and shaking Karine's hand. "Never could get it."

"Ah, it's not my chosen sport either," Karine admitted. "George, can you take the car to the garage and get it washed? It looks like you drove through a mudslide."

"It was raining, Karine," George said out of the window, before looking down at the mud-splattered car and wincing. "Okay."

"This is an incredible building," Rosa said as Karine motioned for everyone to follow her.

"Thank you," Karine said. "I know it isn't mine, but as I live here for so much of the year, it's nice to think of it as my home, too."

They reached the door, which Karine opened, revealing a small wooden-floored foyer and a grand staircase leading up to a small landing, before another set of stairs went up to the floor above. There were pieces of artwork adorning the wall, and at the landing sat a huge painting of wolves moving through a dark forest. Considering the size of the piece, Miles wondered if they were actually done to real-life scale.

"Would your dog like something to drink or eat?" Karine asked Miles.

"Her name is Church," Miles said in English, looking down at her. "You want food and drink?"

Church barked once, the sound echoing around the small foyer.

"That means yes," Miles told Karine in French.

"She understands?" Karine asked.

"English, aye," Miles said. "German, Gaelic, and Russian too, oddly. She probably understands more than we do. She may look like a dog, may act like a dog, but she's a lot more than any usual dog."

Church barked once more.

"Justice Balderas is down that hallway, second door on the left," Karine said. "I'll take Church to freshen up, if you like."

"Tell her," Miles said, pointing to Church.

Karine nodded and crouched down in front of Church. "Would you like food and drink?" she asked in English.

Church barked again.

Karine smiled broadly. "You are a smart dog."

Church licked her face.

"She will be safe with me," Karine told Miles through her laughter.

"I know," Miles said, seeing no need to mention that Church was more than capable of taking care of herself. He looked down at Church. "See you soon."

Karine and Church had gone a few paces when Miles called after her. "Is Charlotte here?"

"Oh, your friend arrived a short time ago," Karine said. "Go right in."

Miles and Rosa followed Karine's instructions, walking down a hallway with art on the walls and several life-sized bronze statues of soldiers in various types of armour. They passed by an open door, which had a pool table and four dark wooden chairs inside, and nothing else. The curtains were closed, keeping the room, and everything else they'd seen, in perpetual darkness.

The second door on the left was actually two doors, both painted white. One was open, revealing a study with a mahogany deck at the end, opposite the doorway. A circular table with four chairs sat in the centre of the room, all made from the same wood as the desk. The furnishings were a mixture of various colours of red and white; the cushions on the chairs were covered in roses. A red chaise lounge had been positioned under the window next to the desk, facing the door.

Miles knocked and beckoned for Rosa to enter the room first.

"Come, come," Justice Balderas said as Miles followed Rosa into the study, taking a moment to enjoy the floor-to-ceiling bookcases along the wall opposite the windows. The justice wore a dark grey suit and sat at a small table where food and drink had been brought. "Coffee?"

"Please," Rosa said, taking a seat opposite Justice Balderas.

"No, thank you," Miles said. "Some water would be nice."

The justice poured water from a metal pitcher into a glass, the ice clanking as it landed inside. Miles took the glass, nodded a thank-you, and went back to looking at the books.

"You can take the House out of the Librarian, but not the Librarian out of the House," Justice Balderas said with a smile.

"I appreciate a good bookshelf," Miles said, placing his cold glass on the table with a coaster, before removing a book from the shelves. "This is a history of the Assembly."

"An original copy," Justice Balderas said with no little pride. "Only a few left."

The book had been written a few hundred years after the Assembly's formation, and hadn't been as complimentary about their practices or creation as some in the organisation had wanted. It hadn't helped that the author had been trying to push an agenda, and had gone on record to say that the Assembly would destroy vampire kind. It was seen as a book that was largely out of date, offensive, and with little historical value. But within the ramblings and decidedly unpleasant and inaccurate statements, it still held value as a reminder of much worse days.

"I like to read it every now and again," Justice Balderas said. "Mostly when I've had a long day and need some levity."

"Didn't the author suggest that vampires who joined the Assembly should be burned at the stake?" Rosa asked.

"Among other things," Charlotte said from the doorway. She walked over and hugged Miles and Rosa. "Did you get started without me? Also, where's Church?"

"Eating," Miles said. "She's had a long few days. And we just got here, so I was admiring the books."

"I guess we should start," Justice Balderas said. "Charlotte has brought me up to date on everything involving Sara Bakos and what she did in Oslo and London. Using the desolate as weapons against vampires isn't exactly a new tactic, but it is one that will get her executed. When we find her."

"Did she tell you about the little home movie we watched?" Miles asked.

Justice Balderas nodded. "I hear you have evidence of it. That true?"

"Yes," Rosa said, although she didn't take the drive out of her pocket.

"That's fine, we can look through it later," Justice Balderas continued. "If Templar International managed to find a way to control the desolate, then yes, it would be grounds for fast-tracking an accreditation."

"The Assembly knew what they were experimenting on," Miles said.

"Almost certainly," Justice Balderas said. "As sad as it is how it ended for Sara and Henryk, that research really could save lives. So long as it was done for research purposes, and not because someone in the Assembly wanted a new weapon."

No one spoke for several moments, until Justice Balderas said, "But we have more immediate matters. Stopping Sara before she hurts more people."

"There's no way she's going to stop," Miles said, taking a seat next to Charlotte and Rosa.

Justice Balderas nodded sadly. "We've had the village that Megan and her team went to scoured. Found nothing. An ATO team did it. You know of Jonathan Holt?"

"Wait, he was in London yesterday," Miles said. "Or this morning. Whatever one of those is true."

"He's the commanding officer of three separate teams," Justice Balderas said. "Twenty-seven members in total. But they're all good at their jobs, and were recommended by one of the other Justices to look for Megan. Nothing to be found. No signs of vampires living there, either. Not really sure where to go from there. We know they're not going to be using the London office again, and it's doubtful that Sara or her allies will be turning up at any other offices. Templar International has officially had its assets frozen as of about an hour ago. Everyone working for them has been told to stay at home. There are hundreds of employees, so it's going to take time to interview them all. Hell, it's going to take time to *find* them all. It's not a small company."

"Anything else?" Miles asked.

"We're looking into the Wolf and his associates," Justice Balderas said. "Trying to figure out if anyone has gone missing. They stole from Templar International, and it's possible that Sara in her current state wanted vengeance on anyone who had done them wrong."

"We also need to talk to Gideon," Charlotte said. "He's been tracking Sara's bloodline, and he thinks he's got something that might help us."

Miles suppressed a groan as Justice Balderas used a remote control to bring down a projection screen which covered the wall beside the four of them. With the push of another button, the lights in the room dimmed and video call software launched. A few seconds later, Gideon appeared on screen.

"Are you wearing a smoking jacket?" Miles asked about the plush purple velvet coat that Gideon wore.

"Of course," Gideon said.

"And a cravat?" Miles continued.

"I like to be stylish, Miles," Gideon said. "I like to look my best for my audience."

"To move things on," Charlotte said, "what have you found?"

"First of all, it's a pleasure to meet you, Justice Balderas," Gideon said. "May I say, it's been a long-held belief of mine that the Justices are the pinnacle of vampire law and order."

"That was the idea," Justice Balderas said.

"Gideon," Charlotte said, her tone impatient. "What did you find?"

Gideon looked a little ruffled at having his ass-kissery interrupted, but continued a moment later as if nothing had happened. "I found a few things. We have an extensive collection of vampire genealogy here."

Charlotte and Miles shared a look of wondering if they could get this conversation to hurry up, but before either of them could speak, there was a knock at the door, and Karine entered. "Apologies for the interruption, but we have a phone call."

"I'll see to it," Justice Balderas said.

"Sorry, sir, it's for Rosa," Karine said.

Everyone turned to Rosa, who looked genuinely surprised. "Who is it?"

"Apparently, it's a member of the Assembly," Karine said. "They didn't want to give their name because this is against protocol, but it's to do with the Templar International building and something they found."

"How'd they know I was here?" Rosa asked. "I didn't tell anyone."

No one had an answer to that, but Rosa got up and left the room anyway, leaving Gideon to continue his talk.

"We need to be careful about this," Gideon said. "Publicly going all guns blazing on Sara and her allies could bring to light what happened all those centuries ago. It could stoke fear and resentment between humans and vampire communities."

"I agree," Justice Balderas said. "We need a careful approach to deal with this issue."

"Okay, so getting back to the matter at hand," Charlotte said. "What did you find?"

"Sara's bloodline, that of House Divinus, is a mess even for our records, as you know," Gideon said. "I decided to look into her own history, and see what I could find there, and to the surprise of no one, the KGB weren't exactly forthcoming with the meticulous details they kept on the people who worked for them. Even so, there are instances of the KGB using vampires for operations that humans simply wouldn't survive. I contacted a friend who still lives in Russia. He worked with them at the time, and he confirmed that there were groups of humans who were turned into vampires to run operations. But that they didn't use any of the Great or Minor Houses to do it. In case it led back to the Assembly, or the Houses themselves."

"What happened to the vampires they used?" Charlotte asked.

"Some were killed, some escaped and were never seen again," Gideon said. "But it's not outside of possibility that one of them is working with Sara after having turned her. But what's most interesting is this."

The image on the screen changed to one of the badges that Miles had seen on the beret of one of the attackers in Oslo.

"You found out who it is?" Miles asked.

"They're a vampire operations unit formed out of the KGB," Gideon said. "I showed it to my friend, and he told me that there was a vampire who led the unit. He was a chatty guy, but scary, and he once saw him turn ghostly. He said he was transferred to another area a few days later. Told to forget everything he saw. I showed him a picture of Sara. He confirmed she was a part of the unit."

"So, how did an ex-KGB operative leave and end up working security for Templar International?" Charlotte asked.

"I asked the same question," Gideon said. "He told me there's no such thing as an ex-KGB operative, which we've all heard a hundred times in our lives, but he also said that the group was tight-knit. If she went to Templar International, the others went with her."

"Like the guy leading the attack in Oslo," Miles said.

"Not to say they all work for the same company," Gideon said. "But there's a possibility they've all remained a network for reasons we don't really understand yet."

"So, there's a possibility that if we go after Sara, that triggers the whole team to do something awful?" Justice Balderas asked. "I'm just thinking worst-case scenario."

"I mean, it's possible," Gideon said. "I'm going to do some more digging, hopefully find someone who might have a clue what's going on. All I know is that Sara and her old team didn't just disband, and Sara is using at least some of those members to carry out the attacks."

Miles was about to say something when he paused. "You hear that?" he asked, looking around the room.

"Hear what?" Gideon asked.

"Yeah," Charlotte said, concentrating.

"An engine," Justice Balderas said. "No, not an engine, a helicopter."

"One of yours?" Miles asked Charlotte. "Drest sending anyone else here?"

Charlotte shook her head.

"Are you expecting anyone else?" Miles asked Justice Balderas.

"Is there a problem?" Gideon asked.

"I don't know yet," Miles said, getting to his feet and walking over to the window. He moved the curtain a fraction just in case the sunlight was strong, and found that the rain was beginning to get heavier and heavier. He looked out over the rear of the property. There was a lake, tennis courts, a swimming pool, and a lot of forest, but in the distance, heading toward them at speed, was the unmistakable shape of a helicopter. Miles opened the curtains fully and stared at the approaching aircraft.

Another knock on the door, and Karine poked her head around the door. "My apologies, the person on the phone would like to talk to you too, Justice."

Justice Balderas came to stand beside Miles. "That's odd," he said. "Let me go speak to whoever it is, maybe we're expecting someone. It happens fairly regularly."

As the Justice left the room, Miles turned back to Charlotte, whose eyes opened wide in horror. He turned back to see the streaking missile as it flew toward them at a speed that made it impossible to get out of the way. Miles moved toward Charlotte, grabbing her and pulling her over the desk just as the missile hit the room, turning it into an inferno.

Chapter Twenty-Six

Miles's entire body was in agony. The blast had thrown the desk back at the far wall, smashing into Miles and Charlotte in the process. He had turned into his vampire beast form, using his wings to cover Charlotte, but the shock wave had been enough to knock them both out.

He didn't know it at the time, but there had been two missiles, with one exploding just outside the room itself—the one that did the damage to Miles and Charlotte—and the second one hitting the wall just above the window. The fact that both had missed actually entering the room had more than likely saved the lives of both inhabitants.

The ceiling above where Miles and Charlotte lay had collapsed, covering the pair in dust, brick, and detritus from the explosion. No longer able to keep the weight it held, a steel beam had crashed through the wall, bringing with it several tonnes of château.

Miles remained in his beast form, heat radiating off his body, his clothes torn apart as he'd transformed. He crouched above Charlotte, holding the steel beam in place, keeping the floor above from completely collapsing onto them. As much as the pain from the blast had torn through his body, the weight above him was beginning to push him down, and he didn't know how much longer he could stay where he was.

Charlotte was unconscious, unmoving, and had blood covering her face and hair. Miles could see one large cut across the side of her head, by her ear. He looked across what had been the study and saw the outside, heard the pattering of heavy rain from above. He looked up, and there was a gap big enough that he could fly out. Fly both of them out. He considered grabbing Charlotte and doing just that, but he wasn't sure he could be quick enough to grab her *and* fly out, before everything collapsed on top of them. He needed her awake, needed her to move over to him, to take hold of him so he didn't have to let go of the beam until the last second.

"Charlotte," Miles said through gritted teeth. "We need to get out of here." He didn't bother adding that he needed to find Church, needed to find Rosa and Justice Balderas, to make sure his people were safe. To make sure everyone was safe.

He looked up at the sound of a helicopter overhead. He'd been deafened from the blast and was only now able to hear again. Probably seconds in real time, but it felt longer.

"Charlotte," Miles said, his body straining as something moved above, causing the weight balance to shift. He dropped to one knee, the beam digging into the flesh at the back of his neck and shoulder. He roared in a mixture of rage and pain, and shifted the weight enough to stop the latter from lacing across his back.

Gunfire erupted from somewhere outside, somewhere close; it was difficult to tell with so much debris around them.

"Charlotte!" Miles shouted.

Charlotte made a murmuring noise and opened one eye. She blinked, wiping blood out of it with her free hand. "Miles?" she asked.

"You need to grab hold of me," Miles said.

"You're not that kind of friend," Charlotte said in a dreamlike tone.

"Charlotte, I am not . . ." Miles paused, and shouted in French, "Goddamn it, Charlotte, open your fucking eyes!"

Charlotte looked up at Miles, and a flash of anger crossed her face. "How dare . . ." She stopped and looked around. "What the fucking hell?"

"Grab hold of me," Miles said. "Or we both get turned to vampire pancakes in the next few minutes."

Charlotte blinked several times, opened her mouth, closed it, sat up, and grabbed Miles around the torso.

"This might not feel great," Miles whispered to her.

"Do it," she said.

Miles braced his legs, shifting down slightly, feeling the tension in them. He brought the beam down slowly, then explosively pushed it up. His wings beat once, twice, and a third time, launching himself off the floor and up through the carnage around him.

Once there was enough space, Miles beat his wings once more, sending him and Charlotte into the sky. The sun was overcast, the rain now a torrent. He looked down at the destruction of the southern part of Justice Balderas's home. The entire upper floor and roof directly above the study had collapsed down, leaving a jagged, raw wound in the building.

Miles unfurled his wings and beat them once more, surveying the devastation all around the property. The helicopter that Charlotte had arrived in was aflame, as were the guest houses they'd driven past only a short time ago. The helicopter that had presumably attacked them had landed in the front garden, and on the horizon a second helicopter was flying away.

Miles looked down at Charlotte, who was staring up at him. "You okay?"

She nodded. "You?"

Miles shook his head, and slowly landed outside of the ruined floor they'd just left. Charlotte dropped to the ground, and Miles noticed for the first time the large cut on the back of her leg. It had stopped bleeding, but like the rest of her wounds, she would need time. He turned to look behind him, and Charlotte gasped.

"Miles," she said softly. "Your back is . . . oh, Miles."

"I'll be fine," Miles said, fully aware that his back was a mass of wounds, of burned flesh, of blood. "I need to find everyone else. Need to find Church. Can you see if you can get upstairs and find anyone still there? I'll go toward the kitchen on the east wing."

"I can," Charlotte said, wincing as she stood.

More gunshots, automatic fire this time. A scream.

Miles looked back at Charlotte. "I'll see you soon." Before she could speak, he'd beaten his wings again and taken flight. He flew over the building, spotting the soldier next to the helicopter. He had a rifle in one hand but was otherwise nonchalant.

Miles flew to the side of the main house, staying above the outer buildings, until he turned and flew across the driveway, over the grass in the centre, and down at high speed. He folded his wings back as he hit the soldier like a bullet, grabbing hold of him by the neck and slamming him down into the ground.

Grass and mud were thrown up into the air, as Miles released the soldier's throat, took hold of the rifle, and used it to swing the soldier headfirst into the helicopter, breaking his wrist with his free hand.

"How many?" Miles asked as he crouched, his voice raw and full of rage. He removed a machete from the rear of the helicopter and held it against the man's throat.

The soldier looked back at Miles, who broke his arm at the elbow, before moving on to his shoulder and tearing it out the socket.

"How. Many." Miles ignored the cries of pain and kicked out the back of the soldier's knee, stamped down on his calf, and with his talons slashed across his Achilles.

"Eight including me!" the man said, screaming.

"Thank you," Miles told him, and cut off his head with one vicious stroke of the machete.

Miles looked over at the garage, where he spotted George's body on the gravel just outside the door. The vampire had been decapitated, his face looking across at where Miles stood. Miles roared as pure, white-hot rage filled his body. He turned toward the main house, beat his wings once, and flew at it low and fast.

He wrapped his wings around him as he hit the set of double windows on the right of the main entrance. Miles had spotted movement inside and was no longer interested in being quiet. He wanted them to know what was coming.

The soldier didn't get his automatic rifle up in time as Miles smashed into him, taking him off his feet and tearing the rifle out of the soldier's hands, tossing it behind him as he drove the soldier through the wall into the hallway beyond.

Before the soldier could react, Miles smashed his taloned hands into his throat, taking hold and tearing the vampire soldier's head off. Miles, now bathed in the blood of not only himself and Charlotte but of his enemies, walked down the hallway, carrying the decapitated head of the soldier. He didn't care about rules, he didn't care about what was right and wrong, all he cared about was pure, undiluted vengeance.

A soldier stepped out of a room farther down the hallway, saw Miles, and raised his rifle. Miles threw the head at him, which surprised the would-be attacker, giving Miles enough time to fly down the hall and tear into the soldier's chest and throat, the stab-proof vest proving no protection against Miles's talons. He threw him back into the room where several of Justice Balderas's people lay dead and continued the assault, until the vampire was dead, his head removed from his shoulders.

Gunfire tore through the wall beside Miles, who jumped back into the hallway until it was done.

"You think they're dead?" someone shouted from inside the room where the gunfire had originated.

"Go check," a second voice said.

Cowards, Miles thought, feeling the rage fill him once more as he inter-cepted the soldier leaving the room, tearing the rifle out of his hands. He smashed the butt of his rifle into the man's head over and over, until the rifle's stock snapped, and he drove the jagged edge into his brain, kicking him back into the room toward the other soldier, who began firing wildly.

Miles stalked back into the room he'd just left, crouched low, and let his wings flutter beside him. His wings beat once, and he took off through the window, moving at incredible speed. He hit the ground outside, rolled to the floor, turned toward the window of the room beside the one he'd left, beat his wings again, and tore through the glass, his talons ripping through the face of the soldier who had been close by.

The soldier fired blindly into the room, but Miles caught his arm before he could get close to aiming at him. He took the soldier by the throat, lifting him off the ground with one hand. With his talons, he cut off the hand which held the gun, before throwing the soldier across the room with enough force to launch him through the wall next to the door.

Miles left the room and used a telekinetic blast on the soldier as he scrambled away, pinning him to the ground. Walking over, he used teleki-nesis to flip the soldier onto his back before crushing his skull beneath his boot.

Five dead of eight. Three to go.

Miles stalked the hallway until he reached the kitchen, and stepped into a scene straight out of a horror movie. Blood drenched every sur-face. Bodies littered the floor, most shot in the head, but two had their heads crushed, bite marks around their faces and throats. "Church!" Miles shouted, looking around.

There was a bark deeper in the house, and Miles set off at a sprint down the hallway beyond the kitchen.

"Church!" Miles shouted again, turning back from his beast form to a more human appearance. His heart was in his throat. Was Church okay?

Church ran out of a room at the far end of the corridor and bounded down toward Miles, who dropped to his knees and welcomed her.

"You're covered in blood," Miles said.

Church barked, turned, and ran back down the hallway, with Miles fol-lowing behind into the room at the far east of the building. The room was a bedroom next to a set of stairs that led to the floor above. The bed had been overturned, the furnishings used as a makeshift barricade to bar the door. Karine was inside; blood saturated her arm and face. She'd taken a blade to the shoulder and was lucky it hadn't severed the limb.

"Karine," Miles said, "are . . ." He stopped when he saw the body of an elderly-appearing male vampire. Bullets littered his torso, the telltale marks of heat rounds around the skin. Someone had hacked at his neck with a bladed weapon, leaving him almost decapitated. Age mattered little against such attacks; even Miles couldn't think of many who would have survived the assault.

"Where's the Justice?" Karine asked.

"I don't know," Miles said. "Are you okay?"

"He tried to stop them hurting me," Karine said softly. "Rosa and me."

"Where's Rosa?" Miles asked, noticing.

"She was dragged away," Karine said. "I don't know why."

"The second helicopter," Miles said. "Fuck. There's apparently another soldier . . ."

More gunfire, this time from upstairs.

"Stay here," Miles said to Church. "Keep her safe."

Miles ran out of the room and up the stairs, running toward more gunfire, accompanied by the sounds of fighting. A soldier ran out of one of the rooms, saw Miles coming toward him, and fired. Miles dove through the door of the closest room, but not quickly enough to avoid the bullet that hit his shoulder.

The room Miles ended up in was another bedroom. Miles rolled over the bed, leaving a smear of blood in his wake, and noticed that the bathroom door was ajar, revealing several people inside. Miles raised a finger to his lips and jumped up to the ceiling, using his talons to hang on as he scrambled across until he was above the doorway.

He'd only just reached his position when the door was kicked open and bullets were fired into the bed where Miles had just been. After a few seconds, the soldier stepped into the room, and Miles let go of the ceiling. He crashed down on top of the soldier, pinning him to the floor. He grabbed the soldier by the face and unleashed his bloodline gift.

The soldier's eyes rolled up into his head as his vampire side was cut off from him. Miles stood, grabbed the rifle, and tore it free from the soldier, tossing it across the room as he looked down at the helpless figure.

Miles was still in his vampire form when he crouched down beside the man and whispered, "Where did they take Rosa?"

"You will never beat the answers out of me," the man said, in a Russian accent.

"You another one of these KGB people?" Miles asked. "Because I've killed a few of you so far, and I can't say I'm very impressed. I guess the KGB never trained you to go after vampires, just humans."

"You will never beat the answers out of me," the man repeated.

Miles grabbed him by his lapel and hoisted him to his feet. "Okay," he said, and casually threw him through the window. He walked over to the shattered window and looked down at the soldier who had fallen twenty feet to the ground. He watched as the soldier tried to crawl along the grass verge outside. A difficult thing to do, considering his foot was facing the wrong way.

On the opposite side of the lawn from where the soldier crawled was the hole in the building where Miles had left Charlotte, but she was no longer there. He hoped she was okay.

Miles dropped out of the window, landing close to the soldier, and used his telekinesis to flip the man onto his back, causing him to cry out in pain. Miles was about to ask a question, when he noticed a small silver pendant that hung around the soldier's neck. He pulled the soldier toward him, tightening the telekinetic bubble he'd encased him in, making sure the hands of his attacker were pinned to his side.

There was a small thud as the bullet in Miles's shoulder was pushed out, landing on the ground next to his foot. "Ah, that's better," he said.

"I will not . . ." the man said.

Miles created a fist in one hand, tightening the bubble, causing the soldier to gasp in pain. "Be quiet," he said, taking hold of the silver pendant and pulling it free with one motion. He stared at it. At the name carved into the face of the silver fang. "You are an ATO." It was not a question.

"Miles," Karine shouted from the ruined window that the soldier had just been thrown through.

Miles looked up without taking the bubble from around the soldier. "He's an ATO."

"What?" Karine asked. "Are you sure?"

Miles let the fang pendant hang from his hand. "I left Charlotte up there; you know where she went?"

"I'll go check," Karine said. "Don't kill him, we need answers."

Miles turned back to the vampire. "Well, I guess you get to live. That's nice." He removed the telekinetic bubble, letting the man drop to the ground.

"Didn't say anything about pain, though." Miles kicked the surprised-looking man square in the chest, sending him sprawling twenty feet away. The man hit the ground, flipped over, and lay motionless on the dirt.

"You killed innocent people," Miles said as he walked toward the soldier, who tried to get up and slumped back to the ground. "You killed people I liked. You tried to kill my friends. You tried to kill my dog." Miles crouched down beside the man.

"You may as well kill me," the soldier said as he rolled onto his back, his expression a snarl of anger. "I won't give up anyone I work for. I won't tell you what's happening."

"Now, I don't think you understand the predicament you're in," Miles said.

"Found her!" Karine shouted from the corner of the building behind where Miles and the soldier were.

Miles turned back as a furious Charlotte marched toward Miles and the soldier. "You sure you don't want to just tell me?" he asked.

"Go fuck yourself," the soldier snapped.

Miles stepped out of the way as Charlotte grabbed hold of the soldier by his neck, wrenched him to his feet, and brought him toward her vampiric face. "I'm going to tear your fucking mind apart," she said, showing the soldier how a snarl was meant to look.

"No," the soldier said as Charlotte mentally ripped into the soldier's mind.

The screams that left his mouth were worse than any that Miles had heard since the attack had started, but he remained where he was and waited for Charlotte to finish. He knew that Charlotte didn't like digging around in people's heads. It was a bit too close to House Umbra's bloodline gift for her liking, and she usually remained satisfied with using her secondary ability to nudge people toward being truthful with her. She couldn't make someone lie, couldn't make someone do something they didn't want to, but she could make them tell her the truth.

"Holt!" the soldier screamed. "Jonathan Holt."

Charlotte looked down at Miles, who was as surprised as everyone else by the name. "He's in charge of your ATO unit?" he asked.

The soldier nodded, his face awash with sweat. He would be able to use his vampire side again by now, although it would do him little good against Charlotte.

"You're going to have to tell us a lot more than that," Charlotte said.

"No, wait, I will," the soldier pleaded, and looked over at Miles as if expecting help that was never going to arrive.

"Now," Charlotte commanded.

The soldier's gaze snapped back toward Charlotte. "We're not really ATOs. I mean, we are, but not exactly."

"You are very bad at this," Miles said. "Honestly, I'm thinking killing you might be a mercy."

"Look, no, please," the man said. "I'll tell you everything. Just let me down."

"Go fuck yourself," Miles said with a smile, and leaned in. "I'm going to count to ten, and you're going to start talking, or we're going to find a more unpleasant way to get answers."

Miles got to six by the time the truth came out.

PART THREE

ᚉ Chapter Twenty-Seven ᚉ

Jonathan Holt was not his real name. He didn't even know his real name. He didn't even know where he'd been born. His accent was fake, his life was fake, his background was fake. He'd grown up an orphan after the Crimean War and made his way to Moscow. He'd joined a criminal gang and lived like a king, until he was found by a vampire and turned, taken to those in charge of the government, and trained to be something a lot more. An assassin. A shadow. Whatever he needed to be. He had been good at it, until after the Second World War, when the Russian government decided he needed to be something else.

He'd been created to be a spy and assassin to use against Russian enemies, and now that enemy was the American government during a period of time in world history when Russia and the USA were both trying to win an arms race. In this case, a vampiric one. He had turned several more humans into vampires before being posted in various American cities. Against orders, they had stayed in touch. It was obvious that any government would disavow all knowledge of their existence, that the Russians would use them and dispose of them the moment they were no longer needed. So the group came up with a plan for just what to do to ensure that it was they who came out on top.

Jonathan played the Americans against the Russians and vice versa, giving information that led to the deaths of soldiers on both sides. All while scheming with his team to use their abilities and knowledge to make themselves rich. Over the years they carried out their plans, the group became rich and cultivated a network of people they could use to give them more wealth and power. Everything stayed working perfectly, right up until he found a better way of acquiring that wealth: the Assembly.

Jonathan Holt had joined the Assembly in the 1970s and had quickly risen to the rank of ATO Commander, having impressed those above him with his ability to do a good job. As well as being able to kiss just the right amount of political ass. They mostly ignored his grandstanding, his need for adulation, or how, on occasion, his methods were not as clean and precise as were expected from ATOs. In many ways, he was given a similar leniency to the Arbiters themselves, although he never made any attempt to become one.

His ATO team was full of highly trained, handpicked personnel. It didn't matter to the Assembly that they were all of a similar age, and all with similar backgrounds. It was suggested that they were good at their jobs, all having left their previous jobs working for the Russian government. It was said that all of them had undergone invasive procedures to turn them into vampires who could be controlled by said government. The Assembly didn't discriminate against where you'd come from, only that you were good at your job, and their results spoke more than words.

Over the decades, Jonathan Holt had been given the command of three more ATO teams, a prestigious level of trust and command. He'd weeded out those who didn't fit his sensibilities, creating one large ATO team with twenty-two agents and two other Commanders. Any suggestion of impropriety was ignored, or passed off as jealousy. They, after all, did a good job. They worked well together, and the streets of the world were a safer place because they *existed*.

Now everything he'd worked so hard for was in the balance, and despite having sent one of the ATO teams who were unofficially his to deal with the problem, none of them had checked in for several hours. It suggested that their mission had been a partial failure. It also suggested that Miles might still be alive. Which was a much bigger problem.

Jonathan paced back and forth across the large open room in an underground bunker in Lithuania. The maze of rooms and corridors covered the area above which was the unfinished village that Henryk had paid to have built. The partially burned mansion sat fifty feet directly above Jonathan's head.

He sighed and looked around the room. It was lavishly finished with two golden sofas, each with burgundy cushions. Marble statues sat in each corner of the room, depicting Roman legionnaires, and art stolen over a career of criminal activity right under the noses of the Assembly adorned every wall. This was a room that Jonathan had designed to come sit and look at all he'd achieved.

His art was the most important thing he'd acquired over the years. He'd even let Henryk borrow some of the artwork to put in his office building in London, and was still upset that he'd lost a few of the pieces before the place was designed to become a death trap for any of the Assembly forces who went to check on it.

Jonathan pressed a small button by the door. Thirty seconds later, Sara Bakos walked into the room. She looked, for all intents and purposes, like a tired but overall healthy young woman. Her eyes were always pools of blood red, the only real indication that something wasn't quite right.

"Yes?" Sara asked, her voice distant and harsh.

"You look tired," Jonathan said.

"I can't sleep," she said softly. "I'll work until I pass out. It's the only way to keep the dreams at bay."

The nightmares had started only a few days after Sara had fed upon the blood and flesh of a desolate, and to Jonathan's mind, they were getting worse. But then, Sara was also getting worse, so it stood to reason.

"You should have let me go to France," Sara said with a snarl. "I would have made sure it was done right."

"Miles would have killed you," Jonathan said matter-of-factly. He'd eventually convinced Sara that Megan was behind her transformation, using her newfound need to hurt anyone she was aimed at as a way to get rid of an ATO team who had been a considerable thorn in his side for a long time, but sending her after Miles would have wasted her potential.

"He deserves to die," Sara snapped. "They all do."

Jonathan sighed. He'd managed to get the Assembly Justice and handler away from the attack zone just in time. He'd initially considered stopping the attack altogether, but had second thoughts when he realised either they would kill Miles, and save him a headache, or Miles would survive and could be used to help him. Either way, Jonathan would use it to his advantage.

Even so, it had been several hours since they'd heard from the few ATO members that Jonathan had spared to intercept Sara's people and remove witnesses. He hoped it was all going to plan.

"Should have let me go after those two bitches in England," Sara continued. "Never got my revenge."

"They are being held in Scotland by House Venator," Jonathan said again. Having to repeat himself over and over was getting tiresome. For some reason, Sara's fractured mind had become utterly fixated on various people being the cause of her current predicament. The two ladies in Southampton who had survived Dominik were just two of the many. He wondered how long it would be before her mind broke completely, the desolate influence making her not only more prone to violence and impetuous behaviour, but outright feral. "There is exactly zero chance you could get to them without being killed."

"You don't think I can take a few House vampires?" Sara asked, a shocking level of aggravation in her tone.

"No," Jonathan said, trying to remain calm. "You couldn't kill Miles, you *certainly* can't kill those who still work for the House. And if you managed to, you'd have First Lord Drest after you, and after us. I've met Drest; I never wish to do so again."

"You're afraid of him," Sara mocked.

"If you're not afraid of the Great House First Lords, you're not paying attention properly," Jonathan snapped, and turned to look at one of the paintings he'd saved from Templar Tower after Henryk's death. The stupid idiot.

A few moments passed, and Jonathan knew that Sara was just waiting to let out her annoyance at having been corrected.

"Go," Jonathan said. "Bring our guests here when they arrive."

"Yes, your majesty," Sara said with a ludicrously overblown bow, before she turned on her heels and left.

Jonathan rubbed his temples and sighed. He'd been introduced to Sara by Henryk back in the 1980s, and had quickly done some investigating of his own and discovered her links to the KGB, and her bloodline gift. He'd found out that she was keeping those pieces of intel to herself, so it hadn't taken much to blackmail her into working for him. All she had to do was look the other way while he used Templar International to run weapons to the more unsavoury people of the world. He'd made a lot of money before switching to making and selling drugs to humans and vampires alike. A career change that had made him a fortune.

A fortune that Megan and her people had threatened when they started investigating the spiked blood pouches, leading them to a gang in Islington a year back. Jonathan had tried to involve himself, but Megan hadn't been interested and had soon set her sights on the higher-ups in the gang's organisation. Who, unfortunately for Megan, was Jonathan.

Things had gone from bad to worse with Dominik's death, and then Henryk's before he could finish those damn prototypes to control the desolate. Jonathan still wasn't sure how Henryk had managed to get hold of even a fraction of the research they were doing in Maine, and if he was honest, he didn't want to know.

He was still in mid-thought about how he'd reached this point in his life from what should have been a very simple way to make a lot of money when the door was opened, and Justice Balderas and Rosa were pushed into the room by Fury, who had worked at Templar International for a long time. He'd only recently been turned into a vampire, but he had taken to his new life with a level of gusto that Jonathan quite admired.

The Justice and handler were forcibly sat on a sofa, before Fury left without a word. They both looked a little dishevelled but otherwise in one piece, which Jonathan was thankful for. He didn't need more complications, and right now that was all Sara was bringing to the table.

"Jonathan?" Justice Balderas asked. "You know, I always wondered which ATO Commander it was who was undermining us. You were on the short list, but I thought you were too self-centred and stupid to pull it off. I'd warned Miles that you weren't someone who could be relied upon. I knew you had your grubby little hands in too many pies, but I didn't think you'd actually try to murder an Assembly Justice."

Jonathan sighed. "I didn't, *actually*. Sara did that. I saved your life, old man. And yours too, young lady. Maybe a little bit of thanks would go a long way."

The Justice laughed. "You want to explain how you saved our lives?"

"I didn't know she'd sent a goddamned attack helicopter to blow up your home," Jonathan said. "I have people watching your property, and I made the mistake of complaining about how Miles and his friends had arrived. I assumed that Sara still had some of her sensibilities left, although considering she decided to fix you as a problem by sending a fucking missile strike, I see that's no longer the case. I made the call that got Rosa and you out of the room, although the stupid idiot on the end only brought Rosa to begin with. I hear it was a close call."

"Why?" the Justice asked.

"You're both going to tell me what you know and who you told," Jonathan said with a wave of his hand.

He didn't feel the need to explain everything to them both. That he had every intention of letting the Assembly deal with Sara once he was far away from her. That he'd brought the Justice and handler to him in an effort to find out what they knew about him, about his involvement with Templar International, and once he had that information, he was going to let his enemies kill each other.

Jonathan had always known that eventually he'd need an exit plan from his work with Templar International, and that good things never lasted, but he didn't think Sara would be the one to lose her mind. That she'd bring down the Assembly on him. His only way out now was to outwardly aid the Assembly in their aim to reclaim a Justice and handler. He considered killing everyone himself, but there were a lot of them, and it was better for others to do the heavy lifting. He would happily cheer the Assembly on as they went to get their vengeance on the murderers of an ATO team, and hopefully an Arbiter. He just needed to be somewhere else when it all came to a crescendo. It wouldn't take long before the Justice, the handler, and Sara were all going to be dead, and someone else's problem, and by then he was going to go into hiding until it had all blown over.

Unfortunately, the longer it went before he heard from his team in France, the more likely it was that Miles had survived. And a living Miles put a very serious mess in his plan. A mess he would need to resolve. That turned the Justice and handler into bargaining chips. And that he could work with.

"But not Charlotte and Miles?" Rosa asked, regaining Jonathan's attention.

"A dead Arbiter is probably a help at this point, which is a shame, as I genuinely liked him," Jonathan said. "I don't give two shits about the House lawyer."

Rosa kicked the bottle of wine off the table at Jonathan and launched herself at him, but Jonathan moved, caught her arm, and slammed her to the ground. He was on her in an instant, pushing her head down to pin her to the floor as he knelt on her back.

"Don't become a problem," he whispered in her ear, looking over at Justice Balderas, who hadn't moved. "Megan became a problem, and you know what happened to her."

"Get off me," Rosa said, trying to push herself up off the floor. "You set us up at the Tower."

Jonathan stepped back. "Nope, that was all Sara, too. I didn't know until the call came through, and I just happened to be in London. Probably fortunate for me; it gave me a chance to get rid of a few things. Sara's been quite busy recently. I assume you know she's all but lost her mind."

"And you want to stop her?" Justice Balderas asked.

Jonathan laughed. "I assume you'd like to see Sara," he said.

"She's part desolate now," Rosa said.

"She is," Jonathan said. "She has some anger and impulse control issues. I had to stop her from turning people into vampires. Or, sort of vampires. They're much more aggressive than usual, and seem to have that same need to hurt people. I think she's infecting others with her desolate side."

"She has to be stopped," Rosa said. "Surely you can see that."

"Oh, I agree," Jonathan said, opening the door and motioning for the Justice and Rosa to leave the room. "I'm working on it as we speak."

The pair walked down the dingy tunnel, past the locked door that had led to the mansion directly above. Right up until some idiot managed to set the mansion on fire and it partially collapsed on top of the exit. Jonathan mentally reminded himself to get it fixed as he exited the tunnel into a large room with two old prison-style cells on either side. A heavy steel door sat directly opposite as he entered.

The door was guarded by two large men, neither of whose names Jonathan had ever bothered to remember. They wore fireproof clothing and each carried a flamethrower with a tank of flammable gel on their backs. They were here for the protection of everyone else in the tunnels. Between them stood Sara, whose head constantly moved from side to side as she looked between the two prisoners.

"You killed Megan," Rosa said.

"I did," Sara said with a creepy smile, her mouth appearing to be just a little too wide. Her eyes, showing nothing but darkness, like a shark. "Her whole team died screaming. It was a thing of beauty."

Rosa dove for Sara but was intercepted by Fury, who quickly got her onto the floor, keeping his foot pressed down on her head.

"I'm going to kill you all," Rosa roared.

"Didn't you just try this a second ago?" Jonathan asked. "Throw her in cell two, let her calm down."

Sara opened the cell door, and Fury launched Rosa inside the pitch-black room. She hit the wall on the far end hard, and fell to the floor as the door was shut. Rosa screamed in anger and flung herself at the doors, her arms through the bars slashing wildly as Sara and Fury laughed.

"You're not breaking these bars," Jonathan said calmly, opening the cell on the opposite side of the room and motioning for Justice Balderas to go inside.

The Justice stepped into the cell, the door shutting closed with a loud clang behind him.

"See how much easier it is?" Jonathan said to Rosa.

"I'm going to rip out your fucking eyes," Rosa shouted.

"I think she's talking to you," Jonathan told Sara, whose smile never wavered. He turned back to Rosa. "My advice would be to calm down, listen to me, and maybe your last few days on earth won't be unbearable. Or you can scream and shout, and make a nuisance of yourself, and I'll have Sara here make your life a living hell."

Jonathan left the cells with Sara, stopping just outside the doorway and turning back to the fractured vampire. "They are not to be harmed, am I clear?"

Sara licked her lips.

"Sara," Jonathan snapped.

"Yes," Sara said, disappointed. "You *need* them alive. For now."

"Yes, for now," Jonathan repeated. "I need to know what they know and who they've told. And then I'm going to use the status of the Justice to make sure that we all get out of this mess you created, so I just need you to behave for a while longer."

"Until Miles comes here," Sara said, still smiling. "You promised him to me."

"And you shall have him," Jonathan said, turning and walking away as a smile passed over his lips. If Miles was still alive, he'd thought of a way to get rid of Sara and the Arbiter at the same time. Everything was coming together again, and soon he'd be rid of Sara, her friends, and anyone else who might be a hindrance to his living a long and happy life.

CHAPTER TWENTY-EIGHT

The ATO had screamed a lot in the hour Charlotte had questioned him. Answering her questions by lying caused him physical pain, and considering lying was all he seemed to want to do, he spent a lot of time lying on the ground swearing.

Eventually, he told the truth, and the pain in his head stopped. He said where Jonathan Holt—the person behind it all—was, how to get there, and even why Megan had died. Apparently, this particular ATO had been there to watch as Megan's team had been killed.

"She was investigating the drugs," the agent said. "Jonathan saw a way to use Sara's insanity to his own ends. Got her to think that Megan was there for her. That Megan and her team were responsible for what happened to Henryk, to her. Sara's completely fucked in the head; she just wants someone to hurt."

"Jonathan is involved with Templar International?" Miles asked.

"Helped them get their accreditation," the agent said. "We used their shipping to get through vampire-controlled docks with the drugs, so we could move them on. Accredited companies aren't checked as much. We managed to pay off who we needed to, and made a huge amount more in the process."

"Why?" Charlotte asked. "Why did Jonathan do this?"

"Money," the ATO said. "He was making a shitload, and Megan's constant investigation into where the drugs were coming from was going to jeopardise it. Then Dominik went nuts, and suddenly she's looking into that, I think she knew the drugs were coming through the vampire-controlled docks, just couldn't prove it.

"Anyway, he got killed, and things went back to normal. But then Henryk is killed, Sara goes fucking nuts, and our money is suddenly not as safe. Jonathan took an opportunity to resolve a problem."

Miles punched the agent in the stomach, making him cough and splutter. "Megan and her team were not *problems.*"

"Sure," the agent said, spitting up blood.

"Why'd he send you to kill us?" Charlotte asked.

"Didn't," the agent said. "Sara sent the attack chopper to blow up this whole place, Jonathan found out, tried to intercept, but it was too late and her people weren't answering the damn phone. So we got shipped in. We were already nearby keeping an eye. Justice Balderas has been looking into Jonathan for a long time, so we just repaid the favour. Saw you all arrive, contacted Jonathan. Next we hear, Sara has sent some idiots here to blow you all up."

"So, Jonathan used a seriously disturbed Sara to kill an ATO team because they were costing him money?" Charlotte asked, disbelief in her voice.

"A lot of money," the agent said.

"So much death and pain because one arsehole wanted to be richer than he already was."

"Like I said," the agent clarified, "it was a shitload of money. More than you've probably ever seen. We were going to be fucking billionaires by the time we were done. Drugs, guns, killings for hire. Jonathan is a one-man criminal enterprise. And no one fucking knew."

"He fooled me," Miles said. "I thought he was an arrogant shitehawk, but I also thought he was good at his job. That he cared about his job, about the people he was meant to protect. Now I find out that he was a lie. How many of your team were turned into vampires by him?"

"A few," the agent said, sweat streaming down his clammy face.

"How many?" Charlotte asked.

"Twenty-two of us," the agent said with a cry.

"Not all of you here had dog tags," Miles said. "The ones in Oslo didn't, I'd have noticed."

"They were Sara's," the agent said. "She overstepped for the first time. Jonathan was *pissed.* Made her swear she'd never do it again. Turns out the word of a desolate doesn't mean shit."

"She's not desolate yet, or she wouldn't be talking at all," Miles said.

"She's unhinged," the agent said. "She kills for fun at this point. She doesn't care about money or anything else, she just wants to hurt the people she thinks hurt her. I think maybe Jonathan's words of who to blame did more harm than good."

"Why take the Justice and Rosa?" Miles asked.

"Value," the agent said. "That's my guess, anyway. He wants them dead where he can control the narrative of what happened to them."

"Meaning what?" Miles asked.

"He puts out that Sara kidnapped them, shows himself as the hero who didn't get there in time to save them," he said. "That's my guess. When he finds out that you're still alive, it puts a damper on it. By now we haven't contacted him to say job done, so he'll have to rethink his strategy. We only came to get them away and make sure the people Sara sent finished their job of making sure there were no witnesses."

"You should have brought more people," Miles said. "Where is Sara hiding?"

"Lithuania. There are tunnels under the abandoned village. The Justice and your friend are there." The agent stared at Miles. "What the fuck are you, man? I've never seen someone take out trained vampires like that."

"All I am is angry," Miles said, getting to his feet and nodding toward Karine. "But I'm nae even close to being as angry as she is."

Karine pushed herself off the wall and unfurled her arms.

"Wait, I told you everything," the agent said.

"We know," Charlotte told him, and with Miles behind her, they left the room to the sounds of the pleading agent.

Miles found Church sitting in the hallway just outside of the room he'd left. She'd barely left his side since the attack had happened.

Charlotte placed a hand on Miles's shoulder. "Are you okay?" she asked.

"No," Miles said. "Not even slightly."

"Haven't seen you turn into your beast form before," she continued. "It was . . . impressive. And a little scary. It's like you're a force of nature or something, the power just comes off you in waves. Reminds me of Drest when he turns to his beast form."

"Well, he did turn me," Miles said. "I guess that power doesn't fall far from the tree."

"I think you're mixing up several metaphors there," Charlotte said.

Miles kissed Church on the head and got to his feet. "We know exactly where Megan and her team went. That's where Rosa and Balderas are. That's where Jonathan is. That's where Sara is. I aim to go and end this."

"I'm coming with you," Charlotte said.

The nearby door opened, and a bloody Karine stepped into the hallway. "He's dead," she said.

"I'm going to call Drest," Charlotte said. "He needs to know what happened here, and maybe we can put some kind of cross Assembly-House unit together and hit these people as hard as possible. We can't let any of them get away."

"Megan and her team were all killed by these people," Karine said.

"They were ambushed," Miles countered. "Had no idea that they were walking into a trap. I'm fully aware I'm walking into one. And it won't make a blind bit of difference to the outcome. Justice Balderas told me to stop keeping my head down. That people who want to come after me are going to do it no matter how much smaller a target I make myself. I was fine with that. I'm nae fine with them coming after people I care for. I'm going to eradicate them for it. Loudly and publicly. There's no sweeping this under any rugs. Everyone is going to know what Jonathan and his friends did, and what happened to them."

"The Assembly might not be happy with that," Charlotte said. "You're talking about killing Assembly personnel, and making sure everyone knows that they betrayed their own kind to do it."

"Yes, I am," Miles said.

"I'm going to talk to the rest of my people," Karine said, leaving without another word.

Miles sat on the floor next to Church, his back up against the wall behind him. He watched Charlotte leave the hallway by the door to the outside. He let out a long sigh, closed his eyes, and took ten minutes to concentrate on his breathing as the weight of Church beside him offered a comfort that words could never quite match.

"I've never had missiles shot at me before," Charlotte said, returning and putting her phone away. "It was an interesting experience."

Miles snorted.

"You think Rosa and the Justice are okay?" Charlotte asked.

"For now," Miles said. "If what the dead ATO said is true, they were taken so that Jonathan could control the narrative. Meaning he's going to want to paint himself as the hero who couldn't quite get there in time, but he'll want the Assembly to know about it all first. Make sure they're aware of his heroic status."

"Drest said he's going to talk to Danica and the other Houses about putting together a joint task force."

Danica was the First Lady of House Barbarous, and was in a relationship with Drest. A secret relationship that if any of the other Houses discovered would cause problems. Miles wasn't entirely sure how he felt about Danica. She was excellent at her job, and her people respected her. And those who didn't definitely feared her. But Miles was wary of House Lords and Ladies. Even Drest, whom he knew as well as anyone else on the planet, had his own agenda. "House First" was a motto for a reason.

"You don't think it'll happen," Charlotte said after Miles had remained silent.

"House Umbra is too insular. House Phalanx might if they realise that doing nothing might come back to bite them on the ass. House Nix has Rosa, and apparently she's an outcast, so maybe they won't care. The Minor Houses might want in, just to hold it over the Great. Vampire politics getting in the way of doing the right thing. Most of the people these arseholes have killed have been Assembly. The victims in Oslo were mostly people linked to the Assembly, too, although thankfully the death toll there was a lot smaller than Sara's people wanted."

"Thanks to you and Church," Charlotte said.

"And Rosa," Miles pointed out. "Jonathan's vampires are just greedy; their primary motive is money, according to the agent Karine just killed. Sara and her people are motivated by a need for vengeance that doesn't exist. That's a lot more dangerous."

"No matter how much vampires want to believe they're apart from the humans, they're not really any better," Charlotte said. "Still petty, still selfish, still capable of greatness but opting to settle for quicker and easier. Sometimes I just find it too endlessly exhausting."

Miles breathed out slowly. "Are you sure you want to come with me?"

Charlotte pulled away before staring at her old friend for several seconds. "How can you possibly think anything else? Do I not seem tough enough? Do I not seem like I can handle myself? I wasn't always a House Counsel, Miles. I've done my fair share of fighting, of hunting, of hurting people who would, or did, hurt me."

"I know," Miles said. "I don't mean because you're not tough, or that you're not capable. I can't think of many people I'd rather have watching my back. I only ask because you keep the House safe. If they lost you, I'm nae sure Drest could replace you. Also because you're better than this. Better than me."

Charlotte said nothing for several heartbeats. "Fuck off, Miles." She shook her head. "You're not my white knight in armour, you're not trying to show that you're worse than I am. I'm not better than you, I'm not better than anyone else. Better than this. We do this to keep our people safe, to stop those who would harm the people we love. It's why you started to work for the Assembly, it's why you worked for the House. Don't give me that *better than me* bullshit. You're not that stupid."

Miles considered her words before saying, "Charlotte, you *are* better than me. A better person than me, anyway. I've spent hundreds of years atoning for what I did as a human. The misery I caused, the lives I took. Balancing that scale is my life's work, and I thank Drest every day for giving me that chance, but I'm nae sure I'll ever truly balance it."

"You're feeling morose," Charlotte said. "Because of all this?"

Miles shrugged. "Maybe. I'm just tired, Charlotte. I'm tired of feeling like I'm standing between monsters and a world they want on fire. I'm tired of feeling like everything we do is only to make things better in tiny increments, and the second we do, someone else makes it worse. People like Jonathan weren't meant to ever be part of the Assembly, but if the last few years have taught me anything, it's that the Assembly isn't actually anywhere near good enough. I just wanted to make sure that you know what's coming when we hunt Jonathan."

Charlotte patted Miles on the shoulder as she got to her feet. "I'm going to be standing beside you every step of the way. And when this is done, maybe you just need to take some time off."

"I've been considering it. Again. This time somewhere that hopefully won't turn into a battleground."

"Church could probably use the break, too."

Church's head lifted up at the mention of her name.

"I already told her that," Miles said.

"Come on," Charlotte said, offering Miles her hand, which he took. "Let's go figure out just where we need to go, and how many people we need to help us get this done. No matter what Sara is, no matter what her people might be, Jonathan is pulling the strings here. Or trying to. All for some more wealth."

"If there is one thing I have learned in this world, it's that for some people, it's never *enough* money," Charlotte said. "There's always a need for more. A need to flaunt that wealth to the world. Sounds like Jonathan's biggest problem is that he wants people to know how clever and good he is."

"That was definitely the impression I got," Miles said.

"So what happens when he's shown to the vampire world as little more than just a common criminal?" Charlotte asked. "A crook who wants to make money and hide with it. A vampiric dragon, sitting on his big hoard of whatever it is that the riches can never satisfy."

The pair walked through the building, with Church following behind. They found Karine in the dining room talking to half a dozen people, several of whom were in need of a shower to remove the blood from them. Bullet holes littered the walls of the room, and one of the windows was broken. Miles realised this was where he'd flown through the window, although the body of the enemy was gone.

"I've also told them they're to stay and await the Assembly," Karine said as the people filtered out of the room, each nodding or saying a thank-you to Miles as they left.

"Good," Miles said. "Do we know where Jonathan lives?"

"Should we?" Karine asked.

"He must have a place he stays," Miles said. "I was just wondering if we know where it is. Might have something there we can use against him. Maybe figure out if he has any other plans beyond making himself ungodly levels of wealthy. This is a lot to go through just to make yourself rich. Feels like something he'd tell everyone just to get them to go along with him."

"Money motivates," Charlotte said.

"So does revenge," Karine pointed out.

"I assume you mean Sara," Miles said.

Karine nodded, a wry smile on her lips. "Yes, Justice Balderas told me about her before our world exploded. It's my job to advise the Justice on such matters."

"I think if I were Jonathan, I'd be looking for a way out that keeps himself in one piece," Miles said. "I don't think Jonathan is the kind of person who would go down with the ship. The hero narrative works here, but with me alive, it won't work. He needs to keep everyone safe until he can make sure I'm not going to spend the rest of my life hunting for him."

Karine's phone rang and she answered it, giving short answers to whoever was on the other end, before finishing the call. "They're a few minutes out."

"We need to get to Lithuania," Charlotte said. "Any of you know how to fly a helicopter?"

No one did.

"So, we need one of the people coming in to do it," Karine said. "Guess we're waiting around here now."

Miles stepped outside as the sun began to set. It had been an exceptionally long day, and a day that would end with Justice Balderas and Rosa still in the custody of people who were happy to commit murder of innocent people.

"Can we walk?" Karine asked as she stood beside Miles.

The pair walked down the bank toward the swimming pool and tennis courts below. "I need to stay here and help," she said after a short while.

"I do understand," Miles said with sympathy, as they passed the swimming pool and continued on toward the large pond farther away from the house. "Today has been a lot."

Karine nodded as the pair stopped by the pond, which Miles noted was bigger than the swimming pool. "I trust you will bring the Justice back," Karine said, looking across the pond to the mass of insects flittering over its still surface. "He's like a father to me."

Miles didn't want to promise anything he couldn't deliver, but the hurt in Karine's voice made him want to anyway. "I'm going to do everything I can," he said, unsure if that was even close to being enough.

"If I go with you, I could lose control," Karine said. "I may as well be vibrating with the need to hurt the people who hurt us, and I don't want to put anyone else in jeopardy. Besides, the people here need me. We've all lost so much today. A dozen vampires and familiars who were just here doing their jobs. They need me here more than I need to go kill those responsible."

Miles nodded. "I think you're spot on. I think your people need you, and the hard thing about being a leader is knowing when to stop and realise that you are more important to them than getting vengeance is to you."

Karine nodded sadly. "I'm not sure this place is ever going to be the same."

Miles looked back at the partially ruined house. "I don't think it should be the same. I don't think you can go back to the time before someone shot a missile at your home, Karine. I think you just need to keep moving forward, however long it takes to get there."

"I've been a vampire for a long time," Karine said without looking back at Miles. "I've killed my fair share of people, vampire and human. I've never seen anything like what happened today. I don't just mean the attack, I mean what you did. You tore those vampires apart with your bare hands. That's First Lord levels of power."

"First Lord Drest is the person who turned me into a vampire," Miles said, looking down at his hands. It had taken a long time to clean the blood off them, but it had been something he'd done more times than he cared to remember throughout his life. "Took me a long time to get my vampiric beast form, but I guess it amplifies everything else."

Karine looked back at Miles for the first time. "Miles, those men were trained soldiers, and you went through them like they were paper."

"They were trained, but not very old," Miles admitted. "Probably only a few dozen years as vampires. Makes things easier."

Karine nodded as if she understood but wasn't entirely convinced, which, if Miles was honest, neither was he. He didn't want to have his power increased to that of a First Lord or Lady. He didn't want to have to get that bullseye on his back.

"I think I'm going to stay out here for a while," Karine said.

Miles left Karine and hoped that she and the rest of the survivors would be okay. Or at least would be able to move forward as best they could.

His phone rang after a few minutes of sitting on the grass, looking out at the rear of Justice Balderas's property. The name above the number on the screen said *unknown*, but he answered it anyway, ready to yell at anyone trying to commit a scam.

"Miles," a familiar voice said.

"Jonathan," Miles said, letting the anger bubble up into that one word.

"You know, I think we might have been friends if not for all of this."

Miles gripped the phone tightly, releasing the grip slightly so he didn't crush it. "I think that if you've hurt Justice Balderas or Rosa, I'm going to find you, and I'm going to make your death long and arduous."

"We need to talk, properly, face to face," Jonathan said. "I need you to know I was not behind the attack in London, I was not behind the attack on Justice Balderas. I had no idea that Sara was going to do anything as stupid as try to kill people, or keep desolate in a publicly used building."

"I heard," Miles said. "We know that you're where Megan went when you killed her."

"Sara killed her," Jonathan interjected quickly. "She's lost her mind, Miles. I'm not saying I'm innocent in all of this, but we need to find a way to stop her, stop her people, before it gets worse. I have the Justice and Rosa, they are safe. I aim to keep them safe so long as I get a few guarantees. Once I have them, I will give you their location, and you go fetch them. Let's not do anything stupid here."

"For you to be free to live without any consequences?" Miles asked, hearing the anger in his voice and being unable to stop it. He knew that Jonathan had been behind Megan being killed. He'd aimed Sara at Megan's team and let her loose, and now he couldn't control her. He considered telling him, but wanted Jonathan to keep digging his own grave.

"No," Jonathan said. "To stop Sara. To stop everyone they're working with. I didn't sign on to kill innocent people, Miles. I didn't sign on to murder Justices and Arbiter handlers. I didn't sign on to have the Assembly hunt me for the rest of my fucking life. None of this was meant to happen." Jonathan paused, sounding exhausted and fed up. "Just meet me, one to one, no games, no ambushes."

"Where?" Miles asked, forcing himself to keep calm.

"Berlin," he said. "There's a cafe there called Kaffee Grau."

"Grey coffee?" Miles asked before he could stop himself.

"The grey city, grey coffee, I don't know, I'm not the person who named it," Jonathan said, a little tension in his words. "Meet me there at nine PM tomorrow night. It's a vampire cafe, so it'll be busy. We can sit outside the front, where there will be plenty of people. I'll not expect you to bring no one, but I assure you, I will mean you no harm. I will bring proof of life for the Justice and Rosa. No harm will come to them. For now. Do not test me, though. As you've already seen, I can't stop Sara forever."

The call ended before Miles could reply. He stared at the phone for several seconds, before placing it back in his pocket and looking up at the sky, the dark clouds from earlier in the day having never left. It felt as if they had been above his head for several days at this point. "Time to go to Berlin, I guess," he said.

CHAPTER TWENTY-NINE

B ut we know he's lying," Charlotte said after Miles had informed them all of the need to get to Berlin in the next twenty-four hours.

"I know," Miles said. "He never struck me as stupid, so he knows his people are dead, and they probably gave up information. Right now, he's doing whatever he can to make sure he gets away. So, we play along until we have the Justice and Rosa back. If I was him, I'd have moved the Justice and Rosa somewhere else, so we need to find out where that is. Once we get them back, we can deal with the duplicitous bastard."

"He might try to kill you," Karine said.

"Possibly," Miles said. "Okay, probably. But my point still stands. I have to try."

Despite there being several minutes of both Karine and Charlotte coming up with reasons why Miles could only even consider such an offer if a battalion of vampires could go with him, he remained steadfast.

Six helicopters landed in the front garden of the property. Four held only Assembly personal, numbering nineteen in total. The fifth helicopter, the only Chinook among the bunch, had brought Halime, along with eight of her soldiers.

"Good to see you," Miles said, embracing Halime as Karine went to talk to the Assembly people.

"Who are they?" Charlotte asked as eight people got out of the helicopter that landed closest to the property entrance.

"House representatives," Halime said. "Those are from House Nix after we told them that Rosa was kidnapped, and they insisted. The other Houses are also helping; they're mostly working with the Assembly to deal with anyone linked to Jonathan. He's about to find out he has a lot fewer allies than he might have thought."

"Guess I was wrong about them wanting to take part," Miles said.

One of the House Nix people, a tall and broad man with brown skin, short black hair, and a serious expression, strolled over toward them. "Are you Arbiter Watson?" he asked.

Miles nodded, and shook the man's hand when it was offered.

"My name is Aamir Lazaar. I've been told that a House Nix member has been abducted. I am here to ensure their safe return."

"It was my impression that Rosa had left House Nix," Miles said.

"It is true that she no longer conforms with what our First Lord believes is the best way forward for House Nix," Aamir said, obviously picking his words carefully. "But she is an old friend of mine, and I would not see her left to her kidnappers."

"Welcome aboard," Charlotte said. "You should know that Miles is in charge here."

Miles resisted the urge to roll his eyes. It was one thing to be in charge of a bunch of ATOs, but quite another to be an Arbiter and in charge not only of people from other Houses, but also other Arbiters.

Aamir's eyes went from Charlotte to Halime to Miles, down to Church. "I have heard much about you, Miles Watson. I will be honoured to serve under you for this assignment."

"Right, well, let's get everyone together, and we can explain what the plan is," Miles said.

"We have a plan?" Charlotte whispered when everyone else had walked off to arrange their people.

"I'm going to Berlin," Miles said.

Charlotte exhaled and muttered something derogatory in French that made Miles smile.

The leaders of the various groups got together in the dining room of Justice Balderas's property. Apart from Charlotte, Karine, Aamir, and Halime, there were two Arbiters and three ATO Commanders, all of whom were more than happy to let Miles take charge as he explained he was going to Berlin.

"But these people who took Rosa and the Justice will be in Lithuania, correct?" Aamir asked after Miles had finished explaining the current circumstances.

"Yes, but we don't know exactly where they're keeping Rosa and Justice Balderas," Miles said. "And Jonathan wants something out of this. He's not going to have harmed his only leverage to stop us going in fangs bared. He wants to live, and he wants to live without the need to look over his shoulder for the rest of his life."

"Are we expecting further attacks?" one of the Arbiters, a Japanese woman whom Miles knew only as Usami, asked. She had long dark hair and looked to have been turned into a vampire in her early twenties. A second Arbiter, a middle-aged looking man with a grey beard and light blue eyes, stood behind her, his hands clasped together as if in contemplation. Despite the number of Arbiters being relatively small, Miles had never met him before.

"We're not," Miles said. "But I wasn't expecting attack helicopters to start launching missiles at us in the middle of the French countryside, so who knows at this point."

"I've worked with Jonathan before," one of the ATO Commanders, a blond-haired, blue-eyed man, said. He's not a stupid man. I agree that if he wants to meet in Berlin, he has a plan to get out of this situation intact. Do we know how far gone Sara is?"

"We know that Sara has drunk from the blood of a desolate and is slowly merging her personality with that of one of the creatures," Miles said to the gasps of those who weren't aware. "She's no longer the Sara she was. She's aggressive and hostile to anyone she considers a threat."

"So we should expect a fight," Halime said.

Miles nodded. "Always. Are we expecting anyone else?"

There were several shakes of the head from the two Arbiters. "The Justices felt that with Justice Balderas being alive and well, as far as we know, that a joint task force was the best bet," the male Arbiter said. "There are over thirty of us, and most of us have been vampires for well over a century. If we can't take down this ragtag band of scum, we're all in trouble."

Ragtag? Charlotte mouthed.

Miles ignored his friend. "Until we know that we can get to Rosa and Justice Balderas safely, we're not taking anyone down. I do not relish the chance to fight an unknown number of assailants on their own territory, without prior information."

"So, you're going to Berlin," Halime said. "How do you plan on getting there?"

"I need someone here to fly me," Miles said. "Church, too. Presumably Charlotte. I need everyone else to prepare for a trip to Lithuania. Whatever happens with my meeting in Berlin, Sara needs to be stopped."

Everyone looked over at Church, who lay on the floor. She glanced up and yawned, seemingly uninterested in what everyone else in the room was doing.

"Any questions?" Miles asked after several seconds of silence. When no one had any, he said, "Let's get ready."

Miles left the room with Church behind him and walked through the mansion to get to the rear of the property, where he stepped outside and took a deep breath as Church looked up at him. "Tired," he said by way of explanation.

"You need food," Charlotte said from the doorway, and passed Miles a blood pouch. "Don't argue. You need sleep, too. You've been running on fumes for hours."

"We're vampires," Miles said. "I can go without sleep for a few days."

"Not after what you did today, you can't," Charlotte countered.

"Valid point," Miles said, tearing off the seal of the blood pouch and taking a long drink of the synthetic blood. He immediately wished he had the time to savour the meal as well as get some measure of rest. The attack on the property had taken it out of him.

"You ready?" Halime said as Miles reentered the building. "We'll have to stop at a nearby airport to refuel before flying on to Berlin, so we need to get going. Charlotte and Church are already in the helicopter waiting, as is my team. Usami is flying with us. The other Arbiter is flying with House Nix's people. Two of the three ATO squads are flying to Berlin and will be awaiting further instructions, and the final one is staying here to aid these people in the cleanup. I know the Commander. He's a good man, he'll make sure everything is okay."

With very little left to do on his part, Miles followed Halime through the house, where he was stopped as they entered the foyer by the surviving members of Justice Balderas's staff. They each thanked him in turn, and wished him good luck in finding the Justice and getting him home safely. A few had tears in their eyes as they spoke.

As Miles and Halime left the house, the latter clasped an arm around Miles's shoulder. "You did good here today," she said.

Miles nodded, unable to voice the idea that he didn't do enough.

"It's a long flight," Halime said, removing her arm. "You need sleep, Miles. We'll get to Berlin, and you can go find Jonathan and make sure he tells you what we need."

"He will," Miles said.

"So confident?" Halime said as they crossed the green mound in the centre of the front of the mansion, the helicopter's blades already spinning in preparation for takeoff.

"I am," Miles said as the sound of the Chinook swallowed any further words Miles might have said. Instead, he got onto the helicopter, strapped in, rested his eyes for a second, and quickly fell asleep.

Chapter Thirty

Miles had fallen asleep almost as soon as he'd sat in the Chinook, and had remained asleep during the entire refuelling time, with everyone else in the aircraft giving him time to himself. They all saw he needed the rest, saw that he was close to burning himself out. After they'd refilled and continued on their flight across Europe toward Berlin, Miles's dreams changed into something more sinister, as he found himself back at the skull-strewn sarcophagus.

A cold fog once again permeated everything around him, punctuated by a burning firepit to his left, although he felt no heat from it. "Did you talk to Drest?" the voice from beyond the fog asked.

"Bit busy," Miles said, finding it odd that instead of fear, he was annoyed.

The same cloaked figure as before floated through the fog until they were still beside Miles, who looked up into the cowl, but saw only shadows where there should have been a face.

"Now, there's the fear," the figure said, sounding happy about it.

"Is this a prophetic dream, or a conversation?" Miles asked, forcing himself to keep his gaze on the mass of swirling darkness inside the cowl.

The . . . *creature* laughed, a rich, throaty noise, not at all what Miles had expected. "Why not both?"

Miles let out a breath. "Just tell me what you want me to know."

"I like you, little vampire," the thing said. "I hope you live."

Miles sat up with a jolt.

"Prophetic dreams again?" Charlotte asked.

"You get prophetic dreams?" Halime asked from her seat directly opposite Miles.

"I had some in the past," Miles said, not particularly feeling like getting into a more detailed description of what he'd seen. "This wasn't the same, it was . . . weird."

"Weird how?" Usami asked, reminding Miles that there was someone else on the flight apart from the House Venator vampires.

Miles tried to figure out a way to get out of saying much, as several of the House Venator soldiers either stared at him in wait of his answer or removed their headsets, knowing that a conversation between Firsts and Arbiters was probably not something they wanted to have knowledge of.

"Fire and ice, and fog, wind," Miles said. "It was weird. Just a nightmare. I haven't exactly been taking care of myself the last few days. Feeding when I can, sleeping little. I think it was just my brain telling me to actually get some rest at some point."

Usami didn't look convinced, but nodded once that she understood. Miles didn't want to talk about it.

"You sure?" Charlotte asked, clearly not getting the memo that Miles didn't want to chat, the concern in her voice overriding anything else.

"I think maybe this is a conversation for later," Halime said. "A tired vampire brain can do weird things."

Charlotte looked between Halime and Miles, and didn't look convinced.

"I'm fine," Miles promised her, mentally reminding himself to actually talk to Drest about it next time. "Just a nightmare. They happen."

"They do," Charlotte said.

Miles got to his feet and stretched. "How much longer?"

"Twenty minutes," Usami told him.

Church, who had already been seated next to Miles, stirred from her own slumber, looked around the helicopter, and went back to sleep.

"Your dog can sleep through anything," Usami said with a smile.

"She has selective sleeping," Miles explained. "She can sleep like a log up here, but other times she'll wake up if I happen to move slightly in bed."

"She is unique," Usami said. "I have never seen a dog like her."

"There's another," Miles said. "They were littermates, but I don't know what happened to him. I hope he's somewhere safe, enjoying a nice log fire and unlimited bowls of his favourite food."

"That sounds like a more pleasant time than being in this," Halime said with a chuckle that several of her people mimicked.

The twenty minutes passed quickly, and the helicopter landed on a helipad at the rear of a large property just outside of Berlin. The Berlin office of the Assembly was, quite literally, in a castle. Complete with a drawbridge that hadn't been raised in centuries, and a surrounding forest full of wildlife. A few minutes' walk from the rear of the property led to the banks of Lake Tegel and a dock which Miles had once sat upon and spent several blissful days pretending to fish.

The main building was made of pale brick with a dark grey roof. Several extensions had been added to the original castle building, which was now used as accommodation for visiting dignitaries. It was an hour's drive from the location to the coffee shop in Berlin, depending on traffic, and the idyllic setting was a place Miles had taken Church several times over the years.

The helicopter landed, and everyone remained seated as Charlotte and Halime left to talk to the staff who came out to meet them. It was just turning dark outside, and Miles decided to leave the helicopter with Church to take a look around, leaving Usami and the rest of Halime's team to sort out whatever they needed.

By the time Miles had walked the few minutes toward the cafe, enjoying the dusting of snow on the ground and the coldness in the air, the Chinook had taken off. He watched as a second helicopter flew in with House Nix and the other Arbiter onboard. Miles stepped onto the dock, listening to the water lap against the bank beneath where he stood.

Church sat beside Miles as he removed his phone and called Drest.

"Miles?" Drest asked. "I wasn't expecting to hear from you. Is everything okay?"

Miles had considered not mentioning whatever dreams or visions he'd been having, but settled on wanting to know what it might have been. They weren't dreams, or at least they didn't feel like dreams, and they definitely weren't visions. Drest listened without comment until Miles finished.

"Are you okay?" Drest asked again, genuine concern in his tone.

"I'm a little freaked out," Miles said. "Been alive a long time, not had anything like that before. Do you know what it is?"

"No," Drest said. "You've had prophetic dreams before. Maybe there's a crypt or sarcophagus wherever you're going. Maybe they've taken their hostages to one."

"Why would they want me to talk to you about it?" Miles asked.

"I don't know," Drest admitted. "If it's prophetic, maybe it's just that someone involved in all of this holds a grudge. When you are done there, come to Scotland, and we'll discuss it further."

"Drest," Miles said, "if you know something more than you're letting on, I'd rather know myself."

"It is strange," Drest said, with no indication that there was anything out of the ordinary about what Miles had witnessed. "But I don't think it's dangerous."

"You don't *think* it's dangerous?" Miles asked. "That's not all that reassuring, Drest. Do you know who it is? Do you know who I spoke to?"

"I genuinely have no idea," Drest said, infuriating Miles further. "The number of people who would live in a sarcophagus in this day and age is almost zero. Vampires have moved on. However, there were vampires in the past who used them. I'll look into things here; there's no point in telling you who I think it may possibly be, when I can't confirm it."

"Someone from House Somnus?" Miles suggested, wanting a more concrete answer. "They can enter dreams. They can change them, too."

"It is possible that it was someone from House Somnus," Drest said. "Although I do not know of any of their House who would invade the mind of an Arbiter just to be cryptic. My guess is you haven't slept for some time and it weakened you enough that they were able to contact you. But I don't know for certain is still my honest answer. I don't know how they did it, I don't know how they found you or picked you. I don't know what they want with you. I don't know who they are. If it is merely a prophetic dream, then I'm sure you'll be seeing parts of it in real life. Just continue on with what you're doing. I'll do the legwork and figure out what might have happened."

"Am I putting people in danger by being here?" Miles asked.

"No," Drest said. "Contacting someone's subconscious is one thing, but they can't do anything once they've made contact."

Miles remembered the cuts in his dream. They hadn't hurt, and had healed instantly. "I'll get this done, and then I'm coming to see you."

"Good," Drest said. "I'll make sure to have something by then. But hopefully I won't need to."

Miles hung up and turned around to see Charlotte leaning up against an oak tree at the edge of the dock.

"How much of that did you hear?" Miles asked.

Charlotte smiled. "Enough."

Miles smiled and waited for her to elaborate.

"You had a vampire contact you in your sleep," she said and whistled. "That's not normal, Miles. Could it be like those dreams you had in Washington state?"

"Nothing about our lives is normal," he pointed out. "I don't know; neither does Drest, though. He's looking into it. In the meantime, let's just go do what we came here to do."

"You've got a few hours," Charlotte said. "You want to shower and change?"

Miles looked down at the tattered blood- and mud-stained clothes he was still wearing from the attack in France. "That would be lovely," he admitted. "Maybe something to eat. And drink."

"I'm sure we can do both of those," Charlotte said as she walked with Miles and Church toward the Assembly building. "You're really not worried about whatever happened to you?"

"Not right now," Miles admitted. "We have other things to do. It's a problem for future Miles to sort out."

"Future Miles is going to hate your guts," Charlotte said.

"I do feel sorry for that guy," Miles replied.

Church barked her agreement as they reached the patio outside of the main Assembly building, which had been taken over by the various House and Assembly personnel.

Miles was taken through the house by a kind young man, who showed him his room. The room turned out to be a suite, complete with hot tub and bar, neither of which Miles had the time or inclination to use. A well-stocked fridge had several blood bags and foodstuffs. Miles grabbed a bag and took enough of the food to make himself a platter of meat and cheese, giving Church her own platter, too, before he went for a long mild shower.

When he'd finally washed off the grime he'd accumulated, which mostly meant watching the water continue to turn pink as it went down the drain by his feet, he got dressed in a pair of jeans and plain black T-shirt, all of which had been left on the queen-sized bed for him. A pair of black and white Adidas trainers completed the look, and Miles checked his watch to see that he had a few hours to wait until he was to meet Jonathan. He texted Charlotte a thank-you for the clean clothes, as he was pretty sure she'd been the one to arrange them, found the TV remote, and settled in with Church to watch whatever terrible B movie he could find on the Assembly's various subscription services.

CHAPTER THIRTY-ONE

After ninety minutes of watching a shark terrorise a seaside resort town, which to Miles's eyes could have been solved by people quite easily if they'd all just decided to stop swimming for a bit, he was ready to go meet Jonathan and hopefully get some answers.

The convoy of three black Range Rover Sports drove through the night-time toward Berlin, which, like all major cities, was still busy with the hustle and bustle of everyday life. The car that Miles was in also seated Charlotte and Church and a driver from Halime's people. The three cars only had House Venator and Assembly people, as everyone thought it best to use as few people as possible. The House Nix contingent hadn't been all that happy about it, but Miles had assured them that the second he found out where Rosa was, they would all go get her.

The car pulled up a short distance away from the cafe, and Miles told Church to stay with Charlotte, who was going to go scout the local area to make sure there weren't any snipers ready to make Miles's day a lot less pleasant. And it hadn't been that great to begin with.

Miles got out of the car and walked to the cafe, taking a seat outside and ordering a cappuccino for himself. The young waitress asked if he would like anything to eat, but Miles didn't want to fill up on cake, no matter how good it all smelled, and declined.

The coffee came a few minutes later, along with a small stroopwafel on the side of the saucer.

"Thank you," Miles said, picking up the small sweet treat and taking a bite.

"They're not German, you know," a familiar voice said from behind Miles.

"Jonathan," Miles said without turning around as he finished the stroopwafel. "Yes, I know they're not German. They still taste good, so I'll try not to hold it against this small family-owned cafe."

Jonathan sat opposite Miles, placing a black leather satchel on the floor beside him. He ordered a black coffee and piece of apple strudel with vanilla ice cream. "Their cake here is delicious. If I was human, I'd be the size of a car with the amount I've eaten. Thank the heavens for our vampire metabolism."

"Are you even American?" Miles asked.

Jonathan smiled. "I was born in Crimea, possibly. My formative childhood years are a bit of a blur. I haven't used my original accent in such a long time. I was always good at voices, at accents. Maybe that's why I was picked. My life is a series of different accents from different places, although I think I like the Tennessee one the most, the drawl that comes with it. It disarms people."

The waitress returned with Jonathan's order, placing the drink and pie in front of him and telling him to enjoy.

Miles stared at the apple strudel and made a mental note to come back and try the delicious-looking dessert when this was all over.

"You want to try some?" Jonathan asked, offering Miles his spoon.

"No," Miles said. "I really don't want to eat pie at this moment in time."

"You want to know where Justice Balderas and Rosa are," Jonathan said, taking another mouthful. "They are safe. They are safe because I made sure of it. I had no hand in the attack on Justice Balderas's people. I actually managed to make sure they both survived. I only wish I could have helped you, too."

"You lie too easily," Miles said.

Jonathan chuckled. "True, but if you're considering reaching across this table to throttle me, just be aware that if I don't report back in, they will no longer be safe."

"Why save them?" Miles asked.

"Because I would rather have a bargaining chip to work with," Jonathan said. "I assure you that's the truth. Killing Justices is a poor life decision. I didn't want to be associated with such a thing. The handler, too. Arbiters die, it's not unheard of, part of the job, but handlers form bonds with their Arbiters, and honestly, if she'd died and you hadn't, I wasn't sure I'd be able to stop you from just killing me no matter what else I'd done."

"Can I assume they're not still in the tunnels under an abandoned Lithuanian village?"

"Like I said, safe," Jonathan replied. "We're going to talk first. I want assurances. I want to make sure I get out of this in one piece. I want to live long enough to come back here and try every single thing on their menu for a second time."

Miles wanted to reach across the table and snap Jonathan's neck. "Fine, Jonathan, what do you need?"

"I did some digging into you," Jonathan said. "Ex-House First Librarian, but before then when you were human, you were a soldier for the British army. You went to war."

"Several times," Miles said. "Against the Spanish and Portuguese, mostly."

"And then you turned to piracy," Jonathan said.

"I was a mercenary for a while," Miles corrected. "Went home with an empty purse and a dislike of authority and those who sent me to fight their wars. Shame I had to go to war to figure that bit out. I'm nae entirely sure how my history is of any relevance here."

"You were a spy," Jonathan said.

Miles laughed. "For a while, aye, I guess you could call me that. I'm good at languages, so I spent a few years in the Russian Tsardom and Ottoman Empire."

Jonathan smiled. "We are similar. I too was a spy for a country that cared little for my survival. So long as I got them what they needed, nothing else mattered. I was . . . disposable."

"So are countless others," Miles said, catching himself before he snapped. "It's pretty clear that authoritarian governments don't give two shits about the people they're being authoritative over. Me with the British Empire, and you with the Russian equivalent. Yet, I managed to grow up. You still seem keen on only doing what helps you."

"Why shouldn't I?" Jonathan asked. "I got sent to countries I'd never been to, to infiltrate their people and get information on things that would have gotten me dead if I'd been caught. They made me a vampire because they figured it would make me a better spy, and they were right. I fucking crushed that job."

"And now you're a murderer and thief," Miles said, taking a drink. "You aimed Sara at Megan. Don't even try to deny it."

Jonathan considered his next words for a moment. "Yes, she was someone who had become a thorn in my side. I didn't know that Sara was also going to try and kill you in Oslo. Had no idea that she'd sent a bunch of people there. I mentioned in passing where you were, I said that you wouldn't be with Megan and her team, and she took that to mean she could hunt you down."

"You know you're going to have to pay for Megan and her team."

"Because she was an ATO?" Jonathan asked, taking a fork of strudel.

"Because she was my friend."

Jonathan's fork paused at his lips, and he swallowed hard. "Oh."

"Fortunately for you," Miles continued, "finding and stopping Sara before the desolate side of her brain takes over fully is my immediate need. You will wait."

Jonathan took a bite of his apple strudel. "Sara is . . . not right. She has turned several Templar employees, most of whom were loyal to her. And they too are . . . unhinged."

"Someone in Oslo said that there was a merc who turned them," Miles said.

Jonathan nodded. "Some old friend of Sara's from before I knew her."

"Where is he?"

"Dead."

"Who killed him?"

"The occupants of Templar International in London," Jonathan said. "He and his team went there to take out some of the desolate. Again, I knew nothing of this. It didn't go according to plan, most were slaughtered. Happened a few weeks back. Those who survived work for Sara now. They seem to believe they follow her out of some misguided allegiance to her. Some of them used to be my people. It's clear that they are uninterested in the original plan anymore."

"Which was?"

"Money," Jonathan said. "I'll admit to the thief part. I've stolen a lot over the decades. Robbed banks, robbed anything that would make me richer. Killed a lot of criminals who had done all of the hard work. You know how hard robbing a bank is in the twenty-first century?"

"But you used Templar International," Miles pointed out. "To smuggle drugs into the country. Guns, too. Probably other stuff."

"I did," Jonathan admitted. "You have done your homework."

"We had a chat with one of your agents," Miles said. "He was very informative."

"You kill him?"

Miles shook his head.

"He's alive?" Jonathan asked, surprised.

"No, he's very dead," Miles said. "It's just that I didn't do it. You pissed off the wrong people with that attack in France. I'm wondering how you managed to get Sara to agree to help you use Templar to make you rich."

"Blackmail," Jonathan said. "I know what she is. I know her bloodline, and she knows what will happen to her should it come out. There's still a death sentence attached to it, after all. Shame she still turned Dominik. I think she thought it would all be swept under the rug, and that they could still keep her bloodline secret. Obviously it didn't work out."

"Turning Dominik wasn't part of your plan," Miles said.

Jonathan shook his head and drank from his coffee. "Not until after she'd done it. And then I had a little chat with Sara about making sure that Dominik was locked up tight, and that's all. And then Sara took her eye off the ball and that stupid little shit escaped and started murdering everyone. On top of which, the Wolf—stupid fucking prick—decided to steal my goods from the Templar port, along with a bunch of weapons, to sell the latter to a group of vampire-hating dickheads."

"You stole weapons from the company and sold them to people who would use them to kill our own people?" Miles asked with a shake of his head. "Was that your silver?"

"It is my silver," Jonathan said. "I should have killed the little shit for stealing it. I knew the twats robbing jewellery shops were using Templar equipment. I found a baton at one crime with their insignia on it. Figured whoever sold it to them might know where my silver was. Turned out it was the same dickhead.

"Also, if it helps, I didn't really *sell* them anything if they were actually scary. The really bad gangs, or whatever, you know, the vampire killers, they got a visit by an ATO team who arrested or killed them all, and the weapons were confiscated. I got richer, I got more accolades from the Assembly. I won twice."

"Do you know that Sara sent the desolate to Oslo as a weapon?" Miles asked, letting more than a little anger into his tone. He was fed up with Jonathan talking about himself and sounding proud about his nefarious accomplishments. He stole, he killed, and he hurt people, all to make money.

"I heard," Jonathan said with a sad shake of his head. "It was something that had been discussed before by the Russian agents who Sara and a bunch of the others worked for at the KGB back in the day."

"The wolf tattoo," Miles said.

"That was their unit badge," Jonathan explained. "When they got out, they kept the badge, went to work for Sara doing whatever needed to be done away from Templar International. They're vampires, and they're not good people. They recruited humans who had similar sensibilities. Created their own little private black ops unit."

"She keep them in check or something?"

"Most of the time," Jonathan said. "But since she went off the deep end, they've been allowed to use their more . . . base desires. They make people disappear, Miles. They're not good people. You met Fury, yes?"

Miles recalled the security guard at Templar Tower. "Aye, I met him. He's human, though."

"Was human. Not anymore. He's well-liked by Sara and the others," Jonathan said. "Sara turned him, and he went from being unhinged to outright horrific. He's one of those people who smiles at you as he talks, and slits your throat when you turn around. Which is something I have actually seen him do, by the way."

"You just surrounded yourself with good people, didn't you?" Miles said sarcastically.

"I surrounded myself with people I once thought I could control and expected to act like professionals," Jonathan almost snapped back. "With Sara's brain being turned to pudding, we are no longer aligned with our aims."

"Where are they now?"

"They're all in Lithuania."

"Did you choose there?" Miles asked.

"Sara told Henryk about her bloodline and past," Jonathan said. "He decided he wanted to give back to the area, so he built a village out there. Was going to make it a vampire settlement for people who worked for him, who needed to get away from the Assembly and Houses. Sara had her people build the tunnels under the village, and then the money for the town dried up, and it just sat there for years."

"Dried up?" Miles asked.

"I embezzled it," Jonathan said with a sigh. "Some of my people staged a few fires, a few attacks. I had Sara tell Henryk that it was too dangerous right now, and said we'd use the money to pay off the local gangs to leave the village alone."

"Except there were no gangs," Miles said.

Jonathan shrugged. "Well, technically I was the gang, but yes."

"I always thought you were a good ATO Commander," Miles said. "I mean, I heard the rumours about you being more interested in yourself, and Justice Balderas told me to stop giving you the credit for what I'd done, but I always thought you at least cared."

"I cared about me," Jonathan said.

"I don't feel that much sympathy for you, Jonathan," Miles told him. "Everything you did was out of a selfish need to help yourself."

Jonathan shrugged.

"Fine," Miles said, getting the impression the meeting was nearly done. "So where are the Justice and Rosa?"

"In the tunnels," Jonathan said with a broad smile.

"You didn't even move them to a more secure location?"

"Why? They're not my problem anymore."

Miles mentally counted to ten. "Any chance you have a map of these tunnels?"

Jonathan reached into the black satchel and removed a folded piece of paper. He opened it, laying it on the table as Miles finished his coffee, using the mug to stop the paper from folding back over. "This do?" he asked.

Miles studied the map. Three entrances and exits. One under what looked to be a mansion—which was no longer usable—one in the woods close to the entrance, and one in the basement of one of the wooden structures, about halfway through. The three marks also had numbers next to them.

"Codes?" Miles asked.

Jonathan nodded. "You need it to open from the outside, but not the inside."

"All of them are guarded, I assume," Miles said without looking up.

"This one here," Jonathan said, pointing to the one in the woods, "is more heavily guarded than the others. It's their point of exit should everything go to shit. It's also how they managed to get around Megan's team."

"The one under the mansion," Miles said.

"Yeah, it's been blocked off now," Jonathan said. "Some fucking idiot set fire to the mansion, partially collapsing it on top of it. They've been cleaning it all up, but it leads to an exposed part of the mansion, and it hasn't been Sara's priority to have people out there fixing it."

Miles traced his finger along the tunnels of the map to where it said *cells*.

"That's where the Justice and Rosa were when I left," Jonathan said. "This room here is where a lot of Henryk's art and stuff is. Well, my art. I'd rather this stuff wasn't destroyed, there's actually a lot of culturally important vampire artwork in there."

Miles looked up at Jonathan. "You care about this stuff?"

"Vampire artists, vampire writers, the arts, they're important to see the world as we see it," Jonathan said. "I'll admit I'm a criminal, a spy, probably a piece of shit, but this stuff actually matters to more than just me."

"Where do Sara and her people think you are?" Miles said.

"They think I went back to England, to the Assembly address in London," Jonathan said. "I told them that I would run interference so they had some time to prepare before hell descended on them for kidnapping a Justice. Which, I managed to explain, was better than if they'd killed him."

"You mentioned," Miles said. "So, you give me this, and we go there, get our people back. What do you want? Specifically."

"Sara and her people have to die, Miles," Jonathan said softly. "They all need wiping out. No survivors. They've gone too far, and Sara is far too dangerous to allow out in the wild, so to speak. Then I want access to my bank accounts, which have been frozen, and which I also know would be monitored even if they weren't frozen. I want my fucking silver, and I want what Templar International owes me. I'm going to lose a lot of money because of all this. I want what I should have made."

"They don't owe you anything; you were using them to smuggle," Miles said.

Jonathan shrugged. "Same difference."

Miles stopped himself from laughing, although it took a lot of effort. "How much is all of that?"

"Two hundred and fifty million dollars," Jonathan said.

Miles couldn't stop himself laughing then. "Are you insane? Haven't you accrued enough wealth to live on for a long time?"

"Yes," Jonathan said. "I have nearly fifty million dollars to my name. I don't care. I don't want to live on it for a long time, I want to live on it for centuries. I want enough to be able to go away and never be seen again. I want to buy a fucking island, Miles."

"Okay," Miles said. "And what's stopping me from just standing up and leaving? We know where the Justice and Rosa are."

"You'll never get in without the codes," Jonathan said. "And if you say no, I call Sara and tell her that you're coming. I won't tell her to execute the hostages, but we both know she will anyway. Slowly."

"Fine," Miles said. "How do you want to seal this?"

Jonathan removed a folder from the satchel and placed it before Miles, who picked it up and started reading. It was several pages long and spelled out Jonathan's confession as well as details of Sara's crimes, which Jonathan was informing on. It also stated what he wanted. Access to his bank account, two hundred fifty million dollars from Templar International, and an agreement that no one would hunt him down. A pardon for any crimes he may have committed. All given within three weeks of the conclusion of this case.

"A pardon?" Miles asked. "You are responsible for the deaths of an ATO team. Even without that, and trust me, I'm nae going to forget it, you've admitted to smuggling, supplying drugs, guns, murder, extortion."

"This is what it takes for me to work with you," Jonathan said. "You need to make a call, make one, but time is ticking on, and you don't have an infinite amount until Sara does something else stupid and dangerous."

Miles was the highest-ranking person dealing with everything that had happened, and while he knew he could contact another Justice and ask them for their approval, it could potentially take hours for them to give it. Hours Miles didn't want to wait around in Berlin, no matter how pretty the place was.

"Fine," Miles said. "You want me to sign it, or dot my bloody finger or something?"

"Blood is better," Jonathan said.

Miles extended his fangs, using their sharpness to nick his finger, which he pressed to the last page of the document. "You now," he said.

Jonathan smiled and performed the same action.

"This stays with me," Miles said, when Jonathan went to take the file.

"That wasn't . . ." Jonathan began.

"I don't like you," Miles said, low and menacing. "I'm keeping this document, I'm going to have it sent to the Assembly here in Germany, and they're going to process it. You have my word that I will inform you of it being handed in. You know full well that once I hand it to the Assembly, it will be logged into the system. No changing things then."

"Once you confirm it's been handed in, I will send you the codes you need to get into the tunnels," Jonathan said. "I have your number."

"Do you have a sarcophagus?" Miles asked, enjoying the moment of utter bafflement on Jonathan's face.

"A what?"

"You know what a sarcophagus is, right?"

"Why would I have one?" Jonathan asked. "Are you high?"

"Is any part of this tunnel system and village near a crypt or mausoleum?" Miles continued.

"What the hell are you talking about?" Jonathan asked, genuine confusion in his voice.

"You don't then," Miles said.

Jonathan sat back in his chair and studied Miles for a moment. "No, Miles," he said. "We don't have sarcophagi, or crypts, or tombs, or anything else like that. We're twenty-first-century vampires, we're not living in the Middle Ages anymore. Hell, I don't even think vampires slept in sarcophagi in the Middle Ages. Who does that?"

"Excellent," Miles said, not sure if he felt relief or not at Jonathan's words.

"You're a very strange man," Jonathan said. "Can I assume that we're now done here? Or do you have questions about temples and pyramids for me to answer, too?"

Miles stood, feeling a need to be as far from Jonathan as possible. "If you screw with me on any of this, there's nowhere on earth you can hide from me, you know that, right?"

Jonathan got to his feet and offered Miles his hand. "Of course. Shake on it."

Miles looked down at Jonathan's hand with open disgust. "Absolutely fucking not," he said, and walked away with the file under his arm.

Chapter Thirty-Two

Miles passed the file to the receptionist at the Berlin Assembly facility the second they returned. He texted Jonathan, who gave him the codes to the tunnels in Lithuania, along with a message showing a countdown. He expected his money and pardon within the next week.

"He doesn't want much, does he?" Charlotte said, when Miles showed her the message as everyone sat in the lounge of the building.

"What a grubby little thief," Usami said. "I would have cut his head off."

"Yeah, well you might still get the chance," Miles said.

"You should not have agreed to it," Usami said.

"I agreed, or everything we've done so far to get Justice Balderas and Rosa back would have been for nothing," Miles pointed out, aware that he had no intention of letting Jonathan get away with all he'd done.

"What if he lied?" Aamir asked.

"Then I kill him," Miles said matter-of-factly. "I have no time to play games here. If his actions end up with the Justice or Rosa being hurt today, deal or not, I will find Jonathan."

"Will the choppers need refuelling on the way?" Charlotte asked.

"The helicopters will have enough fuel to get there," Halime said. "Let's get this done."

Three helicopters landed at the rear of the property, with Miles and the House Venator people getting into the same Chinook that had brought them to Germany in the first place. They lifted off soon after, as Halime went around her team, making sure everyone was geared up and ready. When they were flying over Germany, toward Lithuania, she tossed Miles a stab vest and bent down to put one on Church, who licked her face as she did.

"Did you just giggle?" Miles asked as he put on his stab vest.

"No," Halime said, looking up at him. "And I would suggest you never heard such a thing leave my lips."

Miles smiled as Halime received another lick from Church.

"You are a brave dog to put up with Miles for so long," Halime said, giving her a kiss on the nose. "Much more patient than me."

"I'm right here," Miles pointed out.

Halime looked up at Miles, a smirk on her face. "Oh yes." She got to her feet and made sure that Miles's stab vest was properly fitted and fastened.

"I've done this before," he said.

"Don't care," she told him. "It's a ritual. We do it every time. We didn't do it once, and someone got stabbed in the neck."

Everyone in the Chinook who worked for Halime turned to look at one of their teammates, who had the good grace to be deeply embarrassed about it.

The journey to Lithuania took a few hours as the helicopters flew up toward the Baltic Sea and kept to the coast of Germany and Poland, until they reached Lithuania. The weather deteriorated the whole way, and by the time they'd reached the Lithuanian border, the freezing cold wind was battering against the exterior of the helicopters with unyielding ferocity.

The teams landed in a field a few miles away from the target, the trees surrounding the open area affording everyone some measure of shelter from the weather. The ATO units quickly and efficiently set up a command post using tents, the largest of which held a table and chairs. There was no time for luxury items, but once it was done, the leaders of the teams, along with the two Arbiters, Aamir, Halime, Charlotte, and Miles all stood around the table in one tent. Everyone inside the tent wore an earpiece for ease of communication between teams.

"So, you have a plan?" Usami asked, looking at the map of the area, which had three red *X*s representing the exits from the tunnels beneath the village, and a large red circle representing where Jonathan had said the hostages would be.

"This *X* here, under the mansion, is destroyed," Miles said. "I still want people outside of it, keeping an eye, making sure we're not being lied to. Anyone leaves, you deal with them. I also want one ATO team at each of these other two *X*s. Each team leaves behind a contingent at the helicopters to ensure that no one is stupid enough to try and screw around with our ride home. Considering the pilots will remain here, four ATOs in total should be enough. Figure it out among yourselves who goes where."

The ATO Commanders nodded without comment.

"Halime," Miles said, pointing to the *X* closest to the entrance of the village, "I want your team at this location. You'll be going in with Usami and Charlotte. Aamir, I'll be coming with your team. When all teams are inside, we move slowly, we go room by room. I do not want to turn it into a firefight down there. We have absolutely no idea of how much Jonathan gave us was horseshit. The circle is where our hostages are, and it's also directly under the mansion, which apparently had an exit before it burned down. To those of you going to the mansion, be prepared for anything. These vampires have shown no concern about killing Assembly personnel. You'd best believe they don't much care about doing it again."

"Any really old and powerful vampires?" Aamir asked.

Miles shrugged. "No clue. Probably not, it sounds like all of them are a few decades old, but they're all trained soldiers. They know how to fight, and they won't be doing it hand-to-hand. There will be incendiary and electric weapons down there, so keep yourselves safe, and don't try to rush in."

"Anything else?" Charlotte asked.

"Once in, we clear out and move toward the hostages," Miles said.

"Is this an extermination?" One of the ATO Commanders asked.

Miles looked around at the expectant faces. "No," he said finally. "This is to get the hostages out, get them free and clear. That is the first priority."

"And once they're safe?" Usami asked.

Miles looked over at her. "We go back and kill everyone who doesn't immediately surrender to us. Those vampires don't get to see another day. These people have used the desolate as weapons before, be prepared for them to use them again in a similar fashion. Any desolates are to be exterminated before we leave. No exceptions. Go get ready, we leave in one hour."

Everyone filtered out of the tent, leaving Miles, Church, and Charlotte behind. The latter was still studying the map when she said, "When we're done here, are you really going to just let Jonathan walk away with millions of dollars?"

Miles shrugged. "I signed that deal saying I would. So long as he doesn't break his side of it, it stands."

"I think letting Jonathan live is just going to bite all of us in the ass later," Charlotte said.

"Let's deal with this first," Miles said, not wanting to voice his agreement on the matter. Jonathan was another problem for future Miles.

Charlotte looked down at the map again. "Are there any innocent people around here who might walk into this?"

"Nearest village is about ten miles away," Miles said. "This whole area that Henryk purchased has large fences in the woods, lots of signs about the danger of death. There's a message board online for people who like to get into abandoned buildings. They used to go here, but it's been deemed too dangerous for the last few years. Apparently, the people Henryk employed to look after the place had a bit of a shoot-first way of dealing with trespassers."

"Is that an airport?" Charlotte asked.

Miles nodded. "It's two miles north of the village. Henryk had it built, but like everything else here, it all got left to rot. I considered us landing there, but it's almost certain that Sara, or someone she works with, will have eyes, possibly a standby means of escape."

An hour later, Miles and the House Nix personnel were moving through the forest to the southeast of the village. Several members of House Nix already had their Conjurations out. The small demon-looking entities ran and bounced in front of the group as if they were all going to something exceptionally exciting. None of them spoke, and they all appeared to Miles to know exactly what to do, as if they were somehow psychically linked with the vampire who had created them. They carried jet black knives in each hand, smaller versions of the gigantic sword that Rosa's Conjuration had used back in Templar Tower. Now that Miles had seen her version, he noticed the similarities between them, although he hoped that no one was about to create a Greater Conjuration in a confined space. He did not relish the idea of sitting through their use again.

They reached the hidden entrance, which was exactly where Jonathan had signalled it would be. The exit was a large metal plate in the floor, about six feet in diameter. It was big enough to fit even the largest of vampires. The plate had a code lock beside it and was covered in a camouflage tarp, which itself was covered in leaves and woodland debris. If you didn't know it was there, you'd have never found it.

The ATO unit stayed back as Miles input the code. There was a hiss of air, and the plate lifted itself up slowly on two hydraulic levers, revealing a ladder inside the dark tunnel beyond.

Miles tapped the earpiece. "You ready?"

"Ready," Charlotte said, followed by the voices of others out waiting to start the hunt.

"Let's go," Miles said, and looked back at Church, who had been fitted with her own stab vest. "You good?" he asked her as she sniffed the edge of the tunnel.

Church looked back and snorted quietly.

Miles looked into the tunnel again, his vision picking out the bottom forty feet below. "You want me to carry you?" Miles asked Church, who looked down at the hole and back up to Miles, and let out a sigh of irritation, stepping aside to allow House Nix down first.

When everyone else had descended, leaving only the ATO team above, Church sat beside the tunnel, looked around, and barked.

"You smell something?" Miles asked.

Church let out a low whine.

"You think there's someone up here?"

Church whined, but shook her head.

"There's something bothering you," Miles said. "You stay here. Any trouble, come get me."

Church barked.

"We'll take good care of her," the ATO Commander said. "We'll head up to the mansion; it gives a good view of the village. No one is getting by us."

Church looked back at the Commander before turning her gaze on Miles again.

"Okay, you stay here, you stay safe," Miles said. "We won't be long."

Church barked again, and Miles dropped down into the warmly lit tunnel, landing softly before walking on until he reached the others, who had waited at a nearby crossroads.

Miles pointed to the north as the direction to move in, setting off without another word. After a short walk, the lights in the ceiling started to blink on and off, until eventually giving up the ghost and deciding to stick with darkness. They all continued on nonetheless, stopping by any closed doors to open them and search whatever they found, quickly moving on.

After several minutes of walking, and having found nothing of interest, Miles stopped at another crossroads. According to the map, the second team was somewhere to the left of the rabbit warren of tunnels. Jonathan's map hadn't included as many offshoots and rooms as the real thing had been found to have, and Miles wasn't sure if that was because he figured they were unnecessary, or if he had hoped that Miles and his people would be ambushed.

Miles showed Aamir the map, pointing to the northeast where the hostages were apparently being held, before moving to point at their current location.

Aamir nodded and moved back with House Nix, the small Conjurations having remained behind the vampires, as if to keep an eye out for anyone coming up behind them.

With Miles in the front, they continued on for a short time, until yet another crossroads. According to the map, the two sides looped around a large area, coming together farther north. He motioned for Aamir to go to the right, taking most of his people with him, while Miles and one of the House Nix vampires Miles knew was called Benedict went to the left. No one was thrilled about having to split up, but considering they were all good at their jobs, any threat of ambush or attack of any kind was fairly low.

Static burst in Miles's ear and he winced, pulling the earpiece out, and finding that Benedict had done the same. "What the hell was that?" Miles asked, rubbing his ear.

"Interference," Benedict said. "Hopefully."

Miles replaced the earpiece, tapping it softly before he said, "Everyone good out there?"

More static.

"Too far underground, maybe?" Benedict asked, sounding as hopeful about it as Miles felt.

They continued on without another word, eventually meeting up with the House Nix people. "You hear that static?" Aamir asked.

Miles nodded. "Only one way here," he said, pointing to the large door at the end of the corridor beside where they all stood.

"The other team hasn't arrived yet," Benedict said. "If the comms are out, we won't know about trouble."

Miles passed Benedict the map. "Okay, Aamir, can Benedict and a few of your people go off and take a look?"

Aamir nodded, and Miles watched Benedict and three more House Nix soldiers leave.

"Beyond here are two rooms, joined by another hallway," Miles said. "First room has cells in it, it's where the hostages are. The second is some kind of treasure room, or something equally crass."

"Does the fact that we've met no one concern you?" Aamir asked.

"It doesn't make me feel good," Miles said. "How do you want to play this?"

"We go check the room," Aamir said, looking back at his four soldiers. "We . . ." His words were cut off by a scream from somewhere in the darkness, followed by the sounds of something crackling.

Miles ran to the end of the hallway, his eyes wide with shock as someone walked toward him, a flamethrower in hand. Miles threw himself to the side as fire flicked against the place he'd just been standing.

"Flamethrower!" Miles shouted, running back to the House Nix soldiers, and practically forcing Aamir to get around the corner as the flamethrower user made their unyielding way toward them. "Get inside the room, bolt the door, or barricade it, or something."

Aamir didn't ask again as Miles took off at a sprint, running around the corner of the tunnel as fire lit up behind him. At the end of the tunnel where Aamir and his team had walked only a few moments ago was another flamethrower user.

Miles sprinted toward his target and pushed the flamethrower up with a blast of telekinesis, the flames igniting across the ceiling. He held the flamethrower in place as he barrelled into the man using it, taking him off his feet, and tearing into the fireproof clothing he wore. He kicked the man back against the far wall as hard as he could, sending him into the concrete. There was a momentary *whoosh* noise as the fuel canister on the user's back exploded, engulfing the man in flames, his screams short-lived as he quickly succumbed to them. Unfortunately, the flames now covered the floor and walls, the sticky gel-like substance that had been inside the fuel canister creating a raging torrent of fire that reminded Miles of his dream.

"Fucking prophetic dreams," Miles said as the slow, methodical sounds of footsteps from behind him brought his mind away from the incredible heat in front of him. Fire began to pour into the corner of the tunnel opposite where the dead man was. He had precisely zero good options.

Just as Miles had settled on using his telekinesis again to hopefully pull the same trick as last time, the fire abruptly stopped, followed by a gurgling noise, and the sound of something wet hitting the floor. Miles peeked around the corner as Halime stood behind the decapitated flamethrower user, his body dropping to the floor into the pool of rapidly increasing blood.

"Thanks," Miles said.

"You always get in trouble," Halime said with a smile. "We met some more of these fuckers on the way."

"Everyone okay?" Miles asked, concerned.

Halime nodded. "Everyone is good. We encountered some low-level vampire resistance, a few guys with electric batons and fire rounds, but I don't think these people were expecting so many of us. Although I'm curious about where the rest are. There was a gas that filled some of the rooms, too. It ignited when we opened them, so we have a few singed, but nothing serious."

"Let's go get these hostages first," Miles said.

"I'll bring my people this way, meet you back out here," Halime said, running off.

Miles stepped over the dead body of the flamethrower user and ran to the door where Aamir and his team had gone through only a short time ago. He grabbed the handle and shoved hard, and the door managed to open with some effort, revealing a bloodstained room inside.

He continued through along a hallway beyond, until he reached a closed door at the far end. He pushed it open to find Rosa and Justice Balderas sitting on an opulent sofa. Aamir and two soldiers stood, weapons trained on the door and on Miles as he entered.

"We all good?" Miles asked.

"The flamethrowers killed two of my people," Aamir said. "Including Benedict."

"I'm sorry," Miles said.

"Let's all get out of here," Miles said, looking over at Rosa and Justice Balderas. "You both good?"

"Been better," Rosa said. "You know that Jonathan is behind it all?"

Miles nodded.

"How are my people?" Justice Balderas asked.

"Not great," Miles said. "You lost people. Karine is helping deal with everything, and we've let a contingent of ATOs in there, but knowing you're okay is going to help."

"How many did we lose?" Justice Balderas asked.

Miles told him in a quick overview everything that had happened.

Justice Balderas nodded solemnly and took a deep breath. "Thank you for everything you did."

"Right now, we need to get out of here," Miles said, feeling sympathy for the Justice, but also needing everyone to be on the same page. "That's our priority. Anyone know where Sara is?"

"I don't know," the Justice said. "She took several of her people with her to the airport. We've all been left here for hours. She said that we were Jonathan's problem."

"She told you that?" Aamir asked.

"She's insane," Rosa said. "The desolate and her personality are all but merged, and I think it's completely shattered her psyche. I'm not even sure she knows what she's doing half the time, but she occasionally has these moments when it's like she's waking up. I think she knows Jonathan has royally screwed her over."

Miles and Aamir put their shoulders into the door, eventually breaking the significant number of bolts holding it in place, and revealing a ladder just beyond. Before anyone could go anywhere, the door to the cell area opened and one of the House Venator soldiers entered, looking as if he'd been running.

"We've got a firefight going on above," he said.

"Ambush?" Miles asked, concern in his tone. "Is Church okay?"

"I believe so, yes," the soldier said. "It wasn't an ambush, thankfully. You stationing those soldiers probably made it so we have the upper hand, but they're laying down a lot of fire from the mansion."

Miles looked over at the ladder. "That way?"

The soldier nodded. "You go up there, and there's going to be a lot of angry people pointing weapons at you."

"Soldier, get the Justice and Rosa out of here, back to the helicopters," Miles said.

"Miles," Rosa protested.

"No," Miles said. "You've both been kept prisoner, and we came here to rescue you, not have you killed. Get them back to the helicopter. Aamir, go with them, make sure they all get back safe."

"Who's going with you?" Aamir asked.

"No one," Miles said. "I'm sure I'll be fine. I'll go up, piss everyone off, and leave. You sure this way is clear of debris above?"

Rosa shrugged. "As far as I know. They could have put debris back on top of it, I guess."

"Go, I'll catch up," Miles said. He wasn't going to be able to use his beast form for a while, so this was going to have to be done the hard way.

Miles waited for everyone to get out of the cell area, with Rosa glancing back at him, before he ran into the short tunnel and leapt up at the ladder, ascending it as quickly as possible. It was a longer climb than he'd anticipated, and after fifty feet, with no end in sight, the nothingness in his earpiece was replaced with static, and after a few more feet, the voices of several people.

Miles paused his climb, and with one hand on the ladder tapped the earpiece. "Anyone out there hear me?"

"Miles?" Charlotte asked. "You get Rosa and the Justice?"

"Sure," Miles said. "Ummm, how many attackers are up there?"

"Twenty, maybe," Charlotte said. "We've taken out a fair few. Most aren't even vampires, just human, although they've got some military training. Where are you?"

"I'm about to come up through the mansion," he said.

"There's a lot of enemy fire from there," Charlotte told him. "The ATO unit you sent found them, firefight started. A lot of them were hiding in the apparently empty buildings of this village. They were definitely waiting for anyone coming. Either Jonathan let them know, or . . . well, they knew he had betrayed them."

"Either way is fine," Miles said. "I'll find Jonathan when we're done. What about Sara?"

"No clue," Charlotte said. "I'm not sure that coming up into that mansion is the best idea, Miles. There's quite a lot of people in there with guns."

"I know, see you soon," Miles said, recommencing his climb until he was under the plate above. He looked around and found a red lever in the wall. He grabbed it and pulled, releasing the hiss of air from the plate as the hydraulics moved it up, letting in the sounds of gunfire and explosions from nearby.

Miles waited a few seconds before pulling himself up to look out of the hole. He was in a basement area, with steps in front of him leading up to a wooden door painted white. There was no ceiling, as part of the building had collapsed, leaving a large hole where he looked up at the night sky. Someone had cleared out a lot of debris but not bothered to actually fix the roof or walls.

Miles pulled himself out of the tunnel, turning to his vampire self as he moved silently up the stairs. His hand was almost on the rusty door handle, when the door itself was pulled open, revealing a man in tactical gear, holding a shotgun. Miles quickly grabbed the shotgun, pulling it toward him as he twisted away, the strap of the gun looped over the man's shoulder, and forcing him onto the stairs.

The strap broke, and Miles casually tossed the shotgun down the stairs with one hand as he hit the soldier in the face with an open palm slap, which caused the man to drop to his side, the partially destroyed staircase the only thing holding him up.

Miles grabbed the man around the throat, lifting him off the floor and squeezing, the man's eyes bulging in fear as he tried in vain to get Miles to release his iron grip.

"How many in the house?" Miles asked, his tone making sure that the soldier knew he was only asking once.

"Nine," the soldier said, his voice hoarse and unpleasant.

"All humans?"

The soldier shook his head. "Fury."

"Where are the other vampires?"

"Gone," the man said, trying to pry his fingers under Miles's to release the grip.

"Gone where?" Miles asked.

The man's hand dropped to his hip, coming up with a gun that Miles caught hold of, breaking the man's finger in the process.

"Gone where?" Miles repeated, slamming the question into the man's mind with enough force that he screamed in pain.

"Don't know," the man managed to get out.

Miles wanted to ask more questions, but getting out of here was more important. He crushed the man's neck in his hand and tossed his body down the stairs, stepping out of the basement into a hallway with broken windows and scorch marks all across the bare wood floor and walls.

Miles ran the ten feet to the end of the hallway as another soldier stepped into it from the room just beyond. He used his talons to slit the man's throat, removing the semiautomatic rifle from his hands, and putting a bullet in his head as he pitched forward. He emptied the weapon before tossing it out of the broken window as more gunfire erupted from above.

With the stairs to the upper floor nearby, Miles took them two at a time, reaching the landing above, and avoiding a shotgun blast from one of the soldiers as they left the room just beyond. Miles rolled to the side, springing up toward the soldier, who fired a second shot just as Miles used his telekinesis to push the gun away, forcing the blast to cut a hole in the wall next to him, leaving small fires where the incendiary rounds hit.

A second later, Miles had broken the man's neck, throwing him down the stairs and continuing on toward the mass of gunfire at the front of the building. He stepped into a large room, the windows overlooking the village in front of it.

Three soldiers inside turned and started to fire, but Miles had telekinetically moved the gun from the soldier on the far right, the bullets tearing into the body of the soldier beside him, whose gunfire ripped into the exposed beams of the ceiling.

The third soldier managed to clip Miles's arm with a bullet from his bolt-action rifle, but Miles was moving fast and collided with the soldier before he could load a second round, throwing the man headfirst into the other soldier, who was in a daze from having murdered his own companion.

Miles dove at the two surviving soldiers, tearing the throat out of one and kicking the other out of the window, where he landed headfirst on the concrete below. With all three dead, he looked at his arm. The bullet had grazed his bicep, leaving a deep cut which was bleeding freely but otherwise was okay. He removed the bullets from the dead man's gun: heat-impact, hollow-tip bullets. Not vampire killers, but definitely something that would make a vampire regret their day.

He picked up the shotgun, checked how many rounds there were—six incendiary—and stepped back into the hallway. He moved to the next room, raising the shotgun as he walked inside, killing the two soldiers with head shots before they'd even turned around from their continuous firing at whoever they saw outside.

"Fury!" Miles shouted as the din of gunfire died down. "Where are you?"

In reply, there was a slight click, and Miles threw himself to the floor as gunfire tore through the wall next to where he had been standing. He rolled over, coming back up with the shotgun, and fired twice at the wall, setting it on fire, and removing a large part of the plasterboard that had been there, revealing the face of Fury, who certainly lived up to his name.

Now back on his feet, Miles fired twice more, missing his target as Fury tore through the wall, taking hold of Miles and driving him back across the room, the shotgun knocked out of his hand. Miles headbutted Fury and drove an elbow into his temple, but the larger man threw Miles back, through the wall behind him, having seemingly barely noticed a blow that should have at least sent him to the ground.

Fury kicked his way through the remains of the wall as Miles rolled back, getting to his feet. Blood stained Fury's nose and chin, and he removed a pouch from his pocket, pouring blood into his open mouth before roaring at Miles.

Miles rolled his neck, making his neck crack as Fury came toward him. The larger man was in his vampire form, his talons out, but instead of slashing at Miles, he ran at him, grabbing him around the chest and lifting him up, squeezing tight enough for Miles to feel one of his ribs snap.

Miles drove an elbow down on top of Fury's nose, breaking it, but the other vampire refused to release his grip. Miles grabbed Fury's ear with one hand and smashed another elbow into his face, twisting the ear as Fury tried to move away, tearing the lobe free and causing the high vampire to feel pain for the first time.

Fury punched Miles in the mouth, knocking him to the side. He grabbed hold of Miles's arm, digging his thumb talon into the wound in Miles's bicep, causing him to yell out. Fury drove his knee up, trying to connect with Miles's stomach, but Miles raised his own leg, blocking it. Fury laughed, throwing Miles to the side as he looked down on him.

Miles got back to his feet, never taking his eyes off his opponent, who continued to flex his muscles and laugh. Seeing the opening, Miles kicked out at Fury's knee, which connected with a sickening crunch. Fury grunted and staggered back, giving Miles the chance to drive his own knee into the vampire's chest, before kicking him square in the sternum, sending him flying back through the broken wall.

Miles winced as his ribs healed from the beating, but he walked back over to Fury who was already on his feet, charging back at Miles in his drug-induced haze. Miles moved quickly, stepping to the side and driving his talons into Fury's liver, before stabbing him over and over. He smashed his elbow into the man's sternum, cracking it, before doing the same to his ribs just above the wound in his liver. With multiple cuts and broken bones, not even the drugs could keep him upright, and Miles grabbed Fury and threw him out of the window, jumping down after him.

Fury hit the grass just a short ways from the house, blood pouring from multiple wounds. He backed off, his hand up, trying to get Miles to show mercy that was never coming.

"Sara," Miles said, his voice low and angry.

Fury launched himself up with everything he had, but he was a broken and beaten man, even with the drug enhancement. Miles had considered using his bloodline gift, but hadn't been sure he wouldn't need to use it again, should Sara or someone else join in. Watching Fury whimper as he fell back to his knees, he wished he'd just ended it back in the mansion.

Miles looked up at the ATOs and House personnel moving toward his location. "You want to tell me and die, or you want to go to the Inquisitors?"

Fury got up onto his knees. "Fuck you, Arbiter filth."

Miles picked up the empty blood pouch that Fury had consumed. It smelled strange . . . sweet. He turned it over in his hands. "This is a tainted drug-laced blood pouch. Jonathan was selling these."

Fury said nothing.

"You know he set you all up? All of this was just a way for him to make money."

Fury remained silent, although Miles saw the shade of doubt in his eyes.

"Anyone here got a sword?" Miles called out.

One of Halime's soldiers removed a broadsword from a scabbard on her hip and passed it to Miles, who nodded a thanks.

"I hope you die hard," Fury said, looking up at Miles.

Miles considered the weapon for a moment, then passed the sword back to the soldier. "You know what taking all of that tainted blood does to someone if you're human?"

"What?" Fury asked.

Miles drove his palm into the vampire's chest, unleashing his bloodline power. "When he stops screaming, see if he's more amenable to answering questions," he said to the ATO closest, before walking back down the hill to the sounds of Fury's very human screams.

CHAPTER THIRTY-THREE

It turned out that, yes, Fury was more amenable to answering questions, once his vampire side had been switched back on and he was no longer a blubbering wreck. Even so, Charlotte asked the questions, with Fury quickly discovering that telling the truth was better than screaming in agony from lying.

When Charlotte was done, Usami cuffed him and dragged him off to the helicopters to await extraction. He was going to have a long and exceptionally hard life ahead of him. If he was lucky.

"The airport!" Fury had shouted over and over. "Sara went to the airport."

"Anyone seen a plane take off?" Miles asked.

No one had.

"I'm going that way," Miles told everyone. "Two miles isn't far. Everyone else, get any survivors back to the helicopters. The Assembly is going to want more answers."

"I'll join you," Charlotte said.

Miles shook his head, removing his stab vest and shoes again, before turning into his beast form. "This is quicker," he said, flexing his wings. "Take one of the helicopters to the airport, I might need help if there's more of Sara's people, but if no plane has taken off yet, we need to move fast."

"Be careful," Justice Balderas said.

Miles nodded and looked down at Church. "Ready?"

Church barked and set off at a flat-out sprint north, soon disappearing from sight as she went through the trees. Miles beat his wings, lifting off the ground, and was quickly soaring above the trees, catching the occasional glimpse of Church, who was putting herself through the paces, running as fast as she could. Miles was capable of flying faster than Church and was soon ahead of her, the airport looming up in the distance.

A single private aircraft sat on the runway, a hangar a quarter mile behind it. What was described as an airport was in reality the single hangar and strip of tarmac, neither of which were in their best condition.

As Miles got closer, he noticed that the airplane was at a strange angle, the engines off, the door slightly ajar. He landed on the field of long grass a hundred feet away from the plane, his wings folding behind him as he walked the distance, unwilling to turn back from his beast form in case he was about to face something a lot worse than had come before.

The smell of blood was obvious the second Miles stepped onto the tarmac, and he looked around as Church burst out of the woods, continuing on at speed until she was beside him. She let out a low growl, her hackles immediately up.

"Check the area," Miles said. "I've got the plane."

Church set off at a considerably slower pace, her nose close to the ground as she weaved through the long grass to sniff out trouble.

Miles flew across the airfield, landing at the bottom of the stairs, the smell of blood and death overwhelming his senses. He slowly walked up the staircase, his wings still folded behind him as he pushed open the partially broken door, allowing him to witness the carnage inside the fuselage.

There were multiple dead bodies inside the plane, each in multiple parts. Miles couldn't figure out who the people were, but there was a lot of equipment and weapons inside the airplane, most of it now covered in gore.

Miles looked away from the plane, leaping down the steps to the tarmac and ducking under the plane as Church's barking grabbed his attention from the hangar. He quickly took to the sky again, flying along the airfield to the large metal hangar, where Church lay outside, looking into darkness beyond.

"You good?" Miles asked.

Church barked once.

"Keep an eye out, okay?"

Church barked again.

The gap in the hangar doors was large enough for Miles to walk through, but he stopped, pulling open one of the doors, which was on casters, until there was enough room for him to see the entire interior. It was sparse inside, with some tools and cleaning equipment at the far end, along with several large crates of who knows what, but it appeared to be mostly a place to store the jet.

"Sara," Miles said into the gloom of the hangar as he stepped inside, avoiding the glass from the broken bulb that had once hung above the entrance.

The sounds of an approaching helicopter rang through the night.

"Church, make sure no one comes in here," Miles said without looking back.

Church made a soft whining noise.

"I'll be fine," Miles said, still looking into the darkness, searching the hangar for wherever Sara was hiding. He looked up at the metal rafters above, spotting Sara huddled in the corner, her knees pulled up tight to her chest as she stared at him.

"Leave," she said, her voice hard.

"No," Miles replied, stepping further into the hangar. "You killed those people in the plane."

"They worked for Jonathan," she said. "I thought they were going to betray me. Jonathan betrayed me. I keep forgetting things, I keep thinking people are trying to kill me. I can't sleep, I can't . . . I'm angry all the time. And when I'm not, I'm scared. I just want to hurt and destroy. I can feel it in my brain like a voice whispering all the time. I'm not me anymore."

"We'll get you help," Miles said. He was halfway across the hangar floor, avoiding the remains of lightbulbs. He wasn't sure that he would even feel the cut in his beast form, but better safe than sorry considering he was so close to a vampire who was unpredictable at best.

Sara dropped her legs to either side of the beam she sat on and crawled along it, keeping watch on Miles. "*You.*"

Miles sighed. "You don't want to fight me. Your people are dead or imprisoned; don't join them."

Sara reached out in front of her and retrieved a large broadsword. She grabbed the steel beam with her free hand and swung down under it, letting go and landing on the floor. She was barefoot, and her jeans and T-shirt were both covered in blood.

"That's all your friends' blood," Miles said.

Sara swayed from side to side. "They're all against me," she said. "I need to kill, to drink blood. I *need* to feed."

Miles remained quiet as Sara moved toward him, the sword still in her grasp.

"I was a spy," she said, almost as if in a dream, her head jerking from side to side. "An assassin. A murderer. A soldier. I worked for my country. I killed for my country, and where did it get me? Jonathan said you were like me."

"No," Miles said. "We just happen to have a similar employment history."

Sara's eyes narrowed in the darkness. "He said you would kill me if we fought."

"He's right," Miles said. "You don't want to fight me, Sara. It won't end well for you."

"You're a beast," Sara said. "I only do this." She became ethereal, walking through one of the crates before reforming on the other side.

Miles prepared for the inevitable.

"You killed my people," Sara said.

"Today?" Miles asked. "Yeah, a lot of them."

Sara shook her head as if impatient. "No, not today, you fucking imbecile. My bloodline. All those centuries ago. It was you. I had to hide who I was for so long, but not now." She chattered her teeth together over and over, getting progressively harder until Miles thought she might break them.

"I didn't do any of that," Miles explained, hoping to find a way out of this that didn't involve killing her.

Sara turned her head to the other side. "Shut up," she said. "I know. Shut up."

Miles was pretty sure she wasn't talking to him.

"Your mind is no longer yours, Sara," Miles said. "Your brain is a mess of desolate rage and hate. Did Jonathan tell you what that means?"

Sara nodded.

"He did tell you what was going to happen to you?"

"I'm going to kill you and feast on your blood," Sara said. "That's what I think I should do."

"You're losing your mind," Miles said, pretty sure that part was already done. "You're hearing voices that aren't there, seeing people who aren't there, you're paranoid and desperate, and you're going to kill everyone around you. All of that sound familiar?"

"And then what?" Sara asked, her tone no longer the dreamlike quality it had been.

"And then you're going to die," Miles said.

"Because you'll kill me?"

"No, because your mind will fracture totally," Miles said. "The desolate side will take over completely, but we're not desolate, so it'll fry your brain. You'll become a vegetable stuck in a constant loop of death and pain in your own mind. You'll wither away to nothing, with no part of who you once were existing. Eventually someone will put you out of your misery. Or not. There's nothing good coming your way, Sara."

"Is this where you tell me you can help me?" she asked.

Miles shook his head. "There's no help here. I'm sorry."

Church barked outside of the hangar, and Miles's attention wavered slightly, giving Sara the opportunity to dash toward him. She swung the sword up toward Miles's chest. He stepped to the side and toward her, hoping to stop her before the sword could complete its arc, but Sara turned ethereal, moving through Miles's hand and reforming behind him, continuing the swing and cutting through his back.

Miles darted forward, turning back into his more human form, the blood seeping down his back. No point being stronger and with the ability to fly if there was no use for it.

Sara's attacks with the sword were fast, precise. She glitched through Miles's attacks, catching him with her own swipes, although he was quick enough to avoid anything serious. After she glitched through his arm again, Sara slammed the pommel of her sword toward Miles's head. He caught the sword handle in one hand and struck her in the chest with his palm, but having used his bloodline gift only a short time ago, he was unable to use it again, and only succeeded in hitting her hard enough to send her flying back, leaving her sword in his hand.

Miles wanted to ask her to stop, but it would have been wasted words. Whatever remained of Sara was buried beneath layers of monster.

"You okay?" Charlotte shouted from the entrance.

"I'm good," Miles said without looking back.

"Oh, friends," Sara said. She sprinted toward Miles, glitching in front of him and reforming behind, but Miles was already prepared for her tactic. He grabbed her by the back of her T-shirt and yanked her back, throwing her across the hangar, where she collided with the far wall.

"I'll be right out," Miles said, feeling the surge through his body that suggested his bloodline power was usable once again.

Sara shrieked and charged Miles, glitching over and over as she ran at him. When she was ten feet away, she leapt at him, her talons bared, ready to tear into him. Miles stepped toward the strike, and she glitched through him like before, spinning around to catch him in the back of the head, but he jumped ten feet off the ground, landing behind her. He grabbed hold of her head and unleashed his bloodline gift.

Sara fell forward, clawing at her head, her body, her talons thankfully retracted, but she still left red lines across her face.

Miles picked up the sword from the floor as Sara rolled onto her back, looking up at him. "What did you do?" she asked.

"Severed the vampire and human sides," Miles said. "I wasn't sure if it would sever the vampire and desolate, too, but apparently so. You probably have about ten to fifteen minutes before everything goes back to how it was."

"I don't want that," Sara said, tears streaming down her face. "I don't want that . . . *thing* in my head anymore. I killed so many people who didn't deserve it. Those people in the plane. They tried to stop me. They . . . they worked for Jonathan. They all worked for him."

"He told you about killing Megan," Miles said. "I know. You thought you had to kill me, too, and sent people to Oslo."

"I hated you both," Sara said. "But he told me over and over again that Megan was the main threat. That she needed to be dealt with. I just . . . I wanted to stop hearing the thing in my head. Jonathan said it would help, and the desolate agreed."

"He blackmailed you to go to work for Henryk?" Miles asked.

"I was already working for him," Sara said. "Henryk introduced us, and Jonathan figured out who I was. What I was. He used that information to blackmail me, for me to look the other way, to falsify records, to hire people who really worked for Jonathan. It was easy. And I hated myself for it."

"I'm sorry about Henryk," Miles said. "I saw the video."

"He didn't deserve any of this," Sara said sadly. "Not the lies, not the manipulation. He was just trying to be a good dad to a kid who was deeply messed up."

"You put that device on," Miles said. "It did something to your brain. And then you fed on a desolate, and that sealed your fate."

"It linked me with the desolate," Sara said. "It . . . I *needed* to feed. That was all I could think of. I think the desolate might not have been so thrilled that I drank him dry. Are Rosa and the Justice okay?"

Miles nodded.

"I wanted to kill them," Sara said, her hands covering her face. "But I knew it was wrong. I knew that they could stop Jonathan. That he had to be stopped."

"He will be," Miles assured her.

"He figured I'd kill them both, and that most of you would die in the fight," Sara said. "He told me to tear them to pieces. The desolate liked that idea—it didn't have total control, but I couldn't keep fighting it. Figured I'd get away, hide. Went to the jet, and the people there told me they'd take me to Jonathan. But I didn't want that, the desolate wanted to be fed. *I* wanted to be fed. I killed them all. This is like a nightmare."

"I know," Miles said, knowing there were no words that could possibly comfort her.

"You're bleeding," Sara said, pointing to Miles's arm.

Miles looked down at his bicep. "Twice in one day. Where will Jonathan go?"

"Northern Russia," Sara said. "Village near the shore of the Barents Sea. Teriberka. Not far from there is a dilapidated village with an old church. He used to talk about it. Said it was a vampire paradise. Always cold, dark for long periods, with plenty of humans far from anything close to civilisation. He won't go straight there, though. He'll take his time, make sure he's not going to be followed. I don't know where he'll go before then, and it'll be a few weeks, maybe longer, until he arrives, but that's where he'll end up. You're going after him?"

Miles nodded. "He got a lot of people killed. So did you."

Sara nodded. "I was so full of rage, just wanted you all dead. I killed Megan, killed her team. Killed innocent people." Her face contorted with rage. "And they fucking deserved it. They all deserved to fucking die."

Miles sighed.

Sara's expression crumpled like paper. "I can feel it. Feel the rage and hate inside. It hurts. Every waking moment hurts. It's like a nightmare I can't ever stop. I just want it all to stop. Make it fast. Please." She moved into a kneeling position and bent forward, exposing her neck.

Miles readied the sword above her.

"I'm sorry," she whispered.

"So am I," Miles said, and brought the sword down in one fluid moment, ending Sara's life on the cold floor of an aircraft hangar in the middle of nowhere.

Chapter Thirty-Four

After Sara's death, Miles let the combined force of the Assembly, House Nix, and House Venator deal with the fallout of what had happened. There were several prisoners, none of whom were going to have a fun time of it for the rest of their relatively short lives.

He'd wanted to go straight to Russia and wait, but he knew that Jonathan would have people watching the place, so Miles decided that Jonathan's fate would have to wait. Instead, he went back to London with Rosa, Charlotte, and Justice Balderas, making sure that the Justice and Rosa were okay. They thanked him for his efforts to keep them all in one piece, and for rescuing them.

"I'm going to take time off," Miles said as they sat in the garden at the rear of the Assembly building where they'd first met what felt like a lifetime ago.

Justice Balderas nodded in understanding. "I would too in your shoes. How long?"

Miles shrugged. "Year, maybe. I don't even want to go anywhere, I just want to not have to kill anyone for a while."

"They all deserved their fate," the Justice said.

Miles nodded sadly. "They did. But we're not done yet, and after that, I would like to enjoy some time at home."

"Jonathan," the Justice said, "there are people out looking for him."

"There are," Miles agreed, looking out across the garden toward the helipad at the far end, where Charlotte stood talking on the phone. Church ran around the garden, carefree and full of energy. It made Miles smile watching her.

He'd texted Drest to see if he could narrow down the search given Sara's directions of where Jonathan would end up, but knew that if he mentioned it to the Assembly, they'd want to send teams there to wait for him. Miles didn't want that; he didn't want any chance of Jonathan running off. For now, he was just going to wait and relax.

"You should just tell them where Jonathan is," Justice Balderas said, breaking the spell of tranquillity that sat in Miles's heart.

Miles looked over at the Justice and smiled. "I honestly don't know where he is right now. But I'll find him. This is something I have to do."

"I understand that, too," Justice Balderas said. "Be sure that this doesn't become vengeance."

"Sometimes you need a little vengeance," Miles said, getting to his feet. "Take care, Justice Balderas. Tell Karine and your people in France that I hope they're okay. They didn't deserve any of this."

"I'm going back tomorrow," the Justice said. "Karine was happy to hear my voice. She's a good person. I don't think I could do the job without her. Rosa passed me a USB drive that I'm going to spend some time looking into. Thought you might like to know. I don't think there will be any wrongdoing passed back to anyone who approved their accreditation. You should know that, too."

Miles smiled. "I expected nothing less. I hope whatever you find helps people."

Justice Balderas offered Miles his hand, which the latter shook. "I'm sure it will," the Justice said.

Miles walked off and found Rosa in a room near the reception area. She was talking to one of the ATO teams who had come to rescue her. The agent nodded at Miles, and left them alone.

"I'm leaving," she said. "Taking some time off."

"Me too," Miles said with a smile.

"Why not come with me?" Rosa asked. "I'd like the company."

"I have things to do," Miles said. "Go have some time off. Enjoy yourself. If you're ever near my place, you're always welcome."

Rosa smiled. She stood, walked over to Miles, and kissed him on the cheek. "I'll take you up on that, Miles Watson. Please be careful."

"Always," he said.

Miles and Church travelled via helicopter with Charlotte, who had waited for him, back to the House Venator estate, and was happy to see that Halime and her people had all returned. Drest met them at the heliport they'd used earlier, the snow having started in earnest, as if it had forgotten about the time of year and was trying to make up for it.

Miles and Church spent a few days in Scotland recuperating and taking a well-earned break. After day three, Drest found Miles sitting on a bench overlooking the rolling hills close by. It had started snowing again, and Miles had always liked that particular bench to view the scenery during the winter months.

"You okay?" Drest asked, motioning if it was okay to take a seat.

"Be my guest," Miles said, watching Church play in the fresh snow. She burst out of a snowbank, looking more yeti than dog. "I'm fine."

"Any more prophetic dreams?"

Miles shook his head. "Nope. No tombs or crypts were found anywhere near where Jonathan and his people were hiding. No mountains of skulls. Maybe it was just a dream and there was no relevance to it."

"Maybe," Drest said. "When you're done with all this, I'd still like you to stay here a few weeks, just in case."

"I'm taking some time away from the Assembly," Miles said. "I think it's better that I do that at home. A home you're more than welcome to come visit, you know."

Drest smiled. "That sounds like an excellent way to get out of here for a while. We could all use some downtime."

"Even you?" Miles asked with a sly grin.

"Even me," Drest said, his expression matching Miles's.

They sat in comfortable silence for a while before Drest got to his feet. "Walk with me, Miles."

Miles stood and stretched, and the pair walked back to the main building, with Church trying to catch as much snow in her mouth as possible.

"What is it?" Miles asked.

Drest passed Miles a piece of paper with a set of coordinates on it. "We found the church you mentioned, about a day's walk from the shore. Used to be a village there too before everyone left, or died, no one seems to know which. It's a good place to hide out, as no one ever goes there. Vampires sometimes use it to hide, though."

Miles nodded and put the paper in his pocket. "Thank you."

"You're going there?" Drest asked. "They didn't find all of his ATO team members in Lithuania. Apart from the one who was killed in France, the rest are unaccounted for. They're going to be in Russia with Jonathan. You know this, I assume."

Miles nodded.

"These are all highly trained," Drest said. "They're not the same young vampires you found with Sara. These aren't going to be as much of a pushover."

"I'll be fine," Miles said, completely confident that he would be.

"When are you leaving?"

"As soon as I can get a flight there," Miles said.

"You can use the Chinook," Drest said. "It'll drop you off about five miles away from the village. That's five miles in territory that isn't going to be fun for this time of year."

"Will they wait?" Miles asked him.

"Three days," Drest said. "No longer. We're calling it an expedition into the area. Apparently there are some old libraries that Gideon would like to see. The vampire settlement there has a collector of the weird and wonderful."

"After three days, I'm either done or dead," Miles said. "Gideon is coming with me?"

Drest nodded. "Halime is sending three of her people to protect Gideon. If you want their help, they'll go with you."

"I'll be okay," Miles said.

Drest rested a hand on Miles' shoulder. "You don't have to do this on your own with just Church."

"I'll be fine," Miles said, removing his phone, taking a photo of the coordinates, and sending one message:

Jonathan location. I'm going now. You'll have to make your own way there. You in?

Miles attached a copy of the photo to the message and sent it.

"Backup?" Drest asked.

"Hopefully. I'll leave my stuff here, if that's okay."

"So long as you come back for it," Drest told him, before the two men shook hands and hugged.

As Drest walked away, Miles's phone vibrated as a single message was delivered; *I'll be there.*

Miles was in the Chinook with Church within the hour. He wore snow-camouflaged trousers and matching jacket top, with a black rucksack that had a cooler compartment with two blood packs. He also had a map and compass—because he didn't want to lose his way in the middle of nowhere—along with a combat knife, an electric baton, and several other bits and pieces he was sure would come in handy. He carried no other weapons, although there was a white flag attached to an extendable metal pole in his rucksack.

Once the Chinook took off, Church did her usual trick of immediately falling asleep, while the three guards Halime had sent to keep Gideon safe all nodded a greeting to Miles, who made the same gesture in return. While he had been a member of House Venator for a long time, he was surprised at how many vampires and familiars he hadn't met who worked for the other Firsts.

Like the guards, Gideon sat on the opposite side of the helicopter from Miles and Church. He sat to one side, directly behind the cockpit, reading a book. He looked up at Miles and tapped his headset. Miles inwardly groaned and placed his own headset on.

"Why are you going to Russia?" Gideon asked.

"I felt like having a holiday," Miles said.

"In camouflage?"

"I *really* don't want to be found."

Gideon's eyes narrowed. "You know, I always thought that you were a little off. You were a scholar, a librarian, second to whatever you actually are. You killed Inquisitors in America. Several of them. You never told me how someone who was First Librarian was able to do such a thing."

"And I never will," Miles said with a smile. "Look, Gideon, we both know you can look up my past history. Jonathan managed it, so I'm nae entirely sure why you need me to tell you."

"How did Jonathan manage it?" Gideon asked.

"My history as a human isn't secret," Miles said. "I was a soldier, a mercenary, a spy, a truly shitty person. I killed people for king and country, for money, and because they needed killing. Now I only do it for the latter."

"How did you get so good at it?"

"Everyone has a talent," Miles said. "Mine is just a little more gruesome than most."

"Why did Drest make you First Librarian?" Gideon asked, finally getting to the root of the problem between the two men.

"Ask him," Miles said.

"I have," Gideon replied. "He told me to ask you."

Miles laughed. "I like studying," he said, after considering whether or not to bother. "I like reading. I like history. I like investigating mysteries. I wanted to do something to help people, not just kill those who crossed me or the House. Being a Librarian allowed me to help people. First Librarian is a scholar and an investigator. Seemed a natural fit."

"I find the act of being an investigator secondary to being a scholar," Gideon said.

"And that is why people don't come to you for help," Miles said. "You would prefer not to have to involve yourself in something. We are there to catalogue not just what has happened in the far past, but what is happening now. It means being a part of the House, it means getting to know people, getting to stop bad things from happening, or at least find out *why* they happened."

"People should be more independent minded," Gideon said. "My librarians deal with the investigator aspect of the role. I am too busy to sully myself with the base actions of criminals."

"The First Librarian is meant to help people, not suggest doing so is sullying yourself, or beneath your notice. There are two parts to your job, Gideon. One of them you are excellent at, better than I ever was. But the other, you don't care for, so you don't do it. Drest lets it go because your staff are all good at their jobs, but people want to see the First Librarian help, they want to know that you will help should they need it. All they know with you is you consider helping them to be a waste of your time."

Gideon stared at Miles for several seconds before resuming his book. Miles shook his head and hoped that was the end of the conversation between the two of them.

If he thought that the journey to Lithuania was bad, the flight to Russia was considerably worse. They once again landed in Berlin for refuelling, with Miles taking Church outside to stretch her legs. They had to refuel again in Stockholm, before carrying on to Murmansk in Russia, where a car was to be waiting for Miles and Church. It was a few hours' drive from there to the closest destination to where Jonathan was.

Once they had landed at a private airfield in Murmansk, the pilot reminded Miles of the three-day rule, which Miles promised he would adhere to. He found the black Jeep Wrangler parked just outside of the airfield, and once Church had jumped into the front and he'd stowed their gear in the footwell behind the driver's seat, they set off.

"You know this isn't going to be easy," Miles said to Church as they drove out of the city and were soon on rural roads, where Miles became grateful for having a 4x4 that was actually capable of going off road.

The location that Miles had been provided was a short distance from the rural location of Teriberka. He'd decided to drive to the small village and walk the rest, which was going to take him another few hours, but which he felt was the better way of making sure no one spotted his approach.

The drive was quiet, and despite the occasional bit of traffic and flurry of snow, uneventful. The exact kind of drive Miles could get used to. He stopped the Jeep in Teriberka, speaking to a local bar owner whom Drest had said owed him several hundred favours. The bar owner was a vampire who belonged to no particular house, but who also wanted to remove one of those favours from his long list of debts. He allowed Miles to park the Jeep, and explained that a friend of his had also been in the village a few hours earlier, having also driven from Murmansk.

"Were they alone?" Miles asked.

The bar owner nodded. "You hunting?" he asked. "Actually, I don't want to know. Do whatever it is Drest needs, and be gone."

Miles left the village in the middle of the night and remembered the last time he'd been to Murmansk when it had still been daylight, despite it being nearly two in the morning. It had been unnerving not to see the moon for days on end—and precautions had to be made in case of UV levels—but he was grateful that it wasn't the case this time.

They trekked through the dark, snowy wilderness of northern Russia, keeping an eye out for anything that might cause him pause. Polar bears weren't a big problem in the area, but that didn't mean they weren't around.

Church took the trek as if it were a fun jaunt through the Venator Estate in Scotland, leaping into snowbanks and running on every few minutes, a seemingly boundless amount of energy.

After an hour, Miles stopped at an old abandoned fishing hut, and took one of the blood pouches from his bag, drank it, and carried on. As he got closer and closer to the coordinates that he'd been given, he saw that to the south of his location was a large ridge overlooking the long since abandoned village and the ocean beyond.

There was a flicker of light from the top of the ridge. A momentary thing that happened once, a pause of a few seconds, and happened a second time, and then it was gone. Miles removed the white flag and pole from his bag and carried it up high, the flag flickering in the wind as he walked along the flat, frozen tundra toward the collection of desolate buildings.

"Church, go around to the rear side," Miles said. "Stay low."

Church took off at a sprint, moving between large rocks as she quickly disappeared into the darkness.

Miles continued on until he reached the outskirts of the village, where he was greeted by Jonathan Holt, who wore a thick bearskin cloak over jeans and a thick black jacket.

"I didn't expect to ever see you!" Jonathan shouted as three others left the run-down houses at the far end of the village, aiming weapons in Miles's direction.

"You lied to me," Miles replied. "You told Sara to kill the hostages. You told them I was coming. You set us both up to kill each other."

Jonathan shrugged. "Figured it was worth a try. You were never going to pay me the money I'm rightly due. And it gave me some time to get as far away as possible."

"No, I wasn't," Miles said. "Did you really believe you would get it?"

"No," Jonathan said. "I might have done if you'd been killed back in France, and I'd been able to play the hero who didn't quite save the Justice and Rosa in time, but then you went and survived, so plans had to change. I heard about what happened. You killed Sara. Did she tell you about this place?"

Miles nodded. "She did."

"I figured her too far gone to be able to say anything of worth."

"She was pretty lucid at the end. And then she died. As did Fury. And pretty much everyone else you left there to fight a losing battle."

"Like I said, it was worth a try," Jonathan said as he walked toward Miles. "So, are you here to kill me now?"

Miles shrugged. "I'm nae sure yet. I figured I'd see if you were capable of actually telling me the truth before I decided your fate."

Jonathan stopped walking when he was only a few feet away from Miles. "The truth is, I was going to kill Sara myself, but I figured it better to try and take a few Assembly idiots out at the same time. I plan on staying here a few decades until it all dies down, and then I'll go get my fucking money. Not what you were going to pay me, the stuff I stashed away for a rainy day. You do know, I've been siphoning it out of Templar accounts for years at this point. I need to give it some time before I can risk going back and being spotted by some Assembly bootlicker."

"And you're telling me this because I'm nae going to make it out of here alive, I assume," Miles said, noticing that one of the three men was no longer at his station against the wall of a building. He turned the pole so that the white flag was pointing behind him.

"Yes, pretty much," Jonathan said. "You know you shouldn't have come here. If you were going to make yourself a target, why not just pick us off one by one? You arrogant piece of shit."

The bullet that caught Jonathan in the neck and jaw made a small entrance hole and a gigantic exit, removing part of his jaw in the process. Blood sprayed from the side of his throat as he dropped to the ground, grasping at the wound that was never going to close.

There was a crack of noise as Miles stepped to the side of the village entrance. Bullets peppered the ground where he'd stood just a moment ago, followed by a scream and more bullets.

Miles looked around the corner of the building as Church nonchalantly padded down the main road of the village. She was covered in blood, although she appeared to be completely okay with it. Miles spotted the bodies of two of the vampires.

"You get all three?" Miles asked.

Church barked once for yes.

Miles looked over at Jonathan, whose eyes were still open wide in a pleading gesture. "Stay here, I'll check his buddies," Miles told Church.

Church barked once again and sat close enough to Jonathan to finish the job should it need to be done.

Miles found the three dead vampires quickly enough. Two of them had their skulls crushed, the force of the bite all but pulverising the brain, and the third had been taken in the throat, which had all but decapitated him. Miles dragged all three bodies into the middle of the village, removed a bottle of the same flammable gel that had been used by the flamethrowers in Lithuania, and used it to set all three on fire.

By the time Miles made it back to Jonathan, who was completely done for, Rosa was stood beside him. She wore a white ghillie suit and carried the same rifle she'd used back in Oslo.

"You good?" Miles asked her.

"Am now," she said, looking down on Jonathan with nothing but cold contempt.

"Jonathan," Miles said, removing another bottle of flamer fluid and pouring it over him. "For all of your crimes, you deserve a lot worse than this."

Jonathan still couldn't speak.

"You got anything you want to say, Rosa?"

Rosa stared down at the dying vampire who had been responsible for so much pain and suffering. "Die in agony, you evil motherfucker," she snapped.

"Good choice," Miles said and set Jonathan alight.

The vampire was dead after only a few seconds, but Miles, Church, and Rosa stayed watching until the flames went out twenty minutes later, leaving only a pile of ash in their wake.

"Always surprises me how fast vampires burn up," Rosa said.

"You got a lift home?" Miles asked.

"No, I figured I'd work it out later," Rosa said.

"You want dropping off anywhere?"

"No," Rosa said. "You going anywhere?"

"Scotland," Miles said. "Home, to be exact. But first, I'm going to go to a small cafe in Berlin and try every single piece of cake they make. You want to join me?"

Rosa smiled. "I will, thanks. I think we deserve it."

Miles looked down at Church. "You want cake, too?"

Church barked twice for no.

"You want a nice juicy steak?" Miles asked.

Church barked once and rubbed her bloody nose against Miles's hand.

"Let's get you cleaned up," he said, looking at his hand, before glancing back at the smouldering ash as the wind took it away. "I think we've earned our long overdue holiday."

Acknowledgements

The Assembly is a series I hadn't expected to write. I'd finished *Those Who Dwell in Darkness* and figured if that was all the vampires I got to write, then I was fine. I had lots and lots of ideas, but I'm an author, I always have lots of ideas. So, I'm eternally grateful to Podium for allowing me to continue with Miles and Church, and get their continued adventures on the page.

There are always numerous people who have helped me get this book written, edited, and published.

My wife, Vanessa, and my daughters, Keira, Faith, and Harley. Their support can't really be measured. They're part of the reason I write; they're part of the reason I ever decided to try and get published in the first place. Thank you for everything you do.

To my parents, who have always been supportive of my writing and read every book I publish, thank you for being there all these years, and I am sorry (not really) for the amount of space the wall of my covers now takes up.

To my family, my friends, all of those people who have supported me, who have contacted me to tell me they've loved my work, who listen to me going on about ideas and complaining about how my brain won't shut up for five minutes to let me work on one thing, you're all awesome.

My friend and agent, Paul Lucas, thank you for all you do.

To everyone at Podium. It's been a genuine pleasure to work with you all and I look forward to what the future brings.

My incredible editor, Julie Crisp, who helps make my work better. Thank you for being awesome to work with.

To all of my Patreon members, your continued support is always appreciated. And a special thank you to members Lydia A. Dean and Daniel Humpage.

And last, but by no means least, to everyone else who picks up my books, whether this is the first one or those who have followed my work for years, thank you.

About the Author

Steve McHugh is the bestselling author of the Hellequin Chronicles. His novel *Scorched Shadows* was nominated for a David Gemmell Award for Fantasy in 2018. Born in Mexborough, South Yorkshire, McHugh currently lives with his wife and three daughters in Southampton.

Podium

DISCOVER MORE

STORIES
UNBOUND

PodiumEntertainment.com